Cattle Capers

Cattle Capers

Caper #1:
Search for the MooMoo Pearl

To Shane,
Follow Your Moos!
Dawn

By
Dawn M. Kravagna

Illustrations by
Pun & Oink® Graphics

Avantine Press

Published by Aventine Press
1023 4th Ave #204
San Diego CA, 92101
www.aventinepress.com

ISBN: 1-59330-247-9

Printed in the United States of America

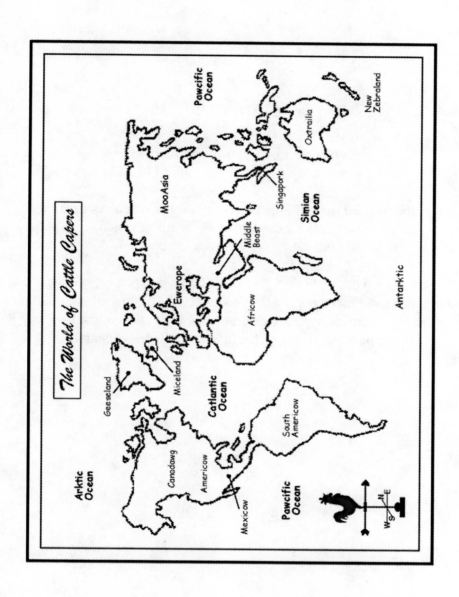

The World of Cattle Capers

Dedication

Dedicated to my family, without whom
I would not be neurotic enough to be funny.

God blessed me with the perfect family to reach my dreams
and goals—I owe them everything: which,
after bills and taxes, comes to about $5.95.

Acknowledgments

Many thanks to my friend Mary Rosewood for the first copy edit—friends like her are precious and few. Thanks to prize-winning novelist Peggy King Anderson for the major edit and valuable opinion; any perceived weaknesses in the novel are not Peggy's fault, as I didn't follow all of her suggestions. Also abundant thanks to Peggy for her positive input on the first chapter created during her Children's Writing Course; I was greatly encouraged to complete the novel: *How delightful is the timely word!** She's a great lady. Thanks also to Jason Carter and David Finley for their insightful commentary and volunteering their lunchtime to read the unpublished manuscript (suckers!)

And thanks to the Lord, who gave me the strength to write when I was weary and the faith to keep trying when I was discouraged. Every day is a gift from Him.

Proverbs 15:23

A cheerful heart has a continual feast.

--PROVERBS 15:15, NASB

Table of Contents

Episode One: Prologue

Episode Two: Fields of Clover

Episode Three (and the longest): The Investigation

Episode Four: Wrapping It All Up

Episode One: Prologue

SCENE ONE: MAYHEM

A flurry of feathers rushed into Precinct Thirteen-and-a-half. "I need your best detective on my case," Madam Portentsky demanded, a strand of pearls swinging back and forth across her downy breast.

"For the love of chocolate, would you close the door? It's raining cougars and Dobermans out there!" Chief of Police Pork didn't bother to look up from his donut: He was busy counting the number of colored sprinkles scattered on the pink frosting. "Dang it! Twice as many red ones than green ones: that means no money's coming my way this week." The wooden swivel chair creaked as he resettled his swine's bulk and placed his donut down amongst a scattered array of arrest reports and restaurant take-out menus. He wasn't going to give the ostrich any attention until he felt good and ready to be annoyed.

"Lordy, the door is closed. With all that pork you're carrying, I'm surprised you'd even feel a cyclone if it was taking you up to heaven," his uninvited guest clucked, pulling her pink feather boa tighter around her shoulders. He could just picture in his mind her high-heeled shoes scratching his newly polished floor as she marched up to the front of his desk. She stood waiting, one wing clutching a bright red vinyl purse (the latest fashion), the other wing pointed at his snout. The sooner he dealt with her silly little problem, the sooner he would be rid of her.

"So what is it this time, Griselda? Diamond ring fall down the drain, love note tied to a brick chucked through your kitchen window? Obviously the cat didn't get your tongue. Meow!" Chief Pork playfully tapped the bird's beak.

"You never take anything I say seriously." Griselda snapped at the chief's hoofed finger with her beak, but he was too quick for her and yanked it out off harm's reach. Tears began to well up in her eyes; however, Pork was not going to fall prey to any emotional manipulations. No dame was going to pull his heartstrings. He played that game once when he was a piglet, naive about the machinations of females and the black-heartedness of crooks. Maturity ruled his reason, common sense guarded his soul from feminine wiles and the treason of sycophants.

"Too dangerous for a swine to do," began Pork, but his response was cut short as the front door slammed open once again and a rooster, handcuffed to a large black rat, burst into the precinct lobby.

"Shut that doggoned door!" shouted the chief. "You're getting rainwater all over my floor! Somebody'll slip and hurt themselves! And why is it raining in August anyway?"

Pork seemed oblivious to the rooster's efforts to close the front door while the rat kept shoving a paw through the opening in an attempt to escape. The pig folded his hooves across his barrel chest, calmly watching the rat fasten his teeth into one of the fowl's wings. Madam Portentsky ended the scuffle, pecking the rat repeatedly in the middle of its back until it quit biting the lieutenant. Black fur, white feathers, and pink feather boa fuzzies swirled together in the air.

"Fat lot of help you are," Griselda scolded the police chief, smoothing the ruffled feathers on top of her head.

"I get paid for shuffling papers, not manhandling criminals. The *Powers That Be* took me off the beat years ago."

"Pork, I'm innocent I tell youse," the rat squealed. He straightened his green beret with his uncuffed paw and shook off the raindrops hanging from his mustache of whiskers. The hair under his chin was combed to a point. Pork also noticed that his fur was not naturally black, but dyed, probably with shoe polish. Obviously the rat was attempting to look like a beatnik—not the best dress code if you wanted to look like an honest citizen.

"Everybody in prison is innocent, but we lock them up anyway. Gotta justify our salary somehow."

"Glad you've finally admitted it!" shouted the rat with a triumphant gleam in his eyes. "That's why I refuse to pay taxes. I won't allow my hard-earned cash go to support squat like youse guys."

"Typical pack rat. Hoarding your money. We'll get you on tax evasion next lock-up," replied Pork detachedly, picking at the frosting on his donut. "Besides, when did you earn anything besides a slap across the chops? Cluck, toss Lenny the Rat into the glass hamster cage this time. I'm always telling you not to put him into the regular slammer. He keeps squeezing out between the bars."

"I'm too smart for the likes of youse," the rat shouted over his shoulder as Lt. Cluck dragged him out of the room and down the cement hallway toward the holding cells. "I will avenge myself. Pork, watch yer backside. I'll be gunning for youse one day, just wait..." was the last of the echoes the chief could hear before the steel door to the cells slammed shut.

Chief Pork put a finger to his mouth, signaling Madam Portentsky to remain silent, and pulled the gold pocketwatch out of his breast pocket. "One...two...three...four seconds," he began counting out. On "ten" Lt. Cluck's head popped around the doorway, a sheepish grin on his face.

"The spare key to the cuffs is on the shelf over the toilet," said the hog before Cluck could open his beak to inquire.

"Thanks, Chief," the rooster replied, disappearing from sight, dragging the rat behind him.

"We'll be moving that key, so don't ask to use the bathroom, Lenny!" shouted Pork after the prisoner.

"Youse just watch yer backside, Pork, just watch..." The threats echoed away.

"Like he said, he's innocent. I'm so scared," said the chief, turning his attention back to Griselda. "Nice job, Grissie. Want to wear the star? Cluck could use all the help he can get."

"The matter that I am about to disclose to you is a very serious one." Madam Portentsky sat down on the edge of the desk and crossed her lanky, ribbed legs. "And I want you to take it seriously. I need your best critter on this case. I need Steer."

"Can't do that, Babe. Lt. Cluck will have to do."

"I must have Steer. Cluck couldn't find his shoe on his right foot without a map."

"Look, I'd love to accommodate you, Grissie, I really would," Pork said, rising to his feet. "But Steer is no longer in the business. He checked out last summer."

Madam Portentsky dropped her purse to the floor. Red lipstick and breath mints fell from between the straps. "Checked out? Why didn't I hear about this? I am the first to know anything of importance in this town. It's my business as owner of the *Cloverleaf Gazette* to know these things."

Chief Pork, realizing that Griselda had misunderstood him, decided to have a little fun and play her like a fiddle. He did not like others dictating his moods, enjoying the sense of power that controlling the emotions of others gave him. And in learning to direct others, he knew better how to handle himself. If Lenny really did try to back his threats up with action one day, being in control of one's emotions was vitally important. A distracted mind missed the subtle clues of danger in the environment.

"Steer went quietly. One day he was a bovine of action, the next, he was strolling in that green meadow."

"Oh, this is tragic, so tragic, I'm doomed, doomed, doomed, I tell you," and Griselda broke down, weeping giant ostrich-sized tears all over the top of the donut box on Pork's desk and on his chrome nameplate. Perhaps he was taking this a bit too far, Pork thought to himself. He still had some latent feelings for Griselda, even though she had broken his heart several winters ago.

"Grissie, I'm sorry. I was just playing with you. I get bored sitting at this desk and do stupid things sometimes. Adam Steer hasn't died: He's just out to pasture."

"What? Out to pasture? How'd that happen? He's too young to retire." The ostrich accepted the linen hankie Chief Pork handed her. She blew her nose repeatedly then returned the mascara-stained cloth to him. He surreptitiously dropped it into the wastecan under his desk.

"Put himself out to pasture. Some guy tried milking his gal, Betsy Moo. He went crazy and nearly gored the chump to death. Before the courts could convene a hearing into the matter, Adam voluntarily checked out of the Force. He hadn't fired his gun the ten years he was on duty, not even drawn blood in a fistfight. Couldn't bear the thought that he'd nearly killed someone."

"What am I to do?" wailed Griselda. "Someone has stolen my precious MooMoo."

Chief Pork leaned back in his chair, his great belly jumping up and down in laughter like a giant bellows. "Are you telling me that your big dilemma is that someone has stolen your house dress?"

"No, listen you airhead," snapped Madam Portentsky, her tears vanishing into a fit of rage. Pork was accustomed to her wild mood swings. "I am surprised that your head stays attached to your shoulders and doesn't float off. Not a muumuu: I am talking about the largest, single black pearl in existence. It's in the shape of a dancing cow. It's a family heirloom that was carved in the Far East and passed down through the centuries from one generation to another. That statuette must be found—and I must have Steer to help me."

"Are we talking reward money here?" Pork asked with genuine interest. Griselda was a widow worth millions.

"Quite possibly I'd be very grateful to whomever can return my precious MooMoo to me." The ostrich pulled the pink feather boa from around her shoulders and teasingly slid one soft end around the edge of the chief's upturned ear. It tickled.

"Then I just might be able to get you Steer. Crazy Cal was put out to pasture with Adam. He was caught trying to steal another cow's cud to chew. He's so disgusting; I can't imagine Steer will remain in retirement with that lunatic sharing his space. He's got to be ready to pop about now."

"Cluck, get the squad car warmed up." The lieutenant dashed into the room at the chief's command. "I want you to treat Ms. Portentsky here like she's the Queen of Sheba. We've got ourselves a very important mission to complete."

"And by the way," Pork added as the three of them stepped out the front door, "What did you do with that spare key for the cuffs, Cluck?"

"I put it back over the toilet," answered the rooster.

"Go get that key before you forget and that rat asks to take a pee!"

Lt. Cluck's top comb went from red to purple as he dashed down the hallway.

"Permit me, my dear," Chief Pork said, offering the ostrich his arm, "to escort you to the car." And when Grissie slipped a warm, soft wing next to his uniform, he recalled the last time her beak left a wet kiss on his snout and quickly pushed the tender feeling out of his heart.

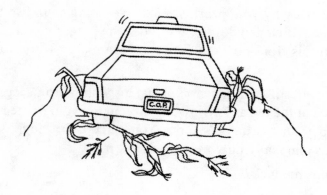

SCENE TWO: FRUITS AND NUTS

"The rain's stopped," observed Lt. Cluck as he led Pork and Madam Portentsky out the front door. He held out a wing and caught a waterdrop falling from the gutters. The sky was fading quickly from cloudy grey into twilight. The skyline of Boville beckoned from the valley below. Red and gold lights twinkled in the distance, the only hint of habitation in the quiet post storm stillness. It was difficult for the lieutenant to believe that somewhere, out there in the glittering silence, someone was committing a crime. Yet statistics didn't lie. A crime was committed in Boville every hour on the average. Just most of the criminals didn't get caught. Cluck saw a worm wriggling across the sidewalk and dove for a late afternoon snack.

Pork wasn't paying attention to what his lieutenant was up to. He delighted in having Griselda snuggled close to his side, her wing wrapped around his arm, yet at the same time was discomforted. It wasn't safe to get too attached to the strong-willed ostrich.

"For heaven's sake, don't do that, Grissie!" he yelled, jerking her to the right and nearly causing her to trip over her feet.

"What, walk under this ladder? I thought you would have grown out of that superstitious nonsense by now." Madam Portentsky pulled her wing out from the swine's grasp. She darted back-and-forth underneath the steel ladder propped against the brick wall of the precinct house while yelling, "Look at me! Look at me!"

"See, that's why your pearl was stolen—doing stupid stuff like that you got yourself cursed." Pork winced as he gingerly pulled his lucky charm from his front pocket, kissing it reverently. He left nothing in life to chance.

"You're not still carrying around that disgusting frog's leg, are you?" She grabbed at the leg as Pork swung around to avoid her reach. "Most animals carry an old rabbit's foot. You carry a frog leg," she added. "And it was one really ugly frog if you ask me."

"It brings me luck."

"Didn't bring the frog much luck if you ask me," interrupted Lt. Cluck.

"We weren't asking, Cluck!" the hog and ostrich swung around and barked at the same time.

"You know, you didn't need to spook me like that, Grissie, " Pork said, shuddering involuntarily as the three of them stepped toward the squad car. "Cluck, where's your manners? Sit in the back seat."

"Regulations state that Griselda sit..." Cluck began, one leg in the front passenger side of the automobile.

"You have NOT been given permission to call me by my first name," Griselda huffed, pulling her feather boa tighter around her neck. "Madam Portentsky to you."

"Madam Portentsky must sit in the rear, sir," Lt. Cluck corrected himself. "Recall the sheriff's new regulation: ever since the last Cowlitz County ride-along guest pulled a gun on his driver, all non-police, arrested or no, must sit in the back behind the partition where they cannot attack the driver."

"Sheriff Hoggsbutter doesn't know his detectives from his directives. You gonna report me if she doesn't ride in the back?"

Cluck opened the back door to the squad car in response.

"You weren't going to attack me, were you, Grissie?" Pork whispered into her left ear as he guided her into the back seat.

"You pink devil," Madam Portentsky giggled, sitting down.

Minutes later they were driving eastward down Hells Highway and out of Boville. Madam Portentsky admired the farmland that whizzed by the window, acres and acres of luscious corn glistening like golden niblets buttered by the rays of the setting sun. Cluck loved the smell of the damp earth that promised hundreds of earthworms would be wriggling near the surface. The chief thought about buckwheat pancakes dripping with one hundred percent maple syrup—which had nothing at all to do with corn or damp ground: he just really liked pancakes and thought about them a lot.

"Your dancing under that ladder has given me the willies, Grissie," the chief said, interrupting the silent reveries of his passengers. "You shouldn't mock the portents of evil."

"You make your own luck, Pork. Intuition tells me that Steer is our critter. He'll be willing to help us. I'd bet my bottom dollar on it."

"There's something I need to tell you," Pork began in an ominous tone. Madam Portentsky heard the back door locks snap into place as Lt. Cluck tripped the button under the dashboard. "We can't allow you to leave the automobile when we talk to Steer."

"What, am I now your prisoner?"

"Yes, a prisoner of propriety. There's something I haven't told you about the detective. In fact, few critters are privy to this information I am about to divulge to you. I want your promise not to print it in your newspaper." Clutching the steering wheel, Pork looked over his shoulder at his old flame, wondering if you could ever trust a journalist.

"Chief, watch the road," Lt. Cluck warned as the automobile drifted over the centerline.

"O.K., O.K.," the hog acceded as he brought the car back into the right lane. "Grissie, I want your promise on this."

"Beaks and feathers. I'm curious as all get out now. What choice do I have?"

"I want to hear the word, 'yes'," said Pork. "Yes, I promise not to tell anyone, Chief Pork."

"Yes, I promise not to tell anyone, Oh Great Porker," retorted Griselda with unnecessary sarcasm, thought the chief. His stomach felt queasy thinking about what he was about to reveal.

"Steer has gone au natural."

Madam Portentsky clapped her wings together, clucking in delight. "Steer has gone naked! I should have my camera! A good reporter is always ready!"

"Grissie, where's your modesty?" Pork was shocked at her unladylike attitude.

Only rebels and barbarians were public nudists since the Great Enlightenment a little over four centuries ago. Steer Isaac Newtoon was sitting under a tree when an apple, drawn by gravity, struck him upon the noggin, prompting the startling realization that he was naked. It was later remarked over the following decades by a bevy of philosophers, debating the necessity of such accouterment, that not only was the hide protected but also the ability to manipulate one's appearance was enhanced. And clothing helped build the economy, putting thousands of once carefree, roaming sheep to work. The privates of mammals were concealed ever since. Only bohemians continued to debate the evils of clothing while smoking clove cigarettes and drinking bourbon in their favorite black light cafes.

"Plumb starkers!" said Lt. Cluck. "Donated his trench coat to the Good Swill charity and hoofed it out of the Force."

Pork yelled something incomprehensible to his passengers. The car swerved suddenly to the right, momentum swinging the squad car into concentric circles. Visibility was zero as they were enveloped in a spray of muddy water and rotated on the fourth revolution off of the street and into the fields. Corn stalks slapped at the windows as the squad car came to an abrupt halt, the tires lodged in the soft dirt.

"Who taught you to drive, Boozo the clown?" yelled Griselda, searching the floor for her purse. Her compact had fallen open and tubes of makeup rolled around on the floor mats. "Look at this," she exclaimed, holding one of the tubes up to the glass partition. "The cap came off and there's grit all over my lipstick."

In response Chief Pork threw open the driver's door and dashed through the cornfield. Cluck leapt out to follow, while Madam Portentsky fumbled with the door handle. Though it was locked she yanked at it anyway, pulling the metal handle out of the door. Trapped in the backseat and holding the dislodged handle, she watched the police officers disappearing through the rows of crushed corn.

Not accustomed to walking through plowed muddy earth, the chief slowed with each step, until his breath was moving faster than his hooves. After reaching Hells Highway a hundred yards up an incline, he could scarcely lift his legs and plopped his bulk down onto the pavement.

"Chief! Chief!" Cluck exclaimed, his breathing also laborious. He'd have to speak to the sheriff about free health club membership for officers of the Force. "Don't run off. It's all right. Not everyone is a good driver."

"No lucky charm could help me get rid of you!" Pork thought to himself as he grabbed the lieutenant by the beak, swinging his addled head to the right like a broken compass point. "Look there."

Hundreds of earthworms, large, juicy, and read to eat, were marching across the highway, some holding picket signs wound into their tail ends, while others shouted slogans. There were a few earthworms that appeared to be about three feet long. Cluck had only dreamt of such edibles.

"You nearly got us killed!" The chief rose to his feet, dropping the rooster to the cement to address the protestors, while fury turned his pink skin red. "I could have murdered several dozen of you, running around on the highway like that! I should ticket the lot of you!"

"If we aren't citizen enough to be covered under the law, we aren't citizen enough to be ticketed!" cried one orange-ringed worm, puffing what appeared to be his chest in defiance.

"Down with authority!" yelled another from behind him, dropping his sign. The sign's lettering was crudely drawn in black ink in Wormese, a language Pork could not read.

"The law applies to everyone," the chief said. He didn't like their attitude. To defy the law was to defy him.

"We are heading to Boville City Hall to protest the new law."

"The new law?" Pork asked, genuinely nonplussed.

Back at the squad car Griselda was picking up the other items that had fallen to the floor from her stylish handbag when she heard the front door open and slam shut. "Pork, do you need help pushing this old rig out of the cornfield?" she asked.

There was no response.

She waited for several minutes in the eerie quiet, apprehension growing with each moment. The hog was not a game player, especially when he was angry. Someone was in the driver's seat, but it was not the chief. Swallowing the lump of fear in her throat, she lifted her head to peer over the seat back. She wished that she hid her head in the sand like other ostriches when afraid, but her journalist's curiosity always got the better of her. She had to snoop and peek and rummage around even when common sense said to leave well enough alone. Besides, the problem with hiding your head in the sand was that someone could sneak up on you and kick you in the butt while you weren't looking. She was glad that thick Plexiglas separated the front from the back.

"Going my way?" a hoarse voice sneered. A pale pink snout pressed itself against the partition. Beady red eyes, framed by an amorphous dark shape, glowed through the mist that the creatures' breath left on the glass. Griselda's knees knocked together. That old hamhock was finally right: She had called up the devil when dancing under the ladder.

The creature pulled away from the window with a chuckle. In the waning sunlight Griselda realized that an unusually large mole was sitting on the front seat. "Are you kidnapping me?" she asked, her eyelids fluttering uncontrollably, a nervous tick that betrayed her intense emotions.

"No, I'm lonely and I want some company," the mole hissed as he shifted the car into drive. The back wheels spun helplessly in response.

"Not too good at this carjacking stuff, are you?" Griselda's fear was momentarily masked by anger at the mole's sarcasm.

"Watch this." The mole put two fingers to his mouth and emitted a high-pierced whistle. The ostrich involuntarily held her breath. There was silence for several tense minutes. Her captor was swinging his head to-and-fro, watching the landscape through the front and side windows. His motion was almost mesmerizing. Searching for whom—or what?

"There!" the mole exclaimed, pointing to the left.

Griselda wiped the fog off of the window with her wing and peered through the shifting swirling haze of dust outside the car. Corn stalks soared through the air. An enormous mountain of earth was rushing toward them. The ground beneath them rocked to the rhythm of a steady thumping sound, pitching her about the backseat, the newly appearing evening stars whirring in an excited buzz outside the window. She screamed as the car suddenly rose several yards in the air while wobbling back-and-forth. They were moving and moving fast, farther and farther away from the highway, farther and farther away from the safety of her companions.

"New law?" asked Pork. Cluck pulled out his *Tweeter's Pocket Guide to Current Law* and thumbed through its pages as his superior spoke. "What problem could you worms possibly have with the law?"

"For a lawman you sure are dumb," the worm retorted, oblivious to Pork's threats. "The Nuts and Berries Law."

"That's the 'Fruits and Nuts Law'," corrected Cluck.

The chief spat on the highway and adjusted his gun belt. "New law? That's been in effect for over ten years now."

The conclusion of the Great International War also ended the Dark Times: The loss of millions of critters in the last century fostered a new appreciation for the value of life. Negotiated at the newly created first World Congress were the No Leather and Feather laws, forbidding the use of animals skins and feathers in products sold internationally. Each annual gathering passed progressively restrictive laws on carnivore activity. Eventually the 55th Congress passed the Doctrine of Lenore, named after the she-wolf from the nation of Canadawg, who refused to eat her prey, a lame duck governor ambushed on its twilight return from a party fundraiser. Lenore took pity on the plump politician with its broken wing and spared its life. Although the Doctrine was only a suggested code of animal conduct, Americow, a civilized nation, followed the lead of the W.C., passing the federal Fruits and Nuts Law, forbidding animals to hunt or eat one another in the States. Non-mammals that were too low on the food chain to be considered animal life were still considered prey: fish, insects, reptiles, and–worms.

Not all nations adopted the Doctrine, a few rogue states even declaring that Lenore was a myth, she never existed, or was a pawn in a capitalist plot to oppress the working class creatures and prevent them from stalking a free meal.

"Really? The law was passed more than ten years ago?" the orange-rimmed worm asked with genuine surprise in his voice. The other earthworms halted their procession, looking at each other quizzically. "We just heard about it the other day."

"Well, if you guys would bother to lift your heads out of the ground once in a while you might know something. Who told you?" asked Pork.

"A little birdie."

"Dumb twit. I'm sure that your dinner guest would be right in supposing the law was brand new."

"New or not," the worm renewed his defiant posture, "it's unjust and we plan to protest it."

"Go ahead and protest; it's all the same to me," Pork said, waving his hands in disgust at the worms. "I don't make the laws, only enforce them. Just be kind enough to clear the road for a bit so we can get our car out of the field and on our way. We've got important business to attend to."

"And so do we," the worm leader responded with a bow. "I hope that we meet in the future under better circumstances." With a swing of his head to the right, he indicated to his followers that they should wriggle to one side of the highway or the other.

"Pompous little pustule," Pork grunted under his breath as he and Cluck began the long muddy walk back to the squad car.

"Seeing all of those worms has made me really hungry." Cluck matched the chief stride for stride. "I hope this conversation with Steer won't last long." He was considering a late night hunting visit to Boville City Hall for a bedtime snack.

"Don't underestimate Gridelda's powers of persuasion, Cluck." Pork slapped aside a stalk of corn and pitched forward into an enormous hole where the squad car had once been.

"I thought you flipped the door locks," the chief groaned from the bottom of the pit.

"I thought I did too. But somehow she must've gotten out of the backseat. Maybe I didn't push the button hard enough." Cluck ran to the edge of the hole, straining his eyes to find the hog in the twilight gloom. "Are you O.K., Chief?"

"Never trust a dame," was the response.

Episode Two: Fields Of Clover

SCENE ONE: STEERING UP TROUBLE

"What a disgusting idea!" Lt. Cluck could hear the two cattle arguing as he approached the rickety fence. The boards were spaced nearly six inches apart and nailed so poorly to the posts that any critter could kick them down: A squirrel walking across the top board could tip the whole fence to the ground. Apparently no one stayed inside the enclosure because they had to—they wanted to. He loosened the buttons on his trench coat, feeling the sweat dripping down between his armpits and the sleeves from the long three-mile hike to Lilah's Happy Farm from the cornfield where their auto was lifted. Chief of Police Pork couldn't keep up the rooster's pace so Cluck left him struggling a mile back. Squinting his eyes to improve his vision, he searched for a trace of the old swine down the spindly road. In the dim light he supposed it might have been the porker framed by the rising moon, trudging along the rutted, dirty path some hundred yards or so away.

"I tell you, NO, NO, NO!" one of the cattle yelled emphatically, redirecting the lieutenant's attention to the pasture. "I don't want anything to do with any of your crazy schemes, Cal, particularly THIS one!" The excited bull turned away from his sidekick and, startled by the sudden appearance of the rooster at the fence, dropped the grass stuffed into his cheeks.

"So, what do you want, Cluck?" The naked bull swaggered up to the fence, his hands upon his hips. "I'm retired now. I haven't got anything to discuss with you."

"Retired, Adam? I can see that," Cluck sneered, his upper beak slightly curled. "Retired from decency. No self-respecting animal would go without some type of clothing on, not since the Dark Times."

Adam Steer pawed his left hoof into the ground, kicking mud into the air. "That's right, Cluck. I ain't got no more self-respect," and turned his backside toward the fowl.

"Chief, did you see that! He mooned me! Swung his big butt around and mooned me!"

Chief Pork struggled to lift his head, huffing and puffing from the exertion of the walk. He had just reached the farm and already Cluck was fighting with somebody. "What did you expect from Crazy Cal?"

"That's not Cal's butt! That's Steer's!" Cluck's overcoat was fluttering behind him as he dashed down the gravel-strewn road toward the hog. He had an amazing amount of energy when he was excited, thought Pork.

"Now how would you know what Steer's butt looked like?" asked Pork. He wasn't in the mood for any shenanigans. His ex-flame was joyriding in his squad car having a good laugh at his expense while his pounding heart felt like it wanted to leap out through his mouth. In fact, he felt like barfing but he wasn't about to let the rooster know he couldn't handle the hike to the clover field. He pulled a rusty tin out of his back pocket and popped a few green antacids.

"It was Adam all right, snorting like a wild bull and chucking mud balls at me."

"Did he hit you?"

"No."

Dang, too bad, thought Pork. It would have been good for a laugh. How could he be so foolish, letting that ostrich back into his life? He should have kicked her scrawny little butt out of the lobby the moment she rushed through the front door. Absorbed in his plaintive thoughts and dragging his weary feet, he tripped over a rock and fell to the ground.

His skull felt like a sack of lead and his chest as if a bowling ball had been bounced up and down upon it repeatedly. Opening his eyes, Chief Pork saw a vision of a white, swirling figure framed by a halo of moonlight floating above him. He smiled in a dreamy reverie. "Sweet choirs of angels..." His mother was singing to him just like she did when he was a piglet in the sty. She caressed his shoulders with one chubby arm and kissed his snout lightly.

"Should I slap him out of it?" asked a voice, clucking excitedly, somewhere out in the fog beyond Chief Pork's consciousness.

"No, I don't think that would be helpful," intoned a somber voice.

"I say we slap him anyway, whether he needs it or not," a third, high-pitched voice said.

The hog leapt to his feet, stamping his hooves in disgust. That wasn't his mother kissing him lightly on the snout: that was Cluck, giving mouth-to-mouth resuscitation. Two naked cattle stood behind the lieutenant. One had two broken horns on his head, the left wrapped with aluminum foil. Obviously Crazy Cal. The other stood arms akimbo, munching on a stalk of wheat, eyes twinkling with mirth: Steer.

"Don't any of you guys tell anyone what just happened here, and I mean NOBODY!"

"Calm down, Chief. You're gonna give yourself another heart attack!" Cluck said solicitously, grabbing at one of Pork's flaying arms.

"You keep away from me, Cluck." The chief pulled his arm out of the lieutenant's grasp, brushed the mud from his shirt and rearranged his belt buckle. Shivering, he brandished a finger at the rooster. "I didn't have a heart attack. I just tripped over a rock, that's all."

"You were out colder than a frozen cucumber," the rooster muttered under his breath, irritated at the ingratitude for first aid services rendered.

"I guess Pork's all right," Steer remarked.

"He looks a little pale to me," added Cal.

"The moon's out for critter's sake," exclaimed Chief Pork. "We all look a little pale in the moonlight." He did feel a little lightheaded and wondered about his blood pressure, but he wasn't about to admit to any weakness in front of his lieutenant or the two shameless cattle.

"Well you didn't come all this way to play speed bump," said Adam. "Where's your car? I know you guys aren't into jogging, unless you've changed your ways drastically in the past year."

"Someone stole Big White."

"Right out from under our noses," added Cluck.

"Well chap my hide." Crazy Cal slapped his sides. "I can sleep soundly at night in the middle of the open field knowing you guys are protecting me."

"Lord, what did I do to deserve this?" Pork said, sliding back to the ground. With a wave of his hand he rejected the rooster's proffered wing. "I'm O.K., Cluck. I just need to rest a bit."

"It's against my better judgment," Steer began, "because I know you guys will rope me into some sort of scheme if I leave this place, but I'd better give the chief a ride back to the precinct."

"You guys don't have a telephone?" asked Cluck. Both cattle nodded "no," while rolling their eyes in obvious mockery.

"We're trying to get away from it all, but you found us anyway." Sighing, Adam knelt down onto all fours. "Hop on, Pork."

"I'm not sure this is kosher," began the chief, "but I'm tired and we haven't got a phone to call back-up." He slid a leg over the big bull and settled his bulk onto Steer's back. His stomach felt a bit queasy as Adam rocked to his feet and started trotting down the road toward Boville.

SCENE TWO: LOTSA BULL

Adam didn't want to admit to it, but he was beginning to tire under the weight of the police chief. Two miles and Boville was still a distant, twinkling, multi-faceted jewel of colored lights. Dilating his nostrils he lifted his head, savoring the smell of wet clover and hay carried by the evening breeze. He had hoped for a brief respite from Crazy Cal, but the nut insisted on carrying Cluck on his back and tailing them. The lieutenant's protestations with regulations gleaned from various codebooks didn't deter Cal in the least: He chased the rooster down the path and knocked him up onto his back with his large head. Adam looked behind to see Cal, grinning idiotically, his passenger popping up into the air with each trot to land again on his bony back.

"I can see why animals abandoned all fours and took to riding automobiles," stammered the lieutenant. "Not that I'm ungrateful, mind you," he said when Cal turned his head to glare at the rooster. "This is much faster than walking."

"So who pilfered your automobile?" asked Cal.

"Be quiet, Cluck. I don't want to know. I just don't want to know anything about what you two characters are up to this time," protested Adam Steer, rearing up onto his hind legs and covering his ears with his front hooves. The chief, caught by surprise, clung to Adam's horns and swung limply against the cow's hairy backside. "The less I know about you guys' shenanigans, the sooner I can get back to a little R and R."

"We got carjacked by Madam Portentsky," replied Cluck, oblivious to the detective's protestations, in a staccato voice in tune with his aerial dynamics. "We thought she was locked in the backseat, but she got out somehow and drove the squad car off."

"Dang, dang, dang," Adam said, prancing about with the hog clinging to his back for dear life. "I didn't want to hear that."

Pork cursed the chatty rooster under his breath for embarrassing them in front of the cattle, but Cluck grinned with satisfaction. He was familiar with the detective's famous curiosity: stronger than a cat's which got him into far more trouble than any feline. The rooster and detective were never close friends when Steer worked for the Force; in fact, no one got close to Adam the ten years he was a Boville detective except for Betsy Moo. But they had a few cups of coffee together on occasion at the various diners in town and shared enough time together on the Force to witness the bovine's famous knack for solving mysteries— and crossword puzzles without the aid of a dictionary. Anything with a question mark was sure to get Steer's attention.

"I just can't stand it. I have to ask!" an exasperated Adam said, stamping his hooves as he settled down to all fours much to the chief's relief: the unanticipated busting bronco ride was stirring up his stomach acids again. "Don't you find anything odd about Griselda carjacking Big White?" Steer asked.

"You mean my ex-galpal stealing an official police vehicle?" Pork fingered his badge with one hoofed hand to reassure himself that it was still pinned to his shirt. "Yes, I find that not only odd but also extremely aggravating. I'd hate to slap the cuffs on the broad, but she deserves it big time for this one."

"When did Griselda learn to drive?"

The chief nearly let go of Steer's horns. He felt the blood draining from his face.

"Now that you mention it," interrupted Cluck, bouncing up and down on Cal's back, "when you two were dating, Chief, either you drove or her chauffeur picked you up in the Catillac."

"I thought she just liked being driven around to show off her money," Pork's normally boisterous voice wilted to a near whisper.

"Unless she took lessons since I left the Force, she couldn't drive a pick up over a cliff," said Adam.

The chief responded by falling like a stone from the detective's back, face first into the dirt. Cluck also dismounted, a little more gracefully, and the trio formed a semi-circle of concern around their fallen comrade.

"He's not used to exerting himself much physically. I keep telling him that we ought to budget for health club memberships," Cluck said, rubbing his sore rear end. "Maybe I should try mouth-to-mouth again?"

"He didn't care much for that last time," replied Cal.

"I believe he's O.K.," said Steer, checking the chief's airway and pulse. "I think he might've just fainted." Seeing the normally self-assured hog in such a helpless state filled Adam with apprehension. Years of being exasperated by Cluck would send any critter's blood pressure careening near dangerous levels. Then add the possible abduction of Pork's ex in his own squad car and a dangerous stress cocktail was mixed. Adam had once been the buffer between the two police officers in the precinct, adding a little levity to the workday, which aggravated the humorless rooster but cheered the responsibility-laden chief of police. Adam sighed. It was obvious that his days of self-exile were ending.

"How can you say he's O.K.? You're not a doctor, Adam. Guess this is a lesson to always have access to a phone to call 911 if you get into trouble," lectured Cluck. "Can we get him up onto your back again?"

As Adam bent down, Cal and the rooster attempted to lift the pudgy hog onto the cow's back, but the burden was too heavy and could not be budged. The police chief lay in a heap, his uniform soiled, his limbs spread outward like he was doing the backstroke in the mud.

"Maybe we can just tie him to your tail and you can drag him home?" suggested Crazy Cal. "That ought to wake him up."

"You'd ruin his uniform. That's against regulations," added Cluck.

"I can live without any more of your suggestions, thank you very much, Cal," said Adam, grabbing onto his tail and pulling it close to his chest in a protective gesture out of harm's reach.

"I have great suggestions. Absolutely the best," remonstrated Cal.

"Oh yeah, real great ones." Steer forgot about the chief's trauma in the heat of the moment. "Like your new business you wanted me to invest into, which has got to be one of the most disturbing ideas I have ever heard."

"I think it would sell and sell well," replied Cal, nervously biting his lower lip.

"Putting our manure into bags and marketing it as fertilizer: like THAT would ever sell. Whoever heard of such a crazy idea?"

"It's win-win, Steer. Recycling to help the environment and garden fuel for farmers. Besides, judging by what's on the boob tube nowadays, poopie sells."

"I'd hate to break up your little board meeting, but I am somewhat concerned about the chief," interrupted the lieutenant. He picked up Pork's fallen hat and gently slipped it onto his superior's head. The tenderness of his action brought tears to Cal's eyes.

"He sorta looks good lying there in the moonlight, kind of like Snow White with a uniform and a snout," commented Cal.

Snorting and flaring his nostrils, Adam instructed the lieutenant to remove his overcoat with which the three of them constructed a sling. Tying one end to Steer's horns and the other end to Cal's, they walked the last few miles to Boville with the chief swinging in the makeshift bed between them in a deep sleep. Cluck walked behind, rubbing his wings to keep himself warm. A few hours later they entered the precinct house and lowered the chief onto the lobby couch. Adam removed Pork's shoes and slipped a wool blanket around his body. He placed the back of his hand against the hog's forehead: cold and clammy; however, his breathing was relaxed and steady.

"If he doesn't wake up soon, I'm calling an ambulance," said Cluck. "Although that'd really cheese him off."

"I hate to bring this up, because I'm more involved now than I'd care to be, but if Griselda didn't drive your squad car off, who did?" asked Adam.

"You think she's been kidnapped?" asked the rooster.

"It's possible. Or perhaps she hired someone else to drive the car for who knows what reason. In either case, it looks like I'm temporarily back on the payroll, until we solve the mystery of her disappearance."

"Glad to have you back, Steer," said Cluck, proffering his wing for a handshake.

"Glad to be back," said Crazy Cal, pushing Steer aside and pumping the lieutenant's hand enthusiastically.

In the background a metal cup was being bashed against the glass of the hamster cage cell in the back rooms. "Youse guys trying to starve me to death?" yelled Lenny the Rat. Suddenly alert, Chief Pork tossed off the blanket and leapt to his feet. The precinct was his responsibility and like a good mother who sleeps lightly, sensitive to the movements or sounds of her children, he was intimately attuned to any disturbance within his jailhouse.

"Can't keep a good chief down," said Cluck proudly.

Episode Three
(And The Longest): The Investigation

SCENE ONE: HOME SWEET HOME

"Didn't the night deputy come in again?" asked Chief Pork between gulps of pink liquid medicine. He wasn't sure if his stomach was more upset at Griselda's possible abduction or at humiliating himself by collapsing twice in front of his inferiors.

"Nah, timecard's not punched," replied Lt. Cluck pulling the deputy's card out of its slot under the time clock and surveying the punches. "Third time this month. For someone with a name like Pepy, he's sure sick a lot."

Chief Pork, surreptitiously rubbing his gurgling stomach, sat down behind his desk. He relished the familiar feel of his swivel chair and the softness of its velveteen seat cushion against his tired limbs. Across from him Crazy Cal sat on the lobby bench, picking at his teeth with a rusty nail and nervously swinging his legs back and forth. Just a few moments ago the loquacious Cal had explained to the trio how minute adjustments of the aluminum foil on his left horn helped him pick up better broadcasts from outside the solar system although he was having great difficulty deciphering the messages he was receiving. Pork wondered, when in the future Cal finally understood the radio messages, whether that would make the bull dangerous rather than just plain crazy. As long as the voices were garbled, then Cal wouldn't be directed into behavior that might be abnormal. Of course, nothing seemed normal about an animal that was not ashamed to go nude.

Lenny's clanging of his coffee cup against the hamster cage and Adam slamming shut the door to a police locker brought the chief out of his reverie.

"Hey, that looks a little familiar!" bellowed the captain. "But I'll make the sacrifice in the name of decency!"

"I guess this coat'll do until I can pick up a new one at The Hoofery," said Adam, slipping his arms though the sleeves of Pork's rain slicker. He pulled the plastic belt tight and examined himself in the lobby mirror. "Yellow was never my best color. Got a hat I can borrow, Cluck? I don't like to leave my head exposed when I'm on duty. Makes me look too vulnerable to the riffraff."

Hurrying to accommodate the master detective, the lieutenant opened his locker and, after reaching into a beat-up military bag, pulled out an old grey fedora. With a stately sweep of his wings he handed it to the detective who promptly slapped it against the locker door, producing a cloud of dust. Adam then adjusted the hat on his head to a fashionable tilt. "Thanks, Cluck." The mirror reflected a wince on the bovine's face as a moth flew out from under the brim of his new accouterment.

"Now that we've rested up a bit, let's get back to Griselda, shall we?" asked the chief.

"He can't do any detecting until he's officially reinstated," interrupted Lt. Cluck.

"O.K., you're reinstated Adam," said the hog without ceremony.

"No, no, no, that won't do," protested the rooster.

"O.K., you're reinstated with the full salary you were getting as of last summer."

"No, no, no, that's not regulation."

Chief Pork screwed up his snout and glared at his lieutenant. "All right already, what's the regs on this one?"

"Well, I don't know," stammered Cluck. "I gotta go check the code books."

"If you don't know what the regs are, then how can you tell me that I'm doing it wrong?" He didn't like the look the rooster returned: the "because you usually are" look.

"This is regulation enough," said Chief Pork, waving his arms around in the air in circles and then flinging the last drops of coffee from his lucky shamrock mug at the detective. "You've been anointed, Steer. So go sue me, Cluck. I outrank you."

"There's paperwork to be done, I'm sure," replied the lieutenant, pulling books from the shelves behind the police chief's desk and rifling quickly through their pages. "We can't just hand someone a paycheck."

"If you'd rather go leafing through old moldy books rather than helping us find Grissie, then help yourself."

"We can handle it fine without you," added Crazy Cal, the iron nail caught between his two front teeth. "We're super detectives, Steer and me. We'll find your gal pal in no time."

Adam winced. He didn't relish the continued company of the nutty bovine, but he was wise enough to realize that no amount of persuasion would get rid of the bull. It would be easier to get rid of a bad flu bug while sitting naked in an ice storm than Cal. No wonder room-and-board came so cheaply at Lilah's Happy Farm: the kook must scare off most of the new boarders after a few days. Only his reluctance to return to Boville and risk a chance meeting with Betsy kept him foraging in the pasture with Cal. And although he didn't want to admit it to himself, the nutcase kept things interesting. Most critters who put themselves out to pasture were either mentally incapacitated or elderly, looking forward to nothing but peaceful strolls in fields of clover. Adam wasn't interested in peace and quiet, only escape. It was even difficult for him to ignore the conversations of the birds chattering in the maple trees at Lilah's: his curiosity made him an irrepressible snoop.

"You want to play detective, fine," said the chief. "But you're not on payroll. Sheriff Hoggsbutter would tan my hide. We can't have you screwing up an official investigation and getting critical evidence tossed out of court. We'll classify you as a 'ride-along'."

"Not a single buck?" asked Cal.

"Not even a donut if you don't get some proper clothes on."

"For a lemon jelly donut I'd do anything," responded Cal. Adam made a mental note to recall that tidbit of information for the future.

Soon Cal was outfitted with Pork's spare yellow raincoat, though it was a trifle short, exposing most of his upper thigh. Wanting to be just like his detective friend, Cal insisted on a proper hat rather than using the hood to his borrowed coat.

"A good detective needs a hat," Cal commented. "Makes you look more mysterious, like you know more than you really do."

"I'm sure that's the truth," Cluck mumbled under his breath.

Not having any regulation caps on hand, the chief pulled the front page of the *Cloverleaf Gazette* out of the recycle bin and folded a hat for the faux detective. Tears prodded at the corners of his eyes as he gazed at the byline on the lead article: Ms. Griselda Portentsky.

"Hey, this won't hold up in the rain," remonstrated Cal. "Can't I have a real detective's hat?"

"We'll laminate it later," responded Adam, fitting the paper onto Cal's broad head. "Besides, what's more mysterious than a bull with a newsprint hat?"

Cal examined himself before the lobby area mirror, nail in teeth, bent horn with aluminum foil poking out between the sides of his hat. He preened at the hair that poked out of his ears, slicking it down with spittle.

"Holy clover and flower petals, I'm a real detective now," enthused Cal.

"We need to put an APB out on Big White," Cluck said, ignoring Cal and reaching for the phone on Pork's desk. The chief nearly tore out a feather on the lieutenant's wing when he slapped his hand away from the receiver.

"Don't alert the State Patrol," protested Pork. "I don't want Sheriff Hoggsbutter getting involved. And The Great Moogah help us all if the sheriff found out we'd lost our squad car. I'd end up a pork roast for sure!"

"But regulations..." Cluck reached for the phone once more, defending his outstretched hand with his other wing.

"We'll find the car ourselves," Adam said gently, placing a firm hand upon the rooster's arm. Cluck winced. He didn't like being touched, particularly to prevent him from performing his duty, but, weary from the night's activities, he pulled his wing back.

Pork grabbed the phone and set it on his chair. That didn't seem safe enough from the fastidious lieutenant, so he slid a paper bag over the top of it, which earned him a stern glare of disapproval from the rooster.

The commotion in the backroom increased. Cluck went to the service quarters to toss a TV dinner into the microwave for Lenny. The lieutenant had protested about covering for the night deputy, saying he wanted to accompany them to look for the ostrich, but Chief Pork didn't like leaving prisoners unattended, even if they were in lock-up. Lt. Cluck wasn't as concerned about finding Griselda as he was about slipping off and visiting the Boville City Hall courtyard in search of a twilight night crawler snack feast—but that was his secret.

"I don't believe we can accomplish much tonight," announced Steer. "Let's agree to meet here at sunrise tomorrow. There's no indication at this time that Griselda is in mortal danger. We've had a rough night and could use some rest." Before anyone could respond to his pronouncement, Adam snatched the paper hat off of Cal's head. "Didn't you say you had Lenny in lock-up?" he asked, ignoring Cal's protests.

"Can't you hear the little noisemaker in the back?" responded Pork.

"Take a look at this." Adam unfolded the hat and spread it upon the chief's desk. There was a large photo on the back page of a merchant ship's prow slipping beneath the ocean waves; a lifeboat bobbed in the foreground. Black thunderclouds pummeled the fragile raft; the occupants, illuminated by a flash of lightning, looked like ghosts emerging out of the gloom in a dark attic. "It's rather obscure, but it looks like Lenny sitting in the front of that life raft." Adam pointed at the indistinct rat in the photograph.

The others crowded about the tabletop and agreed that the rodent in the lifeboat did indeed bear a resemblance to the prisoner banging his cup in the backroom, but the photo had been taken at night and the ship's flares eradicated a lot of the detail of the features of the boat's occupants. But there was no mistaking the beret and the pointed beard on the rat.

"This newspaper's dated May 17, nearly three months ago," said Adam.

"You guys don't empty that recycle bin too often, do you?" commented Cal.

"So what's this got to do with the price of noodles?" interrupted Cluck. "We've got to get an early start tomorrow to hunt down our squad car before that dame…" Pork's glare prompted him to reverse himself quickly. "Before uh…before someone crashes it."

"As you might recall, Cluck, my cardinal rule is: Never overlook anything. And rule number two: patience, so that you don't overlook anything. Besides, my curiosity's piqued. Chief, do you still have that magnifying glass you use to read with?"

Pork, turning red in the face, pulled a large magnifying glass out of his top desk drawer. "I use it for examining paw prints. I'm not that old yet, you know."

"Forgive me if I offended you," said Steer with a wry grin. "It was unintentional." He'd seen the chief using the glass many times to read the lottery numbers in the paper. But it was not his nature to upset others unless necessary.

"Your education starts now, Cal." Steer spit on the glass and rubbed it clean with his hat brim. "The ship went down in the Western Pawcific Ocean the day before the photo was printed in the *Gazette* as an AP feature. It appears that the photo was taken by the rescue crew."

"So what's the significance of that?" asked Cluck.

"It means, gentlemen," replied the detective, refolding the newspaper into a hat and handing it to Cal. "That the ship's log would have a record of who they picked up from that raft, and we have a pretty good guess of which day that was based on this newspaper."

"And what if it was Lenny?" interrupted Cluck again. He was beginning to chafe at the thought of not being in charge of the investigation: he was the Police Force's primary officer before Steer came into the picture. On the other hand, life was getting a lot more exciting since Adam Steer reentered their lives. He would never admit that he didn't like someone else coming up with clues or drawing conclusions that he had totally missed, especially someone who hadn't graduated from Cow Tech in Criminal Studies as he had.

"I don't know what it means, Lieutenant," said Steer. "Probably nothing. But since we've got the little cheese sniffer in the cage, let's see what Lenny's been up to lately."

SCENE TWO: FOWL PLAY

Adam and Cal accepted the hospitality of Chief Pork at his townhouse a few blocks from the precinct for the evening. Between the chief's snoring rumbling through the living quarters and Cal muttering and laughing to himself in his sleep, Adam caught only a precious few minutes of snooze while curled up on the loveseat near the fireplace. He wondered how the other two managed not to wake themselves while he spent the evening hours counting the knotholes in the pine ceiling in an attempt to bore himself into Slumberland. When a rooster in the distance announced the dawning of a new day, Cal rose from the hide-a-bed in the living room, hair tousled but feeling refreshed, while the detective greeted his comrades with red-rimmed eyes and drooping shoulders.

After a breakfast of pancakes smothered with grits and syrup, accompanied with copious amounts of Steerbucks coffee, the trio drove off in the chief's Chevy to meet Lt. Cluck at the precinct. During the ride Pork explained the reason for Griselda's visit to the precinct house and her obvious distress at the loss of the statuette. Adam's first instinct was that the pearl was moved during a redecorating of the mansion and would turn up in a cursory search of the ostrich's estate. An open-and-shut case. Problem was: he had left Lilah's Happy Farm for the first time since he'd checked in many months ago. After getting a taste of the game once again, could he bear to return to the tedium of the pasture? And continue listening to the inane chatter of Cal and the birds into an indefinite future?

"Pepy never showed," yawned the rooster as he opened the front door. "And I scarcely caught a wink of sleep with that rat complaining all night and banging his TV tray against the glass."

"You didn't go sneaking behind my back and call the State Patrol did you?" Pork pointed a hoofed finger into Cluck's beak.

The lieutenant's Adam's apple visibly rose and fell with the hard gulp in response to Pork's threat. "No, no, sir."

"Good." Pork squinted his right eye suspiciously and removed his finger. The telephone was rescued from its brown paper wrapper and sitting on the desktop; next to it lay, opened, a red codebook, obviously removed from the bookcase behind the desk chair. "'Cause if you did," the police chief added, "I'd be obligated to wring your scrawny little neck. Nothing personal, of course."

"Of course, nothing personal," Cluck agreed, placing a winged hand protectively to his throat. He grinned unconvincingly and returned the codebook to the bookshelf.

"This is what we're going to do instead: I'd like you to contact Lt. Sparrow at Precinct 10. He owes me a favor that I've never cashed in."

"I thought you didn't want someone else involved in locating Big White?"

"You're going to tell a little *white* lie. Tell him we're looking for Pepy—that he took the squad car out last night and hasn't returned or phoned in. We're not worried: it's our only squad car and we're just wondering what's causing the delay. Ask him to take a few flights about the county as a favor to me. He won't want to get another officer in trouble and will keep it quiet."

"You want me to lie?"

Pork stretched his arms out in front of him with his hoofed fingers curled halfway as if struggling to prevent himself from throttling his lieutenant. "Lord help me if I have to call Lt. Sparrow myself!"

Cluck snatched up the phone receiver. "I'm dialing! I'm dialing!"

Cal was thrilled at the opportunity of going into the backroom and seeing the inside of a jailhouse for the first time. He was disappointed not to find a dozen cages filled with hardened criminals, but, instead, a dingy grey room illuminated by one low wattage bulb hanging at the end of a crooked wire and two cages: one with a bucket and straw flooring that appeared to require changing after housing a party of drunks and the other made of glass holding two very discontented, but not very vicious-looking, rodents.

"What kind of joint youse guys running here, Pork? I couldn't get a wink of sleep with that danged hamster running on his wheel all night!" complained Lenny, rubbing at his eyes with his front paws.

"Just trying to get away from your whining butt," replied the hamster with a yawn as he burrowed out of sight into the cedar chips lining the bottom of the cage.

"Join the club," interrupted Adam. He pulled up a stool and sat eye-to-eye to the rat. "You needing any seasick pills lately?"

"Whatcha meaning, Steer?" Lenny squinted his eyes, obviously suspicious of the detective's line of questioning. He tugged at his green beret as if reassuring himself that it was still there atop his head.

"He means this, dunderhead," exclaimed Cal suddenly leaping to his feet. Grasping the dangling overhead wire, he swung the light bulb to and fro in a rhythmic motion. "Ocean waves moving up and down, and up and down, and up and..."

Chief Pork clutched at his stomach, still tender from last night's activities, and choked back the bile rising in his throat. "He means did you desert any sinking ships lately?"

"What would I be doing on a ship?"

"That's what we're asking yas, ya dirty rat!" said Cal, grasping the wire near the bulb and shining it into Lenny's face. Adam pushed the bovine aside, reasserting his authority. "Let's try another tactic. Do you know anything about the theft of the squad car last night?" This question produced an ear-to-ear grin from the rat.

"Did you have to tell him that, Steer?" groaned the chief.

"What would I be doing with some pig's car?" replied Lenny. "It's not like I be needing any more attention from the coppers lately."

"Just checking," said Adam.

Without responding to the rat's protestations of innocence and claims of police brutality, the two police officers and two detectives left the jail room to meet in the lobby. Pepy the sloth, who was sliding his timecard into the clock, greeted them. His thick tan fur was matted and his uniform disheveled. Guess not many got a good night's sleep last evening, thought Adam while the chief chewed the deputy out for coming in on the wrong shift.

Fifteen minutes later the four of them were riding in Pork's white Chevy down Hells Highway toward the cornfield where the possible kidnapping took place. At the chief's request, Cluck pulled a compact pair of binoculars out of the bin in the dashboard and scrutinized the landscape for signs of the abduction site. The circling of crows overhead to the right caught his attention and soon they stopped on the shoulder of the highway.

It was a beautiful August morning: yesterday's rain cleared the smog to reveal a crystal blue sky unmarred by grey clouds. A gentle breeze kept the temperature comfortable and the slight humidity refreshing, rather than bothersome. Stepping out of the car, Cal lifted his face upward to bathe in the golden beams. Adam smiled, admiring the bull's simple enjoyment of life. Many times he was caught up in analyzing the clues of a case or the thrill of the pursuit of a villain and would forget that life was to be enjoyed, not just studied or run through at a gallop. He slipped off his hat and allowed the sunlight to caress his wavy shock of brown hair. Cars and trucks whizzed by, often loaded with camping gear, their occupants giving the detectives scarcely a glance of concern.

"That's one heck of a hole!" exclaimed Cal, looking down into the cornfield from the roadside. "You sure that's where Big White was parked? How in rusty cow bells could the car drive out of that?"

"Yes, I'm sure that's where we left the car," Pork replied, his voice carrying a hint of doubt. "But in the dark the hole didn't seem quite so deep."

Pork and Cluck strolled down the embankment and the hundred yards to the edge of the site, which looked like an enormous ice cream dipper had scooped out a twenty-yard chunk of the green cornfield, leaving a large dirty brown hole. Stalks of corn lay strewn to the sides. The police officers searched for footprints or other signs of critters, but most traces of last night's activity were washed down by the evening rain—Pork could scarcely make out his own shoe prints from the previous night and Cluck's claw marks not at all.

A curious crow winged down and settled near the edge of the hole to study the intruders; Pork shooed him off with a wave of his hand. "Stay away, you're messing with evidence," he yelled. But the only other signs of critter activity were multiple bird markings from claws, evidently crows searching for ears of corn shook loose by the formation of the hole. He shuddered. All signs of which direction the squad car had driven off were gone.

Cluck cupped his winged hands around his beak to amplify his voice. "We don't find anything down here," he yelled to the duo alongside the highway.

Adam had borrowed the binoculars and was surveying the cornfield from above. With a nod he acknowledged the rooster's comment. Cal observed him with undisguised interest. There was a line of strewn cornstalks, tossed to the right and to the left, leading from the hole into the midst of the field and eastward toward open countryside. For a moment he watched Pork and Lt. Cluck walk from the abduction site to follow the trail of displaced corn stalks.

"It's very strange," mused the master detective, lowering the glasses and rubbing his chin. "I don't see any evidence that the car was driven through the field. No ruts from tire tracks and the corn isn't squashed or broken as if run down by a vehicle; it's tossed to and fro as if it fell over or was uprooted. It's almost as if a giant picked up the squad car and walked off with it."

"Or maybe an alien beamed the car up," Cal interrupted but without his usual enthusiasm. He looked upward, twisting at the foil on his horn, but the sky betrayed no hint of mystery. "It looks like a giant concave crop circle."

Adam frowned. Maybe Cal hadn't been soaking up rays earlier but was searching for flying saucers. He shuddered and shook his head, as if trying to knock the disturbing thought out of it. Some things were better left not considered too deeply, particularly since Cal insisted on his companionship. But what had happened here? Surely nothing supernatural: There was a logical explanation. The chief believed in omens and superstitions, and Cal in his aliens, but not Adam. The real world was fascinating enough without unnecessary embellishment. Was Griselda in greater danger than he had first supposed? The unknown made the imagination work too hard; fortunately the truth, when revealed, was usually less exciting. It was likely that their worries were unwarranted: Griselda would shortly appear in front of the precinct, honking Big White's horn, and announcing in her typically dramatic fashion that they had underestimated her once again, that she had recently learned to drive, and oh, what fun she had at their expense. Adam wasn't going to express any alarm at this point in the investigation. Pork appeared to have recovered from his fainting spells the previous night, but Adam didn't want to frighten him unnecessarily.

Steer's attention was diverted by the unwelcome sound of a tractor combine coming from the south. He directed the binoculars in its direction: stalks of corn were dropping to the ground like dead flies from the sky. A twenty-five-foot-wide swath was being cut across the trail extant to the abduction site. Adam shouted and waved his arms wildly to catch the attention of the officers in the field—unnecessarily it turned out. The roar of the giant engines caught their attention and they ran toward the mammoth vehicle. But the farmer driving the tractor, an old Springer spaniel with floppy ears, could not hear them over the roar nor see them over the hood, and corn stalks continued to fall and contaminate the evidence site.

Until the hound and the tractor plummeted into the hole.

An angry dog sprang out of the hole and entered immediately into a shouting match with the two police officers. Adam was happy to be up on the bluff and out of harm's way.

"This beats watching television any day," Crazy Cal exulted, moving forward to join the fight.

Adam held him back with a swing of his arm. With amusement he observed the dog and Chief Pork pushing at the front of the engine in a feeble attempt to push the giant machine out of the hole while Cluck ran around the dirt perimeter, pulling at his top comb in anxiety and making a last sweep for clues with his magnifying glass. Moments later the hound waved his front paw in disgust at the hog and marched off in a huff across the cornfield—most likely returning to his farmhouse to call for a tow truck, Adam surmised, to unintentionally destroy any remaining clues to the mystery of the missing squad car. He sighed.

"Couldn't Cluck do air surveillance?" asked Crazy Cal.

"Ever seen a flying rooster wearing a gun belt?"

A few moments later a crow alighted near their feet, a large juicy worm hanging from his beak. Adam winced in disgust while the bird, in obvious enjoyment, sucked down the hapless worm. "Delicious. Like to try one?" he asked, holding one wriggling victim in his winged hand.

"No, I wouldn't feel comfortable doing that," Adam said, pushing the bird's proffered hand away.

"Don't mind if I do," interrupted Cal, snatching the worm out of the crow's hand, and bringing it to his mouth. "Never tried worm, at least, not that I know of. You can't always be sure what's in the hay, particularly if the sun hasn't come up yet." He rubbed his stomach in mock hunger, one eye on Adam to see the result his act was having on the detective. The effect was laughter. With a yelp of surprise he dropped the worm to the ground. It had bopped his tender nose with the edge of a tiny wooden sign.

The crow stepped toward its victim but was intercepted by Adam, who said, "Leave the little fellow alone. It may be of no concern to you, but it obviously values its life."

The worm slipped into the tall grass bordering the incline to the cornfield.

"You know, that trail you're looking at ends about three-quarters of a mile eastward," the bird said, craning his head in search of the recalcitrant worm. "Then there's another big hole like that one down below. And," he flapped his wings, treading the air slightly above, "a mass of worms just begging to be eaten. And the oddest thing is, they appear to be marching in several rows." He flew upward a few yards then abruptly spun around to dive-bomb the cattle's heads, yelling "Yeehaw," and joined a growing number of his feathered comrades flying in a funnel-shaped circle to the east. Adam lifted the binoculars then turned away, wincing at the sight of the crows, diving toward the ground and soaring back up into the sky with several wriggling worms in their beaks. A worm massacre that would whet Cluck's appetite.

"You weren't really going to eat that worm, were you?" Adam asked.

"No."

"Liar!" The worm popped out of the grass and slapped the back of Cal's shins with his sign.

"I've been called worse," Cal responded, scarcely aware of the assault to his shin.

"That's not hard to believe," the worm retorted.

Smiling broadly, Adam bent forward to confront his contentious visitor.

"Thanks for saving my life," the little worm said without a hint of obsequiousness. Though tiny, there was no doubting the authority in his voice. "From that big boob," he added, apparently trusting in Adam to continue to protect him. Cal stomped a hoof in mock anger but appeared more amused than the detective.

"I'm afraid that we can't do too much for your pals." Gently Adam picked up his new friend, cupped into his right hoofed hand.

"The survivors will reconnoiter at the Boville City Hall."

Adam had to admire the little critter for its pluck out of proportion for its size.

"So what can I do in return for you?" the worm asked. "I don't like being in anybody's debt."

Adam explained what he knew about Griselda's abduction as he carried the worm back down to edge of the cornfield. "I'll see what

I can do. But I have to meet my comrades in Boville, that is, what'll be left of them." With a wave of his tail as if in farewell, the worm wriggled down the embankment and burrowed down into the abduction site, leaving his sign behind on the topsoil.

"Not the sentimental sort, is he?" asked Cal.

"His kind can't afford to be."

Huffing and out of breath, Pork trodded toward the cattle followed by Lt. Cluck, gnawing on an ear of shucked corn. "Haven't got a clue how Griselda got that car out of the hole. No tire treads, no evidence of spinning wheels. In fact, we found nothing but those darned worms again," the hog remonstrated. "I should've run them down the first time we saw them."

Fifteen minutes later the four of them were riding in Pork's white Chevy through the entranceway of Madam Portentsky's estate, Grande Le Coeur. The two white wrought-iron gates were laced with feathers and leaves tastefully done in the art deco style and the half-mile driveway was lined with topiary in the shapes of exotic birds: parrots, emus, and ibis. "Wow, I'm really eager to make this chick's acquaintance," enthused Cal as the car came to a stop at the foot of the waterfall staircase leading to the main doorway.

"I strongly advise you to show respect when talking about Griselda," whispered Lt. Cluck into Cal's ear. "The chief has strong feelings for her that he's reluctant to own up to."

"So what's it like kissing a beak?" asked Cal before Adam could slap his hooves over the cow's mouth. Fortunately, as the four of them exited the vehicle, the butler distracted Pork's attention. Stepping down the staircase to greet them, the Dalmatian wasn't dressed in the typical movie film black-with-tails but in a powder puff blue suit coat with a white shirt and bowtie.

"I couldn't quite catch the full account of what you told me over the gate's intercom," the dog said with a stately and proper British accent, "but I do hope that you can shed some light onto the whereabouts of our mistress. She did not come home at the anticipated time last night."

"And when would that be?" asked Adam as the group followed the butler up the cascading staircase toward the front entrance. Lovely art nouveau railings, silvery steel vines twisting and winding along either side of the steps, glittered in the sunlight. It was like entering Camelot. All that was missing were courtiers with horns and heraldic flags fluttering in the wind.

"About 6 PM, sir. She has her bath drawn at 6:15 sharp each evening and her dinner on a tray in her private bedchamber at 7."

"With all of this attention to detail and nobody noticed this?" interjected the master detective, pointing toward a large dagger thrust into the wood in the elaborately carved front door. A piece of notepaper folded in two was impaled amongst images of dancing elephants and mice. Adam pulled two rubber gloves over his hoofed hands. All eyes watched as he pulled the large hunting knife out of the door, unfolded the attached note, and examined the message typewritten in red ink.

"Leave the black pearl cow statue in the blue flowerpot," Steer read silently with Cal peeping over his shoulder, "in the lobby of the Westwind Hotel in Barkerville at 3 AM Sunday morning and take a fast hike out of town or the old dame gets plucked." Unfortunately, it was time to alarm Pork.

"Guess that huge knife blended into the woodwork, eh, Dude?" remarked Cal.

"That's Dudley, if you please," remarked the butler without breaking his composure.

"I guess this answers our question about what happened to Griselda," commented Steer, handing the note to Chief Pork. After pulling on a white glove, the ex-lover read the note with shaky fingers and, snout wrinkling with suppressed emotion, returned the letter to Adam.

"It appears that this investigation now has a change of focus," the detective announced to the others. He examined the hunting knife. It had a black plastic handle and a five-inch blade, somewhat battered from use: nothing unusual and available for purchase in any five-and-dime store's sports department. Looking for its source would be a waste of valuable time, which, apparently from the contents of the note, was now in short supply. He slipped the dagger into a large plastic baggie then into his side pocket and fingered at the notch in the door. It wasn't very deep. Additionally, the blade did not slide in at an angle, but was thrust into the wood straight on. Whoever pushed the knife into the door didn't have a lot of strength or was in a big hurry. It couldn't have been there long: it would've fallen out soon on its own.

"Please, come into the parlor and kindly share the contents of the missive," said the butler, motioning to the guests to come into the mansion. "I am greatly concerned about the safety of our mistress."

"And well you should be," Adam announced when they had all settled onto the white satin loveseats in the parlor. "Pork, buck up. You need to stay strong to help Griselda."

"I'm a professional first and a lov—...friend...second," Pork replied. He and Griselda had broken off their relationship two winters ago, and, until recently, scarcely communicated with each other except professionally. But in every conversation there was an underlying tension of hurt feeling that betrayed itself in sarcasm and sardonic wit.

Adam read the note aloud, watching the response in the butler's face. His expression remained stoic, except for his eyes, which widened with astonishment. Wasn't faked, Adam surmised. But someone with access to the estate was involved. Had to be, unless it was a bird. Could explain the lack of strength in wedging the knife into the door. But how had the bird been able to wing in, shove a note into the door, wing out, and gone unnoticed by the gatekeepers or gardeners? Surely they would've checked out the door right away, found the knife, and alerted Dudley. Someone at the mansion had unknowingly incriminated themselves.

"Well, this is what, Tuesday?" asked Cluck, wincing at the thought of what a plucking must feel like. He'd lost a few feathers here and there, like the time he caught his tail feathers in the squad car door after the wind slammed it shut. "That gives us five days to get the statue over to the hotel." He paused for a moment, a quizzical look on his face. "What statue are they talking about?"

"Grissie came by the precinct yesterday to ask us to help her find a statue stolen from her home that she called the MooMoo Pearl, some family heirloom from the Far East. Said it was in the shape of a dancing cow. And she was very insistent that Adam be the one assigned to the case," answered the chief in a low voice.

"Then we've got to find that statue," announced Lt. Cluck. So that's why Pork wanted to locate Adam the night before! Wasn't he, a high-ranking police officer, capable of locating the pearl without the aid of a lovelorn ex-detective? In fact, if the chief had assigned him the case and not gone joyriding in search of the disgraced sleuth, the old bird might not have been snatched. He had just supposed that Griselda wanted to do an interview with Steer for the *Cloverleaf Gazette*. Since Pork was so sensitive about his relationship with the bird in the past, Cluck had kept to himself, not considering for a moment that she had arrived at the precinct to inquire about a criminal investigation. He had assumed they were merely giving the ostrich a ride, an excuse to tread familiar ground once again with her old beau. He gave Adam a jealous glare that would not go unnoticed.

Adam sighed. There was never a straightforward case for him to solve when on the Boville detective squad. Inhabitants of the small sleepy city of Boville had lots of unoccupied time to think up elaborate schemes worthy of any comic book villain.

"You know anything about a black statuette in the shape of a cow that's been reported missing by Madam Portentsky?" Adam asked the dog.

Dudley, the butler, led them through a long hallway into the receiving room. A mural of capuchin monkeys and palm leaves decorated the far wall while a rush of warm air greeted them from the fire crackling in the hearth. Dudley pointed to the mantelpiece above the fireplace, crowded with a dazzling collection of glass cows in a rainbow of bright colors. "She kept the black pearl here between the red and the green statuettes. I believe she mentioned something about it being missing before she had her chauffeur drop her off at the stationhouse."

"And when did you first see the statue on the mantelpiece?"

"Sometime late last spring. She said it was an heirloom and didn't specify which relative. It was not my place to inquire into the private business of my mistress."

"No, certainly not. Could she have owned it previously and moved it from another room?"

"I do not know, sir." Dudley was clearly insulted. "Please ask the maids."

Adam walked over to the mantel, pulling a pair of rubber gloves over his hands. Gently he picked up each of the glass cows, examining them from every angle. Each piece was formed into a charming dance pose. He wondered if Madam Portentsky had dated animals from other species besides the chief. "Does Madam travel much outside of the States, Dudley?" he asked, replacing the last of the objects back onto the mantelpiece.

The butler was surreptitiously scratching himself with his hindleg when startled to attention. "Not to my knowledge, sir. She was reluctant to travel by airplane and didn't care for the slowness of ships."

"He's found a clue already?" Cal asked with undisguised pride. He was already enjoying this detecting stuff. He and Adam were certainly making a fine team.

"I suppose an old newshound like Madam Griselda wouldn't want to be too far out of touch with her news base for any length of time," Adam responded to no one in particular. "Dudley, old boy, you don't mind helping me out a bit for a moment, do you?"

"If I can be of help, certainly, sir."

"Would you be so good as to take a good sniff about this mantelpiece?"

"Indeed, that's a rather vulgar request." Dudley lifted his muzzle heavenward and away to emphasize his disdain.

"Just take a few sniffs about and tell me if you notice anything irregular. Some scent that's unfamiliar to you, that you don't recognize."

Dudley sniffed a few times about the mantelpiece then wrinkled his nose in disgust. "No, sir, nothing unusual." He paused then grinned, "except musty cattle."

"Don't you find that rather odd?" asked the master detective, ignoring the insult.

"Are you inferring that one of the staff..." began Dudley with disdain curling his upper lip.

"No, no, not implying anything, my good critter."

"The staff regularly uses aerosol to clean the rooms. It's possible that any scent the thief left behind was unintentionally erased by the staff during their daily household duties." Then with a sneer, the butler added, "sir."

"I'd like to examine the rest of the mansion, if you don't mind. I'd also like to talk to all the staff, including the chauffeur."

"Certainly, sir," Dudley said. "We are all quite eager for our mistress's return and will certainly cooperate." Adam and Cal followed the butler out of the room while Cluck and the chief began dusting the statuettes and mantel for prints.

"The butler did it," whispered Crazy Cal into Adam's ear. "Or he smelled someone's scent and he's concealing the fact." Adam just nodded in agreement to end the conversation quickly before Dudley's keen sense of hearing picked up Cal's remarks.

Adam was impressed with the stateliness of Griselda's home. There was decoration without ostentation, clutter with regularity, cleanliness without seeming Spartan. He wondered why Pork's relationship with Griselda didn't last beyond a year and whether it hinged on the obvious fact that they couldn't have children together. He had mixed feelings about interspecies couples adopting. There were just some things ostriches did that piglets shouldn't be doing, and vice versa. He did a cursory examination of the rooms and their closets, taking mental note of what the contents would reveal about the state of the owner's finances and interests. He also checked the bedchambers for evidence of occupation: there didn't appear to be any recent guests. A question to the butler confirmed his observations. He didn't like to rely on household staff for answers because they sometimes lied to protect their employers, or themselves. But it never hurt to confirm whether the answers concurred with his own suspicions.

He asked Cal to continue searching the closets while he questioned the staff. Cal was torn between wanting to accompany Adam or obeying the request, but this was his first assignment from the master detective and he wanted to prove himself worthy of being his partner. Sighing he borrowed a penlight from Adam to continue the search of the closets.

"I noticed that none of the glass figurines on the fireplace mantel were dusty," Adam remarked to the butler. "I would like to meet the maid in charge of keeping that particular room tidy. She is certainly very meticulous. I could never keep all of those tiny grooves clean myself."

"Perhaps you are accustomed to the lower standards of the local government," Dudley sniffed. "Madam hires only the best."

"No doubt present company included," Adam smiled in response. It never hurt to grease the spokes of even the most well-oiled heel.

Adam followed the butler into the kitchen. The housemaid was eating her lunch at a cheap Formica table near the pantry. Startled by the unexpected guests, the French poodle dropped her spoon into her bowl of chocolate mousse and jumped to her feet. Extending a delicately manicured white paw and smoothing her apron, she greeted the detective with a slight curtsey.

"Miss Demeris Oui Oui," Dudley announced formally. "I regret to tell you, Miss Oui Oui," he added, addressing the poodle, "but this detective is searching for the whereabouts of Madam Portentsky. If you haven't heard yet, she didn't come home last night."

"Oh dear, that's just awful. I know that she doesn't like to be out after dark."

The poodle sounded sincere, noted Adam, but seemed a little twitchy. Her eyes darted around the room, and she stole several glances toward the back door. She also seemed a little too jumpy when he and Dudley entered the kitchen and kept her voice low when speaking, as if afraid of being heard beyond her personal space.

"I noticed the excellent job that you do in keeping the furnishings clean," said Adam, observing that Demeris relaxed at the compliment. Her eyes stilled and focused their attention upon his face. "I am sure that you have an excellent memory for the madam's belongings, and," watching the poodle closely, added, "particularly her more fragile and expensive items." Demeris flinched slightly at the word "expensive" and her smile seemed forced.

"Yes, the madam has utmost confidence in my skills in caring for her belongings," the poodle responded. "I can assure you that she never has to question my integrity or trustworthiness."

"No one is making any accusations," responded Adam, "nor questioning your integrity. Do you recall seeing a black pearl statue in the shape of a dancing cow sitting over the mantelpiece?"

"Yes. It's on the mantel in the front parlor." Her eyes leveled with his in a cold stare.

"Are you sure?"

"Yes. It is my duty to clean the downstairs. I don't understand what this has to do with Madam Griselda not returning last night." The poodle was on the defensive, one paw balled into a fist.

"Have you seen the pearl anywhere else on the premises at any other time?"

"Are you accusing her…" Dudley interrupted.

"No. Just fishing for details. It's my job. Nothing more. Nothing personal," Adam said. He pulled his hat off to distract the poodle's attention while he did a quick study of her uniform and hair. Each curl of her white coat was perfectly in line with no hairs straying out beyond her silhouette; her dress with its apron was starched and without wrinkles. Very careful toilette, Adam thought to himself—a critter accustomed to paying attention to detail. Which was why he was surprised to notice the condition of her nails when saying goodbye. As she picked up her spoon to resume eating, he saw that the cuticles were stained black.

He spent the next hour questioning the kitchen staff, the other maids, and the grounds keepers. No one had noticed the statue before May at the earliest and only in the front parlor. They offered no other information that appeared to be immediately relevant. The chauffeur, another Dalmatian, also didn't offer anything that was out of the ordinary: Madam Portentsky hadn't mentioned anything about the reason for her trip to Precinct Thirteen-and-a-half and he presumed she was merely paying an old friend, Chief Pork, a visit. As she didn't request him to wait for a return trip to the mansion, it was the chauffeur's belief that his mistress would get a ride home from one of the police officers. The Catillac remained in the garage, untouched since yesterday's journey.

There was nothing suspicious about the chauffeur's answers or behavior that indicated he was lying, so Adam rejoined the Boville police officers in the parlor.

"No prints, nothing at all," announced Lt. Cluck at Adam's reappearance. "We dusted everything on the mantel and the figurines and even the grating in front of fireplace and there are no prints whatsoever."

"Indeed," responded Adam. "That's rather odd, wouldn't you say, when there are so many servants bustling about?"

Cal came bouncing into the room, his paper hat nearly falling from his head. "Nothing to report except lots of stinky shoes and an enormous brass paperclip that I just had to pilfer." He was holding what was indeed one very large shiny paperclip nearly the size of a cow's hoof. This reinforced Adam's observance of the professionalism of the household staff: not one of them snickered or smiled at Crazy Cal's odd appearance when they were exploring the rooms together. That made Demeris' unsettled attitude all the more noticeable.

"I suppose our mistress could make do without that paperclip," sniffed Dudley as he entered the room. "Did you find anything useful, sir?" he asked Adam.

"Many things useful, but nothing conclusive," replied Steer. "Anything else to report, Lieutenant?"

"Besides that Ms. Portentsky had a weird affinity for dancing cows, I can't say I do," replied Cluck.

The chief was sitting on the white damask couch, wiping his brow with his hat. He was containing his emotions quite well, Adam thought.

"I see nothing odd myself," said Cal, picking a particularly fragile looking figurine from the mantelpiece while Dudley, gesturing wildly, implored him to put it back.

"O.K., O.K., keep your britches in place," Cal said as he put the slender red cow, posed as a ballerina doing a pirouette, back into its place. However, he didn't like taking directions from any stranger and, feeling an impulse to be belligerent, pushed the figurine around to make it appear as if it were giving another green cow a kiss on the lips. He loved the agitated look on Dudley's face when he swung back to face Adam.

"Now, Cal, we shouldn't abuse our welcome," said Steer, approaching the mantelpiece. Nonchalantly he picked up the red cow and returned it to its former—and proper—position on the mantel. "These are quite beautiful, aren't they, Dudley?" The butler was looking concerned about the safety of the Madam's glass collection. Adam picked up a few other figurines and turned them about in his hands, admiring a particularly lovely honey yellow cow doing the foxtrot. "Notice how the skylight above is placed so that the sunlight shines onto the statues, as if it was built specifically to highlight the collection, and not vice versa. The light creates a glistening rainbow of color." He paused for a moment then discreetly slipped a hand into his right pocket. "An opaque black statuette seems a little out of place in this glittering color scheme, wouldn't you say, Dudley?"

The Dalmatian swallowed before replying tersely. "It's not my place to question my lady's decor, sir."

Moments later they were all seated in the chief's Chevy, Cluck behind the wheel, returning to the stationhouse.

"So you gonna keep us in suspense forever, Adam? What did we miss besides the lack of prints?" asked Chief Pork.

"The mansion is exquisitely decorated in expensive furnishings, paintings, and knickknacks that show an utmost attention to detail and upscale taste," began Adam. "However, each piece of glassware on the mantel was stamped with "Made in Singapork." Why would she place a very expensive pearl over the fireplace, which would not only stand out like a sore thumb amongst the brilliantly colored statuettes in color, but also in expense? You said, Chief, she claimed it was an heirloom?"

"That's right. And she was pretty distraught over its loss."

The puzzled looks on Cal's and Cluck's faces encouraged Adam to continue his lesson in good detective work. "Also, Dudley informed us that Griselda didn't care for travel outside the States, so those weren't souvenirs she was lining up over the fireplace. It's unusual that her entire collection comes solely from one country in MooAsia. No other objects in her home were stamped Singapork. And also, coincidentally, she said the MooMoo heirloom came from the Far East although she didn't specify where, did she?"

"Never mentioned it to me, Adam," responded Chief Pork hoarsely. Feeling a sense of doom wash over him, he popped a few antacids from a roll hidden in his inner shirt pocket and nervously rubbed his lucky frog's leg. "But now that I think about it, I don't recall her ever saying she had a glass collection of any sort when we were dat—...fraternizing together."

"How long ago was that, Chief?"

"Together about a year, broken up a few years. But you should recall that, Steer. You were with the Force then." Pork popped another antacid. It was supposed to be cherry-flavored but tasted more like chalk. His mouth was dry: He needed a beer.

"Just thinking aloud, Chief, putting the pieces into their proper places. I don't mean to scratch at old wounds," Steer said as the hog grimaced in response.

"What does all this mean, Detective?" asked Cal.

"It means that we need to pay the mansion another visit when we are not expected."

"You're not saying we should break in, are you?" asked Cluck. "That's not proper procedure. We'll need a search warrant from Judge Bookem first."

"I'm not saying that *we* should do anything at all," replied Adam, pulling a green cow from the pocket of his rain slicker. He gently slid his hoofed finger across its glossy surface. "Just me."

"And me, too!" exclaimed Crazy Cal who was not to be forgotten.

SCENE THREE: ARTISTIC LIBERTIES

"Where's Lenny? I've got a few more questions I'd like to ask him!" thundered Chief of Police Pork as he and Cluck entered the precinct house lobby. Pepy was slumped in the chief's chair, feet up on the accompanying desk and sound asleep.

Pepy yawned to alertness and rose slowly to his feet. "Was bailed out…by some lady…while you guys…were gallivanting…about." He spoke with a lazy drawl, as if each word was taffy being stretched thin. The sloth's slow speech always irritated the chief, but good help was hard to find and sloths were normally nocturnal, which made them excellent night watchmen. They were also painfully slow in their movements, but speed wasn't required in guarding sleeping prisoners. That is, when they came in on the correct shift. Guarding moving and active prisoners in the daytime was another matter. He wasn't surprised to find Pepy asleep on a shift that wasn't in tune with his nighttime biorhythm.

"Bailed out by whom?"

"Someone who called herself…an old biddy,…but she looked… pretty young…to me. Couldn't have been…much beyond…college age,…if you ask me."

Pork swallowed hard, attempting to get his temper under control. Sloths were also notorious for being slow about getting to the heart of a matter. It often took several questions to get to the answer you wanted. Cluck slinked over to the bookcase and ran one forefinger along the bookbindings, as if looking for a particular item. Pork knew that his lieutenant had every code book in the cabinet nearly memorized: Cluck was just trying to look busy to keep out of the middle of an ensuing confrontation.

"What species was she, for heaven's sake?"

"A cow, and…a nice-looking…one too,…if you ask me,…except I didn't care…much for the style…of clothing…she was wearing…Too mod…for my taste."

"The name wouldn't be something that rhymed with biddy, like Liddy or Betty, would it?"

"Could be," replied Pepy, screwing up his face in thought. "You know,…could be…something like…Netty or…Betsy also. Yes,…that was it,…Betsy."

"Betsy Moo?" asked Cluck, suddenly becoming interested.

"No, she didn't…moo at all," answered the sloth.

"Well, isn't this just grand," continued the rooster. "We're gonna have not just one but two cops discombobulated over women."

"I'm not disconbubble-ated or whatever the heck it was you said," shouted the chief.

"No, not at all." Cluck rolled his eyes.

"I want you to sign out," Pork roared at Pepy, "and don't count the time it takes you to get over to the time clock!"

"So who's gonna pull night duty?" asked Cluck, knowing that the chief was taking his frustration out over Griselda's disappearance on the sloth. He liked Pepy who, because he was slow-witted, made the lieutenant his superior in every conversation.

"That's right. Pepy, get back here!" Pork bellowed. The sloth, only managing to lift one leg in the air since his dismissal, didn't have much ground to cover in his return to the chief's chair.

"Some Lieutenant Spiro,…Spiral,…Sparrow,…something like that,…called about…an hour ago," Pepy continued. "Said he hadn't found…anything but since I…picked up the line, …he obviously didn't need…to keep looking…Seemed to think…you'd know what…it was about."

"Uh, good work, Officer," Chief Pork responded distractedly. Where the heck was the squad car? He couldn't write off the mileage while on patrol in his Chevy: how could he explain THAT in the budget? He fingered the ransom letter in his breast pocket, as if placing it near his heart was keeping Griselda herself nearer to him. It was getting tattered from his nervous rubbing. Cluck's attention was drawn to his pocket by his movements.

"Let's take another look at that note, Chief," asked Cluck, proffering his hand to take the paper. Reluctantly, his superior handed the note to his lieutenant. Cluck pulled the note out of the baggie, spread it out on the chief's desk, and examined it closely with the magnifying glass that Steer had left on the desk earlier. He then reached into a cabinet drawer, pulled out a small light box, switched on the light, and placed the note on it. He hummed and hawed for effect until Pork came and peered over his shoulder to also examine the note. Pepy began the slow journey from the chair to participate in the investigation.

"No smudges, no visible latent prints," Cluck announced. "But what can this note tell us about the captors? Quite a bit, I imagine. As you can see, Chief," he continued, pointing at the type, "there is a slight bit of dark ink at the bottom of each letter."

"You're right, Cluck," was the reply. "So what? If Steer didn't think it was worth bothering with, why should we waste time with it? No one has ever bested him yet when it comes to solving crimes."

"That's right, Boss," added Pepy. "He helped me find where I left my badge one night."

Cluck winced at the compliment to Steer. "Uh, let's not touch that one. To continue," he said matter-of-factly, "what this shows is that this was not typed on a computer or a word processor, but on a standard typewriter. And that the cartridge contained a two-toned ribbon: black and red."

"So what are you getting at?" asked Pork, eager to find anyone connected with Griselda's disappearance and belt them one—after reading their Mooranda Rights, of course.

"Well, when I was attending Cow Tech," began Cluck, "before the age of personal computers, I had an old Steers model typewriter that had two-toned ribbon in it. To save money, I would use the red ribbon when typing a draft, flip a switch, then use the black when I wanted to type up the final. That way you didn't use the ribbon up too fast and have to buy another one right away."

"So you're suggesting that this note was a first draft?" sneered Pork. "That doesn't make any sense."

"Perhaps he's saying the letter-writer was an aged college student?" asked Pepy.

"No, no." Cluck picked the letter up in exasperation, waving it in the chief's face. "What I am saying is that whoever typed this letter probably ran out of the black side of the ribbon, so they used the red. That means they didn't have the money to buy a new ribbon. Nor did they have access to modern computer equipment. And this paper's nothing special either, just plain bond."

"Or maybe they just wanted us to think that they were poor to throw us off the track," said Pork, snatching the ransom note back and pushing Cluck's hand away from his face.

"Or maybe they just like the color red," interrupted Pepy in a whisper, "like blood."

"O.K., that did it. I don't think I'm needing any more of your guys' help tonight." Pork gingerly refolded the letter and slipped it into to his breast pocket. "Where are you going, Cluck?" he demanded.

Grabbing a rain slicker from his locker, Cluck slung it over his shoulder and pulled a flashlight out of top desk drawer.

"Gonna go hunting night crawlers, Chief. Gonna go catch me some night crawlers."

Chief Pork screwed up his snout in disgust. The other white meat. "Please, enjoy yourself while I go do something vaguely useful—like try to save some ostrich's life!"

The lieutenant kept his eyes down, testing the flashlight battery, while his supervisor ranted. The chief was certainly being emotional lately. Cluck preferred to keep his own plans—and his secrets—to himself.

"You might have something there, after all," exclaimed Chief Pork. "Could be that the criminal is not poor, he just likes collecting old things. Something a packrat would do. Like that weasely little Lenny."

"But he was in prison during the kidnapping, " said Cluck. The chief was looking a bit wild-eyed for his taste. He was glad that he was parting ways for the rest of the night. "And when the ransom note was delivered also."

"Maybe he has an accomplice." Pork snatched up the car keys from amongst the pile of papers on his desk, following the lieutenant across the lobby. "I know that little runt is involved in this somehow. Maybe Betsy has done us a big favor. That flea-bitten criminal has his paws into everything. He might catch wind of something about the stolen pearl in that grimy little underground world he subsists in. And when he does, I'm going to be there, clinging to his back like a capuchin organ monkey with a bad crush. That little fake in a beret couldn't care less that Grissie is missing; if he gets a hold of the pearl first he'll sell it for the cash and let her rot."

And feeling pretty darned smug, Chief of Police Pork followed his lieutenant out the door and into the drizzle of a light evening rain.

After wriggling into the ground at the abduction site the worm was shocked to find itself falling through the air and landing hard onto earth below. With a shake he rose to discover he was in the largest tunnel he had ever seen, obviously not dug by a worm, but it also did not appear to be artificially created: the sides were rough and crumbling, as if clawed through. He wondered if it had any connection with the ostrich's disappearance. The automobile was nowhere to be seen, so the most obvious conclusion—that the car had merely fallen through the ground into a sinkhole—was no longer probable. The tunnel was large enough to drive a vehicle through. He considered for a moment whether to follow the tunnel or wriggle back into the earth to join his mates at City Hall. Sure, the hunk of walking beef had rescued him from being a snack, but hadn't the consideration to ask his name, as if he was unimportant as an individual. He didn't actually have a name (worms never did due to their short life spans and solitary nature), but that wasn't the point. It was the lack of acknowledgement that bothered him. Still, he owed the big lug something.

He popped his head once more above ground, keeping careful watch for the crows, but neither the cattle nor the police officers were to be seen. Hoping for a short trek, he fell to the tunnel floor once more and began his journey through the darkness.

SCENE FOUR: COCK-N-BULL STORIES

Steer parked his black sedan, retrieved from storage, outside the gated periphery at Grande Le Coeur estate and winced as Cal, stepping out of the passenger seat, slammed the door shut. "You'd be considered sneaky if we were digging up criminals in a cemetery," hissed the master detective, rain dripping from the brim of his hat. "If you want to hang around me, you've got to be quiet and listen. You can't learn much if you're yapping like an excited dog all the time." He didn't appreciate having Cal clinging on while prowling about Griselda's property, but since Cal was determined to be his sidekick, he decided to straighten him out a bit and make him moderately useful. Maybe it was his curse for not going to church and worshipping Moogah since he and Betsy broke it off.

"I wasn't saying anything, nothing at all," whispered Cal, his eyes wide and dewy. He had left his paper detective's hat in the glove compartment and looked pitiful with the rain pelting the top of his head.

"I'm sorry for getting sore at you," Steer said, draping an arm around Cal's shoulders. "In fact, to make up for it, I'll let you climb over the fence first and show me how to do it. Would you like that?"

He almost felt guilty when the goofball enthusiastically accepted the challenge and, scrambling to the top of Steer's sedan, began climbing over the top of the fence. "Hm, no electric wiring," he thought as Cal slipped over without getting zapped. He placed their flashlights through the slots in the grating onto the grass on the other side and waited to see if any guard dogs would streak across the grounds toward Cal. Unexpectedly their intrusion was met with silence. Certainly the dame had some sort of security system, thought Steer, unless she was relying solely on the dogs in her personal service for protection. There had to be some sort of alarm system protecting the perimeter, if not the house.

But then, no one on the staff, including Dudley the Dalmatian, had seen, sniffed out, or heard the miscreant that left the ransom note on the front door. Which was very odd: Someone inside the mansion, if they didn't know about the theft of the pearl, did know what happened to their mistress. The ransom note threatened murder. Was the kidnapper really capable of such a despicable act? Some critters did hold a grudge against the wealthy, even if they were treated well as an employee. Adam tensed up between the shoulder blades. One of the servants did not have a prohibition against lying; the problem was, who?

"Help, Help!" Cal called in an urgent whisper. Expecting to see sparks flying from Cal's horns, Adam looked upward to find him dangling against the fence on the other side, his left hoof caught in the ornamentation near the top. Exasperation pushed out the guilt for his bovine guinea pig stunt. "Can't I take you anywhere?" asked Steer, climbing to the top of his sedan. He wasn't concerned about scratching the paint: the less attention his automobile attracted, the better. He didn't need a tricked-out hot babe magnet to draw unwanted stares. Cars were useful only for doing your job and scouting out the bad guys.

"I'm having difficulty dislodging your foot," whispered Steer between grunts of exertion. "You're going to have to grab the fence and hoist yourself up a bit."

"I don't have the strength to push myself up from behind my back."

"O.K, I have another idea." Adam hopped back down to the fence. "I'll push you up from underneath and you free your hoof yourself."

"Good idea," whispered Cal as the detective grabbed onto his shoulders through the bars. "You're always thinking."

Putting his full weight into the effort, Steer dislodged Cal from the grating. As a result, Cal plummeted down onto the top of his skull.

"You all right?" whispered Adam through the fence.

"I'm fine. I've lived through a few hard blows to the head."

I'm not surprised, thought Steer as he lifted himself over the top of the fence and landed softly on all fours.

After retrieving their flashlights they hugged the perimeter of the vast yard spreading out from the mansion like a green silken cloak. Only two lights were on, illuminating the front porch and the garage door. Signaling Cal to follow, Steer stepped across the driveway and tiptoed toward a bank of English laurel bushes several yards to the left of the lights. They huddled in the midst of the hedge, Adam scrutinizing the exterior. On their side of the mansion there appeared to be five rooms on the bottom and perhaps four on the upper floor. All of the windows were shut, likely due to the rain although it was mid-August and a bit muggy. He was formulating a plan to gain entry when a light illuminated an upper chamber. The window opened and Demeris the poodle looked out, pulling a hair roller out of her topknot and straightening her pink blouse. A blast of wind sprayed her with rain and she shrank back from the window. Just at that moment Adam spied a dark figure slipping across the lawn from the area of the garage and into the bushes under the maid's window. His eyes widened with surprise.

"Hey, help me with this ladder, will youse?" Lenny's shrill voice squeaked softly. Demeris reappeared at the window and grabbed the top of the trellis, holding it tightly as the rat scampered up the wooden slats, dislodging roses in the process, and over the windowsill. After looking to her right and left, Demeris closed the window.

"Was that who I thought it was?" whispered Cal.

"Shhh. Dang, can't hear anything," said Steer.

"Maybe I can pick something up," offered Cal, pointing to his horn wrapped in aluminum foil, "with my radio."

"Thanks for the offer but this might help." Adam pulled what looked like a large, grey, plastic cow's ear from his coat. "This electronically amplifies any sounds within 100 yards."

After slipping the instrument over his right ear, he detected a slight rustling of the bushes behind them.

"Be quiet! We're not alone," whispered Adam, a finger extended to his lips. "Keep still and let our guest reveal himself."

However their attention was diverted back to the mansion. Demeris once again opened the window and Lenny, a newspaper-wrapped package in the crook of his right arm, slipped out and slid masterfully down the impromptu ladder. As Adam tracked the rat, a light suddenly flashed into his face and he was confronted with Cal, holding the lantern full flood at him. Startled, he screamed. Cal screamed. Lenny screamed and dropped the package. And someone else screamed full throttle behind all three of them that made their blood run cold.

Chief Pork parked his Chevy in the parking lot of the Cock-n-Bull Tavern and stepped out onto the gravel. The booming of a base amp or two, accompanied by raucous laughter, resounded from the building through the misty night air. He surveyed the neon sign, twitching on and off erratically and humming like a giant bug zapper, announcing: "BEER AND WINE SOLD HERE," and became acutely aware once again of his need to wet his parched mouth.

A giant heraldry shield posed as the doorknob; pushing at it, he walked into a room full of smoke, the smell of cigarettes and stale beer, and other odors he cared not to identify. The bar was the focus of activity in the neighborhood and not all of it legal. It was possible that Lenny might show. And he'd squeeze the little runt for anything he might know about Griselda's kidnappers with pleasure.

Bellying up to the bar, he reached for the bowl of peanuts, grimacing when his fingers swept across a sticky spot on its lip. The bartender, a goat with matted hair, slapped a once-white towel across the bar, ostensibly to clean the counter, splashing the chief with wet dirty water. Ignoring the insult, Pork asked for one of their finest. After receiving a sarcastic look from the goat, he placed three dollars on the counter: in this dung hole it was cash up front. A mug of maple-colored beer, foam head slipping down the sides, was substituted for the cash. Pork didn't ask for change, although the keep certainly didn't earn a tip.

"Not too subtle, marching in here with your uniform on," said the goat, refilling the bowl on the counter with peanuts.

"Even a cop gets thirsty once in a while," said Pork to no one in particular, although the message was intended for everyone within hearing distance. "I'm just like you boys. I like to kick back and enjoy myself occasionally." He removed the police badge from his shirt and slipped it into his coat pocket and lifted the beer mug in an exaggerated toast toward his waiter. He grimaced when his lips touched the mug and met with crusty tidbits lining the rim. He was sloppy but not a hog: He liked a certain measure of cleanliness that was normal to any animal. However, as the bartender was still eyeing him with hostility, watching each of his movements, he forced himself to drink a few sips of the brew, certain he'd find something nasty floating at the bottom of the glass from a prior "occupant."

He surveyed the room; it wasn't very large: about 25 feet long and about 20 feet wide and filled with the usual miscreants who hang out in bars on a weeknight when civilized folks were home with their families or getting ready for the next day's work shift. They were all too busy playing checkers or arguing about baseball to be concerned about a cop perched on a barstool.

A sudden rush of wind hit the back of his neck. Turning around, he saw a rakish black Labrador with a poodle on each arm, each dame sporting a diamond choke collar, trot through the front door. Trailing were two bulldogs, neither making any attempt to hide the bulge at their hips under their black sweaters, obviously sporting a sidearm of some type.

"Odd place for a chap like that to hang, isn't it?" Pork asked, ostensibly turning to the sodden Chihuahua to his left, but keeping the new arrivals in his peripheral vision. Unexpectedly the goat shrieked at the top of his lungs. Nearly scared off of his barstool, Pork knocked his beer over across the counter. Reclaiming his composure, he swung back around to discover that the Labrador and his entourage were missing.

Deeply disturbed, Pork requested another beer. The goat, smirking, asked for another three dollars. "Hey, if it wasn't for you, I wouldn't need another beer," complained the chief, yanking the towel out of the barkeep's hand and wiping up the spill.

"If it wasn't for guys like you, I wouldn't need to work overtime in this dive."

Sighing, Pork pulled another five dollars out of his wallet, slapped it onto the bar, and received a refill on his original mug. Again, no change.

"Hey, the last beer was three bucks. You owe me, buddy," Pork complained. "Two bucks, as I see it."

"I don't see two bucks myself," said the goat, turning his back and cleaning out a mug with the dirty cloth. "No siree, no deer or elk in here at all." A flea-bitten weasel, a patch over his left eye, came up to the counter and he was given the same recently wiped beer mug, refilled, without the benefit of clean water and soap first. Pork immediately set his glass back down onto the bar.

The door opened once more and a couple of cows with heavy makeup, walking arm-in-arm, pranced in and quickly found themselves a couple of welcoming laps. Again Pork felt a blast of night air against the back of his neck when the ladies, loosely termed, had entered the establishment, but hadn't felt anything when the Labrador and his gang had disappeared. Where did the dogs exit the room? Obviously not through the front door, Pork mused.

"Do you feel that cool air?" Pork asked the Chihuahua when the heraldic door opened once again and a trio of mallard ducks waddled in.

"I don't feel anything at all right now," answered the little dog with a sway. In response Pork steadied him on his stool. The bartender still kept a hostile look on the chief, which was beginning to irritate him. And he wasn't getting anywhere in his investigation. Everyone was either shouting total inanities or keeping their voices too low to be heard over the loudmouths. And the barkeep, quite unlike the sort to work in finer establishments, wasn't being too social, or too helpful.

Pork wasn't quite ready to leave, but he had also lost his craving for the dark brew. Yet he had to do something to justify his presence. Taking a bowl of peanuts and a saltshaker from the bar, he carried his mug over to a table, more in the thick of the crowd and a better location to view the front door. The bartender continued keeping a watchful eye on him. He reached for the peanuts and was surprised when the bowl slid away from him. Looking under the table, he noted that one of the legs was shorter than the other two. Well, he couldn't keep hopping from table to table and drawing too much attention to himself.

"So I hear you're holding out on me, Pork," a voice sneered to his right. It made the hog wince. Turning around, the chief discovered at the next table the face that nearly matched its oily voice in repulsiveness. A grey-haired weasel, dressed in a black raincoat, tipped a black fedora in greeting. It was Wiley, the lead journalist who worked for Griselda's *Cloverleaf Gazette*.

"Like you to meet my brother, Figmund," said Wiley, putting an arm around the shoulders of the weasel with the eye patch who had recently been at the bar. "Figmund and I get along real swell."

"Yeh, yeh, real shwell," echoed Figmund. Pork, ignoring Figmund's proffered limp hand, snatched up his nasty beer.

It was a blood-curdling scream that turned the knees to gelatin and the heart to fluttering like a butterfly caught in a jelly jar. Retrieving his flashlight, dropped in the frozen pose of fear, Steer turned its beams, firstly, on a very ashen-faced Cal, then, secondly, onto their verbal assailant. Cluck stood immobile, slacken jaw nearly grazing his waist, eyes wide as pan-fried omelets.

"Holy cow, you nearly gave me a heart attack," said Steer, switching off his light. "If you wanted to help out on the stakeout, why didn't you just ask to come along instead of scaring the hair off my bottom side?"

"I wanted to keep you guys from breaking-and-entering," stuttered the lieutenant.

"Sorry about that," said Cal. "I thought it might be an alien and didn't want it sneaking up on us. I was trying to keep the flashlight aimed into the bushes."

"I shoulda known it was youse guys," said Lenny, picking up his package and attempting to brush the dampness from it. "I was trying to be quiet out here, no thanks to youse."

"So were we," replied Steer, advancing toward the packrat.

A light came on and Demeris slipped her head out the window once more. "What the heck is going on out there, Lenny?" she asked. "Did you fall and hurt yourself?"

"Got a coupla snoops out here, that's all."

"Should I let the guard dogs out of the kennel?"

"Nah, let them finish their biscuits. I can handle this here problem by myself."

"Who's that out there with you?"

"Think they'd be ashamed to admit to it. But come to think of it, let the dogs out in about fifteen, would youse?"

Demeris scoped the backyard, but the trio of embarrassed sleuths hid themselves in the bushes. With apprehension clouding her face, the poodle closed the window once more and turned out the light.

"With the vigilance of her staff at night, I'm surprised that Madam Portentsky didn't get herself kidnapped years ago," commented Cluck, emerging from the bushes.

"I don't know and I don't care what yer doing here, but you've got yerself fifteen minutes to make yerselves scarce," warned Lenny.

"We're looking for night crawlers," offered Cluck, displaying his flashlight. Cal mimicked the rooster's motion, although he didn't know what it meant. "Sweetmeats, you know. The madam often bragged about the quality of her underground tenants and we finally took her up on her offer to try them out."

Lenny squinted his right eye in suspicion at the two bovine detectives. "Don't know many cattle that are into eating worms."

"We're just into the sport of it," said Adam. "We toss the little ones back." He paused, to emphasize the change in topic. "So what's in the package?"

"A little gift from my sweetie, if youse guys don't mind." Lenny hugged the package protectively to his chest. "I'm a packrat, if youse haven't forgotten." He made a sudden run for it, but Steer grabbed his tail. Startled, Lenny dropped the bundle; it went flying toward Cal. He speared a corner of it with his right horn, which caused the paper to rip asunder and the contents to spill to the wet grass. Cluck scooped it up in one belly-flop. Like a prize-winning mud wrestler the proud rooster held the rescued contents aloft.

It was one giant ball of dirty black yarn.

"I didn't see yer warrant." Lenny snatched the muddy trophy out of the lieutenant's winged hand.

"You risked breaking your neck, sneaking up the side of the house to get a ball of yarn?" asked Cluck, nonplussed.

"No, I risked my whiskers to get me a kiss which ain't against the law, last I heard," said Lenny. "The ball of yarn just happened to be a gift from my sweetie, as if it was any business of yers." He took a few steps, then, flashing a toothy smile, stopped to speak once more. "And it ain't. I'd appreciate it if youse guys kept this quiet to protect the young lady's honor."

"Don't believe the rest of the staff would approve?" asked Steer with a hint of menace.

"Animals are always suspecting the worst of folks, just like youse three lugs. What'd you think I was up to, stealing the old crow's silverware?"

Cluck didn't want to admit that he had, Steer didn't make assumptions because sometimes appearances were deceptive, and Cal was just glad that he didn't let his water loose when everyone was screaming.

"Unless youse all got plans to meet the security staff," Lenny added, once more flashing his very sharp pearly whites, "I'd say it was time to be hoofing it. Although I wouldn't mind watching the action from the other side of the fence when my missie lets the dogs loose."

"Well, that's just swell," complained Steer, stomping around in circles and slapping his hat off of the top of his sedan a few minutes later. "We got lucky to hit the mansion on a night that the security team was kept under wraps by Miss Twinkle Toes, and we had to blow our cover. Thanks a lot, fellas."

"Why on earth would a lovely lady like that want to date Lenny?" asked Cluck, pulling a yellow handkerchief out of his pocket and cleaning the mud from the front of his rain slicker. A hopeless task. "Can you imagine the dingy holes those whiskers have been in?"

Cal shuddered. He pictured Lenny in a junkyard strewn with old bottles, rusty tin cans dripping with unidentified spoiled material that was once called food, and broken glass. The rat, with a twisted crown of laurel leaves low on his brow, lay back upon a tattered satin pillow and Demeris, standing over him, dropped soiled grapes into his yawning orifice.

"In fact," continued Cluck, nervous energy and embarrassment animating his mouth, "why on earth would Betsy have anything to do with him?"

"What do you mean, Betsy?" asked Steer, suddenly still. His heart was thumping almost as rapidly as during the scream fest in the bushes. And he hated it. Wasn't he a master detective? Wasn't he an expert in sniffing out the nuances in another's physiognomy for signs of deception? Yet, he could not lie to himself, no matter how hard he tried to bury his feelings in the past. His blasted heart would betray him every time her name was mentioned. And his brain seemed to have nothing to say about it.

They were interrupted by the sounds of dogs howling and then, barking furiously, rushing from the back door and across the lawn toward the front gate.

"Let's go," said Cal, pushing Steer toward the car. "There's time to fight later."

Pork shivered as the night air swept across the back of his neck. Obviously the door had opened once again. A short dark figure caught the corner of his eye; he tried to track the newcomer, but his attention was once again commandeered by the bothersome weasel.

"Griselda hasn't been around the *Gazette* for two days now," continued Wiley. "Something tells me there's a story hanging in the air here, and I intend to pluck it out."

"Yesh, pluck it," echoed Figmund.

"What am I supposed to know about Madam Portentsky?" With a grimace Pork took another sip of his beer. He tried shunning the weasels by relocating the surreptitious figure. His attention split, his next remark was made offhandedly. "What's she to me?" then realized he was better off shutting up about four words sooner.

Wiley, whipping a notebook out of his front pocket, pulled a ballpoint out from behind his ear and leaned forward in anticipation. The press badge, pasted to the inner cover of the book, reflected the dim light above. "My sources say she was last seen being dropped off at your precinct house yesterday morning. And," he continued, getting uncomfortably close to Pork's right ear, "rumors are that you still have feelings for her."

"I can't deny the past nor can I relive it. What's past is past and I moved on." With a sneer on his face the chief pulled away from the weasel and nursed his beer. The little creep was intruding into his personal space and it made him feel very uncomfortable, like a rock being shoved into his shoes while walking.

"What I am wondering," Wiley's voice took on a more sinister intonation, "is whether the ostrich has moved on also, if you're catching my drift."

"Yesh, catching his drift," repeated Figmund.

"No, I am NOT catching your drift. What are you inferring?" yelled Pork, slamming down his mug. The rickety table rocked, throwing the bowl of peanuts precariously near the edge and in danger of falling off to the floor.

"Not inferring anything," replied Wiley, leaning back in his chair, twirling his hat around his right index finger. "Just that, far as I know, first time she meets up with you since getting a new boyfriend, she turns up missing."

At the word "boyfriend" Pork nervously pulled the peanuts back toward himself, knocking the saltshaker over with the bowl. "Bad luck, spilling salt," he mumbled, picking up the shaker and tossing its contents over his right shoulder into Wiley's and Figmund's faces. "Gotta spill more salt over the shoulder to keep the portents of evil away."

Figmund blinked back tears as the salt hit his right eye.

"No need to get nasty." With a smarmy grin sliding across his face Wiley leaned back into his chair. "I'm just asking questions. Nothing personal. Just trying to track down my boss. Need another raise, you know?"

"Well, *I* intend to get nashty!" yelled Figmund, grabbing the saltshaker, intending to reciprocate in a burgeoning condiment war. Pork ducked and the salt flew into the face of an ox sitting at the table behind them. Throwing the table aside, the ox jumped to his feet, grabbed a red squeeze bottle, and squirted catsup into Figmund's face. "Hey, big boy, pick on someone your own size," yelled a ram in response, which earned him a punch to the groin from the brutal ox.

The next few moments were a whirl of action as tables and chairs were tossed aside and punches thrown right and left, the drunken participants of the bar robbed of their inhibitions. Obviously lacking imagination, Figmund was squirting mustard in all directions while his hapless brother made good friends with several fists. Ducking a punch, Pork dove under his table, and in that moment he saw what looked like a little black-haired rat wearing a beret, slipping in and out under the skewed chairs to avoid the brawl. He stood up, intending to run across the room and confront the little runt, but a flying bar glass greeted his forehead, diverting his attention. As he fell backwards he caught a glimpse of the rodent ducking through the crack of a hidden doorway in the wall. Animated by the discovery of Lenny, he leapt to his feet, blowing on his police whistle full blast. Suddenly everyone froze, punches in midair, victims dangling from the grasp of their victimizers.

"Hey, didn't anybody notice that there was a cop in this joint?" yelled Pork, pulling his badge out of his breast pocket and pinning it onto his uniform. Though the room was dim, the struggling overhead light flashed off the shield's shiny surface. "I could toss the book at the whole lot of you." Several dozen bleary pairs of eyes blinked as the police chief pulled at his belt and exposed his sidearm. With a stately air he crossed the room, stepping over broken table legs and twisted chairs. This was his moment. He was the boss and he was in control.

Pork scanned the knotty pine of the sidewall for traces of the door that Lenny had slipped through, but there was no noticeable entryway in the paneling. He slid on a pile of broken peanut shells and pitched forward, his semiautomatic flying out of his holster and his police badge skittering across the wooden floor. The room immediately erupted into a cacophony of howls as the fighting resumed.

SCENE FIVE: SECRET HANGOUTS

"Well, doesn't this just figure!" exclaimed Ms. Griselda Portentsky of Grande Le Coeur as she lifted herself up off her cot, trying to avoid accidentally scraping her feathers against the dirt wall of her cell. "Two days now and not a hint of a rescue. Guess I'll just have to rescue myself."

She estimated that it must be Tuesday night, unless she had miscalculated and missed the short hand swinging past twelve a time or two on her wristwatch while she languished in the darkness of the hole that was her prison. Wooden bars were imbedded top and bottom into steel grates that lined the roughly circular doorway; a musty odor permeated the area as if fresh air was an infrequent guest. Roots dangled from the ceiling: she couldn't identify the type. In fact, she was fortunate that she kept a small penlight in her purse. Its feeble illumination into the dark corners of her prison kept her imagination in check; she used it sparingly, a few minutes at a time, rationing the battery power.

Her captors—the mole that had kidnapped her and similar rodents that paraded occasionally past her cell—were generally harmless-appearing and, after initial glances of curiosity, ignored her so that her initial fear during the kidnapping had gradually faded into irritation at being detained from her usual business. She was well-fed with corn niblets and meal worms from a plate slid through a slot in the bars and, darkness concealing any possible failure in the decor, she was generally satisfied and took the opportunity to catch up on some much-needed rest. That was, until this moment. Chief Pork and Detective Steer, if he were to be found, should have traced the miscreants that dumped her into this hole-in-the-ground and released her by now.

She sighed. Never let anyone do what you should do for yourself. Besides, an escape would make a far better story for the *Gazette* than a routine police rescue anyway.

Blindfolded by the driver before the squad car had stopped near the base of the foothills, she tried to recall how many lefts or rights she had walked after stepping out of the automobile. But Griselda was led through a series of twists and turns too numerous to keep track of. It was possible that they had tricked her and led her in circles through the same hallways before she entered the barred room. How could she know? There were no unique scents along the trail to identify entry into one hallway or another; everything had a sameness to it: the omnipresent smell of moldy dirt and rodents, the ubiquitous muffled sound of seemingly distant voices throughout the tunnel complex. But one thing was certain: she was underground—just how deep could not be determined. She had only heard about the mole population's labyrinth of dens in haunted fables read to her by her mother as a hatchling.

Fortunately she was alone in the cell. There was no cellmate nicknamed Tiny or Bubba to accost her or interfere with her inspections. She placed a right wing against the wall fronting the cot: still damp as on the first night. Probably not a good idea to try digging in that direction, in case there was a stream running nearby. The other three walls were dry but musty smelling, as if the earth hadn't been disturbed for years. Then a thought occurred to her: moles must generally burrow near the surface as their mounds had often ruined her lawn over the years. However, how expansive was the maze of tunnels?

She tugged on one of the roots trailing down from the ceiling. It didn't budge. She dug around it, avoiding getting the falling dirt in her eyes.

"I wouldn't advise continuing," a hoarse voice cautioned from outside the cell, "unless you'd like to be buried alive. We're standing under a golf course sand trap: dig a hole in the ceiling and you'd be immediately covered with several yards of sand over your head. You'd suffocate before you freed yourself."

"Thanks for the warning," said Griselda stiffly without a hint of gratitude, recognizing her kidnapper. Those beady red eyes that had stared at her from the front seat of the squad car were now reflected in the light of the lantern held in his paw as he stood outside the bars.

"We may be moles but we're not stupid," her captor added, handing a set of keys to a smaller, chubbier mole who unlatched the door. "We wouldn't bother putting doors on the cell if you could just dig your way free."

"No, of course," said Madam Portensky, suddenly feeling very foolish. "I didn't mean to imply..."

"No insult taken," her kidnapper added as the door swung open. "It's not worth the energy to get upset. Please follow me."

"Where are you taking me?" asked Griselda, collecting her purse and feather boa, not really anticipating a response but feeling the need to keep talking to assuage her rising apprehension.

"To see the Big Guy. If you think I'm large compared to this mole," her captor pointed at the guard, nearly six inches shorter, who was returning the cell keys to his proffered hand, "then you're lacking in imagination."

Griselda gulped and almost wished she was digging her way upward through a hill of sand.

"So what's your poison this time?" asked Betsy Moo, pulling at the hem of her skirt which seemed uncomfortably short to her but far too long to suit the male patrons of the Cock-n-Bull's Backdoor Club. Made of red satin, it kept sliding up her nylon-textured thighs. "You're looking a little bit hard about the edges tonight." She leaned over; the bright primary-colored disco lights flashed off her server's tray.

Lenny sat slumped in his usual chair in the corner of the room, nervously fumbling with his left paw at the torn edges of a large bundle of newspaper. He seemed oblivious to the animated dancers a few yards away, gyrating to the frenetic beat and amplified bass of Moodonna, just as the patrons in the front room in the Cock-n-Bull Tavern were totally oblivious to the party atmosphere on the other side of the paneling in the rear of the same building. A few knocks and a password and the privileged left the murky smoky den of the blue-collared class with their brewskis in the tavern and, after passing through a small hallway, entered the neon plastic and aluminum world of chablis and wine coolers. In the tavern cash reigned king; on the other side of the wall, credit—plastic or on the tab—was the rule. It appeared that no one on the rougher edge ever noted that the number of cars in the parking lot surpassed the number of patrons inside the tavern. Or if they had, which was more likely, didn't consider it worth their bother. The blue-collar crowd didn't crave the company of the sort that disappeared toward the back of the room. After a long day at the factory or driving a longbed truck, they needed the easy companionship of a similarly weary soul, not the affected smile and forced conversation of an office worker yearning to break free from their cubicle or a bourgeoisie harlequin parading as a duke.

Lenny also appeared somewhat smaller and vulnerable than usual, quite different from his blustery posture with most critters. But Betsy wasn't most critters. "I hope you don't mind my remarking on your haggard appearance," she asked.

"I appreciate yer helping me out this morning," replied Lenny, feigning his sweetest tone despite his weariness. "I really do. Those swine must miss me: those coppers will use any bleeping excuse to lock me up in their slammer."

"Glad you called. I've missed seeing you about the club." Betsy smiled. She wasn't sweet-tempered with her patrons just to increase her tip pool, but genuinely enjoyed their companionship. Interacting with them helped ease the dullness of an occupation that was far below her mental, but not her actual, capabilities. If only she'd had enough money to finish her Multimedia Certificate at Cow Tech. And the new technology was always advancing faster than the pace of her paycheck. It was unlikely that she could afford to return to school in the near future.

The packrat, functioning out of more self-interested motives, however, was always keen to please the ladies that crossed his crooked path and nurtured such relationships whenever possible. His pappy always taught him that you could never predict the good turn a friend might do you one day. Ladies were attracted to the aura of danger exuded by his bohemian manner, but this appeal was lost on the males that crossed his path; consequently, he didn't bother to waste his energy attempting to charm them, despite their potential usefulness.

"I don't care fer anything to drink right now," said Lenny, pushing at Betsy's tray. "I jist hung out for a few minutes to thank youse before I go in to see the Walrus."

"Always glad to help out a friend. I'm not terribly fond of the Force myself, you know, due to recent unnamed experiences." Betsy meant Adam Steer and the ugly altercation precipitating the break-up of their relationship. Lenny understood the reference and was kind enough not to broach the topic.

"I'm good fer the money, you know."

"Wasn't much. Not worried about it."

An awkward silence followed. After a few moments Lenny stuttered, "Soon as I make my transaction," then thought it better to conceal his intentions at the club that night and fell silent.

"Sure you wouldn't like a glass of water?" Betsy asked. "It's on the house."

"Miss, another tonic if you don't mind, please?" a gravelly voice asked. Betsy turned around to find an extravagantly bejeweled black paw waving toward her from several tables away. It belonged to a black Lab, framed by two similarly bedecked white poodles giggling nervously and snuggling up to their benefactor. Two bulldogs flanked either side, sitting on the floor in front of the circular divan, watching with obvious distaste the dancing crowd of animals gyrating on the raised discotheque floor. The Lab lifted his upper lip in a half-hearted grin, displaying two fangs capped with golden crowns.

"Who gave those creeps the password to get in here?" asked Lenny with disgust and perhaps a twang of jealousy at having his time with the winsome cow interrupted.

"Not for me to say. Good luck. See you later, Sweetie," Betsy said cheerily, lightly tapping the rat's snout with her forefinger then prancing off to answer the dog's call.

"Who needs luck, lady," mumbled Lenny to himself, patting the top of his packet holding the ball of yarn, "when I've got this."

SCENE SIX: BUTTING HEADS

"Been finding you lying on your back quite a bit lately, Old Boy," said Detective Adam Steer with a twinkle in his eye.

"I don't find that funny, Steer, not funny at all," Chief Pork replied from his hospital bed. He attempted to push himself higher onto his multiple pillows to face his visitors on an even level, rather than in recumbent position, but, the effort making his head pound, he merely groaned and slid back beneath the covers.

"You just push this button here on this little control," interjected Cal, grabbing at the little box wired to the hospital bed. "This'll move you forward with no trouble at all."

"Put that down, Cal," warned Lt. Cluck, wanting to show himself useful to his hapless superior. He grabbed at the remote but found it firmly clasped in the bovine's hooves.

"I think I'm quite capable of working these three little buttons," protested Cal with a sneer. "Excuse me, but I wasn't born in a barn."

"You guys are starting to give me another headache," groaned the chief, lying one weak arm across his forehead.

It was Wednesday morning. The drizzle that had accompanied the first days of the week was giving way to the brilliant beams of summer. The sunlight peeping between the long slanted blinds of the hospital room made the legal tenant of the room appear striped like a prisoner. The chief's head was wound in a bandage, swaddled to the tips of his ears. His right eye looked as if a mad cosmetologist couldn't decide what color blue to use as eye shadow and ringed his socket with multiple shades of the pigment.

"This red button here, I think," continued Cal. The television set, facing the bed, flickered to life. Two cows draped in black capes with punk red mohawks, knitting needles sticking out of their bottom lips and up through their nostrils, were explaining to the talk show host, a chicken with a stencil pad, why Goth was cool and other critters were ignorant for staring at them. Cal wondered how they were able to eat without stabbing themselves to death.

"No, this button," said Cluck, attempting to yank the remote out of Cal's hands. As they struggled to be useful, the hospital bed flipped upward, then backward, then vibrated, then pitched Pork's legs up and over his head, then sent the officer into a ball over the back rail of his bed into the wall. He consequently landed with a muffled thump onto the floor, tangled up in his top sheet and blanket, the bed halfway across the room.

"That ought to cure his concussion," commented Adam flatly, pulling back the twisted covers and helping Pork to his feet. Every time he looked at the lieutenant, he felt irritated. In the back of his mind he knew it was because Cluck had revealed last night that Betsy had been fraternizing with Lenny. Betsy had the right to date any fellow she wanted, even a slimy little putrid rodent. But the more he considered not only the rejection of himself, but also being replaced by a scuzzball of a thief, his blood boiled. He gave the rooster the look of death that went unnoticed.

"You two stay away from me from now on," exclaimed the chief to the mortified rooster and the sheepish Cal. "Where's my lucky frog's leg?" He stumbled toward the small armoire next to the bed and opened the door. After fumbling about the pockets in his uniform slung over a hanger, and, finding the precious relic, he placed the withered leg to his lips and kissed it gingerly. A moment later he was frantically pulling at his uniform. "Hey, my gun's gone!"

"I looked into it for you and it's in the hospital safe," Adam reassured the officer. "They don't allow weapons in the rooms."

"Thank great Moogah, I thought..." began the chief.

"You telling me that you lost control of your weapon last night?" asked the lieutenant.

"I'm not saying anything, Cluck."

"You know, Chief, regulations state that a hearing is mandatory in any situation in which an officer, off-duty or not, loses personal possession of his sidearm."

"Cluck, right now I'm not in personal possession of myself, so if you don't mind," Pork said, stumbling onto the bed, "bugger off."

Adam picked the bedding off the floor and tenderly fixed it about the police chief who immediately grabbed the blanket and yanked it over his head.

"Bugger off! Bugger off! He just told me to bugger off! That is *so* unprofessional!" Cluck's protestations met with unsympathetic looks from Adam and Cal. "He's also to blame!" Cluck pointed an accusing wingtip at the aluminum-tipped critter. "Why don't you tell him to bugger off, too!"

The chief peeped out from beneath his blanket. "Why don't the whole lot of you just bugger off," he said and yanked the cover back over his head. A moment later, it came down again. Pork's voice was slightly apologetic in tone. "I think I saw Lenny last night at the Cock-n-Bull Tavern, but I'm not sure. He managed to disappear into thin air."

Adam slapped a hoofed hand across Cal's mouth before he revealed Lenny's presence at the mansion the previous night to the supine police chief. He looked over at Cluck, who was obviously struggling with the urge to spill the beans about their nocturnal visit to the mansion, his mouth in a twisted grimace. It was not easy for the lieutenant to be silent about anything. But, like Cluck, Adam didn't want to answer questions about blowing their cover on the stakeout. They acted like fools last night. Best to remain silent and appear to be competent than to let loose with the lips and betray their reputations. Or rather, his own. He doubted that Cluck or Cal had much of a reputation to worry about protecting. On the other hand, everyone usually viewed themselves more favorably than those who knew them. He winced, Betsy's smiling face coming to mind.

"Adam, did anyone catch wind of the statue last night? Are we any closer to rescuing my poor dear Grissie?" In his dazed condition the chief did not realize that he was betraying his feelings. Steer nodded his head "no." In response the chief sank further downward into his pillows. "My poor dear Grissie," he continued. After a few moments of silent contemplation his face gradually transformed itself from a soft pink to a grimacing beet red, like placid Dr. Jekyll into disfigured Mr. Hyde. "My poor dear Grissie that swore eternal love and dumped me for another jerk. My poor dear Grissie that pretended to be pining for me these past few years and was sashaying around with another two-timing, twittle-nosed, ape-handled…"

"One more good conk on the head outta set him straight," said Cal, lifting the water pitcher from the nightstand over the pig's head.

"Let's continue out in the lobby." Adam snatched the container out of Cal's hands. "And, Cluck, why don't you just bugger off for once?"

"There's still no cause to believe that Madam Portentsky is in any real danger at this time," began Adam Steer to Cluck and Cal. The three of them were sitting on the divans in the hospital lobby near Surgery. Adam slouched deep into the cushions of the chair, weary from a poor night's rest, lacking the energy to maintain his irritation at the meddlesome lieutenant. He and Cal had spent the night at Boopsie's Holiday Inn. Apparently the other tenants were celebrating some happy event as their reveling drowned out even Cal's nocturnal conversations. He might be forced to keep peace with Cluck to find a free bed for the night. Perhaps the chief would loan him the keys to his townhouse for the night? "The only real tie we've had with the purported kidnappers so far is the note in the front door yesterday. There have been no other threats to heighten the sense of urgency. No phone calls that we're aware of. At this point it seems unlikely that anyone on her staff would conceal any. The kidnappers either have a lot of faith that the statue will be traded for Griselda or are so arrogant they don't believe they could be double-crossed. Or possibly detained for some reason and cannot make another threat." He paused in contemplation, then continued. "When it comes to crooks, I vote arrogance most of the time, closely followed by stupidity and greed."

"So weird about that car," mused Cal. "I still think the aliens took it. Maybe the old dame is getting a brain implant and will be returned to Boville to spread death and disease."

"Yes, we'll all sprout wings and start dancing the fox trot," quipped Adam.

"Maybe we should take a trip to Barkerville," interrupted Cluck, ignoring the cattle's bizarre comments. He wasn't in the habit of amusing himself with fantastical imaginings. "Scope about a bit, sense if anyone is acting twitchy at all."

"You got that ransom note on you?"

Cluck summarily pulled it out of his back pocket and presented it to Adam with a reiteration of his masterly summation of the note's clues that he had given to chief Pork the previous night.

"Yes, good examination," Adam said with a slight tone of condescension which Cluck, in his joy of being complimented, missed. "But I'm not certain that a trip to Barkerville will be a worthwhile use of our time. At least this early in the week."

"Ha!" rejoined Cal in glee. "The master's one step ahead of you already. Please continue, Maestro," the bovine waved toward Adam while Cluck, his wounded pride seething through his eyes, pierced Cal through like a meat skewer.

"Despite the obvious surprise on Dudley's face," continued Adam, suppressing a yawn, "I find it difficult to believe that someone could cross the grounds and slip up the driveway of Grande Le Coeur and stab the front door with a very large note and not one single soul witness it. There are a large number of hounds of all sorts on Griselda's staff and I cannot, for a single moment, believe that not one of them caught an odd scent or spied a darting figure at any time."

"They didn't notice Lenny nor us last night," interrupted Cluck, "and we weren't exactly being sneaky."

"Yeah, that's right, Adam" said Cal, changing loyalty. The lieutenant smiled at the approbation.

"That one's got me stumped for the moment," said Adam. "Could be that the staff relies on the guard dogs to investigate."

"And Demeris had them locked up," Cal interrupted.

"The main point is," the master detective continued, "perhaps Dudley nor the staff noticed anything odd because there was nothing odd that day to notice."

"Not catching you."

"What I'm saying, Cluck, is that perhaps Dudley didn't catch an unusual scent because..." Adam paused, giving the officer opportunity to redeem his pride, but Cal jumped in first.

"Because whoever stabbed the note into the door had a scent that was already familiar to the staff, a scent they smelled every day and wouldn't have thought twice about." Cal was exultant.

"That was obvious, went almost without saying," said Cluck, folding his wings defensively across his chest and crossing his legs at the knee.

"Well, let's just continue our summation to be certain that we're all on the same track," continued Adam. "Someone on the inside of the estate placed the ransom note on the door. The question now is: Are they involved in the kidnapping itself or are they merely taking advantage of Griselda's disappearance to enrich themselves? Is that the reason for the absence of further threats? Someone on the inside is already aware of what is going on with the investigation, so they don't need to reiterate? Or they're afraid to duplicate their efforts and be accidentally caught in the act by a fellow employee? Or did they place the note on the door for some reason we don't have enough information yet to consider?"

"Yes, indeed, that's why I was scoping the mansion out last night," lied Cluck. "Looking for further clues." The truth was, he was tailing

Adam and Cal, ensuring that they would not come up with any evidence and leave him out of the loop.

"Yes," smiled Adam, recalling Cluck's admission last night to being at the mansion to prevent them from lawbreaking. His own pride was stable enough to share the limelight. He didn't need continual reassurance of his abilities and therefore did not feel the need to parade them whenever possible.

"But that seems weird to me." Cal wrinkled his large nose. "Why would a staff member kidnap the ostrich when the statue was already sitting on the mantel ready for the taking?"

"They wouldn't. Is it possible that whoever wrote the note was involved in neither the kidnapping nor the theft? But if the motive was to enrich themselves, wouldn't they know that the statue was stolen by an unknown thief and might not be recovered for ransom? It doesn't make any sense. The pieces of the puzzle are not coming together for me yet." Adam tapped at his temple with his right hoofed forefinger.

"And that is just too bizarre for me," said Cal, pulling a kidney bean out of his borrowed rain slicker pocket and impaling it on his unfoiled right horn.

Griselda's knees were nearly knocking against one another as she stood in front of the largest mole she had ever seen. At nearly a story-high, he towered over the other moles that attended to him: they appeared like tiny demons dancing in front of their giant master in the red glow of the overhead lights. Apparently the moles disliked sunlight so much that they didn't even use white light to illuminate their dens. About two dozen female moles carried pitchers of wine or plates of food, which the mole snatched and greedily gulped down the contents. He slurped and belched and smacked his lips for what seemed like an eternity to the genteel ostrich until finally he completed his orgy of gluttony, wiping the back of his paw across his enormous lips. He fixed his eyes upon her. Her legs felt like jelly, but she was determined not to betray her fear to the enormous colossus.

"Imprethive, ithn't it," he bellowed in a guttural lisp. It was as if his tongue was too thick to find adequate maneuvering room in his mouth.

"Yes, the caverns are quite extensive and..." she searched for a compliment to placate her captor, "amazingly similar in circumference." She was both horrified by the slovenly ogre and mildly amused by his vocal impediment.

"I meant mythelf," the mole bellowed again. "Yearth of steroidth and mathive amounth of food sculpted thith beautiful form." He leaned forward into Griselda's face. His breath was both hot and fetid, as if the food was not being digested in his cavern of a stomach. He stared into her eyes, burrowing into them, until she blinked and looked away.

"I alwayth win that one." The Colossus of Rodents laughed, his enormous belly bouncing up and down. His minions clapped their hands over their ears as if in pain from his booming voice.

"So you kidnapped me to win a child's game?" Griselda was angry. She'd been sitting in a dirt cell for more than a night, hadn't had a bath for nearly two days, and didn't appreciate having some moron steaming her feathers with his unpleasant breath. In a matter of speaking, she had just about enough and was ready to fight back.

"No," the mole said. He wasn't intimidated by Griselda's anger. Any physical action she could possibly take against him would feel like the pinprick of a flea.

The jailer with the lantern knocked her in the side with his elbow. "I'd button up if I were you, missie."

"I jutht wanted to know what the great female publisher of the *Cloverleaf Gazette* looked like," sneered the gargantuan mole, "before we got rid of you."

SCENE SEVEN: VENGEANCE

It was Lieutenant Cluck's assignment to visit Judge Bookem and request a search warrant of the servants' quarters of Grande Le Coeur, which they hadn't thoroughly searched on the investigators' first visit as it was not the public domain of Griselda's home. Adam Steer, with sidekick in tow, traveled down to the Port of Boville to check the records of the merchant ships that had sunk about the time of the article featured on Cal's hat. A few hours later Cluck hopped out of his red Cheep Rangler, meeting the two cattle sleuths in the mansion's driveway. "Got the warrant," the lieutenant announced as the trio marched toward the front door. "How was your trip to the port?"

"Interesting," responded Adam Steer without elaboration. He nearly tripped over a powerpuff blue moped parked near the front step of the staircase leading to the entranceway. Pulling on a black glove, Adam brushed away the grime covering the speedometer and other instruments on the front casing of the stumbling block. "I've seen this before," he announced to the other two, "but I can't quite place whom it belongs to." The key was in the ignition but had no identification: the keychain tag was a glow-in-the-dark owl, announcing the opening of a new merchant bank. There was a small brown backpack, well worn, over the rear wheel. Adam opened the bag and scrutinized the contents. Pencils, blue chalk, a half-eaten chocolate bar, but nothing to identify the owner. The bike reeked of spilt oil.

"Seems familiar to me, too," said Cluck.

"It's not familiar to me at all," added Cal, sliding one leg over the seat of the bike. "But I'd sure like it to be!"

"We've no time for that." Adam grabbed Cal by his coat collar and pulled him from the seat. "Besides, Cluck here would feel obligated to cite you for theft, and you wouldn't be much good to me sitting in the pen." He thought for a moment, and then let Cal slide back onto the seat. "Go right ahead; ride it for all it's worth."

Dudley, the butler, opened the door and, with a sniff of obvious disdain, inquired, "Have you found our mistress yet?"

"Yeah, got her right here in this sack!" Cal exclaimed, holding up a soggy brown paper bag. Dudley winced suitably. The reaction satisfying Cal, he slid the bag once again into his coat pocket. "You know, you don't have an ounce of class," Cluck hissed into his right ear.

With a sigh Adam and his two partners walked up the staircase. "We've got a warrant," announced Cluck, pushing the document into the Dalmatian's face as he walked by. Adam did not care for the wry smile on the butler's face in response to the rooster's rudeness. In a moment he found the cause.

"Wiley, you old snake," Adam said as he walked into the lobby. "How unpleasant to see you."

The weasel turned from an intense conversation with the Dalmatian chauffeur near the kitchen doorway, meeting the master detective with a forced smile. "Ditto. You certainly didn't expect me not to look into the disappearance of my employer, did you?"

"I cannot believe for a moment," replied Adam, "that you are motivated by feelings of concern for Griselda."

"Who mentioned feelings?" Wiley smiled more broadly, displaying his yellowed teeth. Apparently the journalist took as good care of himself as he did his bike, thought Adam, surveying the slothenly appearance of the weasel. His raincoat was rumpled, the belt hung too long on one side, and one pocket was shedding stitching. The fedora looked as if someone large had sat on it and then punched it back into shape. It should be a punishable offense to destroy a good hat.

"Yes, haven't had a good story in a long time," continued the weasel. "So, you've got a search warrant?" He fingered the top of the document firmly clasped in Cluck's wing. The lieutenant yanked it out of his reach. "Temper, temper," Wiley sneered. "Looks like my timing's good today. Mind if I tag along?"

"The only tag I'd like to see you with is in a body bag," snapped Lt. Cluck.

"I get the feeling you guys don't like this weasel," interrupted Cal.

"What's feelings got to do with it?" asked Adam. "It's all objective fact, I assure you, Cal." The bovine didn't catch his drift; Wiley certainly did, but it didn't appear to faze the weasel as the smile continued to deck his face. "However, Wiley, I'd rather you joined us in our search rather than print creative innuendos in the *Gazette*."

"I'm glad you're so impressed with my journalistic gymnastics."

"But what is journalism," asked Cal, "but deliberate obfuscation of the facts? A presentation of one egregious worldview—that of the college-educated journalist indoctrinated in a liberal university system—while claiming to represent the community as a whole? Omitting to include details or even whole events that might sway the reader to a conclusion that does not support the editor's doctrines? Claiming to present facts of an occurrence while privately holding the belief that there is no such thing as truth? That all is relative? Then all you are left with is a daily manifesto."

"Whatever," replied Wiley. "It sells."

"Where'd that come from?" Cluck poked Cal's side with his elbow.

"Studied Communications at Cow Tech some years ago. Why do you think they call me Crazy Cal? I wouldn't toe the line. The constant battle for independent thought at that bigoted institution nearly drove me nuts."

"Plus," he whispered into Adam's ear, "maybe a little too much catnip at the Kitty Kat Bar down the street."

"I would never doubt the integrity of our mistress in the running of the *Gazette*," sniffed Dudley with scorn for the uninvited snoops. "Now, if you please, resolve this metaphysical debate at some other time and continue with your purpose at hand. I'd like to get the house back into order as quickly as possible. Your repeated presence here is upsetting to the staff."

"I bet it is," said Adam with a wry grin. "O.K., Cluck and Cal, you take the east wing." He pointed up the spiral staircase to the right. "Wiley, stick with me. We'll work the other side. I want to keep an eye on you."

"Ditto," replied the weasel, pulling a pencil out of his hatband and flipping open a notepad.

Putting a paw up to his forehead in weary submission, Dudley watched the detective and the newspaperman walk toward the ladies' quarters in the west wing.

"Whoa, do you mind?" asked Adam, motioning with his hoofed forefinger for the butler to follow. "We'll need your master keys."

Chief Pork's head still hurt and his ears were tender: both were wrapped in bandages but the hospital staff had discharged him. They needed the bed, was the explanation, never mind that his head felt like a crushed tomato. He wanted to see a chiropractor after his unplanned gymnastics performance due to the fight over the remote. He'd have a good talk later with Cluck about that episode. However, he didn't experience the joy of having his back manipulated as he soon found himself standing before Judge Bookem.

The large rooster would have looked ridiculous in his oversized black robe and tiny wire-rimmed glasses perched far too low on his beak, but Pork was on the wrong side of the bench this time and he knew the reputation of the rotten-tempered fowl: He would not dare to laugh. A careless look or a "gesundheit" in response to a sneeze at the wrong time could land the defendant in the slammer. The judge was an expert at recalling some obscure and moldy law that was forgotten by most of the legal system but was still on the books and quite useful in making an example of a hapless victim to the long arm of the law. And Judge Bookem's reach went back to the founding of Cowlitz County several centuries ago.

"Have you converted to some Eastern religion?" asked the judge in a piercing voice. "Or has the Police Force changed its policy on official attire?" Each of his words had a snap to it, popping out of his mouth like popcorn exploding in a microwave.

"No, sir," the chief laughed nervously, even though he didn't feel like laughing at the judge's pathetic attempt at humor. The old rooster was not known for being a funny guy. Pork wasn't sure why he'd been summoned before the magistrate but hoped it didn't have anything to do with last night's soiree. "I've recently been discharged from the hospital."

"Was that before or after you lost control of your weapon?"

"Dang that Cluck," Pork hissed to himself. "Can never mind his own business." The sound of his voice echoed unwelcomingly in the spacious wooden chamber.

"Speak loudly and clearly for the court reporter," Judge Bookem continued, leaning forward. "And under no circumstances are you to speak again without responding directly to one of my questions." Noticing the sour look the chief gave, he added, "or I'll hold you in contempt of court."

His hand shaking, Pork reached into his breast pocket for his lucky frog's leg, but it wasn't there. Frantically, he patted his shirt and searched his trousers, but no leg.

"What's the matter?" asked the judge. "Catch a flea in the hospital?"

"No, no, my good luck charm," moaned the chief. "I can't find it."

"Guess you've run out of luck. I pity you." Judge Bookem searched around the top of his podium then tossed a shriveled garter snakeskin at Pork. "Will that do as a substitute?"

The hog leapt backward in horror as the snakeskin slapped him in the snout. "Bad luck, bad luck," he said, dancing about and stomping on the skin. Anything associated with the snake was a bad omen.

"Actually, it was quite good luck for the prisoner as he eluded the bailiffs by slithering both out of his skin and out of their grasp," intoned the judge. Pork couldn't tell if he was smiling or not. He'd heard some bird's beaks became dry and inflexible in their older age and not as responsive to muscular impulse. And he was certain if ever there was a bird that resembled a dried prune, it was Judge Bookem. His stomach was beginning to hurt as much as his head.

"I'd like to see the weapon," the rooster requested. The current bailiff, a bull mastiff, handed the semiautomatic to the judge which had been taken from Pork at check-in to the courthouse before proceeding to the courtrooms.

"Is this the weapon you saw lying on the floor of the Cock-n-Bull last night?" Judge Bookem asked, looking beyond the police chief.

With a start, Pork turned around. He hadn't been aware that there was anyone in the room besides the judge, bailiff, clerk, court reporter, and himself.

With a triumphant gleam in his eyes, Lenny leapt up from the prosecutor's chair onto the tabletop before him and pointed a finger at the chief. "Yes, Judge, that's the pig—and that's the weapon that I saw him fumbling about fer on the floor of the bar last night. That is, after he started a fight that nearly destroyed the entire interior of the establishment."

"I concur with that!" A goat jumped out of the gallery: it was the dour-faced bartender from the Cock-n-Bull. "Everything was nice and peaceable last night until that cop waltzed in like he owned the joint. He took off his police badge so he could start a fight without anyone knowing what he was about. And, on top of it all, he was a lousy tipper to boot."

"Two bucks a beer and you call that a lousy tip?" Pork asked, incredulous.

Judge Bookem gave a warning look, which cowed the police chief. "I have in my possession several photos of damage done to the interior of the Cock-n-Bull Tavern." He held the glossies up in the air and then slapped them down onto the podium for effect. "Are you denying, Officer Pork, that you were at the Cock-n-Bull Tavern last night?"

Chief Pork bristled at the slight of being called "Officer" instead of his proper title. "No, sir. Only that I was not the cause of the damage in the photo. Nor was I responsible for the loss of my weapon last night."

"You were not responsible for the physical possession of your sidearm?" the rooster snapped.

"No, what I was intending to say," Pork fished for a quick explanation, "is that I tripped."

"Then why wasn't your weapon soundly snapped into its holster to prevent its accidental dislodgement?"

Pork couldn't respond. The more he spoke, the bigger the hole of trouble his tongue dug. Best to remain silent. He sensed Lenny's smirk rubbing at the back of his neck.

After a brief pause, the judge spoke again. "It could have gone off accidentally and injured someone."

"That's not possible..." Pork protested, his brain once again gearing into automatic butthead mode, but a stern look from the ridiculous-looking rooster with the near-omnipotent authority warned him into silence.

"Then, in accordance with the law, seeing that you are in violation of Code RC15.16.55 for losing possession of your weapon and Code RC15.14.32 for inciting a brawl and Code RC15.13.44 for causing damage to the property and premises of another citizen," the judge stated with obvious glee in his tone. "I suspend your gun license for two weeks effective immediately. You are hereby forbidden to be involved in any manner in police activity during that time." The rooster looked delighted at having an officer of the law in his power, engorging his sense of self-importance. "And your sidearm will remain in the court's possession until the suspension is over."

"Two weeks!" protested the hog. "I have a missing person's case on my hands. It's imperative that I find her before this Sunday!" He was near sobbing, which only contributed to Lenny's glee.

"Leave that to the more competent members of your staff," replied Judge Bookem. "You will attend a firearms safety course during the time of your suspension. Additionally, you are to render reasonable restitution to the Cock-n-Bull Tavern for damages incurred last night. Ms. Shiftkey," he addressed his attention to the courtroom clerk seated below him. "Please, see to it that the owner of the pub is contacted for an account of damages."

"I did not incite trouble last night. Figmund the weasel started it. I blew my whistle and attempted to stop it!"

"That's not what these two witnesses reported," the judge responded, holding up several documents.   And, looking toward Lenny and the goat, asked, "Did either of you observe a weasel named 'Figmund' starting the quarrel last night?"

"He had a patch over his left eye. He came up to the bar! You saw him!" Pork shouted to his mangy persecutors. This interruption earned him another reproachful look from Judge Bookem and a warning. "Intimidation of the witnesses will earn you a night's lodging at taxpayers' expense."

"No, I've got to say emphatically that it was the copper standing there before you who started all the hullabaloo last night," said the goat, pointing his hoofed forefinger at Pork.

"Ditto," exulted the rat.

"I've got to say I'd never question these two reliable citizens of the great town of Boville," muttered the hog with contempt. It came out louder than he intended; the court reporter's fingers recorded the comment for posterity. If he could sweat he would be drenched with anxiety.

Chief Pork realized that he was beginning to lose control and attempted to regain his composure. He had permitted his feelings for the ostrich to influence his thinking and behavior and now he was suffering the consequences. He hated the thought of being without his weapon for two weeks. For the nearly twenty years he had been on the Force, he rarely had cause to fire the gun, but he was vulnerable to attack by criminals without it. When Griselda came flying into the lobby Monday morning, he should have refused to get involved and referred the matter to an inferior officer. Filled with self-disgust, he wiped at his snout with the back of his hoofed hand.   "Would you consider deferring my sentence until after Sunday?" He hated groveling in Lenny's presence.

The little furry black pustule would get his comeuppance one day—and good.

"No." The judge pushed his glasses up his beak and began to read a large book at his podium, ignoring the police chief, and waving his right wing in a dismissive gesture.

Pork could put up with snobbishness but not disrespecting his high position as a member of the Police Force. Those involved with the courts considered themselves better than the grunts putting their lives in danger every day on the streets of the precinct. Book smart but not street smart, was the saying on the police beat. He had worked hard to attain a respectable position and didn't appreciate some dried-up sack of feathers dissing him, especially in the presence of an insignificant rodent. He felt the bile rising in his throat as fury began to overwhelm him.

"I've been avenged!" Lenny shouted, thrusting his fist into the air and dancing with glee on the tabletop.

"Watch it, rat," warned Judge Bookem, looking over the top of his spectacles, "or I'll hold you in contempt also."

"I go now." Lenny, feigning sheepishness, slipped off of the table. As he stepped into the doorway of the courtroom, he turned around to get one last look at the copper being dragged off by the bailiff toward the jailhouse for the night for spitting on the floor in front of the podium. He only wished that the hog had the guts to actually spit on the old rooster himself rather than on the wooden floor, which would have placed the nosey copper out of his path for a longer period of time.

SCENE EIGHT: MERRY-GO-ROUND

"Good," said the pelican as Chief Pork was shoved disrespectfully into his cell, "company for once." The bird was sitting on the bottom edge of an wrought-iron bunkbed and digging at the toenails of his right foot with a metal fork.

Chief Pork straightened his prison shirt, pulling it down to his waist, and retied the string on the matching black-and-white striped pants.

"They don't give you enough rope to hang yourself," the pelican spoke again.

"Didn't need to, had enough already. And I did a good job of it, too."

"I'm Pelly, by the way," the pelican said, proffering his wing to the chief. Pork accepted the handshake and wearily settled his bulk onto a cot against the other side of the cramped room.

"Ignatious," added Pork. "Iggy for short." He didn't want to reveal his surname to a prisoner, just in case there was some past professional connection of the negative kind. He wanted to be able to close his eyes that night without worrying about getting a fork jabbed into his throat by a disgruntled prisoner from a past arrest.

They were silent for a few minutes, Pork pondering the events that led up to his incarceration. What a fool he had been to aggravate Judge Bookem! Griselda was missing and he was unable to assist in the investigation. Since she had barged back into his life, his mind seemed to have softened into mush. He had avoided dating other ladies since their break-up to maintain his emotional equilibrium. Life had been much calmer without her.

Or so he told himself.

"So what are you in for?" asked Pelly. He had a congenial manner, an easy-going personality that was at home in a tavern or the boardroom.

"Spitting on the floor."

"Critters, this is one-hardnosed town. How long you in for?"

"The night." The chief didn't feel like speaking, but he didn't want to be rude. Obviously the pelican was in the mood for conversation and he didn't want to unnecessarily aggravate the convict he was locked behind bars with.

"They got me on driving without a license. Dang," the bird exclaimed as a chip of nail went flying. "Pushed too hard on that one."

"So you've been in here...?" Pork figured there was more to the story than just driving without a license, but didn't want to press, not knowing the temperament of his roommate.

"Miss my sweetie, I tell you," Pelly interrupted, waving the fork in the air for emphasis. "Haven't had me any beak for nearly three months. You know the sweet caress of a tender beak, Iggy? No, I'd say you wouldn't." The bird returned his focus to his toenails. "No, a pig wouldn't know. Now chicks ain't got lips, I tell you, but lips ain't everything."

The sound of Pelly's voice faded into the background. He was sitting in the back of Griselda's limousine. The ostrich lightly brushed her beak against his cheek, which flushed red in response. He slipped his arm around her feathered shoulders, pulling her toward him, and then the chauffeur opened the sliding window panel between the front and back seats. Pork was transported back to the present.

The chief was normally untroubled in his thoughts, filing away disturbing emotions and focusing on the facts and details of the moment, but his mental drawers appeared to be full, the files kept falling to the floor of his mind. Despite the trouble she had caused him, Pork was worried about Griselda's safety. She had been missing for more than two days. It was uncharacteristic not to make her presence known: loving attention and admiration, she was definitely being held somewhere against her will. What a fool he had been to lose his temper! In exchange for one brief moment of satisfaction in the courtroom, he was cooped in a tiny cell with a loquacious bird and detained from aiding in the search for Griselda. At least for the night, he'd have to rely upon Adam and Cluck to find her.

Moogah help Griselda!

Cluck and Crazy Cal systematically searched the rooms on the east wing, starting with the door closest to the grand staircase and working their way to the back of the mansion. Wanting to ditch the ditzy bovine, the lieutenant suggested that they split up and search each room individually, but Cal, not wanting to miss a moment, would not be ditched. Flashing the warrant before him, the rooster opened each bedroom door and barreled into each room without knocking, hoping to catch one of the servants "in the act." But, generally, the rooms were empty, the occupants being at their posts this early afternoon.

"Do you suppose they'll really pluck her?" asked Cal, riffling through a drawer of men's cotton socks in the top left of a dressing table. "I wonder if that'd be anything like having each hair of my skin yanked out?" He shuddered.

"They don't mean 'pluck' literally." Cluck pulled up a wool rug from the side of the four-poster bed, slid his wing underneath, and searched for hidden doors or secret notes. "If we don't find that statue by Sunday, they intend to kill her." He paused for a moment. "You ever catch a message with that, er, transmitter of yours?"

"Receiver," Cal corrected him. "Not transmitter. No, never have, but I'm ready for them when they decide to return Big White."

"Who's 'they'?"

Cal merely smiled and pointed upward. Cluck wished he hadn't asked.

"Nice paper hat your friend's got," Wiley sneered, his voice dripping with sarcasm as he stepped onto the first landing.

"That hat provided us with a very important clue," replied Steer. "So I'd appreciate it if you didn't mock my friend and associate."

"And what would that clue be, sir?" asked Dudley.

"In good time."

"You plan to clue me in? What the heck are we looking for anyway?" asked Wiley.

"You're a reporter for the *Gazette*, go figure it for yourself," snapped Adam. "Don't you read the newspaper you work for?"

"That's what I thought, didn't really have anything." The weasel flashed a smug smile but stuck close to the steer in case he came up with something important. Anything newsworthy. With the old dame gone, it was his chance to run the *Gazette*—*his* way. Which would be the *right* way.

"The ladies' hall." Dudley pointed to the hallway to their right. Before them lay a beautiful cream-colored rug adorned with twisting green vines and pink roses.

"Guess that's rather obvious," Steer replied. Pre-Raphaelite paintings of beautiful cows and chickens paraded down the walls and the light scent of lavender wafted down the hallway. "Seems like the old dame took pretty good care of her staff."

"Indeed, sir," continued Dudley. "We do not have anything to hide here. Search about all you like. As I said yesterday, " he added with another sniff, "I do not care for the implication that someone on our staff is involved in this catastrophic affair. I thoroughly research the backgrounds of all potential employees and only hire those with the most impeccable resumes."

"Past performance is not always indicative of future results." Steer scrutinized his IRA statements and was quite confident in the veracity of his statement. "Which room belongs to the poodle, I believe her name was Demeris?" He was being coy and knew perfectly well what her name was; better to be thought somewhat of a dunderhead and catch the butler off-guard, if he had anything to conceal. It was a strategy Adam often used playing chess: make a few really bad moves; then, when his opponent had relaxed his guard and was focused intently on his own strategy, zero in from unexpected quarters for the kill.

"Shouldn't we start at one end or the other and work through them systematically?" asked Wiley. "We don't want to miss anything."

"No, I want to avoid sounding a warning." Steer held out his hoofed hand, waiting for Dudley to give him the master key. "This was the room I intended to search from the start. I just wanted Cluck and that crazy bull out of the way for a while so I can hear myself think for once."

"I can't imagine Miss Oui Oui would have anything to do with Madam Griselda's disappearance," the butler protested as he handed the key to Adam. If he had refused to cooperate, then the detective would believe that he was covering for Demeris. And Dudley felt very uncomfortable having strangers searching the female quarters, not knowing what kind of character this detective and newsman had. But they had a warrant and he had no choice.

"Maybe I just want to see how the French do things," Steer replied. Walking on tiptoe to the door identified by Dudley as belonging to Demeris, Steer signaled the others to stay back behind him. He knocked on the door and waited a few moments. No response. He slid the key into the lock and gently twisted the crystal doorknob. The room was empty. The window was open, the same one the poodle had leaned out of last night to help Lenny up the trellis. The lace curtain sheers fluttered away from the window, blown by a warm summer wind. Adam signaled, waving at the other two to follow.

"Boy, guess I'm in the wrong business," Wiley exclaimed when he entered. "I need to get out of journalism and into the domestics."

Gilded mirrors adorned the center of three of the walls. A canopy bed with ivory curtains, stitched with red- and melon-colored roses, dominated the room. Marble candlesticks in the shape of penguins, holding large double-wicked green candles, sat atop her dresser which was in the art nouveau style, curvaceous and lined with leaves. A delicately woven pink and green rug covered the floor. Steer walked over to the dressing table and looked thoughtfully into the large ornate mirror. After a few moments he opened a heart-shaped silver box with a bronze clasp that rested on top of the dresser. It was a music box; "Somewhere Over the Rainbow" tinkled from a hidden source while a golden sparrow twirled round-and-round from a tiny pedestal amongst the red velvet and pearl earrings nestled in the interior.

"This how the guys live in the other wing?" asked Adam.

"No, sir," replied Dudley, clearing his throat and wiping at his forehead with a white silk handkerchief. His paws shook with restrained nervousness.

"Dang," said Wiley. "Time to ask for a promotion, eh, old bowzer?"

Dudley frowned at the disrespectful reference.

For a few moments, Adam contemplated the music box, then, closing the cover, announced to the others to commence searching the room. "That is, if you'd like to help out," he added to the stately Dalmatian.

"I'd prefer not to stick my nose into a lady's private business."

"Suit yourself. But hang around in case I have a few questions to ask you."

To the butler's disgust, Wiley rushed toward the dresser and began yanking out the drawers, tossing lingerie and other personal articles in all directions. The weasel was quite impressed with the fine quality of the satin slips and other toiletry items. "This dame's got class," said Wiley.

"It's apparent that you don't," remarked Adam. "Try to show a little more respect for the lady's personal items, would you?"

After searching under the mattress and the edges of the Turkish carpet, Adam opened the single door to the closet. It was a walk-in with three racks packed with clothing lining the walls. He noted that there were no slacks, only the shirts, aprons, and skirts of the mansion's staff uniform and various evening dresses. Rose-scented perfume hung heavy in the air. Pulling the rope to the light bulb, which oddly enough, was without any sort of shade, Adam found that the floor was littered with boxes from different department stores: dozens of pairs of shoes from the continent of Ewerope and personal laundry. He examined one of the boxes: Ritzles, a store known for its exclusivity—and expense. Picking up several other box tops, he noted that they too originated from department stores generally frequented by the well-to-do. The items in the boxes varied from the mundane, a treetop angel for the holiday evergreen, to beaded purses and more shoes.

"Mighty high-living for a maid, wouldn't you say, Dudley?" asked Adam.

"I prefer not to jump to conclusions, sir," the butler replied gravely. "Demeris is a fine lady. I wouldn't be the least surprised if these were gifts from some of her suitors."

"She date a lot?" asked Wiley, pulling the pencil from behind his ear.

"She has been out at night recently," answered Dudley. "I won't presume why."

"For how long?" asked Adam.

"About two weeks, sir. But again, there is no cause to jump to any conclusions about her guilt in relation to Madam Portentsky or the theft."

"Or jump to conclusions about her innocence either," added Adam, pulling the laundry basket toward himself.

Walking down the main staircase after having completed their assignment with nothing of consequence to report, Cluck and Cal heard the slamming of pots against a floor and a shouting match between a male and a female. It came from the kitchen. Together they raced into the kitchen, slapping the swinging door to the side and sliding into the marble-floored room. There was Lenny, standing on the countertop below the row of hanging pots and pans, brandishing a skillet while Demeris cowered behind the kitchen table, shouting at him to calm down.

"Youse trying to get me killed!" Lenny was screaming. "The Walrus don't take too kindly to having his time wasted! It'll be a miracle if he ever lets me in again."

"Honestly, Lenny, I didn't know," Demeris shrieked, her forelegs protecting her muzzle. "It was a mistake."

"It took me years to build up that relationship..." The rat stopped and turned in surprise at the two intruders.

"Holy cheese bits!" exclaimed Cluck. "What in the name of all mothers are you doing here, Lenny?"

"He sure gets around," commented Cal.

"What, youse guys again?" asked Lenny. "Can't a rat have a little privacy once-inna-while?

Like taking a mask off of her face, the poodle's mood suddenly switched from desperation to cool and composed. Demeris smoothed down the wrinkles in her apron and primped at her pompadour. "Just a little lover's spat, boys," she purred, sauntering over to Lenny and scratching at his goatee. The rat thumped his left leg several times in automatic response but his eyes flashed with anger.

"I be needin' another wax job. Grey's starting to show again."

"I'll fix you right up, Sweet Meat," the poodle replied, opening the pantry door. She pulled out a small tin can of black shoe polish and a dirty rag. With a swirling motion Demeris pushed the rag about in the polish then slid it over Lenny's fur.

"Oooh, oooh, that feels good, Babe," Lenny said, his snout lifted high in the air, twitching his whiskers in ecstasy.

"O.K., it worked. I'm thoroughly disgusted. I'm leaving." Cluck turned toward the exit to the entrance hall.

"I like to watch," Cal said, pulling out a chair from the central table and sitting down, one leg swung around either side of the back.

"I guess I wasn't thoroughly disgusted yet," Cluck continued, pulling Cal by the collar of his raincoat and nearly knocking the paper hat from his head. "NOW I'm thoroughly disgusted." He pushed the bull through the door so hard that it swung back and hit him square behind the shoulder blades, sending him flying into Cal. The two of them sprawled to the base of the grand staircase.

"Why can't I ever have my camera with me at the right moment?" asked Adam, stepping from the stairs to the entryway. In his hands he held an object tightly wrapped in a pink terrycloth bath towel.

"Help, help, I've fallen down and I can't get up," yelled Cal from beneath the rooster.

"Now ain't they a lovely couple?" added Wiley. "Kind of pulls at the old heart strings."

Dudley was the last to enter the hall from behind the other two. He was silent, absorbed in his thoughts, obviously disturbed, nervously swinging his tail to-and-fro—which was quite unusual for the reserved butler. One of the maids, a Yorkie, entered from the sitting room with a silver spoon resting on a satin pillow. Seeing the disturbance, she turned around and exited without comment.

After explaining to the recently arrived trio from the ladies' wing about the disturbance they had witnessed, Cal and Cluck led them into the kitchen. Once again Lenny was brandishing a pot but also chasing Demeris around the room while shouting obscenities. Spotting Adam, Demeris ran toward the back door and unbolted it. But in her haste she forgot that it was a split door and, neglecting to unlatch the lower half, fell face first over it. Grabbing at her ankles, Adam pulled her back into the room while looking away from her exposed undergarments. Allowing Demeris a few moments to compose herself and primp her uniform, he invited all the occupants of the room to sit about the kitchen table. There weren't enough chairs, so Dudley volunteered to stand with Cluck.

"What's going on, Demeris?" demanded Lenny.

"I don't know," she replied with a stammer, her eyes downcast, avoiding the gaze of the surrounding crowd.

"Oh, but I believe you *do* know," said Adam. He watched her eyes as he set the pink wrapped object down in the center of the table. She tried to look attentive but her lips were curling back in an expression of dread. With a shaking paw she pulled at a curl of hair from her opposite wrist and nervously played with it. Adam slowly unwrapped the towel as the others watched in rapt attention. Even Lenny leaned forward with curiosity.

A moment later the towel fell to the tabletop. The onlookers gasped, except for Demeris.

"Look familiar?" Adam asked the maid.

It was the MooMoo Pearl, just as Chief Pork had described it. A black cow in a ballet pose perched upon the right back leg, one arm upward and the other downward, the left leg swung backward. Even though it was dark-colored, the kitchen light danced upon its glossy surface.

"It's beautiful," Cluck commented; Cal nodded in agreement.

"What's the explanation for this?" Lenny demanded, leaning into the maid's face.

"I don't know," stammered Demeris. She nearly yanked a curl out of her wrist. "Last I saw of it was on the mantelpiece."

"You're telling me that the madam's life is in danger and you've been hiding the statuette that could save her life!" shouted Dudley in increasing volume. He raised a paw as if to slap her across the face.

Demeris swung her forelegs up in defense but Adam, slipping between her and the butler, gently lowered them again. "You have the answer, don't you, dear?" he asked sweetly, smothering the anger seething inside.

"I...I don't know anything about Madam Portentsky being in danger." Tears began to flow from her eyes. "I was cleaning the statues on the mantelpiece the other day and when I turned around to leave, I accidentally bumped the big black one with my elbow and knocked it to the floor. Of course, with my luck it didn't hit the rug, it hit the brick in front of the fireplace. You can see here," she said, pointing to the top of the cow's head, "a bit of its left ear broke off. I was going to fix it and then put it back. But before I could do so the madam discovered that it was missing and ran off helter skelter to report it to the police chief. I didn't think she'd spot it missing that fast." Demeris was sobbing now, mascara running down her face and staining her white fur. "It's a really expensive statue, she was always telling the staff, and I was afraid to admit that I'd broken it. I couldn't afford to pay to replace it. I really did intend to return it when I'd fixed it, I really did."

Dudley's look of anger relaxed into sadness. It was obvious to Adam that the butler was very fond of the poodle, maybe even attracted to her physically, which would make him an easy mark for manipulation by a clever bitch. Dudley pulled a large white cotton handkerchief out of his back pocket, which was gratefully received by the poodle.

"How come nobody explained to me why my boss was at the Precinct House Monday morning?" exclaimed Wiley to inattentive ears. "What's this about danger and a missing statue!"

"She's really good at ceramics," Lenny said with a sneer that surprised the detective. "She woulda fixed it up real good so that nobody'd noticed."

Adam slipped a comforting hand around Demeris' shoulders. "So you didn't know about the ransom note?" he asked.

"Ransom note?" the poodle replied with genuine surprise on her face. "Did something happen to Madam Portentsky?

"Ransom note?" asked Wiley. "Hey, how come you guys have been holding back on me?"

"Yes, she was kidnapped," added Cluck, enjoying having one up on the odious weasel. "And the kidnappers wanted the statue in exchange." He scratched his top comb as if perplexed.

"Don't think they'd be too happy if they saw it looking like this," interrupted Cal, always eager to put an optimistic spin on events.

"What's the ransom demand?" Wiley's voice, though rising with excitement, was without a trace of concern for his employer.

"That's confidential," Adam said distractedly, not wanting to reveal all of the details of the case to the oily reporter. He was holding the base of the statue, examining the damaged ear.

"Hey, if you think I'm going to stand for…" Wiley began but was interrupted.

"Ladies and sirs," Adam continued, turning the dancing cow around to reflect the light from different angles, "we are all looking at what may be the largest single cut black pearl in existence; in fact, the largest single cut pearl in history—period.

Everyone gasped in awe except for Demeris, who began to cry again. She appeared not to find it comforting to be reminded of the value of the broken item.

"Well, we've got the statue," Cluck said. "Now we wait till Sunday and trade it in for the ostrich."

"It's damaged, though," exclaimed Cal. "Think if we used a nail file to smooth the rough edge the kidnappers would notice?

"That's statue's still very valuable," squealed Lenny the packrat, "even busted up a bit. Are youse guys sure the madam, as you call the old bag, I mean, lady, would want youse to be handing her valuable prize off to a bunch of strangers? Maybe they ain't got her. Maybe they's just bluffing. What proof have they given anybody that they've really got her? Maybe she's jest missing for some reason and somebody in-the-know is taking advantage of the situation to pick themselves up a pretty little penny." He wriggled his fingers continuously as if itching to get them on the statue but dared not with the police around, leaving him like an automobile in high gear but with the brakes still on.

"That's right," Cluck interrupted. "We don't have any evidence that these shmoes really have Madam Portentsky. We're just taking their word for it, and they're criminals, for holy guacamole's sake. They might just grab the statue and take off, leaving us standing there in the lobby feeling like a bunch of fools."

"That's what it takes to make you feel like a fool?" asked Cal. He was irritated that the persnickety rooster beat him to the observation first. "Or have you just become inoculated from years of practice?"

"I don't have to put up with you!" Cluck jammed a finger into Cal's large pink nose. "You're not a real detective! You're just a bad actor in a borrowed raincoat!"

"Please, let's focus on the situation at hand, shall we?" Adam interrupted, pulling Cluck's wing away from Cal's nose. "There's plenty of time for squabbling later. Time's short and we need all the help we can get, professional or not."

Cal grinned in mock triumph at the rooster. Demeris sniffed and rubbed her muzzle with a handkerchief.

"Lenny's right," Adam continued. "We need a game plan. Let's assume the path of least resistance for the time being that the kidnappers are the same individuals who sent the ransom note. We need some way to get Griselda back and keep the statue at the same time. It's an heirloom, and I'm sure she values it dearly."

Still holding the base of the statue, Adam placed his chin into one hoofed hand, appearing to be deep in thought. The others held their breath. "Eye-catching isn't it?" To which everyone replied with a nod "yes," except for Demeris who was wiping at her eyes with Dudley's hankie.

Adam lifted the statue slightly, running a finger along the site of the damage.

"You got the piece that's broken off, Miss?"

Demeris nodded in agreement and pulled a black shard from the front pocket of her apron. Silently, she handed it to Adam. He touched the broken piece to the damaged site, examined the end of it, and then dropped it to the table.

"Be careful, sir," said Dudley reaching forward as if to catch the broken ear. "Even a bit of the pearl is considered valuable."

"Noted." Adam replied flatly, absorbed in thought. Again he pulled the statue toward himself, turning it one way and then another. Suddenly he pulled a large hammer out of the pocket of his raincoat and slammed it full force onto the top of the pearl. Myriads of shattered pieces, varying in size, flew in all directions, slapping the shocked onlookers in the faces and chests.

"I always keep one of those handy myself," Cal said, pointing to the hammer. "You never know when it'll be useful."

With their mouths frozen open in horror, the group turned toward Adam who was grinning ear-to-ear, obviously enjoying their reactions of surprise.

"I'd like to see the poodle fix it now," commented Wily. His eyes were as large as fifty-cent pieces, and a pencil, in danger of falling to the floor, dangled loosely from between his furry fingers. It was a frightening look, thought Cal, a weasel with large eyes. No wonder the Great Moogah saw fit to make them naturally small.

In their shocked state nobody noticed Demeris sliding a small key from the debris and slipping it into her handkerchief. She wept some more, looking askance to each side, but nobody wanted to stare at a crying poodle.

"Wait a second, if you please." Dudley reached down to the table top, scattering the glittering confetti. He pulled a strip of paper from amongst the broken pieces, grimaced, and handed it to Adam.

"Help, I'm being held captive in a Chinese ceramics factory," the detective read aloud from the scrap.

"It's a fake!" shouted Cluck, slapping his thighs. "They kidnapped the old bird for a fake! Boy, are they going to be surprised!"

"So, it's a fake," hissed Lenny. Adam was surprised to see the rat glare at the distressed poodle with undisguised hostility.

"We all believed the statue was a real pearl. How'd you know it was a fake?" Dudley asked Adam.

"I didn't. I just thought it was ugly," was the reply.

The worm had almost given up following the tunnel to rejoin his buddies at the Boville City Hall when it ended abruptly at what appeared to be the bottom of a hillside. A large wooden split door covered nearly the entire exit and was secured by a large bolt-and-lock combination. But not secure from a worm. He wriggled through the crack between the two doors.

SCENE NINE: SURPRISE! SURPRISE!

"I think I'm going to faint," announced Demeris, leaning backward in her chair. Dudley caught her around the shoulders before she slid to the floor. The butler lifted the poodle up into his arms as if she were as light as a puppy, gently cradling her head against his breast without regard to decorum. "Good day, sirs, " he added with a nod. "This has been quite enough excitement for the both of us," and he, his tail whipping to and fro in anger, carried Demeris out the kitchen door and toward her room.

Adam stared after them, absentmindedly twisting a shard of the broken statuette between his hoofed fingers. How convenient for the poodle to faint and avoid further questioning. And did Dudley really still believe that Demeris was uninvolved in the theft? Was he shielding her from scrutiny out of a sense of duty to the staff under his care? Or just shielding himself from learning an unpleasant truth about someone he apparently was emotionally attached to?

"I guess she doesn't have to worry about fixing the statue anymore," stated Cal. "Anyone for a game of pick-up?"

"Yeah, here's a broom and a waste pan," was the response from Lenny, proffering the domestic instruments to Cal. "Knock yerself dead."

Nearly an entire day had passed since her visit to the gargantuan mole, and Griselda's legs still felt weak. Accustomed to the company of governors and corporate giants, the interviews of murderers and fiends, she wasn't the type to frighten or intimidate easily. But, for the first time in her life, standing before the colossus of a rodent made her feathers bristle and stand on end. It was not fear but horror: an innate dread of the malformed and defective. She dreaded losing a wing or having her beak damaged in an accident; it caused her to be reluctant to confront the odd or the misshapen, the misfortunate freaks of nature. She was not a humble bird. Deep down she feared dependence, facing life unable to care for herself. Perhaps that's why her relationship with the police chief didn't work out: She faced life boldly, ignoring her fears and pushing the obstacles out of her path, while Pork relied on superstition and old wives' tales for a sense of control, which she considered crutches for the weak.

"Pssst, come here," she hissed when her former illicit chauffeur walked by her cell door. The mole, flashlight in his hand, shuffled closer to the wooden bars. "I've been in here nearly two days and I'm getting a little lonely. What's your name?" The mole didn't appear as intimidating in the dingy corridor as he had the night of her abduction; in fact, he had lost his aura of menace and almost seemed like an average Joe—except that he was a criminal.

"Edwin," was the simple reply.

Edwin? Griselda thought to herself. Edwin the mole? That was like naming a salamander Gertrude or a crocodile Harvey. She suppressed the impulse to smile. After all, she'd heard a lot of odd names as publisher of the *Cloverleaf Gazette.*

"Why are you asking my name?" asked Edwin. Very few critters in the burrow ever took much notice of him as he was a favorite of The Mole's: They didn't want to make themselves too conspicuous and subject to the giant's bizarre whims. Edwin, therefore, wasn't use to being asked questions. It made him suspicious.

"I'm a journalist; it's my nature to ask questions," she replied. Edwin appeared to relax a little, his shoulders slumping forward. "Kind of quiet down here with the dirt walls, sound doesn't travel much. Conceals the presence of the others when their voices don't carry. Makes you feel kind of lonely sometimes, doesn't it?"

"Yeah, sometimes."

Griselda fell silent a moment, sizing up what type of critter Edwin might be. Despite his regal-sounding name, he didn't appear to be the literary sort.

"You got any playing cards on you?" she asked.

"No, but I can get some," he replied, suddenly gleeful. "You like to play cribbage? I've got a beautiful ivory playing board in my hole."

Good heavens, she hated cribbage. "Yes, that'd be lovely. Can we play in your room?" She hated hypocrisy, but the situation forced it.

"No, but I can bring the board down to you." Edwin whipped around and dashed off down the hall. The omnipresent dirt of the tunnels immediately swallowed up his receding footsteps.

A few moments later Edwin returned to the cell, jumbling the board, the cards, and the keys to the cell door. In his haste he didn't notice that Griselda had pulled the feather boa around her neck and had her purse clutched under one wing, prepared to leave.

"This will be much easier than I supposed," thought Griselda.

Edwin rifled through many different sized keys before coming up with the square-headed one that opened the lock. "Yes, Jack said this one," he muttered to himself. As he entered the cell, he slipped with his paw and dropped the cribbage board and the cards, which went flying in 52 different directions. Griselda and Edwin simultaneously bent downward to pick up the board. She grabbed it first and slammed it up under the mole's chin, sending him flying backwards. With a squawk she darted out the door while Edwin shook his head and lifted himself from the floor.

"Ah, the heck with it," he said, waving a paw in defiance after her. "Where's she gonna go?"

Griselda wished she had prepared her flight more thoroughly. She ran through several tunnels, being careful to check for other moles before crossing intersections, but after running down dozens of nearly identical tunnels she didn't appear to be any closer to escaping than she had ten minutes prior. The air was still dank and musty, obviously not fresh. She paused a moment at the next intersection, hoping to discern any change in temperature in any of the four directions. The air felt cooler to the right, which might lead deeper into the mole's city of burrows. She tried the left. After several paces she felt a gentle puff of fresh air and raced toward it.

She stooped slightly to enter the tunnel then skidded to a stop. It opened up into a large rock cavern filled with precious items of all sorts. She felt like Aladdin entering into the forbidden cave. Golden plates were strewn carelessly about; strings of pearls were wrapped about the bases of antique Tiffany lamps; and many other items of silver and marble too numerous to properly appreciate in a few minutes filled every nook and cranny of the enormous room. Unlike the rest of the mole's habitation, the chamber was brightly lit with numerous chandeliers; the treasure reflected the artificial light like a giant glittering crown of diadems. Looking upward to the ceiling, which was many yards above her, she saw a ceiling fan, whirling about and creating the breeze she had felt a few moments before. There was no other visible sign of entry or aperture besides the door she had entered. There was no way out but backwards.

Yet, there was the sound of a hinge turning and a bolt sliding to the side. A large hidden door flew open in the wall to her right. Dozens of rats scampered into the room. She felt a sharp object in her backside—a large rat was poking a scabbard into her feathers. Edwin stood with his flashlight at the rat's side, obviously happy at finding Griselda trapped in the room.

"Welcome to my world," the colossus said, arms spread wide in a mock embrace, riding into the room behind the rats on top of Big White's roof.

"I don't trust her," Cluck said as the three investigators stepped down the curved landing into the driveway. "I can't tell you why, but I don't." He watched as Wiley hurried past without acknowledging them, hopped onto his moped, and cruised toward the main gates. Always so friendly, Cluck thought. He wished the gates wouldn't open so Wiley would crash into them, but the daytime gatekeeper was watchful, and the two iron giants pulled slowly to the side, leaving a slit just narrow enough for the weasel to slip through.

"I agree. I don't trust fainting females," replied Adam, pulling his hat off. For a few moments he traced his fingers about the bill, pinched at the creases in the top, and brushed at the wool. "It's too storybook. Modern gals don't faint."

"So what do we do now, Boss?" asked Cal.

"Persuade Cluck to put us up for the night so that we can sleep on it," Adam said, slapping his fedora back onto his head and pulling it down over his bloodshot eyes.

"Uh, yeah, sure," the rooster agreed with obvious reluctance. "If you don't mind the couch."

"Right now I'm so pooped I'd settle for a pillow on a hard floor and a bottle of wine for dinner," Adam replied.

"I'll just settle for the bottle of wine," added Cal, "or two."

"Hey, I nearly forgot my old pal," Adam exclaimed when he saw Lenny walking down the front walk. His whiskers twitching nervously at hearing his name called out, the rat reversed directions to scamper back toward the mansion, but Crazy Cal grabbed him by the tail. Lenny shrieked in rage, which startled the three investigators.

"I'm just inviting you to supper, Lenny." Adam slid his right arm around the packrat's shoulders. From the other side Cluck also hugged the reluctant rat while Cal continued to hold onto the tail. After Adam steered Lenny into his sedan, Cal ran around to the other side to welcome the new occupant to the vehicle. "There's just a few little questions I'd like to ask, real friendly like. Just pretend we're pals for the night and enjoy the company. In fact, I'll even foot the bill." Adam slid into the driver's seat, wedging Lenny between himself and Cal. "Make sure he stays put," he whispered to Cal who responded by grabbing onto both of Lenny's ears.

No one noticed the earthworm wriggling up the back tire and onto the bumper of the police vehicle. The attention of everyone in the treasure room was centered on the giant rodent.

"Bring back any memories?" The colossus laughed maliciously then stepped down from the top of the squad car onto a red velvet cushion proffered by one of his servant moles. He reached through the open driver's window past the rodent chauffer and honked the horn several times. "Beep. Beep," he mimicked, keeping his eyes fastened on Griselda. She swallowed hard, her throat feeling dry and swollen with fear. No words came, but the look on her face obviously satisfied the malicious streak in the monstrous rodent and he laughed again.

"Thee how my little palth keep everything tho nith and shiny?" the mole announced, pointing to the packrats. The rats were scampering across the mound of precious articles, picking up items here and there and polishing them with rags smeared with some type of white goo. The giant picked up a large serving platter and admired his reflection in the silver. "I love packrath. They know how to get the goodth."

Griselda held onto her knocking knees, willing the fear to leave her body. The massive mole was doing an excellent job of intimidating her, and she resented him for it. She who had rubbed wings with royalty and exposed the dark dealings of the highest politicians. Hard work earned her every cent and item she had, while this pest pilfered it from the sweat and efforts of others. Fear began to give way to anger.

"You're not taking my attempt to escape personally?" Griselda asked Edwin.

"No, not at all," said Edwin, rubbing his chin where Griselda had hit him with the cribbage board. "Added a little bit of excitement to my evening. Where the heck did you think you were going? Even I can't figure my way out of this maze without a map."

"I didn't know that," Griselda sniffed.

"I would've told you if you'd just bothered to ask." Edwin appeared to be sulking and was still carrying the ivory cribbage board.

"You know that I can't let you live now that you've dithcovered my little thecret," the mole said nonchalantly as if he were brushing a piece of lint off of his fur.

Griselda clutched her purse and wriggled herself free of the scabbard poking into her back.

"Jutht kidding." The giant leaned his gargantuan face into Griselda's. She grinned weakly but didn't find his pronouncement of her doom the slightest bit amusing.

"I thuppoth you want to know why you're here in our burrow?"

"That might be nice," she answered nervously, pulling her face away to escape the mole's foul breath.

"As thoon as your buddieth give me the pearl you can go free."

"You mean the MooMoo Pearl?"

"Yeth, of courth. You thee, I thought it wath juhth a myth, but then one day my friend the Walruth callth me and heth bragging about thome big pearl heth going to thcore thoon. Thayth heth going to make my collection look like an amateur didn't know what he wath doing. Everybody thought that the MooMoo Pearl was jutht a myth, a folk tale old thailoreth been thpinning yarnth about." He looked for a nod of understanding from Griselda, who returned the obligatory nod although she was struggling to understand him through his lisp. "But then thome old dame, thome old othtrich with a big mouth goeth to hith nightclub and ith bragging about thome big black thtatue her boyfriend had given her—lookth like a dancthing cow, and then the Walruth knowth that the pearl ith real and not a myth."

"Most wives' tales have their origins in truth," Griselda stammered. On a night out with her gal pals several months ago she had bragged to Betsy Moo at the Cock-n-Bull Backdoor Club about the expensive gift her sailor boyfriend had given her from overseas. She had told her staff, when placing it upon the mantelpiece, that it was an old family heirloom as she was uncomfortable announcing her relationship to the sailor. So, she was the old dame with the big mouth. She had inadvertently set her own trap to be ensnared in.

"However, I have to tell you, at the risk of making you angry," Griselda continued with trepidation with the gargantuan mole looming over her, "someone has stolen the statue from me. Asking my staff to ransom me for the pearl won't do you any good if they don't know where it is."

"Oh, yeth, I heard about the theft," said the mole looking unconcerned. "You thee, I have ear-th everywhere. Rath work cheap. But if your buddieth ever want to thee their little othtrich galpal again, your little piggie cop friend better find it—and quick! I have a thort attention thpan and don't have the patienth to wait long, ithn't that right, Edwin?" Edwin nodded. "You thee, I named my little buddy here Edwin becauth Edwin got no eth in it." He placed an enormous paw around the shuddering mole's shoulders, nearly covering him in a furry grey blanket.

"Yes, Boss, no 'S's'," repeated Edwin nervously. Griselda took note of his fear. Perhaps that knowledge could be put to use somehow.

"What the heck, maybe I'll write a great editorial about my escapades and win a Bullitzer Prize," Griselda said to Edwin as he led her back to her cell. Unexpectedly the mole closed the barred door behind the two of them and, grinning, held up the cribbage board and pack of game cards. "We've got plenty of time to play," he announced in response to the bird's groan.

"Let's arm-wrestle." It was a command and not a request. Pelly pulled a small table between him and the hog. It looked too rickety to be a suitable pivot point, but the pelican slapped his elbow down in the center of it and invited Pork to grab hold. Sighing, the chief pulled his cot over and grasped the wing. At that moment he noticed an area devoid of feathers on Pelly's left forearm, which showcased a faded blue tattoo of an anchor and gull.

"Merchant Marine," stated Pelly proudly in response to the hog's stare. "Ten odd or so years now. Pays well," and added with an easygoing laugh, "that is, when I'm not spending time in the slammer."

"You spend much time in the slammer?" asked Pork, grunting with exertion as they commenced the match.

"In the past they've clapped me in chains and cuffs and dragged me back to the ship's brig from time to time," grunted Pelly in response, slowly working his arm toward the chief's side of the table, "in a port or two." He grimaced as his wrist was slowly pushed back the other direction. "A little boozin' it up. But nothing that I couldn't sleep off and be ready for duty the following afternoon. A little morning medicinal cocktail, if you knows what I mean, and I'm shipshape and ready to roar." He pushed Pork's arm once again to his side of the table, "Nope, this is my first time in the big house." In triumph he slammed Pork's hand down to the tabletop, nearly knocking the table over. "Isn't too bad. Been in worse places. I mean, look at the great company I get to keep!" He spread his wings wide to encompass Pork in his allusion.

"Is it true that sailors have a gal in every port?" Pork asked, rubbing his bicep: it felt like an overstretched rubber band. He was irritated that the bird didn't appear to be sore at all; Pelly was flexing his muscles like he was in the Mr. Universe contest.

"At one time I did. But that's a young bird's trade." He leaned forward toward Pork and smiled, winking knowingly. "I had a nice lady in town here, a real upper class chick, but she don't know where I am and I didn't have the heart to tell her she's dating a convict."

"So you haven't spoken to her in over two months? She'll think you skipped town and dumped her."

"I know. But maybe she'll forgive me. Better than admitting the truth."

"She may find lying less forgivable."

"Well, if she don't," Pelly said, picking up a wide-toothed comb and brushing his feathers on his right hip, "there's always another port of call."

"Evening paper." One of the polar bears that watched their cellblock tossed a copy of the *Cloverleaf Gazette* through the bars. It flew into separate sections across the floor.

"What's this?" asked Pelly, picking up the front page.

"KIDNAPPED," the headline shouted in all capitals.

"I don't read too well," Pelly said, handing the newspaper to Pork. "Please read it aloud to me." He crawled to the top bunk and leaned on one side, head resting upon his wrist. "I'm a bit farsighted."

Pork, being nearsighted himself, lifted the paper to nearly the end of his snout. After clearing his throat, he read:

"It was a diabolical deed far too dastardly to be the
handiwork of any one of the fine citizens of Boville..."

"This guy gunning for the Bullitzer Prize or something?" interrupted
Pelly. "What a load of bull puckies."

"Byline says, Wiley Weasel," replied Pork. "I know him. You're
right: he's full of bull puckies."

"I've got that talent for appraising other critters. One look and I'd
know a fake from the genuine article."

"I could tell," agreed Chief Pork, swallowing a chuckle at the
pelican's inability to recognize a cop sitting in the same jail cell with
him. "To continue..."

"...yet involves one of our city's finest. The First
Lady of our lovely town is not the mayor's wife nor even
the matron of our own world famous art gallery, The
Gullery,..."

"Never been to the Gullery," Pelly interrupted again. "You ever
been there?"

"No," said Pork, feeling anxious, not wanting to read any further. He
had flipped the front page over to reveal the bottom photo—a large spread
of Griselda. Blast that Wiley! He had wanted to keep the investigation
low key, firmly in the jurisdiction of Precinct 13-and-a-half, and out of
the hands of the County's Missing Person's Bureau, particularly out of
the hands of that egotistical cigarette butt sucker Sheriff Hoggsbutter!

"I've been to a gallery once," Pelly continued. "All these snooty
people sitting at the front counter, looking down their beaks and snouts
like they was better than a blue-collar fella like me. So's, even though it
was a free day for the gallery, I drop five bucks into the donation bucket
to impress the old bags at the front counter and goes on in, thinking that
there's something wonderful hanging on those walls on the other side."

"So what did you find?"

"There's some weird-looking woven stuff like large picnic baskets made out of bark and then pinned to the wall. And stuffed toy pumpkins sitting on a shelf with steel hooks stuck into them and a fishing pole nailed above them. And then I turns the corner, and there's these large pieces of white butcher paper thumbtacked to the wall. But it looks like someone messed up and tore one corner, so someone uses some masking tape and fixes it back up. There's one paper that used to be two separate pieces and scotch tape was used to tape them back together again. There's no attempt to hide the tape at all."

"Maybe it was posted to let kids get a chance to draw?" suggested Pork.

"No, no, there's these pencil slashes on the paper, like just a regular lead pencil was used, and I'm thinking, someone got confused and put this up by mistake, picked up the wrapping for the paintings and stuck it to the wall. So I goes over to the plate on the wall, you know, those little plastic signs that tells you all about the artist and their picture and stuff, and it says, you're not going to believe this..."

"Believe what?" asked Pork, surreptitiously folding the newspaper and sitting on it.

"It's got the title, "Pencil Drawing 99" or something like that and some fool is asking $250 for this piece of bull puckie. Can you believe the guts that guy's got asking $250 for butcher paper that looked like a three-year-old was scrawling across it?"

"If the guy can talk someone into hanging it up in a gallery and then get someone to pay $250 for it, then he can't be too much of a fool."

"Well, not me," said Pelly, sitting up and crossing his legs. He pounded on his knee for emphasis. "I know quality when I sees it. I know the genuine article when I sees it. I know a fake from the real thing, an artist that's just got their pants full and someone who's got real talent. I know it because I can feel it: hits me deep in my guts."

"You've got an amazing talent," Pork said, resisting the urge to roll his eyes.

"In my travels I've gotten my wings on some beauties that you can't describe." Pelly was becoming excited, leaning forward and talking in a loud whisper. "And I know how to unload them too. Some people are just content to look at beautiful things hanging in a museum someplace; me, I know people who live with beautiful things every day. They don't need to jump into their cars to go visit it."

"For someone who calls himself 'blue-collar' you seem to hang with quite a highfaluting crowd of folks." Pork suddenly was interested in Pelly's monologue. If the bird knew how to unload precious artifacts or paintings, perhaps he would have some clue as to who might be interested in purchasing a large black pearl, or would even go to the lengths of robbing one. Pelly might be able to lead them to Griselda's kidnapper.

"It's just that when it comes to cash, a bird's gotta keep his options open. I'll never become a millionaire working for the Merchant Marine. Like my pappy always used to say, 'you'll never make money working for somebody else.'"

"So you found a way to meet up with the right folks to sell what, black velvet rock star paintings or Fiestaware?"

"No, not that junk most folks collect," Pelly whispered as if revealing a long-held secret. "Good stuff. High-class stuff."

"So any of those folks live around Boville?"

Pelly pulled back on the cot and crossed his arms in a protective gesture.

Drat it, thought Pork. Eager, he had overplayed his hand.

"Enough talking about myself," Pelly said. "I'd like to hear more about that newspaper article."

"I'm tired. I don't feel like talking anymore," Pork said defensively, sitting down onto the lower bunk.

"Read the blasted paper, Pig!" Pelly whipped out the fork and pointed it menacingly at Pork. Reluctantly the chief unfolded the newspaper. He had acted foolishly in arm-wrestling with Pelly; it only now occurred to him that the seabird wasn't acting friendly: he was testing the strength of his new cellmate and had come out the winner.

"How about the comics page? There's this great dog and cat strip..."

"Read the bloody front page! Critters, you'd think I was asking you to read the entire blasted phone book, A to Z."

"You're not asking, you're telling." Pork put the paper down and crossed his arms in defiance.

"You're right, I'm not asking, I'm telling you." Pelly hopped down from the top bunk and pushed the fork into the pink flesh of the hog's throat. "Read the blasted paper!"

"O.K., O.K.," Pork said. Pelly appeared satisfied, released his throat, and crawled back onto the top bunk.

"The entire police staff is horrified over the abduction of such an excellent lady," Lieutenant Cluck of Precinct 13-and-a-half said to this reporter earlier in the afternoon.

Chief Pork could feel the blood rushing to his skin and his face turning red. That blasted Cluck! Could never keep from showing off what he knew. The twitty little creep. Never thinking about the consequences of his foolish ramblings.

"Keep reading," was the threat.

"And just who is she?"

As if the picture and its caption didn't tell you, you dumb twit, thought Pork. Where'd you get your journalism license, Wiley, from a dog pound?

"Ms. Griselda Portentsky, Grand Dame of Grande Le Coeur, and publisher of this fine, every day increasing in sales, newspaper."

"What was that you were saying?" Pelly bolted upright. "Griselda Portentsky?"

"You heard of her?" asked Pork, curious at Pelly's interest in the missing ostrich. His stomach tightened at the thought of another critter paying attention to his ex-girlfriend.

"A potential client, just a potential client," reiterated Pelly, suddenly becoming repetitive. "She likes fine things. Keep on reading."

Really? wondered Pork. Was Griselda connected with the kidnappers personally somehow, or did she just run in the same circles? Did her abductors find out about the presence of the pearl in her home?

> "The butler and the chauffeur are baffled as to her
> whereabouts. She is not in the habit of leaving the premises
> after dark, yet her staff has not seen her for over two days.
> There is a ransom note but neither the Police, nor the staff,
> will confirm or deny the contents of the letter. And in the
> interests of protecting Madam Portentsky, some details are
> not being reported, such as the Sunday deadline for the
> ransom."

The ambitious fool! Wiley had revealed important information in the last sentence. Pork would be certain to inform Griselda of her employee's duplicity. A lump formed in Chief Pork's throat at the reminder of how long his past lover had been missing and how little time they had to find the statue. He wagered that Cluck was also the one who let loose about the ransom note, but at least he was able to keep most of the details secret: it was a small pinprick of hope in a dark night sky of gloom. He continued to read the article, growing increasingly curious himself as to how much of the case was being carelessly tossed into the public domain like a cheap dog biscuit into a hound's tin dish.

> "It's unconfirmed, but Madam Portentsky's kidnappers
> are demanding that a costly black pearl be traded for her
> safe return,…"

"What was that?" Pelly shouted.

The bird's oddly excited about events that seemingly didn't have any relationship to himself, thought Pork.

"...a family heirloom and treasure from the Far East, nicknamed the MooMoo Pearl."

Pelly leapt from the top bunk, nearly landing on the central table. "I gotta get out of here Pork, and you're going to help me."

"You're breaking out?" Pork asked incredulous, putting down the newspaper.

"That's what I'm telling ya," Pelly said, pulling off his striped shirt.

"Hey, I'm outta here tomorrow. I'm not going to get myself into trouble helping you bust out of prison."

"You're only going to get into trouble *if* you get caught," Pelly continued, pulling down his trousers and stepping out of them. "And you ain't." He pulled at the edge of the bandage wrapped around Pork's right ear.

"Hey, that hurts. If you think abusing me is going to get me to help you bust out of here, you've got a big disappointment ahead of you! Even if I wanted to help you, how would I know you wouldn't betray me and turn me in when they catch you!" There was no way in Swineville Pork was going to help his only link to the pipeline of precious artifacts slip from his grasp until he had pumped the fowl creature for the information he needed to help Griselda.

"Just pull the stupid bandage off and rewind it back up with me sitting inside," Pelly said, ignoring Pork's protestations. "Then pretend like you're really sick and let them take you to the infirmary. When we're there, you just unwind it enough to let me free myself and, viola, I'm gone, and nobody's gonna finger you for it."

"You thought all of that up on the spur of the moment?" asked Pork.

"No, been thinking about it ever since I saw your fat head come waltzing through that cell door." Pelly continued tugging at the bandage on the hog's head. "I've been going nuts sitting in here by myself for three months and I don't want to sit here for several more just over some dumb jalopy."

"You don't think they'd notice that my head got a lot bigger all of a sudden?" Pork asked while wondering silently, What, was this bird crazy or something?

"Not that fat head of yours. I couldn't tell your snout from your butt end when you first came lumbering in."

"Insults aren't helping your cause."

"I thought it was a compliment, myself."

Pork pulled the bandage out of Pelly's grasp. "I'm not cooperating. I plan to walk out of here on my own two feet." He had the impulse to reveal that he was a police officer in an attempt to intimidate the pelican with his title, but decided that Pelly was much too excited at the moment and didn't need an excuse to feel more aggressive toward him. His cellmate might think he was an undercover cop and not a genuine prisoner for the night.

"So you're not cooperating?"

"Not in the slightest," said Pork, folding his arms defiantly across his chest.

"You won't fake even a teeny weeny little stomach ache to help out a new pal?" Pelly's voice carried a hint of menace to it.

"No, certainly not," Pork said firmly. He was beginning to wonder if he was making a mistake by not revealing he was a police chief.

And before he could cry out or protest, Pelly grabbed the table and landed a full force blow across the back of the pig's skull. His head already causing him a great deal of pain, Pork's knees buckled beneath him and he passed out.

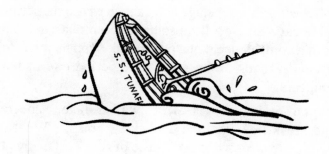

SCENE TEN: SCRATCH AND SNIFF

"You know, we still might've been able to trade the statue for Griselda," commented Lt. Cluck as the motley crew of four slid into the booth at the Little Chick Diner. "The kidnappers might not have noticed that it was a fake until after the switch was made. You didn't need to destroy the statue to prove your point."

"The main point is," unruffled by the intimation that he was pompous, Adam interrupted himself to thank the waitress for the menu, "that it was a fake and I noticed it. If our villains were willing to risk kidnapping a prominent bird in our town, they most likely could distinguish a fake cut pearl from the real article. And perhaps injure Griselda in revenge. Oh, quit squirming, Lenny. I've never known you to turn down a free meal yet."

Adam had Lenny in a near vice grip around the shoulders, seated between himself and Cal. While they were cramped, sweaty, and sticking to the cheap vinyl seat, Lt. Cluck sat luxuriously by himself, reveling in the comical view on the other side of the Formica table.

"Smashing that statue was a moment I won't soon forget. You've got quite a flair for the dramatic, Old Boy," said Cal. "Ever thought of becoming an actor?"

Adam was going to respond, "No," but then Betsy Moo came to mind. She was sitting in his black sedan next to him, wind from the open window whipping her luxurious hair across her face, her rose-scented perfume blown forever into his memory. "Every day's an act," he replied. "The world's our stage and chance writes the script, wouldn't you say?" He gave Lenny a little squeeze to emphasize his point. "So isn't it a bit of a coincidence that a packrat like you happens to be dating one of Griselda's maids in the same time period one of her priceless statues disappears?"

"Look, you proved it yerself it was a fake," sneered Lenny, struggling to break free from the detective's grasp. "What would I be doing attempting to steal some fake piece of rock? The guys I deal with only want top quality; they'd kill me if I tried to pass off a fake as the real deal."

"And who would that be?" Adam asked, giving Lenny another big squeeze. It was meant to threaten, but Lenny didn't intimidate easily.

"Look, youse guys inviting me to dinner or some hippie love-in?" protested the rat. "Let go of me, you big gasbag. I ain't no squeeze toy. I've got nothing to be ashamed of, nothing to hide. Youse can let go of me. I ain't gonna go nowheres until I get my free meal. No use'n wasting my time now that youse dragged me this far."

Adam released his grip. Lenny brushed himself off with both front paws and straightened his beret. "Near kidnapped me, youse have, and youse call yerselves Officers of the Law. I call youse guys pissants, that's what I call youse."

"Always ingratiating yourself." Adam pulled a few napkins out of the metal container by the window.

"Ain't polite to sit at the dinner table with your hat on." Cal yanked the beret off Lenny's head and tossed it onto the coat rack by the front glass doors. Amazingly, it landed on one of the outstretched elk horns adorning the length of the rack.

"Yer one fer preaching politeness," sneered the rat, "with a paper hat on yer own skull. Guess they don't pay junior detectives much these days."

The waitress, a tabby cat wearing a pink uniform and white apron, asked for their order. Adam requested a spinach salad and bowl of squash bisque; Cal dittoed, not having been in a restaurant for some years; Cluck had the mealworms with red sauce and a small bowl of corn chowder; and Lenny ordered squid, extra crispy, and chips.

"Thanks for reminding me, Lenny," Adam said, pulling the hat off of Cal's head. "Mind if I borrow this?" Cal nodded in assent and Adam unfolded the paper to reveal the photo of the sinking ship with its accompanying article. "Bring back fond memories?"

"I don't know what yer talking about?" Lenny said, squinting one eye.

"Been in Singapork lately?"

The rat's whiskers froze, his eyes widened in surprise. Realizing that he was betraying himself by his behavior, he recovered his composure by shaking himself all over. "I've got a lot of friends and relatives. Rats got big families, you know." He rubbed at his goatee nonchalantly, but his tail, up in the air, slapped against the back of the cubicle.

"May 17th," Adam continued, smoothing the wrinkles out of the paper. "To summarize this rather lengthy article: The S.S. Tunafish, a ship returning to Americow from Singapork, goes down in the Pawcific Ocean. We all know that rats desert a ship about to sink. And it appears to me, and my highly distinguished colleagues," Cluck and Cal grinned in response, "that it is you sitting in the life raft in this photo."

"Yer mistaken," sneered the packrat. "Youse can scarcely make out what type of critters is sitting in that raft, let alone identify their faces." His tail thumped more loudly against the vinyl back of the bench.

"I took a little time to visit the Port of Boville," Adam said, unruffled by the rat's defiance, his voice smooth as skates sliding across ice. "Asked a few questions at the shipping company, I.L.B. Wayward & Associates, which chartered the S. S. Tunafish. Of course, they keep a passengers manifest, which they were kind enough to permit me to peruse. Your name was on the list."

"That's a Merchant Marine vessel! They wouldn't have a passengers manifest!"

"Now how would you know what type of ship it was?"

Lenny's tail stopped thumping. He had been caught in a poorly contrived lie.

"If the traveler is willing to forego a few cruise ship luxuries, many merchant vessels take on a few outside passengers who want to purchase a cheap ocean crossing or satisfy a longing for adventure." Adam thanked the waitress who was setting their plates and bowls, pouring forth delicious aromas of tomatoes and squash, onto the table. "And knowing how stingy you are, Lenny, I'd say you were taking a cheap trip, not satisfying a youthful fantasy."

"So I took a trip to Singapork, what's that got to do with anything? It's not a crime to travel outside the country. I had a passport." Lenny nibbled nervously on a slice of breaded squid.

"Theft and accessory to kidnapping," snapped Adam, "is definitely a crime and will get you at least ten to twenty in the slammer."

"Why would I steal a statue and then kidnap the old bird to get it back again? Doesn't make any sense, does it?" The packrat squealed, biting his cheek rather than the squid; a tiny drop of blood dribbled down his chin. He brushed it away in an angry swipe with the back of his paw.

"He's got you there," quipped Cal. "I'm not too bright and even I figured that out."

"You know, these mealworms are a little too chewy," interrupted Lt. Cluck, his cheeks stuffed with worms and red sauce. He signaled to the waitress. "Miss, I'd like to have this redone."

"Wouldn't want chewy mealworms." Cal rolled his eyes in disgust.

"Doesn't matter if you're guilty or not," threatened Adam, pressing his face into Lenny's. He pulled a piece of squid from the rat's plate and stuffed it into his mouth, intimating he could take anything from Lenny anytime. He intended to continue vocalizing his threats but found the squid was indeed very stringy. He chewed for nearly a minute while the others watched with amused fascination, and then with a grimace, spit the cud out onto Lenny's plate.

"Hey!" Lenny's voice squeaked when he shouted. "There's no need for that. I may be a rat but I'm sanitary! Youse guys really disgust me. All of youse. I'm not sure this kind of sordid company is worth keeping fer a free meal." He attempted to rise but Adam, placing a firm hold onto his right shoulder, forced him down again to the bench.

"Word's been out in the field for some time that you're into fencing goods," continued Adam. He was taking a chance of being caught lying: He didn't know if the rat was into fencing goods or not, but most packrats were.

"Yeah, that's right. I overheard the birds at Lilah's talking about that a few times," interrupted Cal with enthusiasm, glad to be back in the conversation. Adam gave him a look of surprise: Cal had never mentioned it, possibly denying him a valuable clue in their investigation. On the other hand, the bull was not a professional and perhaps didn't consider it apropos until now. Or Cal could be lying just to back his partner up.

"Miss!" Cluck spoke a little louder this time, waving a wing toward the waitress. She had a carafe of coffee in her paw and was pouring a round into the cups of the customers sitting near the back of the diner. Apparently the rooster was more interested in his supper than the increasingly heated discussion across the table.

"I don't fence anything," Lenny said, trying to pull out of Adam's grasp. "I procure fine items for cultivated clients, quite unlike present company, and sell them fer a tidy profit. Again, youse guys got nothing on me." The rat tried once again, unsuccessfully, to rise from his seat. "Unhand me, you hoofed fiend."

"Melodramatic, ain't he?" asked Cal. He thrust his nose into the squash bisque and slurped. He swished the mixture around in his mouth, grimaced, then transferred it from one cheek into the other, a circus performance that caught both Lenny's and Adam's morbid attention. "I thought it looked like puke," he announced, following the long-anticipated swallow with a loud belch, "but it's pretty delicious."

"You doubted my good taste?" asked Adam.

"I sure as flipping do," added Lenny, looking at the wad of chewed squid on his plate.

"You help us, and we won't drum up any charges against you."

"I haven't done anything wrong...in this instance."

"You give us a little information and we won't try too hard to find something," returned Adam. "I've never been to Singapork. You have."

"Miss, Miss!" Cluck exclaimed, wildly waving his wings, trying to catch the attention of the pussycat as she rushed by with the coffee pot.

"You ever seen anything like this, Lenny?" asked Adam. Out of his trench coat pocket he pulled the green dancing cow that he had purloined from the mansion and set it down on top of the napkin holder.

"Yep, cheap tourist trinkets. Street vendors sell them jest about anywhere in Singapork. Cost a few bucks apiece."

"Any reason why a very wealthy woman like Madam Portentsky would have a mantelpiece full of inexpensive souvenirs when she doesn't travel outside the States?"

"Bad taste?" Lenny quipped.

Lt. Cluck caught the edge of the waitress's dress as she hurried by the table once more. "This tastes old, like it's been sitting on the counter for several hours before you served it to me. I'd like you to replace this plate with fresh mealworms and red sauce."

"Look, buddy," the waitress warned, obviously irritated at Cluck for the insult. "It took me less than ten minutes to get your food to you. It's fresh."

"That proves my point. You couldn't have dished it out so fast if it hadn't been pre-made and sitting around in a pot on the stove for a while."

"So, Lenny, were you making some sort of procurement overseas?" asked Adam.

"This ain't a fancy restaurant." The tabby had one hand on her hip and the coffee pot brandished menacingly close to Cluck. "And I don't care if you're a copper or not. You're eating what's already on your plate!"

"See if I leave YOU a tip."

"Like I was expecting one anyway." The waitress rolled her eyes.

"You're inferring I'm cheap?" Cluck's voice was rising in pitch.

"No, I'm outright saying that you look cheap." The cat's ears pulled down flat against her skull and her eyes narrowed.

"Cluck, please, we've got something a little more serious to attend to at the moment," Adam pleaded. He swallowed hard, his heart pounding. There was one question he was dying to ask the rat, but wasn't sure how to do so without revealing his Achilles heel to a potential adversary.

"So why'd Betsy bail you out Tuesday?"

"Guess she likes me," the rat replied, his eyes intently focused on Adam's face. He was looking for signs of betrayed feelings and received it; Adam's face paled and his left eye twitched nervously. "Or perhaps she prefers the superior company of rats to the more unsavory members of her own species." He stuck the knife in between the ribs and was rewarded with another twitch of the left eye. Only the most practiced liars, like himself, could bury their emotions under a layer of deceit. "As do many other young ladies."

"I insist that you take this plate and give me a new one." Cluck pushed his dish toward the waitress and, unintentionally, into her stomach, which caused the cat to pitch forward and drop the pot of coffee into the rooster's lap. The lieutenant shrieked and jumped from the bench, pulling his officer's shirt out of his slacks and splashing coffee everywhere.

In the chaos Lenny slipped under the table, grabbed his beret off the rack, and darted out through the glass doors. Trapped on the bench by Cal, who was trying to mop up the spilled coffee from off of the newspaper with his napkin, Adam watched Lenny rush by the window. The rat couldn't resist a good opportunity; anchoring his thumbs in the corners of his mouth, he pulled it apart and razzed Adam. Then he darted down around the corner of the diner and out of sight.

Adam slammed his hoofed hand atop the table, startling the others into momentary inaction. He should have asked Lenny who his connections in precious artifacts were, not wasted his time asking about Betsy. What a fool he was! Master Detective indeed. With the discovery that the statue was a fake, searching for the MooMoo Pearl was no longer their most likely route to finding Griselda. It made more sense to discover who in town was interested in procuring expensive collectibles and perhaps, at the same time, find the kidnappers. He had acted like a lovesick cow and was now paying the price with the disappearance of his best lead.

"Uh, Miss, could I have my coffee warmed?" asked Cal, moving his cup to the edge of the table. The waitress stood dumbfounded with an open mouth, the empty pot dangling from her right paw.

An hour later the three failures sat in the living room of Cluck's townhouse. Cluck had a cloth napkin in his hand and was rubbing baking soda into his shirt, attempting to work the coffee stains out. Cal batted a wet wad of newspaper between both hoofed hands, lamenting the demise of his impromptu detective's hat due to the spilled coffee in the diner. Adam pushed himself as far as possible into the soft cushions of a misshapen loveseat, the evening edition of the *Cloverleaf Gazette* in his hands. Only his strong desire not to sleep in a hotel that evening had prevented him from throttling Cluck when the rooster complained that Adam's sedan was blocking the townhouse driveway and should be parked in the street instead. The detective had given the lieutenant the "look of death," and the car continued to block the driveway. Even the rooster showed a modicum of common sense at times.

He sighed, leaned forward toward the coffee table, and began folding a new hat for Cal from the front page of the newspaper. Looking at the photo of Griselda on the cover just cheesed him royally. It was inevitable that the story of the bird's abduction would eventually be publicized, as she was the owner of the city newspaper, but did Cluck have to feed information to Wiley? The bird had been careless at the mansion, not considering who was listening. The lieutenant had never said anything directly to the reporter, Cluck had protested: the weasel had pieced it together when they were assembled together at Grande Le Coeur. It was possible that he was telling the truth, as Wiley was not known for his ethical standards, and it could be likely he only surmised information then presented it as a direct quote. They had certainly leaked plenty of details at the mansion earlier that day.

Adam preferred to work with a degree of anonymity to avoid tipping off the suspects or enduring interference from amateur sleuths not fully cognizant of the dangers, or the repercussions, of their investigations. He could most likely accomplish more by acting on his own, rather than putting up with the companionship of the two doofuses who considered themselves detectives. A more accurate term would be gumshoes: They were like gum stuck to the soles of his shoes that he couldn't remove. Cluck was part of the Police Force and was on the case by default; Cal was unpredictable—and interested in the kidnapping: it was better to keep an eye on him than allow free reign to the rogue cow to pursue the case on his own, which he most certainly would do if tempted. And, unlike Cluck, Cal was amusing at times and tolerable company.

But on the other hand, perhaps alerting the public through the press would set more eyes and ears looking for the ostrich. Hopefully, any critter with pertinent information about the abduction would call Precinct 13-and-a-half rather than circumvent official police processes. A phone number had been published at the bottom of the newspaper article requesting information regarding Griselda's kidnapping, and it was not the number of the police station, but rather, that of the *Gazette*. Would Wiley keep information back from the police? Blast Wiley for being there that afternoon! Yes, he would. And perhaps endanger Griselda in his lust for glory.

He handed the newly christened official detective's hat to Cal who proudly placed it upon his head. Adam had been careful to fold the picture of Griselda into the inner folds so as not to upset the chief the next time they encountered him. He felt a pang of guilt, realizing that the three of them hadn't thought to check to see if Pork had been discharged from the hospital that day. If the chief had been released, he wouldn't be surprised if the old hog was intentionally ignoring them.

It was dark and difficult to breathe, as if a wet suffocating blanket was wrapped about his head. Pork panicked, waving his arms and kicking his feet in an attempt to free himself. Pelly was trying to kill him! After a few moments he discovered he was actually wrapped in a blanket. He ceased struggling and, with embarrassment, realized that he was being observed. A cross-eyed goose with a wry grin on her face stood next to the bed with a clipboard in her wings, clucking to herself. Pork was in a room of about a dozen wrought-iron beds with cheap box springs and white bed sheets. It was the prison infirmary. One other inmate, some type of hound, lay in one of the six beds on the other side of the room, groaning and clutching at his stomach. As Pork watched the dog upchucked into his bedpan and then began lapping it back up.

His stomach would have troubled him also at that moment if his head didn't ache so terribly.

"I'm not sure how you sustained such a blow to the back of your head," the nurse said, scribbling something onto the chart in her hand. "I thought maybe you'd fallen off the top bunk, but I would've expected the knot to be on your forehead or somewhere on the side of your skull, not on the back."

"It was Pelly." Chief Pork gingerly worked his fingers around the large bump on the back of his head. It hurt, but morbid compulsion made him continue to touch it, to feel the full extent of the injury.

"Pelly?" the nurse asked. "Do you mean, jelly? Did you spill some jelly and slip on it?"

"No," Pork groaned. He rolled to his right side, away from where the bump sat. "The pelican that was in my cell."

"There was no one else in your cell when you were found lying on the floor. And the gate was locked tight."

"No, no, indeed," another voice added. One of the polar bears that had been guarding his line of cells stepped to the foot of his bed. "There was just the hog."

"That's not..." and then Pork's protestation trailed off. The bear slid a night stick under the bedcover and gave a warning tap against the bottom of his hoof. "No one was assigned to that cell but this cop here," the bear added with another tap. Pork was too weary and in too much pain to protest. Whatever was going on it didn't have anything to do with Griselda's abduction and therefore wasn't really his concern. If the County thought they were so superior and so much more brilliant than the poor City Police Force, then let them inspect and clean their own dirty laundry. He'd had enough of the County to last him for months.

"Poor dear." The nurse brushed a wing across Pork's forehead. "He's really suffered quite a blow. Hallucinations. Buster," she said to the correctional officer, "we might have to keep the hog an extra day for observation." Her eyes were bright and soft, peering gently over the top of her wire rim granny glasses. Pork savored the soft wispy touch of her feathers. So much like Griselda's. Tears welled up in his eyes and he rolled over to his other side to conceal his emotions from the nurse.

Adam, still nestled in the armchair, was working on the crossword puzzle in the Want Ads section of the *Gazette*. Cal was placing two blankets and a large piece of plywood across the arms of two different loveseats, creating an impromptu bed for himself. Cluck entered the room with a large silver bowl of popcorn, poured part of the contents into a paper sack, and handed it to the nutty bovine. "Now this is what I call room and board!" Cal exclaimed, reaching for the television remote. Cluck glanced at Adam, surmised that the detective was not interested in a snack, and settled down into a rocking chair. The antique rocker made an annoying squeak as the rooster absentmindedly pumped it back-and-forth while absorbed in the opening credits of the monster movie about to start on the boob tube.

"What's a six-letter word for idiot?" Adam asked, his nose buried in the paper.

Cal pulled his own nose out of the popcorn sack and shouted back, "Doofus!"

"That doesn't fit the puzzle, Cal."

"Moron!" Cal shouted back.

"No, that's only five letters," Adam said, looking up at Cluck, and flipping the black marker back and forth between his fingers. "Try again."

Takes one to know one, Cluck thought silently to himself.

"Nitwit!"

"Yes, I believe that fits," Adam responded, ostensibly writing the word into the puzzle boxes.

A monster's voice roared from the television set. Startled, Cluck tossed the popcorn, intended to go into his beak, across the room. Then the squeaking of the rocking chair resumed.

Squeak. Thunk. Squeak. Thunk. Squeak. Thunk.

"How about a five-letter synonym for idiot?" the master detective asked.

"Booby!" Cal cried gleefully. Cluck stopped rocking, focusing his attention on the two crossword sleuths.

"Try another one," Adam said, staring Cluck in the eyes.

"Dunderhead, numchuck, twit, spaz, numbskull, lamebrain,..."

"Those might fit." Adam rolled the tip of the pen in his mouth.

"You must really think I'm a nincompoop if you don't think I understand what you're doing!" the lieutenant screeched, jumping excitedly from his chair.

"Oh, nincompoop! I forgot that one!" Cal exclaimed.

"If you're so doggoned brilliant, how come we aren't any closer to solving this case than on the day the old broad got snatched?" Cluck's face, despite being covered with feathers, was turning nearly as red as his top comb.

"Well, I wasn't the idiot that got her snatched to begin with!" Adam lost his temper, a rare occurrence, and also jumped to his feet. He hated violence but sometimes, despite your best efforts to maintain self-control, when you're tired and you're fed up, you lose it. And Cluck could push a duck to losing its beak!

"Sticks and stones will break my bones but names will never hurt me." Cluck held his beak high in a smirky grin that nearly drove Adam nuts with exasperation. The detective hated twits, but was usually wise enough to conceal his true feelings.

"Names won't, but this will!" Adam balled his hoofed hand into a fist and pulled his arm back, as if to throw a punch, then relaxed and fell back into the marshmallow chair. He was more than a match for the spindly rooster and it was against the law to hit an officer, no matter how irritating he might be. He sighed and wiped his hand across his damp brow. "We're tired, boys. Let's just get some rest and resume in the morning."

"Let's not resume like this, screaming and yelling," Cal said, snuggling under the blanket on his makeshift bed. "I may be crazy, but I do prefer a more civil atmosphere. Makes it easier to digest your dinner. Good night, Cluck. And," he turned his face toward Adam before closing his eyes for the night, "Good night, Detective."

Cal smiled, revealing a genuine affection for his mentor which did not go unnoticed. Adam wondered if Cluck had deep feelings, even superficial, for anyone, or was his life merely a maze of regulations and rules that didn't require involvement of the affections, just obedience?

"If you don't mind," Cluck announced, removing his shirt, "I'll take a shower first. I don't want to use the tub after you guys. It'll probably take me days to get the ring out."

A cool breeze snaked across the back of Pork's neck. He pulled the blanket tighter about his shoulders and looked upward. Except for the twittering snore of the hound across the room, he was alone. Twilight obscured the timbered ceiling. A sheer curtain flapped like a dying trout from an open window several yards above his head. With his nearsighted eyes he could scarcely make out the half moon, but he could have sworn the shadow of a large bird darted in front of the glowing orb and into the night.

SCENE ELEVEN: BUMPS AND BRUISES

Adam woke somewhat refreshed in the morning but rather embarrassed for losing his temper the night before. He was becoming accustomed to Cal's sleep talking and more adept at ignoring it while resting. The hide-a-bed was not very comfortable, but it was better than sleeping on a hotel mattress that had supported the weight of various creatures from bulls to rodents—lumpy and sagging. And the rooster's couch smelled better too: there was a lavender sachet in each pillowcase. Say what you would about Cluck, but there was no denying that he was neat. The apartment was clean and had a slight odor of disinfectant. The books on the four shelves of the bookcase were neatly stacked in rows by ascending height. Matching coverlets graced each arm of the chairs and where the head lay. Magazines were neatly displayed in a semi-circle on the coffee table. The color scheme was steel blue and grey, not a comforting color combination but showed some class.

The problem was breakfast: grits. Adam politely refused and sipped at his Steerbucks coffee. In a whisper to Cal he promised a bowl of Wheaties later on. It was the breakfast of champions—and bovine detectives.

It was a very pleasant August morning. The back porch door was open, birds were chirping in the trees in the yard, a lawnmower was buzzing, and the sweet scent of cut grass blew into the room. Everyone sat comfortably around the kitchen table in their boxer shorts. Cal and Adam had borrowed from Pork the other night, respectively, a blue pair of shorts with strawberries on them and an orange pair with pineapples. The lieutenant sat in woolen green-and-navy checked shorts like a lumberjack hibernating in a log cabin in the wintertime.

Cluck pulled a large plate of biscuits out of the microwave and set it down onto the table. He buttered a biscuit and reached for the strawberry jelly in an appropriately shaped berry container. His way of apologizing for the scene the night before was not to mention it, as not commenting on anything was difficult for the rooster. Giving his opinion was almost his birthright and he was very generous. His mother used to say that she could hear him talking in his egg. "Pork mentioned that he saw Lenny at the Cock-n-Bull. Think it means anything?"

"Maybe," Adam answered. The scent of the warm bread was intoxicating. "Toss me one of those biscuits, will you?"

"Me too," added Cal. He was feeling sleepy and was content to listen to the conversation rather than participate. His eyes felt crusty about the lashes also. But his mouth was watering profusely in anticipation.

Cluck literally tossed two biscuits to the two cattle then slid the jelly container toward their side of the table.

"Or it might not mean anything at all," Adam continued, chewing a hunk of biscuit. It tasted good: warm and soft with a hint of butter. He wondered if Cluck cooked it himself or got it at a bakery, but although he no longer felt angry about the events of the previous evening, he wasn't in the mood to give the rooster any compliments. "Let's summarize what we do know. Lenny admitted to being in Singapork. Madam Griselda doesn't travel, but she's got an entire mantelpiece full of cheap trinkets that come from the same country. Is there a connection?"

"Why would Lenny give the madam souvenirs?" asked Cluck. "I wouldn't think she would be hanging around with the likes of a packrat like him."

"No, most likely not," Adam said perfunctorily. "We do know that he's involved with Demeris, the maid. Did he give the trinkets to her, and she passed them on to her employer for some reason?"

"Could they be booby trapped?" asked Cluck. "Or have teeny tiny little cameras in them to watch her movements for some reason?"

"You examined them yourself."

"Oh, yes, that's quite right," Cluck said, pulling his jaw in defensively.

"Besides, why would Demeris want to spy on an employer that she could freely eavesdrop on nearly anytime with little effort, since they lived in the same household?"

"Just brainstorming, like they taught us at the Academy."

"Cluck, why don't you check with the servants and get a time for when the souvenirs first appeared. And be sure you ask Demeris and corroborate her remarks with a few of the others."

"Of course," the lieutenant snapped, feeling insulted. "How else would I go about it?"

Adam smiled. He wouldn't expect any other response than a defensive one. He continued his summary. At this point they didn't have much and it was necessary to glean whatever details they could from what they did know. "Lenny was most likely in Singapork procuring some item or items to sell in the rare goods market."

Cal couldn't remain silent any longer. "I don't recall the birds at Lilah's Happy Farm ever talking about Lenny specifically," continued Cal. "How'd you know he was into the rare goods market?"

"I didn't," Adam replied, glad to feel like he was the knowledge master again. "I just threw out a line to see if I'd reel anything in. But if he traveled all the way to Singapork, he had a darn good reason for being there—he's not the sentimental sort to be visiting family. He's also involved with a gal who works for a fowl who's had a priceless item stolen. Lenny doesn't have a reputation for deep devotion to any particular lady; if he's involved with Demeris on more than a casual basis, he's got an ulterior motive than just being love-struck. Unfortunately, he returned to town several months ago. It's going to be tough scaring up his contacts before our deadline this Sunday." He sounded cold-hearted to himself, as if Griselda was just an insurance policy he was handling and not a bird whose life was possibly in danger. "He's had plenty of time to contact a buyer and unload it."

"Maybe he didn't get a good enough offer from his local contacts. Maybe he's still in the process of locating new buyers—it takes awhile when you're being discreet. Maybe he was scoping the millionaires at the club for a better offer."

"Club? You mean tavern, don't you, Cal?" interrupted Adam.

"No, club." Cal tore off a piece of biscuit and stuffed it into his mouth. "Haven't you guys ever been to the club at the back of the tavern?" His question was answered with blank looks from the police officer and sleuth. "The Backdoor Club?" More blank looks. "Some detectives you two are, not knowing about the private club in your own back yard." He swallowed and reached for another biscuit. "Guess you guys don't have much of a night life."

Cluck was obviously unwelcome by the look of distaste on Dudley's face when he opened the front door, but the lieutenant stepped inside anyway, brushing his wounded feelings aside. He knew that a cop shouldn't be overly sensitive for, as an officer of the judicial system, he represented law and judgment, which often made people feel uncomfortable, even when they were innocent. He had potential power over, and the ability to change, the lives of others for good or bad. And officers of the law often discovered secrets that others preferred would remain hidden from scrutiny or to disregard and maintain their blissful ignorance without disturbance from the ugly realities of life. It was apparent that Dudley had feelings for Demeris, although Cluck had no idea whether these were ever expressed to the poodle or if she had ever regarded the butler with more than a semi-professional interest. Yet the lieutenant wanted to be liked and it was apparent that Dudley did not like him.

The little Yorkie named Gladys and Dudley corroborated Demeris' contention that the figurines began to appear roughly a year ago and were not a gift from Lenny. About that same time the Madam was often returning late from the newspaper, sometimes after dark, which was not her custom as she hated being out after twilight. She was not a bird given to being fearful, and had a chauffer to take her about, so it wasn't a case of night blindness; but there were rumors that something had happened one starless night when she was a teenbird, an incident only whispered about in the servants' quarters but never directly referred to. In any case, she was frequently late and the staff wondered if she had a new interest of some sort, a social club or a possibly even a boyfriend. They hadn't seen any beaus about the mansion since Chief Pork some two odd years ago, but perhaps the couple's blowup in front of the servants pushed her into being more discreet with her relationships. Or so Dudley, Gladys, and later, the chauffer, had said.

"What do I care about my mistress' love life?" asked Demeris, lifting her muzzle high into the air and looking down her nose at the lieutenant. "I have plenty of my own interests; I don't need to go snooping into my employer's affairs."

Cluck blushed. He was not insensible himself to the French poodle's charms and certainly believed her statement that she had plenty of males in her life. Her fur was delicate and neatly curled, her perfume was light and floated on the air like a fragile soap bubble. Her limbs were strong yet lithe, not overly muscular. Her uniform was neatly pressed, her grooming impeccable.

"Did you ever bring any of your boyfriends to the mansion?" Cluck asked with some reluctance. "Perhaps someone you didn't know as well as you really should?" He could feel his face turning red with embarrassment.

"I don't invite males..." Demeris began to protest then realized to her chagrin that Cluck had twice witnessed her involvement with Lenny at the mansion. She cleared her throat and smiled. "I don't normally invite my masculine friends to the mansion. My employer frowns upon that sort of thing. Lenny is an exception."

Cluck noticed that her paws were black near the cuticles in contrast to the pink polish on the rest of her nails, the only discrepancy in her immaculate toiletry: perhaps from weeping yesterday, her mascara running into her fur, or more likely... Cluck recalled the scene in the kitchen, Demeris rubbing black shoe polish into Lenny's dingy fur. It didn't seem to be particularly demure or ladylike behavior. Maybe the little packrat just brought out the worst in a critter's character.

With a slight awkward bow Cluck bid Demeris goodby and with an affected air of nonchalance, pushed by Dudley, standing guard at the front door, and into the driveway.

"You've been lying about on the job quite a bit lately," Adam said with a wink. He was standing next to Pork's bed in the prison infirmary; Cal, being neither a relative nor an officer of the law, was not permitted to go into the jailhouse and had to wait in the outer lobby.

"That's starting to get a little old, Steer," the chief replied, rolling over onto his right side to get a better look at the detective. "I thought you had more imagination than that." He wasn't sure he was happy to see Adam or embarrassed at being found, not only in another hospital bed, but also in jail. It suddenly occurred to him, seeing the concerned bull's face looming over the top of him, that he hadn't had any good luck since leaving the precinct to retrieve the detective from retirement. Perhaps Adam was bad luck—some critters were. Wasn't their fault: it was part of their genes, like brown eyes or acne. Even Adam himself had an unlucky life: no gal, no calves, and no living family that he knew of. Pork wondered if he should avoid further collaboration with the bovine sleuth after his release from captivity. Even his lucky frog's leg didn't carry enough good fortune to protect him from Adam's aura. He shook himself out of his reverie; Adam was waiting for him to speak, perhaps to explain himself.

"And I'm not on the job anymore. Had a little falling out with Judge Bookem yesterday," Pork began. "He decided that I was stressed out and insisted that I get a little R and R, a little break from police work for a while." It was somewhat the truth. He didn't want to admit that he'd lost his temper and been chucked into the can for spitting on the courtroom floor.

"The judge sentenced you to two days of hard labor in bed?" Adam's eyes were twinkling with amusement.

Pork was not feeling similarly gleeful. His head no longer hurt: it ached, a deep, all-encompassing ache that throbbed in a full circle from the back of his head toward his temple. It ached more than his heart did for Griselda. It ached more than losing his dignity in the tavern. It ached more than the humiliation of being denied his gun for two weeks.

"I met this odd bird in my cell." Pork ignored Adam's question, holding his left hand up to his forehead. His voice was halting and punctuated at intervals with slight gasps as if struggling to breathe. "He struck me in the back of the head in an attempt..." Pork gulped, looking embarrassed, "to break out of jail."

"Didn't he know you were a cop?" Adam interrupted.

"No. I'm not sure if it would've made a difference, except he probably would've hit me harder with the table. Pelly suddenly went wild, desperate to escape. I don't know if he actually made it: haven't caught wind of any news around the ward at all."

Adam looked across the room at the other patient: an old hound dog, scratching at his big floppy graying ears with his hind leg. "I imagine you caught wind of *something* since last night."

Pork caught his drift and laughed despite his pain. "Most likely. I wouldn't want to tell you what he did with his bed pan this morning." He paused a moment, letting the throbbing in his head settle down into a dull ache, then continued. "Odd thing is that no one seems to recall that the bird was a prisoner here. But he claimed to have been jailed for months. I'm sure that the polar bear watching our cell block knew the guy."

"Maybe the guard is crooked. In on a scheme of some sort with the jailbird."

Pork did not respond for over a minute, as if deep thinking were painful for him. When he spoke his words were slow, as if they were taffy being pulled out of his mouth in long, stringy pieces. "That could be. But I don't have time to concern myself with anything that doesn't pertain to our case at hand." Another pause. His mind filled with Griselda's image. "The bird was a pelican. Name was...Pelly, I believe. Yes, it was Pelly. He was in the Merchant Marine."

"Did you say Merchant Marine?" asked Adam, suddenly enlivened. He leaned further over the bed, his left ear closer to the chief's mouth.

"Yes. And what upset me most about his disappearance is that he was into the antiquities market. I wanted to milk him for information about his contacts, thinking that perhaps one of them would be interested in procuring the MooMoo Pearl. Perhaps so much so as to commit a felony kidnapping to obtain it."

Adam was giddy with delight. This could be their first big break in the case. Pork had been in the hospital and didn't know anything about the information the trio of sleuths, loosely put, had obtained the last twenty-four hours. He removed his hat and sat down on the edge of the bed. "Did this bird, Pelly, tell you what ship he sailed on?"

"No. I was a little too obvious in my initial questions and he played duck-and-cover. I wanted to broach it later on, when he relaxed a little, but then he made his great escape and I ended up with a tour of the infirmary." He sighed and rolled onto his back. "I'm feeling a little tired now, Adam. If you don't mind, I think I'll take advantage of their kind hospitality and nurse my wounds for another day. Grissie's in your hooves."

Adam was struck by how old the chief suddenly appeared. It wasn't wrinkles or sagging skin, but a drooping attitude. Quite unlike the fiery obstinate police chief he had known for years. He recalled Pork lying supine on the ground under the night sky. A shiver scuttled up his spine. Pork was like an anchor that kept the precinct firmly in place. Without him, the department would drift in the wrong direction.

Pork noticed Steer surveying him. "Grissie got herself a new boyfriend not too long after we broke up. Wiley told me. Delighted in rubbing my wounded feelings into the news."

"Chief," Adam interrupted, feeling a little rude. "Did Pelly seem eager to escape when you first met him?

"No, not at all," the hog responded, pulling his blanket and sheet tightly about his neck. He closed his eyes, as if telling Adam to go away, let me sleep now. "But I wouldn't expect him to betray that type of knowledge to a stranger he'd just met. I could've been a stool pigeon."

"What made him suddenly so eager to escape?"

"You know, it was the oddest thing," the chief's voice trailed away in the initial stages of slumber. "He made me read the newspaper to him and then he got very excited over Wiley's article about Griselda. Wouldn't explain why." His eyelids flew open. "You think there's a connection between him and Grissie?" He bolted upright. "In fact, it was right after I read about the theft of the pearl that he said he needed to escape."

"Chief, I love ya, you big porker!" Adam grasped the hog's chubby face between his two hoofed hands and squeezed his cheeks. "You're one heck of a detective—even lying down on the job you beat the pants off of the competition."

Pork watched Adam as the bull thanked the nurse for permitting him the time for the interview and slipped out through the bulky infirmary door. He flipped onto his right side once more and pulled the blanket protectively up to his ears. He didn't admit to himself that he was pleased that someone cared about him, even though it was only Adam. His heart felt stabbed through with a dull arrow by the thought of Grissie with another critter. Closing his eyes, he fell asleep and dreamt about his gentle mother.

"You probably don't want to hear me saying this," Cal began. He was sitting in the passenger seat of the sedan with Adam at the wheel. "But I think we might have to talk to your old gal pal, Bitsy, to find Lenny." He watched the detective's reaction from the corner of his eye. Adam paled visibly, but his response did not betray the emotions that were stirred up by the comment.

"Betsy," Adam corrected him tersely. "Betsy, not Bitsy. Have you ever heard of anyone named Bitsy?" He realized he made a mistake as soon as the words had slipped out of his mouth.

Cal smiled. "As a matter of fact I have. A little mouse that used to share an apartment with me after I left Cow Tech. We'd go the local smorgasbord restaurant on Tuesday nights for their all-you-can-eat pizza night. She used to get a little bitsy of this, and a little bitsy of that, and..."

Adam held up his hand to stop the chatterbox. "I get the point." He suspected that Bitsy was interested only in the cheese, not the pizza itself.

"So I nicknamed her Bitsy. Place was quite a hole-in-the-wall," Cal added, which made Adam forget himself for a moment and laugh out loud. "Made her feel right at home."

"But seriously." Cal furrowed his forehead as if in consternation. "If you're afraid to go to Betsy's place, where do you suggest we start looking for Lenny? Or for where to find our local proprietors of fine goods?"

"I'm NOT afraid of going to Betsy's!" Adam shouted louder than he had intended. "I just don't BELIEVE we NEED to go to Betsy's. If anyone would know where Lenny is, wouldn't it be Demeris?"

"I don't think so. Demeris has a reason to lie, it seems to me, and Betsy probably doesn't."

Adam spun the wheel quickly at the next left turn. Cal was unprepared for the sudden move. His head flipped sideways and smacked into the door window, then rebounded to its proper position.

"Sorry about that," Adam said in a low voice. "Unintentional. Trying to avoid an old cat stepping off of the curb." Unconvinced, Cal rubbed his head but got the drift and fell silent.

"I'm thinking we need to check out the local pawn shops."

"Yes, the Savings and Loan for the down-and-out. But how would they know the type of critters that would have the cash for precious artifacts?" Cal interrupted. "Pawn shops are for losers."

"Not necessarily." Adam winced. He recalled the time he had to hock his uncle's antique accordion to pay for his last quarter of Criminal Studies at Bovine University. Then after two years of near poverty in apprenticeship under a bumbling private detective who was so cheap he couldn't locate his wallet, Steer took the State Licensing Exam. But even with his P.I.'s license it took several months before he found a position with Cowlitz County, which was at Precinct 13-and-a-half in retainer under Chief Pork. And then he had to go to the Police Academy to qualify to work as a police detective. More schooling, more money. In those intervening years he never got up the cash to retrieve the accordion out of hock. His uncle, in the first stages of senility, never noticed that his instrument had been borrowed. Pangs of guilt temporarily erased his angry memories of Betsy. Steer was one of the few animals that actually enjoyed accordion music: he had hoped to inherit his uncle's antique one day and learn to play it. He had just hurried up the timetable a bit. Now someone else was probably dancing the jig to its music without any idea of its precious ancestry.

"I'm thinking that the pawn dealers probably get some fine goods they can't sell to the locals at a good price and, consequently, have a network of clients that can afford the more expensive items," Steer continued, emerging from his reverie. "And we need to check the antique shops also. I'm sure someone in town has procured at least one old antique or two that's worth far more than the original owners had recognized and therefore have a few favorite resell markets."

"I wouldn't be surprised if the old bird herself was a favored client," Cal said. An idea struck him that he thought was particularly brilliant. "You don't suppose that the statue was not an heirloom but something she procured at a bargain price, say at a pawnshop, that the original owners didn't really want to part with permanently? And then when the owner went back to pay off the pawn ticket they found out that their statue was gone? So they discovered who bought it and stole it back?"

"Ingenious idea. I should have thought of it myself. But doesn't feel right to me. And intuition plays a big card in the detective game. However, I like the fact that you're thinking." Adam turned his attention from the road and smiled warmly at Cal.

"Then I guess we don't really need to go see your old girlfriend anyway," Cal said, returning Adam's smile with a bit of a smirk. This time, however, he was ready: as the car swerved sharply in the intersection he held onto the dashboard with both hooves for dear life.

Griselda dreamed she was lying snugly in a bun. Warm mustard was slowing oozing from her toes up to her neck. With a start she awoke and realized that muddy water was dripping onto her blanket from the earthen ceiling above. She jumped out of her cot and pulled it away from the wall. Drat it all. She was getting fed up with being held hostage in the dirt cell. The air was rank and close and every draft carried with it the foul scent of unwashed moles. She was also bored and wondered how Wiley was running the *Gazette* in her absence. In the past the sneaky little weasel could scarcely wait for her to call in ill with the flu so he could take over running the show. She didn't particularly like him, and wondered if there was anyone in Boville or anywhere else in the vicinity of Cowlitz County who did; however, Wiley never gave up on a good lead and was unmatched at ferreting out information that no one else was able to procure. Perhaps he would be the one to find her kidnappers before the authorities did. Then she thought it over again. Wily had more reason than anyone *not* to look for her. He was in charge now that his employer was away. She swallowed hard. Hopefully that wouldn't be too long.

She had lost over a dozen games of cribbage last night. Edwin, with boyish enthusiasm, never seemed to lose his interest in playing throughout the evening; Griselda finally developed the nerve to kick him out so she could get some sleep. She would probably like the mole under different circumstances: he was honest, sincere, and did what he was told. Maybe make a good gopher at the newspaper. But he was in the employ of the obese mole and had been her kidnapper, which was a felony and could not be forgiven, no matter how fond she was becoming of him. Well, she could go visit him in prison one day. That was, when she had escaped her own.

As if he had heard her thinking about him, Edwin appeared at the cell door.

"My blanket is all wet," Griselda complained, holding it up for the mole to see. "It's dripping water from the ceiling."

"Uh, oh," Edwin said.

"Uh, oh? I don't like the sound of 'Uh, oh.' Particularly when I am stuck in this lousy stinking cell!"

"Might be the pool near the sand trap." Edwin paused and cocked his head for a few moments as if listening intently. "Maybe someone dug their golf club in too deeply trying to get their ball out of the sand, instead of taking the penalty stroke."

"You're saying..." Griselda nearly dropped the blanket.

"Yes, look out!" he cried, scrambling to get the key into the door lock. The ceiling broke loose and a wave of water rushed into the cell.

"So what are you doing here again?" the large crow, his left eye squinting with suspicion, asked from behind the counter. "I don't traffic much with snoops, I told you that yesterday."

Adam and Cal had walked into the Human Relations Department of the I.L.B. Wayward & Associates Shipping Company. The place smelled rank, of old mold that had been swiped at with years of floor cleaner but never fully removed. And the ever-present odor of dead fish around the port permeated the air, flowing in through the open glass front doors.

"I'd like to check again on the S. S. Tunafish that foundered last May," Adam said cheerfully without any trace in his voice that he acknowledged the hostile stance of the crow.

"You got a short memory or something?" the crow asked although he wasn't sure himself what the something might be. He was more comfortable dealing with ledgers and lists than interacting with other critters. And it was a hot summer day, the type of day to kick back a bit, put the claws up, and chug down several soft drinks—not deal with chatty snoops that disturbed the languid atmosphere.

Adam placed his right elbow on the counter, his eyes burrowing holes into the worker's dull pupils. "I'd like to take a look at the sea critters' list, the guys that shipped out from Singapork on the voyage that sank. And yes, my memory is in quite good shape. Thank you for your concern."

The crow grumbled a few inaudible words under his breath and sauntered to one of the several PCs at a desk behind the counter. He pushed the errant papers aside that covered the keyboard and sat down to type. Suddenly the lethargic bird was a flurry of speed, his winged fingers racing across the keys. "Who you looking for?" he asked. "I'm not going to give you a copy listing the entire crew. Would be an invasion of privacy, at least I'm supposing there's some law against it."

"Certainly," Adam continued cheerfully. "That's why your help is so much appreciated."

The crow stopped typing and turned to face the bovine sleuths. "My bull detector is running full blast right now. Is this how you detectives normally operate?"

"No, sir." Cal puffed out his chest. "This is how master detectives operate."

"Well," the crow turned back to his screen, "if the delusion makes you happy, who am I to interfere?"

"The individual I'm looking for is a pelican," Adam said.

"Sweet serenity, never heard of a pelican in the Merchant Marine before." The crow rolled his eyes upward. It was common for seabirds to enlist in the Merchant Marine, as most of them loved the ocean. "How long did it take you discover that vital clue?"

"Actually, a few days," Cal confessed, which earned him a light slap with Adam's fedora.

"We're looking for a critter named Pelly," Adam continued.

The crow cut him off. "First or last name?"

Adam looked at Cal. "I don't know," he confessed. "But I'm guessing first."

The crow keyed in the name. "Don't find a Pelly. But of the eighteen or so pelicans on that voyage, two come up with the letter "P" for first initial."

"And their last names would be?" asked Adam.

"Sandwich and Pickle."

"You're serious?" Cal interjected.

"No. I can't give you their full names. Be invading their privacy. I need to see a warrant first."

Adam thanked the crow for his time and walked out onto the pier. He bought a packet of fries from one of the fish stands and tossed them to the seagulls hanging out at the end of the wharf. The panhandling gangs of gulls were notorious throughout Boville for their ferocity if their beggarly requests were not met. Mild satisfaction touched his lips as he watched two gulls pull knives and fight for the last fry.

"Forgot how entertaining a day at the pier could be," commented Cal, walking beside Adam. "When I was a calf my Momma used to take my brother and I to the boardwalk for cotton candy."

"I hate sweets," Adam commented with unanticipated antipathy. "I ate cotton candy once at the local fair and barfed it all back up onto the sidewalk before my folks made it to the automobile."

"I'd say they were pretty lucky you didn't make it to the car." Cal smiled. He almost hoped that they wouldn't solve the case or that the kidnappers would extend the deadline for the delivery of the pearl. He enjoyed Adam's company and playing detective; after all, he had wanted to be a journalist at one time to ferret out injustice and fight for the common good of the community. The old flame was being reignited and he didn't want it to go out again. He wondered how he could manage to remain in the detective's life after the case was resolved. After all, at some point Adam would find the kidnappers and life would return to its usual dull routine: the bull had a reputation for being an excellent sleuth and certainly wouldn't fail this time, particularly with Cal there to help. Lilah's Happy Farm seemed more and more like Lilah's Boring Farm.

"It's not definite," Adam continued, tossing the empty wrapper into a garbage can and plunging his hooves into his coat pockets. "But it doesn't discard the possibility that Pelly was on that boat. And what would be the odds of two critters on the same boat being in the same business of trading precious artifacts and not knowing each other?"

"I'd say the odds were pretty good they did know each other."

"And that is one reason that I keep you around," Adam said, placing an arm around the nutty bovine's shoulders, "because you make me feel smart."

Cal smiled in appreciation of the compliment, and then caught the sparkle of amusement in the detective's eyes.

"What kind of kidnapping do you call this?" Griselda shrieked. She abhorred raising her voice, particularly in an environment where her authority was not respected, but her patience was waning. Her boa was soaked in mud and ruined, her purse was buried somewhere under an enormous mound of sludge, and there was water in her nostrils. Edwin handed her a white hankie. In a quite unladylike fashion she blew her nose into it and then began wiping the mud off from around her neck.

"You know, that's never happened before." Edwin's voice was very apologetic.

"The ceiling caving in or nearly killing off your prisoner?" Griselda snapped. She was attempting to use the only dry corner of the handkerchief to wipe her feathered fingers clean.

They were sitting in the hallway outside of what had previously been her cell but was now a mountain of mud. At the first initial moments of the cave-in Griselda had hoped that she could swim through the sea of cascading dirt and out into freedom. But if Edwin hadn't gotten the key into the lock and yanked her forward, she would have found that her bid for freedom would have been permanent—in heaven.

"Uh, well," Edwin fumbled, "I'd say both. But I've only lived in this particular burrow for a few years. Can't say what happened before that." With feelings of guilt he watched her pathetic attempts to wipe her winged hands clean. She was only smearing the mud around.

Their conversation was interrupted by a cadre of moles with shovels and wooden beams.

"The cave-in stop?" one of the moles asked. "Is there any further danger of a slide?"

"No, I'd say not," Edwin replied. "But I'd think it'd be a waste of time to clean up. Just board the room up and call it a loss."

"So what are you going to do with me?" the ostrich asked, tossing her ruined boa to the floor.

"Well I hope you're not going to try to escape again. My leg's a bit sore today and I really don't feel like chasing you down the halls."

"Sitting too long in one place playing cribbage." Griselda watched the moles placing the planks against the cell bars. The thought of digging through the ceiling to the outside was buried with her purse in the muddy hill in the next room. Along with her hope of escape.

"Come on." Edwin grabbed one of her wings. "I've got an idea."

He escorted her down seeming endless winding tunnels. Most of the moles skittering by scarcely paid her a moment's attention. Apparently they were either accustomed to visitors or so nearsighted, as most moles were, that they weren't sure what they were looking at. "In here." Edwin gave her wing a forceful yank that caused her to knock her head against the low ceiling of the tunnel. A few sprinkles of dirt trickled down in front of her, causing her to freeze in fear.

"Really, I don't expect another cave-in," Edwin reassured Griselda. She ducked her head to enter a small cavern. Grey towels hung from two towel racks. Red lights flicked in the corners. A pool of clear blue water filled the room. The water seemed illuminated from below, sending shimmering waves of flickering light cascading across the ceiling with every gentle ripple. Under other circumstances it would have been romantic.

"After you clean up," Edwin continued, turning his back to the ostrich, "we'll see about getting you out of here."

Chief Pork pulled the blankets over his head, but he could only drown out the sight, not the noise, of Sheriff Hoggsbutter. The clanking of metal against metal, most likely the sheriff's gun holster against his enormous silver belt buckle, and the jingling of boot spurs could not be ignored. And the odor of his ever-present clove cigarettes was overpowering.

"You just going to lie there like a darned fool or are you going to tell me just what the heck in hogs' heaven's been going on lately?"

Pork detested Sheriff Hoggsbutter. He was a poorly trained hog with delusions of grandeur who got his post by appointment of the governor, not because he had earned it honestly with hard work and professional expertise. And he was so incompetent, rumors were that his position was bought by greasing the politician's palms under the table. But despite the backroom gossip, Hoggsbutter was the ultimate police authority in Cowlitz County and could wield that power over Pork at any time—usually when it was most inconvenient and endangered the current caseload. He pretended to snore with short, raspy, guttural gasps that were not quite convincing to himself, let alone to an observer.

"You need to wake up there, boy!" The sheriff smacked Pork across the back of his skull with his ten-gallon hat, which successfully got his attention and ended his pretense. Bolting upright in bed and clasping the back of his head in his hands, Pork yelped in pain.

"This is a sick ward, not a darned roller derby!" Pork shouted.

And there the old fool stood: Sheriff Hoggsbutter. He was unnaturally thin for a hog, his gun holster threatening to pull his loose pants down to his ankles were it not for the large belt buckle with the Cowlitz County seal on it. His right eye drooped to the side, visible reminder of the losing end of a knife fight some years back from breaking up a domestic quarrel, and was underlined with a purple scar. His skin was pocked with teenage acne that was picked at too often. He fingered the end of his handlebar mustache, the perfect caricature of an Old West antique, and chewed the end of an unlit clove cigarette, tiny leaves peppering his teeth. Pork grimaced.

Hoggsbutter was unperturbed. On the exterior. But internally he was upset by the blast of emotion from an inferior officer. He observed Pork for a minute, chewing silently. "I talked to Judge Bookem this morning," the sheriff began slowly, as if measuring out each word. "And I reviewed the court records. 'Behavior most immature and unbecoming an officer.' And the guys at the precinct confirmed that you've been unusually emotional lately."

"I've been ill," Pork lied, hoping he wouldn't reap the deceit he was sowing. He'd have to get a new lucky charm and anoint himself with holy water—just in case. "Swine flu. We're short-handed." With horror he realized the error he'd just made. The sheriff was fishing for a way to interfere with the kidnapping case and he was handing him the opportunity on a silver platter.

"I realize that and am offering the services of myself and my associates." It was an attempt at diplomatically stating he was taking over the case. He bit off the end of his cigarette, grimaced, and tossed the butt to the floor. The attending nurse, the cross-eyed goose from the previous evening, banged a bedpan against the wall and pointed at the floor. With a wink of acknowledgement Hoggsbutter picked up the butt and stuffed it into his shirt pocket. Pork found his attempt at being charming pathetic and sickening to his stomach.

"That won't be necessary," Pork exclaimed, pushing aside the covers and leaping to his feet. "I've got Cluck on the case." He resented the sheriff's not-too-subtle implication that his precinct was incapable of handling the situation.

"After last year's fiasco with the Buttermuffin Case I'm really impressed." The sheriff screwed up his face. "I can get two of my boys onto the case pronto."

He had a point, Pork admitted to himself. Cluck had investigated the spiking of jelly donuts with rum sold in local supermarkets: it was discovered that the tampering had originated at the Buttermuffin Bakery. He had arrested two grocery attendants at the Drop-On-In supermarket for selling the doctored donuts, which should have pulled from the shelves after the recall notice was promulgated, to minors. When Cluck was out on the beat, the two clerks were released with a warning and their records surreptitiously purged by Pork from the computer system.

But Pork didn't like having his investigations pulled out of his department by some know-it-all of a scarecrow not worth the silver in his belt buckle.

"Thank you for the sacrifice of your staff..." Pork hated kissing Hoggsbutter's butt, and the sheriff knew it: He wasn't fooling either of them, but the appearance of civility had to be maintained. Sucking up left a bad taste in his mouth. "...as I know your department is quite busy. But we've got everything under control and a breakthrough is imminent," he remonstrated while tightening his pants string. He bent over to put on his shoes, purposely turning his butt end to the sheriff. His superior. Hardly. Superior Numbskull. He pictured the sheriff rescuing Griselda from a back alley storeroom. His two guns blazing, kicking in the back door to a card room, and finding the ostrich tied to a wooden chair in the corner. And undoing her bonds while placing his bony hoofed fingers on her shoulders. "I've got two other detectives on the case, the absolute best. Wouldn't want to waste your resources."

"And those detectives would be?" Sheriff Hoggsbutter asked, sounding totally unconvinced.

"Adam Steer. And he's got a new trainee working with him, highly intelligent and a very promising future recruit for the department." It was another lie: Pork considered Crazy Cal potentially dangerous. He was too unpredictable in his behavior. Cluck was very predictable, exasperatingly so. He was a royal pain in the posterior but he knew his regulations. And the rooster had been right: It was against the Police Code to lose control of his gun. He had been justly punished to have it taken away for two weeks. He just wished that Cluck was less rigid and had cut him some slack by not reporting the incident, would value comradeship above strict obedience. But ultimately landing in prison had been his own fault, not Cluck's. Seeing that little pustule Lenny in the courtroom had tested his endurance to its limits and he had lost control. He hated being emotional. Perhaps he was approaching a mid-life crisis? No female could have that much influence over him!

Or could she? Perhaps the sheriff should take over the search for Griselda. He had not acted like a professional since she rushed into his precinct and back into his life earlier that week.

"Adam Steer, huh? Hadn't heard he was out of retirement. Problem is," the sheriff replied, "I've received a complaint from a friend of Ms. Portentsky who feels you folks aren't making any progress locating her kidnappers and they're concerned for her welfare."

"And that would be?"

"Confidential." Hoggsbutter grinned and pulled out another cigarette to suck on. "But not to you. One of her co-workers. A weasel. I believe he said his name was Wiley."

Pork placed his hands upon his hips and snorted with disgust. "He doesn't care a flinging fig about her. He's a reporter for her paper, the *Cloverleaf Gazette*. We've been keeping a lid on the details of the case. He's just fishing for a way to get more information to push newspapers."

"And you think my department's incompetent enough to feed it to him?" Hoggsbutter leaned into Pork's face. His breath was as nasty as the chief had imagined it would be. He rubbed at his snout in a feeble attempt to wipe away the smell.

"No," Pork said hastily. "I'm just saying that Wiley believes that to be so."

The sheriff squinted in obvious disbelief. He pulled a red tin out of his back pocket, slid out a stick of gum, and placed it between Pork's front teeth.

"You've got three days." Sheriff Hoggsbutter pointed his right forefinger in warning at Pork as he walked toward the infirmary door, then, looking back over his right shoulder, added in an ominous tone, "If you don't have the ostrich by Saturday night, my boys take over. And it won't be a social visit when I call on you."

Adam sneezed and pulled out his handkerchief. Cal sneezed and wiped his nose on his coat sleeve. They were exiting the sixth shop in the Antique Mall along the Boville waterfront of Foggy Ghost Bay. Near the ocean seemed the best place to look first, since Pelly was in the Merchant Marine. A sailor, constantly shipping out from port to port, would most likely make contact with critters that were conveniently located, particularly if he was carrying expensive goods that he wished to conceal. The dealers had answered Adam's questions with undisguised loathing. Somehow they sensed he was a detective and wouldn't proffer any information regarding their clients or procurement routes. However, if he wanted to buy some furniture, they were all ears. Steer decided to try another tactic.

He took a gulp of fresh sea air and stepped into Barbara's Reel Deal. All of the waterfront shops smelled faintly of mold and were dusty, the furnishings looking like they were allergic to the touch of a cleaning cloth. He heard the bell above the door ring behind him as Cal stepped in. An elderly female rat greeted them. Her shoulders were painfully stooped and she walked with tiny steps. She also smelled of ginger and wore an abbreviated version of a kimono. From her features it was apparent that her ancestry was MooAsian.

"You're Barbara?" Cal asked before Adam could prevent it.

"No," the old lady smiled without offense. Apparently she'd been asked the same question before. "Bought the shop from Barbara. My name is Kuniko. How can I help you?"

Adam was elated. He was not interviewing an employee, as in the other shops, but the actual proprietor. Someone who had more control over the finances of their store and would be better connected with the community.

"My associate and I are representing a lady of high distinction. She is looking for a particular item of rare value and would pay handsomely to obtain it," Adam answered.

Kuniko motioned to them to sit in the wicker chairs surrounding a black lacquer table that was inlaid with mother-of-pearl in rose patterns gracefully coiled about the inner edge of its surface.

"It's so beautiful that I'm afraid to touch it," Cal said, wiggling his fingers above the table.

Kuniko smiled in return. There was no hint of suspicion in her face or in her voice. She accepted them at face value. And there was no taint of greed in response to Adam's request: no sign of eagerness, just polite hospitality as if she were receiving visitors and not a potential kill. Antique dealers were notorious for wrangling the lowest price out of a hapless client, ignorant of the item's true value, and reselling it for a tidy profit. Perhaps she was accustomed to dealing with critters who preferred as little personal contact as possible, and she wore a social mask to conceal her dirty dealings, Adam mused.

Kuniko left the room and returned a moment later with a pot of tea, dainty cups, and ladyfinger cookies. She poured green tea for each of them and sat at the table, folding her hands in expectation. It made Adam feel slightly guilty for lying. But sometimes dirtying yourself was the price to pay for being a detective. Sometimes necessary information was obtained no other way.

"She's a collector of pearls." Adam jump-started the conversation again.

"Oh, I have some very fine strands of pearls," Kuniko answered with a gentle, measured voice. "And not cultured. The real deal."

Cal chuckled at the allusion to the shop name.

Adam picked up a cookie and snapped it in two. "This particular lady has very unusual taste. She's a collector of carved pearls and would pay beyond their value to obtain particularly fine items that catch her fancy." He watched Kuniko's face for betrayal of any sign of anxiety or guilt. But her face beamed with the same sweet expression that greeted them at the front door.

"Any particular..." she paused, her eyes swinging to the front door in response to the jingle of the bell. Adam followed her gaze. A large grey rat with drooping ears and whiskers stood in the doorway. His nose twitching uncontrollably, his head swiveled back and forth to survey the cluttered room. Kuniko's smile faded.

The intruder settled his beady red eyes upon her face. Then acknowledged the presence of her two guests with a sneer. "Keeping odd company these days, I see? Business must be slow." His voice had an oily tone that greased Adam's eardrums unpleasantly. Dressed all in black with a belt about a loose-fitting ghee, the rodent appeared to be an aged martial arts aficionado. Or perhaps he just liked the look. Adam hoped he wouldn't have to test which one applied.

"Just customers off of the street," she replied casually, keeping her eyes focused on the rat's movements throughout the shop. The rodent gently fingered the top of a leaf entwined brass lamp stand then, with his thumb, squashed a ladybug sitting on its top edge.

He looked up at Kuniko as if suddenly caught in a dirty deed. "Oh, dear, that wasn't very polite was it?" he stated without sincerity. "I forget myself." He lowered his arm in a fluid slithering motion that reminded Adam of a snake.

Though angered at the thoughtless destruction of a useful insect, Adam remained silent. What unspoken relationship bound the two rodents?

"That's bad luck," Kuniko said.

"Oh, yes, that's right," the rat replied in mock surprise. "But for whom: the one who destroys or the one who housed the destruction?"

"Oh, please," Adam said, pulling his grey fedora off of his head and fanning himself. He could handle only so much pretentious melodrama. "Have I stepped into a bad soap opera?" Cal suppressed a laugh when Adam shot him a warning glance.

"Excuse me?" The aged rat tightened his belt and, arms akimbo, stepped forward toward Adam. He was obviously irritated. "Were you making fun of me?"

"No, certainly not," Adam protested, placing his hat back onto his head. "I must've heard incorrectly. Ears are plugged. Allergies you know," and he hocked a large sneeze in the rodent's direction. In response Cal also blew out a big one then smothered his resulting laugh in his coat sleeve.

The rat knew he was being mocked but didn't take up the gauntlet. He was in a hurry. "Do you...?" He searched Kuniko's face for the answer. She looked downward. "No, you don't." He paused a moment, slapping his belt back and forth in deep thought, then continued. "Make it soon," he threatened.

"Would you like to join us for tea, Sum Ting?" Kuniko asked sweetly in response, although her nervous eyes betrayed her true feelings.

The rodent laughed, sliding his right hand in a mock farewell, and trod out of the room, banging the door behind him. Kuniko released a small gasp of tension.

"Who was that?" Cal asked. "With a red nose he would look like the twin of Boozo The Clown." He pretended to sip from a bottle comprised of his two hoofed hands.

The others responded with laughter.

"Is he bothering you?" Adam, suddenly serious, asked their hostess.

"Vee have our vays," Cal added with a wink.

"No, no, I'll be fine," Kuniko said, but her voice faltered. "Just an old...acquaintance from Singapork. More cookies?"

Adam's ears perked up at the allusion to Singapork, the origin of Griselda's souvenirs. He trembled with suppressed excitement, but, not wanting to appear overeager, refrained from asking about the pearl. If Kuniko was connected to the theft in any manner, she might be on the alert for undercover police. However, despite her distress, the rat appeared determined to continue their prior conversation. The trio finished their snack and discussed the various items inlaid with pearl that had recently passed through the shop, then some furniture Kuniko planned to procure from some estate sales in nearby towns. Although Adam made his best efforts to appear sincerely interested, it was fifteen agonizing minutes of desultory conversation.

"Do you ever come across anything that is carved from one single black pearl?" asked Adam, scrutinizing the face of his hostess, and was rewarded with a slight darkening of her expression.

"At times," she responded carefully, matching his stare. "I sense you are looking for something in particular?"

"Yes," Adam answered in a low voice. "Word has it that there is a shop on the waterfront that has a bite on an item of quite unusual and spectacular value," he lied, hating himself for it and, doubly, to someone who appeared so sweet.

"And you think I might be able to procure this…item?"

"It's rumored that you have valuable connections in Singapork." Adam was taking a big chance by getting too specific. He didn't know the strength of her connections and didn't want her to spook any of them into hiding. Was Sum Ting, the rat, one of them?

"Your associates know much about me." Kuniko nervously pulled at the fabric on her right sleeve, her eyes darting toward the door the rat had recently exited. As if realizing she was betraying herself, she lowered her eyes toward her teacup and took a sip. "Singapork is the country of my ancestors. Many members of my family still reside there."

"And Sum Ting…" Adam ventured.

"Is NOT a relative." Kuniko's eyes narrowed, her lips tightened.

Adam was afraid that he had pushed too hard, appeared too nosy. Cal was nearly convulsing with the effort to suppress himself from interfering. But Griselda's life was ticking away with each minute. Adam decided to take a chance.

"I want to be frank with you. We're looking for the MooMoo Pearl. It's rumored that it has entered the country."

"The MooMoo is a myth," Kuniko said evenly.

"I've heard otherwise." Adam matched her eyes and poked Cal in the side to remain still.

She paused for a moment, then, picking up a pair of tongs, plucked a cube of sugar from the bowl and dropped it into her teacup. She stirred in silence. "You believe I have the resources to obtain such a valuable statue?" The voice was demure but the eyes were suddenly hard, a mixture of anger and hidden knowledge.

"I'm hoping so," Adam said casually, concealing the excitement welling up within him. The lady knew something, but how much? He had to draw it out.

"I believe you are overestimating the power of my connections," she continued in the same measured tone, "or of my abilities."

There was no humility in her answer. She was definitely concealing something. "You get a different fish if you toss your bait into the ocean rather than into a stream in the mountains," he said.

"What is the bait?" Kuniko asked. She sipped at her tea and observed him over its brim.

Adam pulled a silver dollar out of his pocket and tossed it to the floor. The three of them watched as it spun on its edge and fell, rocking back and forth in alternating flashes, then finally coming to a stop. They stood in silence for several moments. "My client wouldn't even bother to stoop to pick that up," Adam added.

The elderly rat bent down, snatched up the coin with fluid grace, and slipped it into the side pocket of her kimono. Rising to her feet, her formerly placid face was transformed by revulsion. "I'll do anything to keep the pearl from Sum Ting. Come back tomorrow and you'll get what you're looking for." The sudden venom in her tone surprised her two guests.

Adam smiled, his heart thumping so hard against his chest he thought the others could hear it beating. "I'm more than happy to oblige." He took her fragile paw into his hoofed hands.

"What guarantee do we have that you won't cheat us?" Cal asked, placing his hand upon theirs.

Kuniko's steely-eyed response frightened him.

"My hatred."

SCENE TWELVE: DOUBLE CROSSES

How Griselda had obtained the MooMoo Pearl was still a mystery to Adam, but Kuniko told them the history of the pearl while they finished their tea. Griselda had claimed it was a family heirloom, but Adam was unaware of any MooAsian heritage in her family tree: She hailed from Ostrichland in the South Pawcific, she had once told him.

The pearl, Kuniko said, was rumored to be at least a thousand years old. A mighty emperor on the MooAsian mainland had a calf, a beautiful daughter he treasured greatly and did not want to give away in marriage, although she had many worthy suitors. Her laugh tinkled like bell tones upon his bovine ears and she was an accomplished dancer, her delicate steps entertaining him greatly. The emperor's name was Sickkow and hers, Tea Blossom. Tea Blossom insisted that her father provide her with a husband so she could bear him a grandson. So the old bull sent a dozen heralds throughout his kingdom announcing an impossible contest: the hand of the princess in marriage to any bull of noble blood who could procure a pearl larger than his fist. It was to be a diving contest conducted between sunrise and sunset on a day to be set by the rolling of three twelve-sided dice carved from the bones of the first Emperor of the House.

There was one suitor that Tea Blossom particularly favored, a bull with long black hair and lashes named Wu; and one she did not: Igcowa, famed for his brawn and bravado which overshadowed his brain. That spring, when the waves were still unsettled from the winter storms, the pearl diving contest took place at the cliffs on the nearest shore. As the morning sun stretched its rosy beams across the sky, critters from many villages crowded dangerously near the ledge, watching the brave bachelors oil themselves down and strap their knives to their forelegs. Igcowa spat at the ground when he saw Tea Blossom blow a kiss to Wu. When the ceremonial gong sounded, the divers flung themselves heedlessly past the cliffs and into the foaming ocean.

Many hours later the contestants slowly wound their way up the trail leading from the shore and toward the waiting throng near the underbellies of the clouds. Many had pearls, but most no larger than a pea. Tea Blossom anxiously searched the faces of the returning divers but could not find her precious Wu. They shared a secret: The previous night she had helped him hide a large black pearl, stolen from the temple of a rival kingdom, in the contest waters. Her mother, who knew her husband would never let his daughter go willingly, financed the thief. His reward for robbing the temple of its idol, unknown to the princess, was beheading to ensure his silence. A product of theft, the pearl was bad luck, Wu had cautioned, but Tea Blossom laughed it off as she placed her hooves over his, helping him to slip the pearl into a hollow in the side of the cliffs just below the surface of the ocean. She had cautioned him not to return the next morning with the pearl too quickly so as not to raise her father's suspicion, but was now feeling uneasy with the continued delay of his appearance.

The sky turned to coal and still Wu did not appear. Her father, pleased at the small size of the divers' trophies, commanded Tea Blossom to return from the cliffs to the victory celebration in the palace square, but she refused, desperately scanning the waves for her beloved. It was Igcowa who eventually emerged from the surf. Onshore he was handed a torch by one of the Emperor's guards and then moments later was standing before them and bowing down with a large black pearl cupped in his hoofed hands. It was the pearl that Tea Blossom had helped conceal the night before! How did had he found it in the rapid waters near the cliff? Did he see Wu recover the pearl and then kill him for it? She believed that the oafish bull was capable of treachery—but of murder? Yet she could not protest Igcowa's recovery of the pearl, for it would mean admitting to cheating, which would bring shame upon Emperor Sickkow and demean his authority in the eyes of his subjects. So she submitted that evening to the ceremony of engagement to the critter she hated.

Several days later Wu's body washed ashore, his right hand and foreleg badly mutilated. One of the fishermen who found him said it looked like his hoofed hand was torn apart by one of the eels that lived under the shelves of the cliff. Tea Blossom was horrified: the stolen pearl was indeed cursed. They had most likely hidden it in the den of an eel.

Or so it seemed. Was it really an eel or Igcowa? But she had no evidence other than her own suspicions.

With a heavy heart the father gave his daughter in marriage to Igcowa, who turned out to be a domineering and ruthless husband, driving Tea Blossom into an early grave with his cruelty. Emperor Sickkow, in his sorrow, commanded his best craftsman to carve the sleek pearl into a representation of his daughter, forever dancing. But, once the precious artifact was completed, the grieving father could not bear to look at it and traded it to the emperor of what is now called Singapork for a hundred famed porcine warriors to guard his palace. He no longer trusted his own Imperial Guard, who hated him for the unhappy death of their beloved cheerful princess, and sent his personal guardians to the farthest reaches of his kingdom to guard the Western border. The ferocious hogs, possessing no loyalty to an emperor of another species, betrayed him one night and deposed him from his throne, lopping off his head and tossing it into the same bay where the diving contest had taken place.

"That was really depressing." Cal wiped the tears from his eyes with his napkin.

"That is the legend," Kuniko said, putting the cups and empty teapot onto a silver serving tray. "Whether it is true or not, I cannot verify."

Adam agreed to contact Kuniko again by phone the following morning and exited the shop with Cal. He stood at the end of the pier, watching the waves, trying to calm the motion of his excited heart. Could the rat really obtain the pearl for them that quickly? It seemed odd to him that what was, until recently, considered a legend could be promised so easily. What did she know that she was not telling them?

"Wait until Pork finds out that the statue we're looking for is bad luck!" Crazy Cal exploded in laughter, slapping his thighs.

"You stay here. I have to sign out for a map of the burrows before we can leave."

"No, I'm going with you." Griselda put down the wet towel she was using to mop the mud off of her body and spread her wings wide, shaking off the water from her recent bath. It felt great to be clean again. "I don't trust you. First you kidnap me, and then you want to free me. It doesn't feel right."

"I simply took a liking to you, that's all. Nothing more."

Griselda considered his simple statement. The mole had indeed relaxed and become quite chatty when playing cribbage.

"You're not afraid of the Revenge of the Mutant Rodent?" She leaned forward, her eyes level with his. He blinked rapidly, obviously nervous, then turned away from her gaze.

"I'm always afraid of him," Edwin answered in a low voice. "That's why I snatched you to begin with." He made a move to the cavern exit but Griselda grabbed his arm and prevented him from slipping out.

"I've been wondering: How'd you find me anyway in that corn field? It's not like it was on the itinerary that I left with the butler."

"You leave an itinerary with your butler?" Edwin asked with eyes wide with surprise.

"Not always an honest one. I like to have some freedom. But if there's an emergency, he can get a hold of me."

"Followed you on my scooter, of course. You didn't have any reason to keep an eye out for me. I was just another critter out on the highway. I intended to make my move after the chauffeur dropped you off at your destination, but you stopped at the police station. Not a great place to perform a kidnapping. I got lucky when you guys ran off the highway. I ditched the scooter and one of the rats retrieved it for me later. And The Big Guy gave us a lift home."

Edwin tried to pull away once more, but Griselda kept him tightly in her grip. "Look, I have to go. They aren't going to sign me out if you're hanging around me—it'll make the Officer-in-Charge-of-the-Keys suspicious. And I don't have much time. Once it hits the Burrows Warden that your cell was where the cave-in occurred, they'll be looking for you. They aren't going to allow you to wander freely."

"I thought I couldn't get out on my own without a map?"

"No, you couldn't. But when they need you for the switch, it'd be embarrassing to admit that they'd lost you."

"So they do plan to ransom me; they aren't going to kill me?"

"Look, and I'm serious about this." With a swift angry motion Edwin pulled his arm out of Griselda's grasp. "I can be intimidated by that big oaf into doing a lot of things I'd prefer not to, but murder is not one of them."

"What about the other critters?" Griselda's voice carried a hint of fear, which she tried to disguise with a tone of authority. "Would they kill if given the command?"

"I can't vouch for them." He moved toward the exit and she followed him.

"You just told me that the other moles might consider killing me. I'm not hanging out down here anyplace by myself. Seems like you're my best bet at this point to keeping my scrawny throat intact."

"O.K. But you'd be better off staying here at the spa instead of sneaking around with me near the map room." Edwin paused a moment, then looked back over his shoulder at her with a look of consternation on his face. "And to be honest with you, I've never been asked to kill. Maybe I can't be sure what I'd really do when it came down to deciding between saving my own neck—or yours."

Griselda gulped back a ball of fear rising in her throat, but continued to stick close to the mole's side. A known danger was better than the unknown. And she could always try to ditch the mole when it appeared they were breaking free of the tunnels.

Edwin peered around the corner, looked both directions down the dirt tunnel, and motioned for Griselda, who needed no encouragement, to follow. Two torches lit the width of the corridor running for nearly sixty yards before branching off once more into the darkness. "This," he whispered, pointing to a tiny wooden lacquered plaque set into the wall about eye's height for a mole. It was decorated with black scratching resembling the slithering dance of a sidewinder. "This is the mole language. These markers direct you to the next location, but never beyond. Without a map no one knows the entire layout. I've tried to memorize them to chain-link a trail out of here, but it doesn't work if you don't know your destination."

Griselda realized that Edwin was just as much of a prisoner as she was. In her eagerness to escape it never occurred to her to consider the condition of her own captor. He had expressed some anger during their card games at the relative freedom that the rats, who procured the precious goods for the giant mole, seemed to enjoy, far beyond his fellow moles who had to do all of the burrowing. The rats carried special passes and could exit the burrows at any time, for they negotiated the deals and purchased the valuables that the colossus enjoyed so much. Little credit was given to the moles that discovered the ancient artifacts or treasure chests buried beneath ground—only the rats received payment for their labors. She wondered if there was enough anger boiling beneath the surface for the moles to erupt into rebellion if the flame was fanned a little bit, say by an intrepid journalist? And a big rebellion would make a great Sunday spread detailing the secret inner workings of the mole's burrows. Top dwellers were largely ignorant of the complexity of the villages that lay below their feet. As long as the moles didn't break any laws above ground, the civic authorities weren't concerned about their activities below the earth. She wondered why she hadn't thought of doing a feature on mole society previously.

Once again Edwin looked both directions at the next intersection, ostensibly not to discern his direction but to avoid detection.

Unexpectedly he turned around and, after quickly pulling a rope out of his vest pocket, slipped a makeshift handcuff about Griselda's left wrist. A trick! He was deceiving her after all, to keep her from running away! She balled her feathered hand into a fist to smack the mole a good one then froze as a black packrat suddenly appeared before them to their right out of the darkness of the tunnel.

"Oh, hi, there!" the mole said in a feminine squeak, gasping for breath between each syllable. "I've been looking everywhere for you two." She held a flickering torch in one paw and a picnic basket in the other.

Edwin softly touched the underside of Griselda's palm and pulled gently on the rope. It signaled her attention to the fact that the rope handcuff was loosely held. She relaxed a little. For the benefit of their audience he was merely giving the appearance that she was his captive.

"How lucky we are that you found us," Edwin said. "Who sent you?"

The newcomer continued to chatter excitedly, seeming oblivious to the sarcasm in the mole's voice. "Burrows H.Q. heard about the cave-in. I'm glad you're both safe. Got lunch for you." She held the basket up to emphasize her point. The delicious smell of baked cinnamon rolls filled the air.

As a mere pawn in a ransom scheme, Griselda doubted her sincerity.

"Someone saw you guys run down the hall before the mudslide blocked the tunnel. They thought maybe you guys got lost. So the Burrows Warden sent me to find you."

The little mole seemed pleasant enough, a teenager, giggly and still naive about unpleasant adult critter relationships and the workings of the real world. Edwin gave a slight tug on the rope. Griselda caught the slight shift of his gaze directing her to note his hold on the other end. It was a shame to have to resort to violence against such an innocent. But perhaps she was hurrying the little mole's baptism into life's hard lessons.

In a simultaneous move Edwin and Griselda brought the rope up into the air and down around the waist of the teenager. She stopped giggling.

"Hey, what are you doing? Uncle won't be happy with you."

With pangs of guilt, Edwin pulled the rope tight while Griselda slipped it from her own wrist and snatched away the torch. After binding the hands of the mole, he led her around the corner and into a small room where he tied her feet together.

"Got anything to gag her with?" Griselda asked.

"Not needed. The dirt walls will swallow the sound. Somebody'd have to be in the same corridor to hear her."

"When would that be?"

Edwin rubbed his two palms together as if they were dirty, but they looked clean to Griselda.

"Don't know. Let's hurry." He grabbed the ostrich by the wing to lead her forward, which irritated Griselda but, being dependent upon the mole at the moment for her freedom, she acquiesced reluctantly to his aid.

"Grab the basket, will ya?" Edwin asked, pointing to the picnic basket that their captive had brought. "I haven't eaten all day and I imagine you're famished too." Griselda handed Edwin the torch and picked up the basket.

They slipped hurriedly down one corridor then another, each one appearing the same to Griselda. Apparently they did to Edwin also as he had to check the plaque at each intersection to find their way. They were half-way down one tunnel when two voices sounded from around the corner: two large-sized moles, one with a set of keys jangling from a silver belt at his waist, stepped into view, illuminated by the torch at the corner. Griselda recognized the smaller one of them as the mole that had fumbled with the keys the first night Edwin came to her cell and would most certainly recognize her. She froze in fear.

A hand yanked her into a cubbyhole, which was scarcely more than a three-foot-wide slit in the wall at an oblique angle. Edwin was inside, bent over the torch to conceal its light. Griselda hunched behind him, hoping that her tail feathers weren't sticking out into the hallway. They had been in the darkest end of the hall when the moles first appeared and she hoped that their tiny flame hadn't been seen before Edwin pulled them both into hiding.

The voices approached, the first shrill, the other as if talking through loose teeth.

"I haven't seen the two of them since the cave-in."

Her heart beating with morbid anticipation, Griselda held her breath. Each heartbeat pounded at her eardrums. The gentle cadence of her comrade's breath sounded like a wind tunnel in their shelter.

"You don't think Edwin would help the old chick to escape, do you?"

The jangling of keys drew closer. Griselda involuntarily balled her hands into a fist, furious at being called "old."

"Don't really know the guy. I'd hope not, for his sake. The Mole wouldn't like it."

"I would. I'd like to see that smarmy little upstart get his comeuppance. Never liked the squeaky little son-of-a-biscuit eater. Thinks he's Lord of the Lair," the sloppy toothy voice said.

Griselda wondered what Edwin thought of that comment. He remained still and didn't betray any hint of emotion.

"Don't see why he should get any special treatment."

"I'd like to treat him really special myself." It was a threat, not an invitation.

The voices halted near their slit in the wall. Griselda sucked in her gut and pulled her butt in as far as she could, feeling like a squeeze ball without air.

"I gotta take a pee," the shrill voice said.

Griselda froze. In her nervousness she hadn't paid much attention to the disagreeable smell in their hiding place. It smelled like old urine. Apparently they were concealing themselves in a mole toilet! The realization made her nostrils itch and tickle, as if the two holes didn't want to take in any more of the rank air. And she felt like she had to sneeze. She clapped both wings over her beak. She could feel Edwin turn toward her in response to the sudden movement.

The keys jangled again. Griselda could hear a slight wheezy breath coming from just behind her. If they were caught, she'd most likely remain unharmed as the large jackass of a mole needed to ransom her for the pearl; Edwin, however, the two intruders had intimated, would suffer a much more severe fate.

"Hey, what's that?" the toothy voice exclaimed.

Griselda stiffened. Reflexively she placed her wings protectively around Edwin, uncovering her beak. The impulse to sneeze returned and one slid past before she could fully halt it. She slapped her wings back over her nostrils, which helped to choke back the sound and deaden its force. But it was the same as the booming of thunder to her ears.

"A feather. A large feather!"

Oh critters! They were found out! She turned to face her captors.

"You think Kuniko can come up with the pearl before Sunday?" Cal asked, both hands pushed deep into the pockets of the yellow rain slicker.

"How should I know?" Adam snapped. "Just because I'm a trained detective doesn't mean I know everything!" Cal looked stunned. "Who knows if she's telling the truth anyway?" Adam asked in a smoother tone, ashamed for his anger. It was his belief that any case could be settled if given enough time, but time was running out. "Perhaps Kuniko figures if she delays us long enough, maybe we'll change our minds and settle for something that's already in the shop."

"So we keep looking?"

"What else are we going to do?"

Cal lowered his head, and Adam couldn't tell if the bull was considering his question or still nursing hurt feelings. He opened his mouth to apologize but remained silent. As the two of them turned the corner on the wharf, they found the side street a hubbub of activity. Adam involuntarily ground his teeth in irritation. Not only was there an ambulance in front of the sundry line of ragtag shops, but a County patrol car. He hoped it didn't signal the entry of Sheriff Hoggsbutter into their lives, and fought the impulse to avoid approaching the vehicles. Any activity on the pier might be related to their case, and if the County were to intrude, it would be necessary to know that also. He didn't admit to himself that his own insatiable curiosity might be the true impulse for continuing down the planked walkway.

He pushed aside the sundry onlookers peering into the doorway and stepped into the Pawn 'n Spawn, Cal short on his heels. It looked like your typical pawnshop: banged-up electric guitars, saxophones, and SLR cameras in the window; pistols under glass at the counter; amplifiers and banjos hanging from the walls. With one notable exception: The right wall was covered with fishing tackle and baskets, huddled around a sign that screamed in large red capital letters, "BAIT—SQUID and COD." A warthog, rubbing at his scalp, sat on the wooden floor. An aardvark EMT, pushing aside the hog's lumberjack red-and-black cotton shirt, held a stethoscope up to its hairy chest. A County officer, identifiable by the patch on his arm sleeve, stood nearby, writing quickly upon a form attached to a metal clipboard. Adam let out a sigh of relief. The officer was a portly hippopotamus and, being someone he had never met before, would not recognize Adam as the former (though reactivated) detective for Precinct 13-and-a-half.

The hippo glanced up from his clipboard with a look of irritation on its weary face. "You're interfering with an investigation," the officer said blandly as if taking an inventory. "You'll need to step outside until we leave."

Adam opened his mouth to protest but was interrupted by the EMT, who stood up and pronounced the warthog totally sound, without any noticeable injury. "I don't believe there's any cause for going to the hospital for x-rays. You're not dizzy and your vision's fine. It doesn't appear that you've suffered a concussion. In fact, the lump on the back of your head is scarcely detectable."

The officer turned to issue Adam another warning to leave the premises. Steer didn't want to waste any time by returning later and took a chance by sputtering out, "I've got a big pearl I'd like to sell, black, carved like a cow."

The warthog suddenly expressed interest in Adam's presence. "That's all I know, officer," he said, rising to his feet, ignoring the EMT. The aardvark rolled his eyes and without even a "good-bye" picked up his medical bag and walked out of the shop. The hog was suddenly eager to get rid of the County cop. "I'd sure appreciate it if you could find out who the thief was, officer. It cost me a pretty penny and I can't afford to lose it. I suppose you'd like to get right to it."

The hippo eyed Adam and Cal suspiciously, aware that the two had something to do with his being summarily dismissed. But, apparently, he wasn't interested in pursuing an incident where the victim was clamming up and, tipping his wide-brimmed hat in adieu to the warthog, he walked away. He slapped his clipboard into Cal as he passed toward the doorway. "Oh, sorry," he said without disguising the tone of insincerity.

"Touchy chap, isn't he?" Cal remarked, brushing at his coat sleeve with his right hand as if it were dirty.

"O.K., so what do you know about the pearl? If I don't get it back my wife'll kill me. I could've sold it and made a bundle." His eyes were narrowed and his voice hard as flint.

"I know that it was stolen." Adam didn't get the reaction he was expecting.

"You're really some fountain of information, you are. Danged right it was stolen! Guy hit me on the back of the head with it. Pretty near killed me." The pawnbroker rubbed at the back of his skull.

"They stole the MooMoo Pearl from you?" Cal asked incredulously.

"Stole the what?" the hog asked, looking to Adam who in turn gave a stern look to Cal for interrupting. Cal shifted his shoulders up and down in a "what was I to know?" shrug.

"Dealing in stolen goods is a felony," Adam continued.

"Dealing in what?"

Apparently the pawnbroker had survived the blow to the back of the head because he was so thickheaded, Adam thought.

"Stolen goods!"

The warthog immediately demanded to see some identification from Adam. He wasn't going to continue to proffer any further information without his lawyer present.

"Look, I'm not after you," Adam continued, throwing away his opportunity to strong-arm the broker into cooperating. He didn't want to take the time to threaten a dunderhead. "I'm a private detective and someone's life is depending upon our locating that statue."

"Well, would that person be willing to reimburse me for expenses?" The hog squinted with suspicion, still uncertain whether to cooperate or not.

"Perhaps even a reward for its return." It was a lie. He had no idea if Griselda would offer a reward or not. Scarcely being able to afford a hotel room, he certainly couldn't offer one himself.

"A reward, eh? Well, I'm willing to admit that I'm mercenary. Why else would I be in business if I didn't like money? The more the better." The warthog hesitated, his eyes widening. "That's honest money, though. Yes, I know I'm supposed to check all serial numbers with the database to be sure that the goods someone is hocking isn't stolen, I know that. I'm not stupid. But this lady comes in full of confidence and poise and offers this gorgeous pearl statue without so much of a bat of the eyelashes. I wondered how she came by it, might be a little funny deal, but how can I check? It doesn't have a serial number." He walked around behind the glass cabinet containing the handguns and sealed himself away at arm's length by lowering the heavy partition completing the counter.

Steer knew that the pawnbroker could've checked the municipal database on stolen goods, but since Pork wanted to keep a low profile on the case, the statue had never been officially declared stolen or missing, except by Wiley in the *Gazette*. The hog looked like he couldn't read the wanted ad on the side of a milk carton, let alone a newspaper. Or if he had read the article, wasn't letting on that he knew it was stolen.

"What did the lady look like that hocked the statue?"

"Very pretty, a white poodle wearing a beautiful blue dress. She spoke with a slight French accent."

Adam was stunned with excitement. This was too good to be true! "Did she happen to mention her name?"

"Got a copy of the ticket somewhere in the book." The warthog disappeared behind the counter and returned with a spiral-bound receipt book, the common type found in office supply stores. Humming aimlessly to himself, he thumbed quickly through several pages. "Oh, yes, here it is. Demi O. Rice."

"Demeris!" Cal exclaimed.

Adam ignored the interruption. "When did she come in?"

"Came in twice," the broker said, closing the book. He explained to the two sleuths how the poodle came in, he believed it was last Saturday, and pulled the statue out of a duffel bag. He had examined it and was surprised to discover it was not a cheap painted hunk of plaster but appeared to be made out of pearl. He gave what he thought was a reasonable, though underestimated price, not having purchased anything with such a large amount of pearl in it before. Though having obviously underbid (he had to make a profit, he had explained to her), he was still dismayed when she shoved it back into her bag and said she'd think it over.

It appeared to Adam that the warthog didn't realize that the statue was not covered in mother-of-pearl but was actually one single, large, carved pearl. He poked Cal in the ribs as a signal for the steer to remain silent and not divulge this essential information. If the pawnbroker had any inkling of the true value of the statue, it might make him clam up and decide to trace the theft on his own, delaying their recovery of the item.

The warthog continued his story. He'd been pleasantly surprised when the poodle returned yesterday and offered the statue for sale.

"How much?" Adam asked.

"About one hundred dollars."

Adam could scarcely contain his shock. Didn't Demeris suspect the true value of the statue or did she merely believe it was another cheap Singapork trinket and was cheating the gullible pawnbroker? The pieces of the puzzle were finally coming together, and he had a strong suspicion of what the final picture would look like when it was completed.

"And you're expecting a reward for the recovery of a hundred-dollar statue?" Adam had caught the hog in a bald-faced lie.

"I told you I undersold her. Couldn't make a profit if I gave market value for everything that came in here."

Adam suspected he was being lied to again, but didn't see the point in pressing the issue, pushing the pawnbroker into clamming up again. Surely the warthog gave her more than a hundred dollars. If he believed a large profit could be made, he wouldn't risk alienating Demeris a second time by another gross underbid. But what did it matter? They weren't after the broker, just the statue.

Cal was getting impatient. "So what happened to the statue?"

"It was getting late, near closing time, so I put it up on the top shelf, thinking I'd take it down to the auction house this afternoon and scope out how much I might get for it on the block."

Adam sighed. This goof obviously had a poor talent for appraising items AND retailing on the secondary market. If he was checking out the local barn door auction house, he obviously didn't have a pipeline set up to resell precious artifacts in the underground market.

"And?" Adam cajoled.

"This pelican and big polar bear came prancing into my store earlier today. The pelican says he's looking for this black statue that looks like a dancing cow and will pay plenty for it. I figure, what the heck, I could waste my time selling it at an auction house, which takes a cut of the profit, or pry some heavy cash out of this sucker who obviously wants to be plucked. In fact, the bird seemed so anxious to obtain the pearl, I offered it to him for a thousand dollars."

The pelican? Could it be Pelly? It had to be! How many pelicans ran around town accompanied by a polar bear, which must be the warden Pork had mentioned.

"The bird agrees, maybe a little too eagerly to my high price, I'm thinking, but I turn around to get the statue down anyway, ignoring the gut reaction I've got in my stomach. I put it down upon the countertop and hold my hand out for the cash. And then next thing I know, I get whacked on the back of the head and I wake up to find that the statue and the two sons-of-a-biscuit-eater gone."

"So this was what, an hour ago?" If the theft had just occurred, it was perhaps still possible to trace the two miscreants down before they had traveled far.

"I think so. I'm not sure. Things seem a little blurry to me right now. I don't mean my eyesight, just my recollection of things exactly."

"You're not seriously hurt?" Cal asked, sensing that the pawnbroker was beginning to weary of them. He thought if he turned the conversation to a more personal matter the hog might continue to offer information.

The warthog rubbed the back of his head again. "My wife always said I was thickheaded. Guess she was right."

"You *must* have a concussion," Adam said with a wink, "to agree with your wife."

"Took a good hit to do that. But don't tell her. Might give her ideas."

"No, I wouldn't want to do that." Adam hoped that the hog didn't catch the hint of undisguised sarcasm in his voice. He was eager to leave, to hunt down Pelly and his friend.

"I don't think she gets many ideas, marrying a guy like that," Cal whispered into Steer's left ear. "Gives me the willies to imagine what she must look like."

The bell above the door jingled and one of the onlookers, a timid-looking koala bear with granny glasses, peered in through the opening. "Is it O.K. to come in now?" he asked in a hesitant voice.

"Yes," Adam answered quickly. "I'll be keeping in touch," he pointed toward the hog as he left the shop, Cal trailing, "You might want to rethink keeping those guns up front like that. You got lucky this time."

"No ammo," the pawnbroker called out after him, opening the partition and coming out from around the counter. "And you do that. You keep in touch. You find it, I get a cut, you hear me?"

Adam frowned, slamming his hooves down in quick, angry steps. "He wants to profit from a stolen artifact, can you believe that?" he said to Cal, without caring if the bull was within hearing distance or not. "Some critters don't have any conscience at all."

Cal scrambled to catch up to the detective. The sun was setting and its waning beams slid over Adam's hat, the brim casting a shadow across his eyes. The quick goose steps and the darkened eyes made him look sinister. Cal wondered if he really knew the detective or only imagined he knew him. Perhaps he wouldn't have made a good journalist after all, if he had graduated from Cow Tech. He tended to take critters too much at face value.

"But this confirms what I suspected," Adam said, lifting his face slightly upward and his eyes brightening. "There is more than one statue. Two at least. Is this it? Or are there more? And are any of them the real item?"

"Holy cow! I hope the next one you smash is made out of chocolate!"

They both laughed.

They approached Adam's black sedan. As he placed the key into the door lock on the passenger side, the detective looked to his left and startled Cal by exclaiming, "Oh, no!"

Griselda caught herself just in time. She was ready to leap into the hallway to announce her presence to the two intruders, distracting them from discovering Edwin in the background, then realized that the two moles were not looking in her direction. They were several feet to the right down the hallway, stooped over, examining something on the ground. She pulled back into the darkness of the toilet and heard Edwin sigh in relief behind her. Squinting, she craned her head to see what the two moles were looking at. It was one of her feathers! They would know for certain that she was somewhere in the vicinity. She pondered whether to reemerge. The smaller mole with the keys, holding the feather, stood up and looked about. No point in aiding and abetting the enemy until necessary. She remained concealed.

The moles lifted their noses and sniffed the air. Their little wrinkled floral snouts looked obscene in the dim wavering light of their torches. There was a short muffled discussion and the two rodents took off in the opposite direction, disappearing around the bend.

"They've gone off in the wrong direction," Griselda whispered to Edwin behind her. "The toilet odor must be concealing our own scent." She felt irritated by Edwin's response, a tug at the feathers on her back. "What is it?" she hissed.

"Would you mind stepping out for a moment? Been squatting in here too long. I gotta pee now."

With a despairing sigh, Griselda stepped outside the toilet and waited for Edwin to do his duty. He emerged a few moments later with a sheepish grin.

They continued their silent excursion through several more identical tunnels. No wonder the moles needed a map, Griselda thought. How did they find their own bedrooms without one?

"We're nearly there," Edwin announced. "You know, aren't you tired of carrying that picnic basket? I'm famished. Let's duck aside for a moment and eat lunch."

Griselda was eager to get the map and exit the tunnels, but she recalled that Edwin had said earlier that he hadn't eaten all day. They might not have another chance for a meal once they obtained the map. Besides, she was tired of carrying the basket and didn't relish the thought of lugging it through another maze of tunnels.

"In here. It's one of many prayer temples in the area. We value our secrecy in prayer so once the door is closed, no one will disturb us."

He pointed to a wooden door that was a little shorter than Griselda's height. He knocked warily, opened the door, and signaled for the ostrich to enter. She considered for a moment that it might be a trap, that he was leading her on a wild goose chase to keep her occupied until the time of the switch for the pearl, but what choice did she really have? She had tried to escape twice and failed gloriously both times. She pulled her head down and ducked inside and was happily surprised to find herself in a cedar chamber, nearly indistinct from a sauna, with a large, gold leaf framed portrait of the Great Moogah on the far wall. His bovine face with its long brown hair, cascading down from the top notch, was parted down the center; the large benign eyes gave her a temporary feeling of security.

With a sigh she sat down on one of the two wooden benches lining the walls to each side. It was great to sit in a room that didn't have visible dirt in it: even the floor was cedar rather than bare earth. Edwin sat to her right; she placed the picnic basket between them. She was pleased to find it filled with cucumber and alfalfa sandwiches, plastic commercial bottles of lemonade, several cinnamon rolls, and napkins. They ate their meal in silence and wiped their mouths in satisfaction with smiles upon their faces. Edwin stood up and crossed to the door, cracking it open to peer in both directions. He signaled to her to follow. She set the basket down under the bench, hoping it wouldn't be discovered too quickly, and slid through the door.

Several tunnels later and heaven knows how many minutes, it could have been hours, they arrived at a brightly lit intersection of five tunnels. Griselda was becoming increasingly nervous. The longer they remained in the tunnels, the more likely they were to be caught. She didn't relish meeting with the mutant rodent once again. And, surely, somebody back home had to be worried about her.

She hoped.

"You can't come any further," Edwin whispered. "You're sure to be seen. Traffic is too heavy here. You lay low and I'll be back in a few minutes." He scurried off to the right. Griselda watched him hurry down the tunnel then trailed him. She wasn't taking a chance of being double-crossed.

Every now and then she had to duck into an open doorway to escape the glance of a passing rat or mole, but was able to keep Edwin within her sight. A couple times she had to slip around a corner when Edwin looked over his shoulder. He didn't trust her. Well, he was right not to. The dirt swallowed up the sound of her footsteps, but also that of anyone else walking through the tunnels. Outside a large locked door set into the wall, Edwin eventually pulled the chain of a cowbell. The door swung open and he stepped inside.

Griselda ducked out of sight around the corner and found herself face-to-face with a large grey packrat. He had a smirk on his face and was absentmindedly tossing an apple into the air like a stray coin.

"What are you doing here alone?" the rat asked with suspicion in his voice. "We don't normally find alien residents wandering about by themselves."

Griselda swallowed hard and decided the best lie was a mixture of truth and falsehood. "I'm waiting for Edwin to get a set of keys to a new cell."

"That's the map room."

Well, at least Edwin hadn't lied about their destination. She tried to think quickly through the haze of nervousness. It was her habit never to look afraid, even when she was. "What I meant was, he got the keys and is looking for the map to find the cell."

The rat fell silent for a moment, tossing the apple back-and-forth into the air and pondering her answer. "I'd like to check it out myself, if you don't mind." Griselda tried to look nonchalant, but her long, lanky legs felt shaky. He grabbed her left wing and steered her into the map room.

A tall counter bisected the room; behind, square wooden shelves labeled with plaques in the sprawling script of the moles lined the back wall. What appeared to be scrolls, obviously the burrow maps, lay rolled inside each cube. Edwin, standing on a wooden box to see over the counter, was speaking to an albino mole, listening intently but eyeing him suspiciously with red beady eyes. They both turned around as the packrat pulled Griselda into the room.

"Is something wrong? I had her roped to the doorknob." Edwin's voice had a strange lack of emotion in a dangerous situation. What was wrong was the tempo of his voice. It sounded like an old LP that was playing in slower than recorded speed. Griselda shook her head, wondering if she'd heard correctly or was just tired. Red spots began clouding her vision. A big ball of panic began to rise in her throat as Edwin tumbled from the footstool backward to the floor.

At one time roped and left in the tunnels but now free and smiling, the teenaged mole entered the room. Following her was the mole with the keys whom had nearly discovered the two escapees hiding in the toilet; lifting up the ostrich feather found in the tunnel, he tickled Griselda under the chin. She wanted to slap his paw away but suddenly her wing weighed like a ton of lead and couldn't be lifted. Swaying, she dropped to her knees, the teen mole's childish laughter echoing through her head.

"We've been drugged. She...set us up. I should've...figured that."
Edwin gasped in a hoarse whisper. "She's a niece of...the Officer-in-
Charge-of-the-Keys. Sorry...I was so stupid. He's got over...two dozen
of them. I'd...forgotten her."

With a start Griselda realized that the lunch they'd eaten in the
temple was drugged. The giggling mole was indeed looking for them,
but not out of concern for their welfare. They had been foolish enough
to take the basket with them and complete the little mole's mission.

The rodent introduced himself to Griselda as the Officer-in-Charge-
of-the-Keys. He kicked Edwin in the side. "That's for tying up my
niece." Edwin groaned. Griselda wanted to run over and belt the bully a
good chop in the muzzle but was unable to move. Her thoughts seemed
to be suspended in a pound of clear gelatin.

Adam slipped around the tail end of his black sedan. At the other end
of the pier Wiley was standing on the street corner. Leaning against his
scooter with pad and pencil in his paws, he was speaking to the County
officer who had recently interviewed the pawnbroker at the Pawn 'n
Spawn. Steer ducked down to avoid being seen but Wiley spotted Cal
before he could slip into the sedan.

The weasel smiled, tipped his hat to the officer, and sauntered down
the walkway toward Cal and Adam.

"If we try to run off, he'll tail us," Adam whispered. "He'll think
we're trying to hide something from him."

"We are," Cal whispered back.

"That's beside the point. I don't trust him and want him involved as
little as possible in this case. That weasel has the nose of a bloodhound
and the heart of a badger. It's difficult concealing anything from him."

"So what do we do?"

"I'm thinking." Adam stood up and placed his chin into his hand,
resting his elbow upon the window ledge of the car, watching the
approaching weasel out of the corner of his eye. He didn't want Wiley
to know that he had been spotted. His visage suddenly brightened.
"What fortune!" he whispered to Cal then shouted in the direction of the

main street. "Hey, Cluck! Great work! I'm really impressed! The chief tells me you've solved the kidnapping!"

"You're my hero!" Cal added.

Lieutenant Cluck was racing down the main boulevard toward the corner where Wiley stood. At Adam's shout he paused, scratching himself underneath his beak, in obvious perplexity at the greeting. He kept a shortwave radio in his Cheep Rangler to listen in on police communications and was responding, albeit a little late, to the report about the mugging at the Pawn 'n Spawn. Wiley spun around to face Cluck, who immediately began to remonstrate that he knew nothing about the solving of the case. But the bloodhound of a weasel wasn't about to let the rooster put him off the trail of a hot story, particularly when it involved the status of his employer—dead or alive.

Adam slipped into the driver's seat, accompanied by Cal through the other door. They shared a round of laughter as the two drove off, pausing only to share a quick glance at the hapless rooster and his tormenter.

An interpretation of my characters by my friend and superb artist Louis Scarborough Jr. (I changed Adam's appearance after this illustration was completed.)

SCENE THIRTEEN-AND-A-HALF: CURSED

"Great trick, Adam." Cal was holding onto the dashboard for dear life as Adam swept through the intersection and took a right turn a few mph over the posted speed limit. "But I don't trust you anymore."

"You were naive to do so in the first place." Adam returned a smile. "I believe we've got this case about cracked. The pawnbroker claimed that Demeris accepted only a hundred dollars for the statue, yet this same hog with the brain of a titmouse has the guts to try to sell it to Pelly for a thousand dollars."

"So what's that tell us?"

"Think this through. There's obviously more than one statue. How did that happen? We know at least one statue is a fake—maybe there's an original version someplace. Maybe not. Demeris is willing to sell the pearl to the warthog for so little and yet Pelly, who Pork told me was experienced in the fine antiquities market, is willing to nearly kill a guy to get the pawned item."

"So that tells us that Demeris is a poor judge of value."

"But consider this, also. Try to put together all the facts that we've gathered over the past few days. Didn't she weep at the kitchen table after we discovered the first statue? She claimed to have hid it in the laundry basket out of fear it would be discovered that she'd accidentally broken it and couldn't afford to pay for the damage. Yet her room shows an obvious source of income from somewhere beyond that of a mere maid."

"Or really stupid guys that give it all to her."

"The point is: she wouldn't be weeping near hysteria over having to replace a statue she believed was worth only a mere hundred dollars."

"Maybe she was desperate for money. Maybe all those fine things in her room were bought on credit and the bill is coming due."

"Or she's one heck of an actress and knew it was a fake all along."

Adam gave the wheel another spin and the car came to a sudden halt in the lot of the Veggie Hamburger Drive-In. Cal was unprepared for the change in direction and flew forward, bumping his muzzle off of the front dash, the seat belt holding back his body but not his large head.

"You hungry again, Adam? We've already eaten at the wharf."

"All this thinking makes me hungry. You burn more calories in deep thought that you do operating a backhoe."

Cal rolled his eyes. "Hey, as long as I don't have to pay, I'm always game for a bite to eat."

Circular with windows running along its perimeter, candles flickering through the panes, and a satellite dish perched on the center of the roof, the diner resembled a flying saucer. At the front counter Adam ordered two alfalfa burgers with fries and tartar sauce from a penguin who had difficulty punching the keys on the cash register with his flippers.

"Must be tough getting good help nowadays," Cal commented as they took their trays to a booth near one of the windows, convex for an eerie effect but distorting the images of the outside. He pressed his nose to the pane. "I wonder if we look like aliens to the pedestrians passing by."

"If your nose freezes in that position, I'll guarantee it."

"Cool! Maybe I'll make contact!"

"If you had graduated in journalism, you'd have been great at the National Inkquirer."

"You don't need a journalism degree to write that stuff. Just a great imagination and the effrontery to deceive others."

Adam dipped a fry into his paper cup of tartar sauce and sucked it down before Cal saw it hit his mouth. "Like I said, we know there is at least one fake. We also know Lenny is involved in this thing somehow. We assumed that the package he dropped the other night on our stake-out was just a ball of yarn, but we never checked to see if the string was wrapped around anything."

"You think it was the pearl? Would he be greedy enough to steal the statue knowing that Griselda's life might depend upon it?"

"We had quite a few run-ins with Lenny during the ten years I slaved for the Force. He's a packrat with sticky fingers and a lust for luxury. Nothing that little runt does would surprise me. Lenny is in the game of life for himself and plays to win, regardless of the consequences to others. This I know: our little white poodle is going to have a rude awakening one day. As long as that rat needs her, she's in the game. Soon as he has what he wants, she's yesterday's stale bread." He paused and sucked down another fry. "Problem is, their little game might turn deadly. There's more at stake now than just money."

"So that night when we were outside the mansion, Demeris might have passed the real statue off to Lenny for a cut of the take, and replaced it with two fakes: one for Griselda's mantel and one to pawn? So there might be at least three statues. Where are they all coming from?" Cal was so engrossed in the conversation that the burger and fries on the table in front of him were being neglected.

Adam took a bite out of his burger and spoke with his mouth full. He was famished but didn't want to waste too much time eating. The excitement of nearly finishing the case, and possibly before the ransom date, accelerated his movements. "These are the possibilities. One: there is no original statue. All the dancing cows are cheap fakes that can be easily purchased in Singapork; Demeris pulled a fast one on the pawnbroker and Lenny. But what shoots a hole in that theory is that Pelly must obviously believe there is an original statue in the area or he wouldn't have escaped from prison and then risked being arrested again by knocking out the warthog. Also, Lenny has been to Singapork himself and would recognize the souvenir as a fake. So that leads to the strong possibility that there is an original. Question is, who has it? And where did the fakes come from?

"Two: we know that both Pelly and Lenny visited Singapork at the same time. Did one of them obtain the original statue for resale and lose possession of it for some reason? Did Demeris get ahold of it somehow? Rather than Lenny using her, is she using him?"

"Maybe Lenny wasn't first to ask Demeris out on a date. Maybe *she* asked *him* out on a date to lift the statue out of his possession. Maybe that's how she gets all her stuff—by stealing from her boyfriends," Cal added.

"No, I don't think so. Lenny most likely has the connections to drop a valuable item quickly and make a fast buck. If he originally had the MooMoo Pearl, it would have been sold off before Demeris could get a paw on it."

"And three," Adam continued. "Did the original statue ever sit over Griselda's mantel or was it another replica? Is she telling the truth that it was a family heirloom? Did her family do business in the Far East in the past? And what did Demeris give Lenny? There are still a lot of unanswered questions."

"She visited Chief Pork to report the statue stolen. She must have thought it had some value to make it worthwhile."

Adam was silent, chewing on his cud in deep thought. Kuniko, the owner of Barbara's Reel Deal, had immigrated from Singapork. And her nasty rat visitor also. Did everyone connect up somehow?

Cal interrupted his reverie.

"Lenny was seen by Pork going to the Cock-n-Bull and I know that a wealthy crowd hangs out in the back club, certainly with deep pockets worth picking. Maybe that's where he ditches his purchases."

"Can you get me into the Backdoor Club?"

Cal scrutinized the detective's attire: from his grey fedora hat down to his yellow rainslicker and bare hooves. "Sure, but you'll have to get more suitable clothing. They've got standards, you know, a dress code. They don't allow slobs in." Cal finally took a bite out of his burger. The taste of ketchup and alfalfa was delicious; he greedily took several more bites, stuffing his cheeks full of food. "Lenny was really angry at Demeris at the mansion. They were fighting terrible before you came into the kitchen."

"So you think she might've double-crossed him?"

"Yes."

In his mind Adam reviewed Tuesday afternoon when he met Demeris in the kitchen. She seemed nervous and a little overeager to be rid of his company. Something niggled at the back of his mind, something he'd noticed about the immaculate poodle that didn't quite rub him right. He pictured her at the kitchen table in her white apron, delicate manicured paws holding a teaspoon. He finished the burger and swirled several fries at one time into the tartar sauce.

They left the diner and climbed back into the sedan.

"Dang it!" Adam slapped his hoofed hand against the center of the steering wheel. "I remember what was bothering me about that poodle! We're going to need that search warrant to get back into the mansion and Cluck's got it!"

"And Wiley's got Cluck!"

The information cost him several more dollars than he would have liked, but bribing the pelicans and rats on the wharf eventually led Sum Ting Wong to its location. Patience, carefully biding his time while the police ran around in a flurry of confusion, had also paid off. He had trusted Lenny, taking the promissory note instead of cash: His generosity was repaid with the nuisance of wasting several weeks of time and the additional expense of an ocean voyage. The money used for the bribe was, therefore, minor in comparison to the loss, but it irritated him, being customarily parsimonious with his money.

The little grey rat held its pink paw out, palm up, waiting for the promised two dollars. Sum Ting pulled his coin purse out and dangled it from its chain with his right forefinger, letting the change inside jingle. The rodent twitched its whiskers but didn't protest the delay of payment. Smart fellow, the older rat thought to himself, while enjoying the delicious torment of keeping his informant waiting. A few more moments, and he slipped the purse back into the pocket of his black kimono.

"When I get my paws on it, then you get paid." Sum Ting's voice sounded more derisive than he intended, but so what? Who cared what this little pissant thought? The rat was merely useful for the moment and then was no longer worthy of notice.

The rat quickly turned on its haunches and scurried out toward Pier 68 where the ferryboats picked up passengers during the daily commute from the islands in Foggy Ghost Bay to Boville. Sum Ting had to run to keep up. It was now twilight and the pier stood like a silent sentinel. A small tugboat tied to a ring drifted quietly on the water rolling gently past the supporting pillars. The rat darted into a glass-fronted building at the edge of the wharf. Panting, Sum Ting cursed the rat for making him run.

Up a tiled staircase and then the informant stopped and pointed to a yellow locker, number 47. It was secure: the key missing, the door tightly shut.

"Time for payment," the pursuer said.

The little rat's whiskers froze in horror.

Sum Ting pulled a crow bar out from under his kimono.

When Adam and Cal walked into Precinct 13-and-a-half they found Chief Pork standing in the front office chatting idly with Officer Pepy. The hog was dressed casually in a white short-sleeved polo shirt and tan khakis.

"Well, I finally caught you standing up," Steer said with a smile.

"Very funny, Adam." Pork chuckled while Pepy the sloth slowly worked up a smile. "I may have lost my dignity, but I still have my sense of humor."

"I thought you were suspended for two weeks. What brings you here?"

"He's been suspended?" Cal asked in surprise, his eyes wide. "How come nobody told me? For what?"

Ignoring Cal, Pork slid into his familiar wooden chair behind his desk. He picked up the brass gun-shaped paperweight from the desktop and fingered it idly. "You know what brings me here, Adam."

"Just stating the obvious to break the ice. But the judge cou[ld] you drummed off the Force if you ignore his dictate."

"So who's gonna tell? You?" Pork pointed at Cal who shook h[is] head. "You? Or you?" Adam shook his head and Pepy began the effort to do so. "Besides," Pork put down the paperweight and sat back, placing his feet upon the desk and crossing them at the ankles. "I'm just here in an advisory capacity."

"Cluck would…tell," Pepy said in his slurred monotone.

On cue the front door opened and slammed shut. Lieutenant Cluck skidded into the lobby. "Thanks a lot, Steer. It took me over an hour to shake off that pesky reporter. What the heck got into you, anyway?" Adam put up both hands as if saying, "What? Me?" The rooster then spotted the chief behind his desk; his beak opened wide in surprise. "Hey, Chief. You aren't supposed to be here! You're suspended for two weeks!"

"Why won't anyone tell me what's going on!" Cal yelled.

"I'm just here keeping Pepy company," Pork replied.

"Cluck, you still got that search warrant on you?" Adam asked.

"What? Of course I've got the warrant. You think I'm a big boob or something?"

Adam resisted the impulse to answer in the affirmative. "We need to go back to the mansion. The judge issued it for a week, didn't he?"

"Five days. But daylight hours only. Why do we need to go back there? It's been a dead end so far. I asked about the trinkets over the fireplace—they began appearing about a year ago. So what's that prove?"

"That Griselda has a friend or friends who visit Singapork where the MooMoo statue may have originated," Cal offered.

Adam didn't like Cluck's defensive attitude, but instead of confronting the rooster, he chose to ignore him. "Chief, you got any clothes Cal and I could borrow to do a little nightclubbing?"

"If you promise not to spill anything on them." Pork pushed himself out of his chair. He was looking good, Adam thought. Just a change of clothing seemed to breathe a little life into the old porker.

ld get

is

199

n around the chief's shoulders as they headed turned to point back at the lieutenant. "Cluck, ...ide Le Coeur at 10 in the morning. Cal and I ...ork tonight."

...e cattle and the hog walked out the front door, Cluck muttered ...nself, "I'm working myself to the bone and all they can think of is partying."

Sum Ting laughed heartily to himself. The little rat had scampered off in fear before he could pull out his coin purse and give him the promised dollars. He looked both directions past the lockers down the corridor. As the ferries only made their runs during the day, the hall was silent and dimly lit by overhead lights that were powered down for the night. There was really no reason for anyone to be in the terminal except to check the posted schedules or grab a bucket seat and spend an uncomfortable evening waiting for the morning ferry run. And that was usually on the weekends when traffic was heading away, not toward, the city. He should not be in danger of being interrupted tonight.

He shoved the crowbar into the edge of the locker; it snapped open easily. What kind of security should anyone expect for fifty cents? Inside was a faded army duffle bag. He pulled the bag out of the locker and slid his long snout into its opening. The item was wrapped in newspaper. He reached in a paw then froze at the sound of fluttering in the hallway to the right. Slipping the satchel over his shoulder, Sum Ting ran in the opposite direction, the crow bar conspicuous in his right hand. He preferred not to resort to violence, but if he had to, so be it.

"No, no, no," Cal laughed, bending forward and clutching both hoofed hands before his waist. "I can't picture you in that. No, wait a second, yes I could—in a conga line!"

Adam was primping in front of Pork's full-length mirror hanging from the inside lip of the bedroom door. A little too disco, but the black slacks, though snug at the waist and a little too short on his legs, looked good with the pink silk shirt, Adam thought. It hurt when the bristles on his tail were pushed back as he shoved it through the slit in the pants created for a small pig's tail. The slick black patent leather shoes were a little large for his hooves, so he shoved toilet tissue into the toes. Overall, he didn't look too bad. A little hair grease to tame his cowlick and he was set to party.

Cal ended up looking like a bad Christmas tree with his red, ruffled velveteen shirt and green slacks. Pork regretted having to loan the crazy critter his good pair of brown loafers, but the Backdoor Club had a "no hooves" policy to protect the flooring, Cal had claimed. Pork wondered what the two cattle had worn before going "out to pasture." Didn't they keep anything in storage? He decided to stick with his casual look. Why change when you're already looking good?

The three of them headed out the door looking more like a motley crew than a trio of bachelors out on the prowl.

Still carrying the duffle bag, Sum Ting Wong laughed to himself as he strolled along the pier in the moonlight. A little too jumpy. There'd been no one in the terminal. He tossed the crowbar into the bay, unconcerned with whether he would hit anything beneath the surface of the water. Now what to do? Return to Singapork right away or try to unload the statue himself locally? He pondered the question a moment, then decided to quit Boville and try a different port on his ship's route. Better to lie low. Lenny might've promised the statue to one of his clients and would still be looking for it. Technically it belonged to Sum Ting Wong, and he was merely reclaiming his property. Lenny had promised payment and hadn't delivered.

In his musing he hadn't noticed the small flock of sparrows until they were upon him. Fool! Why had he tossed the crowbar? Sum Ting beat wildly with his arms, trying to swat the birds away. But the seeming hundreds of birds swooped and pecked and beat about his face with their wings. Frantic with confusion and anger, Sum Ting swung the duffle bag in circles, intending to frighten the sparrows away. He screeched when the newspaper wrapped object slid out of the bag and clattered some several yards off onto the wooden boards of the pier. Diving forward, the rat tried to retrieve it but a dozen sparrows were quicker and, grasping the package in their claws, rose up into the air above the rat's head and flew off over the bay. Sum Ting hopped up and down in a hopeless and desperate effort to lift himself high enough to retrieve the package. His effort was rewarded with several dozen wet white surprises delivered to his face and shoulders as the flock of birds disappeared into the night.

Hurling threats of violence with his tongue, Sum Ting searched for whatever departing sparrow he could snatch up in his paws, intending to tear it to pieces in revenge. One little bird lay panting by one of the posts at the end of the pier, exhausted from its recent aerial exertions. The rat grabbed for its tail feathers but found his path interrupted by a gang of seagulls. It was a trap!

"Want to play a little game of hide-and-seek?" one of the gulls asked. He was nonchalantly slapping a chain back and forth between both winged hands.

"Yeah, yeah, we seek whatever it is you've hid in your clothes!" another gull laughed, a potato fry drooping from the corner of his beak like a bad cigarette.

While the rat from Singapork screeched in rage at the end of the pier, another little grey rat held out a pink paw for his reward. He curled his fingers around the five-dollar bill that the elderly female rodent gave him and scampered off, three dollars richer than he'd originally hoped to be at the end of the evening.

SCENE FOURTEEN: DISSED COW FEVER

About 10 PM they emerged from Pork's white Chevy and pushed through the heraldry shield into the Cock-n-Bull Tavern. The crowd sitting at the tables toward the back was sparse, ensconced in a cocoon of cigarette smoke and the rank smell of spilt beer that hadn't been wiped up for a week. The goat tending bar still had matted hair and an attitude. He squinted suspiciously at the trio as if they had just brought a contagious disease into the room.

"Don't buy a beer from that guy," Chief Pork, pointing toward the bartender, whispered into Adam's right ear. "You'd have to take out a loan to afford it. And believe me, it ain't worth it."

"So, Cal, how do we get into the club at the back of the tavern?" Adam asked.

Crazy Cal, trailed by the others, crossed the room and knocked his fist against the far right back wall. The three of them stood there waiting for a response, while the assortment of hoofed and winged misfits in the tavern watched in amusement. Silence. Cal banged harder on the wall a few times, bruising his bovine knuckles. No response. Finally, he placed his ear against the cedar boards and listened.

"You don't know what the heck you're doing, do you?" Pork crossed his arms.

"Well, I only SAID there was a club at the back of the tavern, NOT that I'd actually been there, " confessed Cal, grinning sheepishly.

The patrons in the tavern exploded in laughter. The bartender slapped his dirty towel onto the countertop before him and wiped it down. "You guys gonna order some brews or you gonna entertain us with a pantomime?"

"I'd have to knock over a bank first to afford it!" Pork yelled in response, which earned more laughter from the onlookers.

"Anybody know how to get into the club in the back of the room?" Cal yelled to the crowd over the din.

"If you don't know how to get in, you obviously don't belong." A low masculine voice that slid smoothly like scotch over rocks answered from behind. The three sleuths turned to find themselves facing a black Labrador retriever and his entourage of bejeweled poodles and gun-toting bulldogs. The Labrador's fingers were laced with large gold rings and a diamond stud was conspicuously jabbed into the side of his stubby nose. A trench coat was tossed loosely across his shoulders and he clutched, in his left paw, a shiny black cane, its gold head shaped like a Great Dane.

"Oh, won't my smoochy woochy help the widdle guys out a bit?" one of the poodles cooed into the right ear of the Lab while running her manicured paws under his chin. "We could use a little excitement for once. We see the same crowd nearly every night."

"And the goofy-looking one with the bent horn is kind of cute," the other white poodle purred, winking at Cal, who responded with a blushing face.

"What do you say, boys?" The Labrador turned to face the two bulldogs standing at military alert behind him. "Tossing these three stranded fish into the frying pan might liven things up a bit for us."

"If any of them guys gets outta hand, we can takes care of them and pronto!" one of the bulldogs answered, placing his paw not too discreetly upon the gun bulge under his sweater at his hip. To which braggadocio the other bulldog nodded in agreement.

You don't know how exciting it could be if you try a swing at me, Adam thought to himself. He hoped that Cal was not leading them astray and wasting precious time. They had a little over forty-eight hours to come up with the pearl to meet the kidnapper's demand. For all they knew the nutty bovine just wanted to take the night off and party. And Pork, with his recent fainting spells, certainly was in no shape for dancing. Hopefully the hog would remember that.

"Ah, well, I had wanted to dispense with your company, but it seems I am outnumbered," the Labrador said wearily, waving his paw lazily through the air. He crossed the room and stood at the same spot where Cal had recently been pounding at the wall. He knocked out "shave-and-a-haircut, two-bits." A moment later a panel slid to the side to reveal the hostile face of a grizzly bear.

"Why didn't we think of that?" Pork asked Adam, who merely shook his head in disgust.

"Glad I didn't," added Cal, pointing toward the bear.

The Lab slipped a few greenbacks through the cubbyhole and moments later the sleuths followed the dog and his entourage through a doorway that had opened up in the wall. The secret door slid slowly to a close on a silent hinge behind them as they followed the grizzly bear through a dimly lit hallway. Black tarpaper was staple-gunned to the walls; a torn piece of green outdoor carpeting loosely covered the center of the cement floor. The grizzly scarcely squeezed through the narrow corridor. Adam wondered if they'd find themselves entering into the backside of a horse barn rather than a flashy discothèque. They turned to the right and came to a dead end.

The bear pushed against the wall. "Boogie down," he declared in a jaded, deadpan monotone. An indiscernible door opened up amidst the sea of tarpaper and the partygoers stepped into a glittering world of spinning lights and tinkling wine glasses.

"Care to join me at my table?" the Labrador asked, pointing a gold-ringed finger toward the booth across the raised dance floor. The poodles, draped in the dog's arms like velvet bedspreads over a railing, implored them to assent with their large brown eyes. Cal moved forward to accept the offer, but Adam pulled him back, grabbing his shirt collar.

"Thanks, but I believe the ladies here have all that they can handle at the moment," the master detective said with a wink. The alpha dog merely smiled, revealing two gold fangs, and steered his two ladies toward their familiar spot.

Adam chose an open table near the dance floor under one of the multifaceted spinning silver balls. Dancing pools of light reflected across their faces.

"Hey, we don't want to be too conspicuous," Chief Pork protested, recalling his last altercation in the tavern.

"Conspicuous is why we're here," Adam answered, pulling a silver chrome chair out from the table and motioning for Pork to sit down. "We've only got two days until the exchange for Madam Portentsky. If there's anyone here interested in buying rare artifacts, we need to capture their attention fast." He looked Crazy Cal up and down in his gaudy discotheque outfit. "And I have a feeling that isn't going to be too big of a problem."

"Well, if you want to capture their attention, I've got the net to pull them in." Cal jumped forward before the others could protest and scurried over to the Lab's booth situated across the dance floor. "May I?" he asked, holding a hoofed hand out to the bejeweled poodle snuggling in the right shoulder of her master. The bulldogs lurched forward, reaching toward their bulging hips as if threatened by the intrusion. Their master pulled his arm out from around the surprised lady and waved at her to rise. With graceful movement she stood up and slid a paw into Cal's hand.

And found herself yanked to the middle of the dance floor while she struggled to maintain her balance.

As the tinny march of the disco drums thumped in the background, Cal bounced his hips to and fro and spun the delicate white poodle in a series of loops. She took a few stumbling steps before Cal grabbed her about the waist and pulled her into a deep backward lunge. The other patrons, in their glossy futuristic outfits that appeared to have been stolen from a series of well-dressed robots, gave them a wide berth.

"I think I'm falling in love," Janeece giggled into Cal's ear. "But then, maybe I'm just confusing the spinning in my head with turmoil of the heart."

"A few more loop-de-loops and then you can decide."

"What'll it be, boys?" an overly familiar voice asked. Adam's heart nearly stopped in his chest—he feared to turn from watching Cal making a spectacle of himself to the source of the voice. Slowly he faced the waitress. It was as if his neck was frozen to his spine and needed axle grease to function properly. It was Betsy Moo. He hadn't expected to find her here in the Backdoor Club and certainly not in the evening. Hadn't she been attending night school for some sort of computer classes?

She stood nestling her silver server's tray upon her hip, dressed snugly in her red satin two-piece waitress outfit. The lights flashing from the dance floor lit her tawny brown top locks from behind with an ethereal glow: she looked like a fairy without wings. He noticed that the skirt was a trifle too short for modesty. Seeing his eyes tracing her thighs, Betsy pulled uselessly at her skirt to lengthen it. It only brought more attention to her shapely legs. She frowned at the obvious intrusion into her personal space.

"Betsy," Adam said lamely, then kicked himself under the table. He'd been pining over her for months, rehearsing over and over in his mind a multitude of phrases to impress her with when he saw her again. And not a single one came to his befuddled mind. He might as well just cut out his tongue and be mute.

"That's what the plate says," Betsy responded, pointing to her nametag.

A song erupted over the loudspeakers, and The MooBelles bleated the lyrics: I like to eat lots of hay and chew my cud every day.

"Two brewskis." Pork held up two fingers. "Without the floaters, if you don't mind."

"The floaters are extra," Betsy said with a wink, obviously steering her eyes away from Adam. "Still the same cheap son-of-a-gun, I see." She walked off without even a glance toward her ex-boyfriend. Then she stopped and looked over her left shoulder toward their table.

Unconsciously, Adam held his breath. "Good to see you again, Chief," she added. "It's been too long."

"Oh, and a large plate of super nachos!" Pork called after her. "Well, I can see you're going to be a big help tonight, Adam." Relaxed, he leaned back in his chair. "It's obvious why you've earned yourself a reputation as a ladies' man."

"You're enjoying this, aren't you?" Adam was sulking, the harpies of misery biting at his heart, momentarily forgetting the purpose of their visit to the Backdoor Club.

"I haven't been out on the town for nearly a year. Not since that ungrateful bird left me." Pork playfully punched Adam in the bicep, then frowned, staring beyond the steer's shoulders. "Holy catacombs! There's Wiley and his blasted son-of-a-biscuit-eater brother, Figmund! I hate those guys!" He turned away and pulled his collar straight upward toward his face as if he could somehow conceal himself in the meager fabric. "I hope they don't come over here. Boy, oh, boy, I'm so glad that we want to be conspicuous!"

"Where are they?" Adam asked without turning his head.

"Next to the booth the filthy rich Labrador and his bitches are sitting at."

Betsy startled Adam by slapping a heaping plate of nachos, laced liberally with jalapeños and avocado slices, down in the center of the table. With the same élan, she dropped two brown bottled Buckweiser beers in front of them.

"Running a tab?" she asked the hog, ignoring Adam.

"Yeah, sure," Pork said, trying to catch her eye without betraying his profile to the two weasels behind them.

Adam's mouth felt dry. He wanted to say something pithy, something witty, anything to rekindle a spark of interest for him in Betsy's heart. Instead, his tongue stuck like glue to the roof of his mouth and, without uttering a word, he watched the love of his life trot off.

"Well, I see I'm not going to ask you for any dating tips once I get back into the swing of things," Pork said amicably. He pointed at Cal, doing the bump with Janeece on the dance floor. "Now there's a cow that knows how to have fun."

"AND HE'S ALSO TOTALLY CRAZY!!!" Adam's tongue suddenly came loose and the words shot out like cannon fire, ripping through the noise of the disco beat and the chattering crowd. Everyone quieted and turned their attention to the embarrassed detective.

"Well, I guess that's another way to get attention," Cal commented to Janeece. She cooed in response, "You've certainly got mine."

"Just give a moo and I'll follow you into alfalfa paradise," the disco speakers blared.

Cal slipped into a seat next to Pork and waved to Janeece, who was also resuming her couchant pose next to the Labrador. The dog bared his teeth, revealing his gold fangs, in response to something she whispered into his ear. "Boy, that pooch can sure trot!" the panting dancer exclaimed as he reached for the nacho chips. "Where's my brew?"

"Here, knock yourself out!" Adam slammed his untouched bottle in front of the steer.

Cal was going to protest then, following the chief's pointing finger, noticed Betsy speaking to a customer. "Oh," he said knowingly. "Here's the information I charmed out of the poodle."

"The Labrador's name is Antonio, a dealer in rare bones. He's not into antiques—he prefers flash over substance. See all the gold he's wearing? Antonio sends his bulldogs out to scope the pawnshops for jewelry that hasn't been picked up within the retainer period. He's one cheap, cheesy, old son-of-a-biscuit-eater. I don't think he'd spring the money for an oil change let alone a priceless heirloom like the MooMoo Pearl." He looked over at Janeece, receiving a smile in return from the poodle and a glare from Antonio. "She's so bored I could probably buy her off of him with a pack of chewing gum and box of biscuits. But I don't think I'd live too long."

"Yes, I agree," Adam said, acknowledging the Labrador's menacing stare.

"You know, I think I've heard about him." Pork's vocal pitch rose with his excitement. "Rumors are Antonio's been digging up and selling off dinosaur bones for canine customers who want the biggest and the best."

"He's got the best," Cal responding, pointing to the poodles, "but I have my doubts about the—"

"Cal, you're with gentlemen," Adam reminded him with a smile on his lips.

Pelly held the MooMoo Pearl in his hands. It reflected an amazing amount of light from the moon shining through the windshield of the Catillac. "I almost hate to part with it," the pelican remarked to the polar bear sitting in the driver's seat. The car was parked on the shoulder in the darkness between floodlights along Hell's Highway just outside of Boville.

"We've got a deal, 50-50," the bear growled. He pulled open his black quilted vest, revealing the silver handle of a pistol. "I didn't risk my job breaking you out of prison for nothing. It ain't worth anything if we keep it."

"After I negotiate the purchase with The Mole, then, we'll talk about the split."

"I'm all for the split." The white of the polar bear's teeth flashed in the moonlight.

"My dogs are barking," Betsy said. She slid her silver server's tray underneath the plate of nachos and joined the police officer and detectives at their table. "I'm beat." She appeared confident but slyly stole a glance at Adam who, in turn, snatched up Cal's beer and raised it to his lips to avoid speaking. It wasn't that he didn't want to say anything to her, but each word grew larger as it came up from his diaphragm and got caught in his throat. He cursed himself silently for being such a maudlin fool.

"Betsy, you read the newspapers lately?" asked Chief Pork.

"No, I'm ashamed to admit I haven't. Been busy." She looked over at Adam who responded by gazing at the lip of his pilfered bottle. "Really busy."

"Busy springing budding felons out of the slammer." Adam's jealousy motivated him to show signs of life.

"Like doing whatever the heck I feel like doing. Like it's any of your business."

"You're right, it isn't." Adam leaned back in his seat, suddenly aware of how poorly his pink shirt and black slacks fit. He must look to her as if he'd picked out his wardrobe at the Good Swill charity. Which, in a matter of speaking, he had: Pork's charity. But why did he care? He couldn't hold a civil conversation with her, and yet, he couldn't keep his eyes away from her lovely face either.

"Griselda's been snatched, Betsy," Chief Pork continued, his cheery demeanor waning.

"Snatched?" the cow asked, baffled. "When?"

Pork explained to her the circumstances of the ostrich's disappearance, the theft of the MooMoo Pearl, and the subsequent ransom demand.

"That's odd. Just a few months ago Griselda was in here with some of her lady friends, bragging about a large black pearl that her boyfriend had given to her."

Pork whinced visibly at the mention of Griselda's boyfriend, which did not go unnoticed by Betsy, who was usually considerate of other critter's feelings. Although she had initiated the breakup, Adam's presence was disconcerting her, despite her attempts to appear nonchalant about his sudden reappearance into her life. "I'm sorry," she said to the hog. "I didn't mean to poke my finger into a raw wound."

The master detective sprang to life. "Did she mention who her boyfriend was?"

"If she did, I don't remember, but I believe he was a sailor of some sort."

Simultaneously Pork and Cal's mouths froze in the midst of chewing on a nacho chip.

Incredulous at his good fortune, Adam asked, "Why did she tell you about the pearl? What initiated the conversation?"

"She didn't tell me. I overheard her boasting about the statue when I was serving them their drinks."

"Who else may have overheard?"

"Oh, I'm not sure." Betsy screwed up her face in recollection. "It was some time ago, you know. It was a weeknight, that I do recall."

"Who's usually here weeknights?" Excitement overcame Steer's anxiety at speaking with his newly rediscovered lost love.

"Well, look around you." She swung her hand idly in a circle to encompass the room. "Just about everyone here, except I don't see Lenny in his usual spot."

"Lenny the rat? Does everybody in this town know about this place but us?" Pork asked. Cal shrugged his shoulders in response and surreptitiously slid a hand along the table to retrieve his stolen beer.

"How long has Lenny hung out here?" Jealousy over the rodent tinted Adam's words with bitter green, betraying his bruised emotions. "A few months?"

Betsy understood the source of the harsh inflection and, being an independent spirit, resented it. Nonchalantly waving a nacho chip in the air, she leaned back in her seat as if deep in contemplation. "Oh, no, no, not a few months. A few years, actually. One of my best customers. Doesn't tip much, but he's entertaining." Adam tried to maintain a cool demeanor but his rage at hearing her praise Lenny turned his face red. "Sometimes he does business with The Walrus." Suddenly she bolted upright and leaned forward over the table. "You don't think The Walrus stole the statue, do you?"

Adam was surprised by her sudden outburst. "Why would The Walrus do that?"

"He's into that scene: expensive paintings and antique furniture, statuary, the like; you know, the stuff you see advertised in the back of archeology or collector's magazines. Lenny cons the big guy into purchasing a few items now and then." Betsy was enjoying being the fulcrum of their attention and the slight sense of power it gave her over them. "The Walrus owns this place, you know, all of it. Front and back."

Of course, Adam didn't know, and he didn't like the cow rubbing his face in his ignorance.

"What type of items?" Pork interrupted to Adam's annoyance.

"Don't know specifically, if you mean anything like the pearl." Betsy dropped a nacho into her mouth and stood to her feet. "Break's up."

Adam reached out, grabbing her hoofed hand as she reached for her serving tray. "Can you help us see The Walrus?"

"No!" Her mood suddenly darkened. Shaking her head for emphasis, Betsy snatched up her tray. "And don't ask again...please. He's been really cheesed-off lately about something and he doesn't like strangers."

"Cheesed about what?" Adam jumped to his feet to prevent Betsy from leaving but, instead, found himself face-to-face with Wiley. He watched the cow trot off into the sea of tables.

"I was quite amused by your buddy's performance on the dance floor, Adam." Wiley's high-pitched voice slid across his tongue like thin syrup running down the side of a bottle. He nodded his head toward the hog. "And Chief Pork. What strange company you're keeping nowadays, Steer."

"Yesh, shtwange," Figmund agreed, stepping to the side from behind his brother Wiley.

"That's CHIEF Pork," the hog snarled and picked up his Buckweiser. "You seem to forget that I was promoted a few years ago."

"I didn't forget," Wiley smiled.

Pork looked the weasel up and down. He was wearing the same rumpled raincoat and weathered fedora when on the beat as a journalist. "This place has a dress code. I guess the bouncers have poor eyesight."

"They let YOU in." Wiley leaned into the hog's face. His breath was fetid, as if dead meat was putrefying in his stomach and intestines.

"Yesh," Figmund agreed.

While the hog traded insults with the weasels, Adam slipped away and found Betsy in front of the backbar. She was yelling her drink orders to the bartender, an emperor penguin, over the din of the critters sitting around the countertop. She was startled by Adam's touch on her elbow.

Her eyes met his: big, brown, and soft. A smile touched her lips then vanished at his question.

"Lenny..." The mere mention of the rodent's name made Adam's tongue feel slimy and contaminated. "You expect him tonight?" He could feel Betsy stiffen and pull her elbow back out of his reach. Avoiding his eyes, she glanced at her wristwatch. "Maybe. But probably not. He's usually here by now."

"Could you help us out?" Adam was embarrassed at the slight tremble in his voice. He wanted to run in the other direction. Betsy didn't seem interested in speaking to him. But Griselda's life was in danger. He had to grasp at any possible chance of cracking the case wide open, even if it was his own heart that ended up cracking instead. Betsy knew the rat well enough to post his bail; she could pass off information to him without raising his suspicions. "I need you...I mean, we need your help. Next time you speak to that little....to Lenny, let him know that we've got the black pearl ready for the drop-off at the Westwind Hotel lobby in Barkerville, Sunday, 3 AM But don't tip him off that I asked you to tell him. You got that? Sunday, 3 AM, The Westwind Hotel..."

Her tone sullen, she interrupted him. "I got it. Westwind Hotel, Sunday, 3 AM, Barkerville. The black pearl."

Adam lowered his tone to a hoarse whisper that she could scarcely discern. "If he's got anything to do with Griselda's kidnapping or the statue, he'll try to intercept the drop." Betsy placed a pencil behind her ear; Adam noticed her downcast demeanor but didn't know how to interpret it. He took pride in his investigative expertise, but felt he could never figure out his ex. "It's important. Griselda's life may be at stake."

"Yes, I know it's important," Betsy snapped, turning away from Adam and stacking the bottles and wine glasses onto her tray that the bartender set up onto the countertop.

Adam opened his mouth as if to add something, then decided otherwise and walked away. Betsy would help. Not because he had asked, but for Griselda's sake. Afraid that the other patrons would see his eyes glistening and sense weakness, he shook his head and forced his mouth into a smile.

Betsy watched him for a moment, then muttered to herself, "It's always important …someone else, never me."

A few moments later a dark shadow slipped among the booths, mysteriously evading the swirling cascade of multi-colored lights in the discothèque. Ever on the alert for a beckoning customer, Betsy caught the discrepancy in the corner of her eye. The shadow hissed at her, nearly startling her into dropping her tray. With apprehension she inclined her head toward the source of the beckon.

"Gads, I thought youse would never leave that trio of boobs." Lenny, his tail whipping anxiously to and fro, was standing under a table in a semi-circular corner booth near the bar. "I had to duck when I saw them stroll in here looking like a pack of unwrapped Pop-Tarts. That hog's got it out for me, and that ex of yers bin a little too friendly toward me himself lately, if youse knows what I mean." He paused, then squinted an eye in suspicion. "Youse the one that let them in here?"

Betsy smiled. The rodent looked silly hiding under the table in the crowded room. "No, Lenny, I've got standards. It's not like I've been anxious to see Adam. You ought to know that."

"Youse coulda fooled me. Didn't look like youse was in too big of a hurry to stay away."

She bent down and rubbed Lenny under the chin behind his goatee. "You're all the male I can handle right now."

Lenny smiled despite his suspicions, always appreciating a good physical and mental stroking.

"You want a drink?"

Lenny slipped onto the seat in the booth. "If I sit to this side, I don't believe them pathetic wretches can see me." He pointed a finger toward Betsy and motioned for her to draw near. "So tell me, what was they about? I know they're up to something, that's fer sure."

Driven by his thirst, Figmund left his brother to purchase another root beer. He was reluctant to flag down the bovine waitress to serve him, not wanting to feel obligated to give a tip. But after leaving the bar with his drink and returning to what appeared to be an increasingly heated discussion among his brother, the hog, and the two cattle, he noticed the waitress talking in a low voice to the rat in the nearby booth. She had been fraternizing with those danged cattle and the police chief. Walking behind her, quickly enough not to be obvious, but slow enough to catch a good portion of her conversation, the slinky snoop overheard Pork's name mentioned. If it was damaging information, perhaps it could be useful to Wiley.

"I overheard Chief Pork saying he's dropping off a statue this Sunday at the Westwind Hotel, Barkerville. 3 AM, I believe he said," Betsy cooed. "You're my quality control expert. Recognize quality when you see it. You know anything about a big black pearl, Lenny?"

Figmund smiled to himself as he popped the cap off his root beer and enthusiastically joined Wiley in the altercation at the hog's table.

"Hey, who spit into my beer?" Pork yelled.

An hour later the trio of sleuths readied themselves for bed at the chief's townhouse. Cal flopped onto the couch and pulled at the gauze bandage wound about his right hand. "You know, Chief, you didn't need to throttle Figmund around the neck. That's police brutality."

"YOU didn't need to knock Wiley over the head with that beer bottle either."

"And YOU didn't need to pull the table up by its legs and knock our plate of nachos to the floor. I was still hungry."

"So was I."

The two of them broke out into laughter, simultaneously snorting merriment through their nostrils and nursing their bruised hands.

"And you guys and the weasels didn't need to get us all tossed out on our keisters. We don't know if The Walrus connection is going to lead us anywhere. We might've uncovered some more leads if we'd stayed longer." Adam paused for a moment, picked up the *Cloverleaf Gazette* from the coffee table, turned to the crossword puzzle page, and plopped himself down into the loveseat. "And next time, Pork, when you're pulling the punches, be sure that Lenny is one of the recipients."

And the three tired sleuths giggled like silly teenage girls preparing for their first dates without a chaperone.

Wiley rubbed at his chin, inspecting the damage to his face in the bathroom mirror. His left eye was red and swollen and a dark bruise encircled the other. Behind him Figmund craned his neck to view his own reflection; he pulled a tuft of fur from his scalp and gingerly touched the resulting sore.

"Ouch!" Figmund yelped at the touch of his finger to the wound.

"That was brilliant."

"Jusht like shlapping that hog acrosh the fashe with your notepad."

"He bothers me. That fat creep has always bothered me. Never liked him poking around the *Gazette* when he was hanging with the old bird." Wiley opened a small white jar and slathered some yellowish ointment around his left eye. "And it's time I did something about that." He revealed two rows of pointed teeth in a wicked smile. "Thanks to you."

"He doesn't want to see you."

Lenny stood his ground and did not betray fear, even when the grizzly bear reared up on its haunches to intimidate him. Trapped in the back lobby of the discothèque with this monstrous creature and secreted from the view of the crowd behind the false wall, he definitely was afraid, but had learned to disguise his true emotions after years of dealing in the black market.

"Fine with me," Lenny bluffed, for he was very interested in selling the pearl for a nice price to The Walrus. "If he's no longer interested in the MooMoo Pearl, there'll be somebody else who is. I was jist giving him another stab at it, being how we'se had such a long history of doing business together."

The bear had a glazed, uncomprehending look in his eyes. Then his pupils focused and he grinned, pushing his muzzle downward into the rodent's face. "Oh, yes, I remember now. The black pearl." And he snatched the rat up into his two paws and bounded through the paneled door before Lenny could catch his breath to scream.

No one from the other side of the wall would have heard him anyway.

SCENE FIFTEEN: ARRESTED DEVELOPMENT

Now Lenny was afraid. The grizzly bear tied a leather strap around his ankles and with the loose end swung Lenny in circles above his head. The back office became a whirr of bleeding colors; voices and laughter swarmed in the rat's disoriented thoughts. Was the bear going to fling him into the wall like an organic shot put? His heart skipped a beat when the grizzly let go of the strap. But rather than flying into the wall, he bounced face first into the plush grey carpet. Sprawled on his stomach, his mind swimming, he tried to access the danger of his situation.

"Nicely done," The Walrus bellowed in his gruff voice.

Lenny lifted his head, struggling to focus his thoughts. He could feel the hot, heaving breath of the grizzly against the fur on his back. During his last business visit with The Walrus, he had narrowly escaped the clutches of the two rhinos by slipping through the space between the ill-fitted electrical outlet and the wall near the bookcase. Rats could squeeze through a hole the size of a dime. Disoriented, he would have difficulty running away. He closed his eyes for a moment, allowing the adrenalin of anger to sharpen his senses, then reopened them. Apparently The Walrus was holding a grudge even though Lenny had not accepted any money during his last transaction. His last escape was an understandable reaction to a mountainous outburst of rage.

The Walrus, his half-ton girth proudly displayed, was stuffed into a leather chair wedged behind a desk covered with sharkskin and trimmed in brass. Two gold-plated tusks draped themselves across his enormous belly and his whiskers formed a handlebar mustache. Flanking him on either side were two rhinoceroses, their horns also plated in inferior silver; their tiny eyes were magnified behind thick bifocals.

Several shelves on the wall behind the desk displayed a portion of The Walrus' hobby: antiquities, most likely secreted out of a burial ground or tomb and destined for sale to the highest bidder. Several jade statuettes of various exotic MooAsian birds and golden idols of extinct creatures were nestled amongst sundry shards of pottery and reconstructed red-figured amphorae. Revenge stirring in the back of his mind, Lenny filed away the contents of the room in his memory for possible future procurement.

If he lived through this night.

Lenny scanned the room for a new escape route. So far his wit had enabled him to survive in the netherworld of the black market. Many of the critters he dealt with were large and lumbering. If he could distract the rhinos, he might be able to squeeze under the door and scramble down the hallway to the Backdoor Club before any of the louts caught him. Of course, that would anger The Walrus and end their tentative financial partnership.

"I must say I am amazed that you would return so soon after your last visit. You are either very brash or very foolish. I cast my vote with the latter." The Walrus clapped his hands. Lenny's heart leapt. He thought a gun had gone off. He squeaked in terror, which evoked laughter from the others. The grizzly grunted and left the room. Lenny felt foolish. The clap was a signal to the bear to exit.

Studying the rat, The Walrus picked up a glass of sherry from the desk, downed the drink in one gulp, and belched unapologetically. He touched a lace napkin to his mouth and then contentedly laid his flippers upon his belly.

"So why should I allow you to live?"

Determined not to embarrass himself again by showing fear, Lenny dragged himself to his feet and looked The Walrus in the eyes as he responded. "I had my paws on the real pearl. I ain't lying. I bought it off an old rat in Singapork. Jist fer you." He watched the two rhinoceroses out of the corners of his eyes for any sudden movements. "But my partner who helped me finance it got greedy and didn't want to share the profits." His voice was rising in pitch with his increasing anxiety. Hopefully The Walrus would not detect his slight embellishment of the truth: There was no partner initially and the statue was not paid for. Demeris had entered the transaction only after he had lost possession of the statue. He needed someone on the inside of the mansion, and, naturally, had used his bohemian charm upon the poodle to persuade her to pilfer the pearl back for him.

"I know youse," Lenny continued, trying to calm his voice. "I wouldn't deal dirty with youse. The bitch double-crossed me. And I think youse knows me well enough that I wouldn't risk my reputation passing fakes. Bad for business."

"Indeed, one thing I can count upon is your greed," The Walrus said with a detached air, as if merely discussing the weather and not a potential murder. He slapped his flippers together. This time Lenny steeled himself and didn't jump. The rhino to the left of the desk turned, opened the top drawer of a file cabinet, and removed what appeared to be the MooMoo Pearl. He set it onto the desktop in front of his employer. Light danced across the surface of the statue: Tea Blossom was in the midst of a ballet pose, one arm stretched upward and the opposite leg balanced on the toe of her hoof.

"If you are not passing fakes, what do you call this?" The Walrus roared, enjoying being unpredictable, watching others flinch in surprise. "Apparently I can no longer depend upon your judgment." Lenny opened up his mouth to protest the insult, but The Walrus held up a flippered palm to silence him. "If you cannot tell the difference between ceramic and genuine pearl," he snapped off the left arm of the statue for emphasis, "I would say that your skills have deteriorated dramatically— or your eyesight. Take your pick; it does not matter to me. Maybe time does not mean much to someone who subsists on your grubby little level, but I do not care to have mine wasted. Time is money, they say. And it is true." He paused for a moment, lifting his glass for another sip of sherry. He grunted in disappointment when he realized it was empty.

Lenny stole a step backward toward the door. The two rhinos edged closer in response.

"The grizzly has informed me that you have another line on the pearl. Well, that had better be so." The Walrus changed the tone in his voice, speaking nonchalantly as if lying in the sunshine and not in a stuffy backroom. "Because I don't suffer fools lightly. One less rat in the world wouldn't be missed. In fact, it would garner applause."

A brief thought raced through Lenny's mind: Would anyone miss him if he disappeared? Well, it was not the time to be maudlin. Survival came first. There would be time to ponder his relationships later.

When in danger, Lenny did what came most naturally to him, second to running away: lie. He hastily explained that the cops had the real MooMoo Pearl and were planning to make a ransom drop that Sunday in exchange for Griselda Portentsky. He planned to intercept the transaction. Surely The Walrus had seen the newspaper articles about her kidnapping?

Lenny didn't know if the cops had the statue or not: He was buying time to save his scrawny neck. He told a second lie: Demeris had stolen the statue from him and traded it to the cops in exchange for avoiding jail time for another crime. He particularly emphasized that Demeris worked at Grande Le Coeur, with the hope that The Walrus would wreak his own revenge against the poodle for interfering with Lenny's business.

"You're sure these police officers are willing to make the trade for the bird?" the flippered behemoth asked with incredulity. "They might decide to sell it themselves and split the profits."

"I'm sure that they haven't a clue as to what it's really worth." Lenny licked his lips nervously and discreetly looked for another escape route besides the slit beneath the door. The two rhinos followed his gaze like two mechanical arms on a pivot. The space along the outlet had been duct taped over. "And the chief hog has an emotional attachment to the dame. Her life depends upon that statue. Or so they believe."

The Walrus laughed, not the tinkling laughter of mirth but of smug corruption.

"As does yours."

Friday morning Cluck was waiting at the foot of the waterfall staircase at Grande Le Coeur when the chief and two bulls pulled up in the hog's white Chevy. The rooster pointed at his wristwatch.

"Three bloody minutes late, Cluck," Pork remonstrated. "Do you always have to be so precise?"

"What are you doing here anyway, Chief? This is official police business."

Pork, dressed in civies—black jeans and a pale blue short-sleeved shirt—gave his junior officer the look-of-death. "Someone had to give these two cattle a lift." He stared the rooster down, daring him to question him again. Cluck dared.

"Don't you have a firearms class you're supposed to be attending?"

"That's next week." Pork began climbing the stairs, pushing the lieutenant aside. "Don't worry. I'm only here in an advisory capacity." He tried to sound jovial but his patience was already running thin from a slight hangover. And Cal's sure-fire hangover Rx for breakfast needed its own cure: No amount of antacids could tame the taste of Tabasco and soy sauce coating his mouth and churning in his stomach.

Cluck stood on the steps looking wounded.

"Look, if the higher-ups question me, I'll take the hit. I'll claim you were totally ignorant of my wanton wiles."

"I'll back up his claim that you are totally ignorant, also," Cal said. Adam popped him a playful punch in the bicep.

"I'll be so glad when this case is over," Cluck mumbled under his breath, climbing the staircase after the others. "And you fat cows go back to the farm."

Dudley's face clearly mirrored his distaste at finding the police on his door stoop once more. He tried to close the door in Adam's face, but Cluck unceremoniously pushed back the door and shoved the warrant into the Dalmatian's face. With obvious reluctance the butler stepped to the side while his unwelcome guests marched into the lobby.

Adam informed the others what to look for and the search was on. With Cal accompanying, he knocked and entered the room of Gladys the Yorkie and pulled a small tape measure out of his pocket. After taking the dimensions of the closet—all sides, top and bottom—he and his bovine companion marched to Demeris' room. The poodle, polishing her nails with pink, was lying on her stomach on her bed. Dressed in a light cotton yellow nightie, she started at the rude interruption. Ignoring her protests, Adam flung open the closet door and used the tape once again to measure the closet's interior dimensions.

The master detective's face visibly paled as he hit the rewind button on the metal tape and slid the compact into his coat pocket. "No difference," he stated to Cal. He hesitated for a moment, then began knocking on the closet walls with his right hand.

"Hey, don't go putting your grimy hooves all over my clothes!" Demeris protested, slipping on a black fleece bathrobe and pushing her way past Cal into the walk-in closet. Unperturbed, Adam continued knocking on all four walls, then on the ceiling. A sprinkle of plaster cascaded down and Demeris coughed demonstrably. "I need to get my allergy medicine." She found Cal, leaning against the now closed bedroom door and biting at his cuticles. Her egress blocked, she reached for an empty glass on top of her dresser and slipped into the bathroom.

Pushing aside the assortment of department store shoeboxes and knocking on the floorboards of the closet, Adam heard a hollow sound, noticeably different in tone, in response to his rapping toward the front of the closet. Pulling a penknife out of his pocket, he knelt down and slid the blade through the scarcely discernible crack in the floor. His efforts were rewarded when he yanked several connecting boards upward to reveal a cubbyhole containing three black statuettes nestled in a blanket. Smiling broadly, he pulled out three dancing black cows and set them in a row outside the doorway. Reaching further into the hole, he fell upon his breast and reached blindly for other secreted items. His hoofed fingers met with plastic. Cal was now standing over his left shoulder as he retrieved a two-part plastic mold, a metal dinner tray with unfolding legs to stand upright, and a box full of paints, varnishes, and brushes.

"Our little counterfeiter has finally been caught," Adam announced with a wry smile. Lying on his right side, he continued reaching around the dark hole for further evidence. With a scream he bolted upward, knocking Cal backward, and hitting his head under a clothing rod.

"Spider," Adam explained while Cal rubbed his jaw.

The bathroom door clicked shut. Demeris slipped across the room toward the hallway. But Cal was quicker and grabbed the back of her robe.

"Let me go, you masher!" she protested, tugging at her bathrobe. "I haven't done anything wrong."

"Then what do you call this?" Adam motioned toward the row of statues and artistic supplies. "And this?" He grabbed her right paw and, pulling it toward his chest, pushed back the white fur from her nails. "Black paint on the cuticles!"

"Ah, that's what you noticed about her that day in the kitchen," Cal said in obvious awe. "Your subconscious clued into it. I'm quite impressed."

Demeris struggled to pull from Cal's grip.

Dudley stepped into the open doorway; Demeris slipped out of the robe and into his arms.

Downstairs Cluck and Chief Pork searched the rooms in the lower half of the mansion. There was nothing of significance in either the waiting or dining rooms. Stepping into the kitchen, the rooster opened cabinets and drawers and slammed them shut once again with scarcely a glance at their contents. "We're wasting our time down here," Cluck remonstrated. "I think Adam's just trying to keep me out of the way again." But Pork wasn't listening: He had opened the upper half of the kitchen door and stared out toward the backyard.

"Didn't Adam say Demeris kept looking nervously toward the door when he was interviewing her here in this kitchen?" asked the temporarily defrocked police chief.

"Mmmm," his number one lieutenant replied with apparent disinterest. "I don't trust Steer. Doesn't like to share the glory. Likes to keep us in the dark."

But Pork, opening the lower door and stepping outside, didn't hear his response.

A few minutes later Cluck found the hog standing in front of a metal tool shed and inspecting the dead bolt on the chain draped through the connecting holes in its two doors. Pork attempted to pull the shed doors apart and peer between them, but could move them only a half-inch, not far enough to discern the contents.

"Help me find a crowbar or key or something, would you?" Pork asked as he checked around the upper rim of the doors for a key.

"The search warrant only covers the mansion, not the grounds. We, I mean, I don't have the authority to get into the tool shed. You, on the other hand, don't have any authority at all."

"I believe you enjoyed saying that, Cluck," Pork said, unperturbed, stooping down and running his fingers along the lower rim of the shed. "Do something useful, will you, and get me the crowbar out from under the front seat of my Chevy.

"You carry a crowbar under your car seat?" Cluck's eyes were wide open with surprise. "That's a concealed weapon."

"I'm not concealing THIS weapon." Pork stood up and held up his right hoofed fist. "And I ain't got a permit either."

Cluck, recalling that his quarterly reviews and employee job performances were conducted by Pork, left immediately but returned with a giant metal cutter instead. "I keep these on hand in my 4x4," Cluck explained, as he handed the shears to the chief. If someone was going to get into trouble for search-and-seizure without a warrant, may as well be on Pork's head.

Pork grunted with satisfaction when the chains cut easily and the shed doors flew apart. Cluck smiled, seeing the grease stain on the hog's nice blue shirt, which would not have been soiled if the chief had stayed home where he belonged and trusted his lieutenant to conclude the investigation. But his superior officer did tend to be emotional and did not fully appreciate the value in court of a job conducted strictly by code: it gave the defense attorney less opportunity to find a loophole to rescue the offender from his deserved fate.

"Well, what do we have here?" Pork asked as sunlight revealed a small kiln about waist high to a standing hog. "Just the right size to bake a few statuettes."

A few minutes later they found Adam in the main lobby placing a pair of handcuffs onto Demeris' wrists behind her back. Cal held a cardboard box of art supplies.

"We've got a counterfeiter on our hands here," Adam said to the butler while the poodle cried out to him: "Dudley, don't let them take me. Lenny framed me. I haven't done anything wrong."

The butler seemed undecided. He allowed Demeris to lay her head upon his breast and wet his shirt with her tears; his face displayed obvious distress, but his arms hung loosely to his sides.

"Found these in her closet," Cal announced to Pork and Cluck as they approached. He pulled one of the counterfeit MooMoo Pearls out of the box. The bottom of the plaster was unpainted and the varnish had not yet been applied that gave it the glossy, imitation pearl appearance. Dudley's jaw hardened at the sight of the statuette and he pulled away from Demeris.

"Somewhere there's an original that she lifted these copies from," Adam announced to the butler. "And I believe her partner is looking for it."

"The Madam's life is in danger and you are hiding the ransom!" Dudley's voice was nearly a shriek. Demeris appealed to him with wide-open, mascara rimmed eyes, but his face was set like steel and devoid of compassion. She surveyed the faces of the detectives and police officers; her gaze was met with the same hard resistance. She turned as if to run, but Adam grabbed her by the right arm.

"Found the kiln in the tool shed out back," Pork announced while Cluck winced in horror.

"I'd say she was looking at ten to twenty, wouldn't you, Chief?" Adam asked while the poodle twisted in his grasp.

"Oh yes, most definitely," Pork agreed. Cal smiled but Cluck was nonplussed by the cat-and-mouse conversation.

"Ten to twenty for what?" Demeris sneered, dropping the helpless female act.

"Cluck, this is your specialty," Pork said.

The rooster preened his top comb with the palm of his winged hand, gloriously pleased at this acknowledgment of his capabilities. "Conspiracy to defraud, hindering a police investigation, forgery, resisting arrest—"

"Look," Demeris interrupted in an anxious tone. She twisted her head to look back at Steer. "You cut me some slack for cooperating, and I'll lead you to the original statue." She ignored the look of disgust that Dudley aimed at her.

"You'll show us where the original is," Pork said through gritted teeth, thinking about the anxiety Griselda must be experiencing while this poodle concealed her salvation from them. "But we won't cut you any slack. Cluck, read this poodle her Mooranda rights. And let her get some decent clothes on."

SCENE SIXTEEN: EATING CROW

Adam was unsure if he should believe the look of horror on the poodle's face when she discovered that the door to locker #47 was pried open, hanging loosely from one of its hinges. Pork wanted to take the key from Demeris and haul her straight from the mansion to the jailhouse, but she threatened to swallow the key if they didn't take her to the ferry terminal where she claimed to have stashed the pearl. Her hardened face didn't give the impression of repentance as she sat, arms crossed, in the backseat of Pork's Chevy (which was against regulations, Cluck said, to transport criminals in an unofficial vehicle, to which Pork said his presence made it official, to which his lieutenant reminded him he was temporarily unofficial) and seemed to scan the passing landscape for an opportunity to elude them. But now she stood in front of the locker bay with the key extended in one delicate paw, her eyes wide, her jaw dropped open in a very unladylike fashion. Then she began to weep and this time the tears appeared to be genuine—weeping for herself, not for her employer whose life depended upon locating the statue.

"You're certain this is the locker?" Adam asked. She nodded her head, handing him the key. Locker #47, Boville Ferry Terminal, was imprinted in its head. Chief Pork reached to grab her roughly by the handcuffs but Adam, placing an arm around her shoulders, steered her to the side. "Can you think of anyone that could have seen you place the bag into the locker?"

Demeris looked into Adam's face with a wry grin. "Look around you. This is a ferry terminal. There's critters everywhere. It was the middle of the afternoon. Anyone could have seen me. But I had the statue stashed in the bag from the time I left my room at the mansion and never removed it." (Pork winced at the mention of Griselda's home.) "It was an old duffle bag. How could anyone possibly know that it had anything in it worth breaking into the locker to steal?"

Adam paused in reflection, placing his chin upon the back of his hand. "It would have to be someone who knew you, perhaps suspected what you were doing and followed you here."

"Son-of-a-biscuit eater!" Chief Pork yelled, slapping his thigh with his right hand. "I bet it's Lenny! If I get my hooves on him, I'm going to kill that rat!"

After agreeing to meet the others in the near future for an early dinner, Pork and Cluck escorted Demeris in grand style to her new home with the decorator bars, while Steer and Cal followed up with Kuniko, the antique dealer at the pier. Adam was surprised to find the glass front door ajar several inches, allowing moist ocean air to enter into the shop, risking damage to the priceless wooden antiques crowded inside. With a forefinger held to his lips, Adam signaled Cal to remain silent. A small bell, hanging from a chain attached to the top of the frame, jingled as he gently pushed the door open wider. He froze, holding his breath while surveying the room for signs of Kuniko. The shop was silent. With Cal close to his backside, he tiptoed forward.

"You think she's got the pearl already?" Cal asked in a hoarse whisper. Swinging around to admonish the bull to remain silent, Adam's elbow knocked a yellow mosaic table lamp from the top of a three-drawer chest; its bronze base smacked against the wooden floor. The sound echoed throughout the room, seeming like a sonic boom to the two sleuths. "And you're telling ME to be quiet?" Cal asked.

The announcement of their presence was met with the sounds of breaking glass and several strangled shouts coming from the back of the store. Adam rushed through the gauntlet of priceless antiques and through the swinging double doors in the back. He was surprised to see Sum Ting Wong forcing Kuniko to straddle a large oak desk backwards; she was struggling to break free from the choke hold he had on her neck. With a roar of anger Adam tucked his head into his chest and rushed at Sum Ting, as if he were a red flag waving in an arena. His fedora flew to the floor with the impact of his horned head into the odious rat's back. With a screech of pain and surprise Sum Ting was tossed into the window above the desk, then fell to the floor, panting in anger.

As the rat fought to catch his breath, Cal lifted a black lacquer vase from a cabinet. Kuniko shook her head "No!" Cal replaced the vase and pointed at a leather-bond glove box. Kuniko shook her head "Yes" and the box found its new home against Sum Ting's forehead.

"I think our dear lady has procured the statue," Adam announced to Cal as he lifted Kuniko from the desk to her feet. He then bent down, picked up his fedora, and straightened out the red feather protruding from the hatband.

Wiley couldn't suppress a smile as he exited the office of Sheriff Hoggsbutter. As he had rightly suspected, the police officers at Precinct Thirteen-and-a-half weren't keeping the sallow hog informed of their progress on the kidnapping case: He was totally unaware of the ransom drop to occur at the Westwind Hotel. Walking out of the brick building, he found Figmund still perched on the back of his moped. He flashed his brother the victory sign.

"Found someone to keep Demeris company," Adam announced as he roughly pushed Sum Ting Wong into the lobby of Precinct 13-and-a-half and into a chair in front of the main desk. Officer Pepy yawned and slowly began his trek from the time clock back to his seat. As a nocturnal creature he hated dayshift, but since Chief Pork was temporarily dismissed from active duty in addition to running around as if he was still on the beat, the sloth was stuck covering the front desk pulling double shifts. He hoped that the upcoming budget review would yield enough money to hire another police officer.

The phone rang as Lt. Cluck and Pork entered the lobby from the back room. Pepy lifted the receiver before Cluck could get a wing on it. "Sheriff Hoggsbutter," the sloth drawled in long, drawn-out consonants in response to the voice on the wire.

Pork froze. "Don't tell him I'm here!" he hissed.

"Sure,…I'll get the chief…for you. He's right…here!" Pepy said into the receiver as the hog waved his arms frantically to and fro in a futile effort to signal to the sloth not to reveal his presence. As Pork nervously reached for the handset, Pepy smiled and pulled it back toward his chest with his usual lack of speed. "Just kidding. It's…the wife. Wants…me to pick up…some June bugs at…the supermarket."

"You're so funny I'm going to call the circus and volunteer you for the clown corps. Who's this?" Pork pointed at the surly rat slumped in the chair in front of Pepy.

"Assault and battery," Steer stated blandly.

"I'll book him." Cluck pulled the rat to his feet and led him toward his desk in the corner. "It'll take that sloth all afternoon to do it."

Pepy watched Steer settle down onto a bench in the lobby next to Chief Pork before he lifted the receiver back to his mouth. "Listen, Sheriff,…I'll get back to you…later." And nestled it back into its cradle.

The chief pulled a plastic baggie of carrot sticks out of his breast pocket and proffered it to Adam who politely refused. The bench fully occupied, Cal slumped against the wall to listen in to their conversation.

"Got quite a story out of the little lady in back." Pork smiled ruefully, then bit into a carrot stick. "Seems your suspicions were correct. In order to save money, Lenny took a berth on a Merchant Marine vessel, instead of a regular passenger ship, to Singapork to do a little business. Met and became friends with the pelican, Pelly, whom I just happened to share a cell with earlier this week. Lenny got to boasting about his prowess and took Pelly with him to meet the dealer in Singapork who had the MooMoo Pearl. Due to its high value, it seems that Lenny procured the statue on a promissory note rather than putting cash up front. And our suspicions were correct: on the way back to Americow, the ship sank. Lenny had to take a life raft. Pelly lifted the statue from Lenny and flew off with it. Since he owed money to the dealer in Singapork, Lenny was anxious to track Pelly down and retrieve the pearl once he returned to dry land."

"You're all a bunch of geniuses," Sum Ting muttered. In response Cluck yanked his right paw forward toward an inkpad to record his prints.

"However," the chief continued, "our good pelican friend didn't know where he could locate buyers who were willing to purchase the statue for anywhere near its true value. He wasn't familiar with the underground market like Lenny is. All he knew was that Lenny lived in Boville, so he assumed the rat had regular contacts in the area. But he was also afraid that Lenny would return and reclaim his property, so he gave it to a girlfriend of his for safekeeping as a gift with the idea of stealing it back once he had found the right buyer."

"Place of birth?" asked Lt. Cluck.

"Singapork. Heard of it before?" The rat glared at the hog.

Pork pulled a handkerchief out of his back pocket and wiped his forehead. He couldn't sweat but felt warm with anxiety, thinking about Griselda with another critter. "However, he didn't plan on being arrested on a reckless driving charge and landing in prison, where he was immobile."

"So Lenny's not a thief after all," interrupted Cal.

"No, unfortunately not," Pork said. "As much as I'd like an excuse to use his verminous face to clean out our toilet bowl, he's actually one of the victims here."

"I'm crying my eyes out," Steer said.

"No doubt," Pork replied, replacing his handkerchief into his back pocket. "To continue my lurid tale: Lenny overhears Griselda at the Backdoor Club bragging about this gift her boyfriend gave her. Realizing it's the statue Pelly stole from him, he links up romantically with Demeris as his foothold into the mansion. However, the cagey poodle begins to suspect she's being used, that Lenny couldn't care less for her. Being a user herself, she sneaks behind his back and gets a line on what the statue is worth. Then decides to cut Lenny out of the deal and keep all the money herself. So she creates a fake and gives it to Lenny. And here she was telling us the truth: She did break the statue that was on the mantelpiece, but it was another fake that she made to prevent Grissie from noticing that her gift was missing. Griselda noticed that the replacement was missing right away. She rushed over here to the precinct to report the theft before Demeris could make up another fake to replace the damaged one."

"Who did Demeris intend to sell the statue to?" Adam asked.

"To discover who Lenny's buyer was, Demeris claimed she was planning to follow the rat the night she passed off a fake to him, but you and the Boozo brothers showed up, forcing her to remain inside the mansion. Could be she's lying and had someone in mind to sell it to. In any case, she supposedly hid the original in the locker at the ferry terminal, but for all we know it could also be another fake."

"The statue's mine!" Sum Ting Wong suddenly shrieked, rising from his chair and rushing over toward the startled cattle and hog. "That rat didn't deliver on his promise to pay me back! I traveled all the way from MooAsia to reclaim it!"

"So you're the dealer in Singapork," Adam commented. "Small world."

"You know where it is! Give it to me!" The rat, arms outstretched, rushed at Adam with the intention of grabbing him by the throat.

Adam drew back his arm and slapped the rat so hard he dropped to the floor. "You want more of that, try it again," Adam said. He hated violence but wasn't reluctant to use it to protect himself. "And even if I knew where it was, I couldn't give it back to you right away. Someone's life is depending upon that statue—and you're not going to lay one finger upon it until we're certain she's safe."

"It's going to be a few months until he can get his paws on the pearl anyway, " Lt. Cluck said, walking over to Sum Ting and yanking him to his feet by the scruff of his neck. "He's not going to want to display it on the shelf at the hotel where he's going to be staying." Sum Ting demanded to call the Ambassador of Singapork as the rooster dragged him toward the backroom to the main jail cell.

"Don't put him in the..." Pork called to the rooster.

"I know, I know," Cluck interrupted. "I'll use the glass cage."

"And don't let him use the bathroom. He can use the chips in his cage."

"Poor hamster," Steer remarked.

"He's not back there anymore, " Pork said. "He made bail. But to finish my summary: What really frosts my flakes is the ransom note."

"What? Did the poodle write the ransom note?" Cal asked puzzled. "Then we don't really need to drop the statue off tomorrow night. She should know where the old bird is."

"I wish it was that easy. Demeris didn't compose the actual ransom note," Pork answered. "She found it taped to the front gate. Fearful that the wind would blow the note away, she moved it when no one was looking, stabbing it into the front door. That's why nobody, particularly the dogs, noticed any unfamiliar scents about the mansion. Figured it was a great way to take suspicion away from herself while she spent time trying to find a buyer for the statue. Or so she says. She fooled us once already."

"Unbelievable," Cal interrupted. "Cared more about the money than her employer."

"Problem was, Lenny is the only one who has the ready-made connections to dump an invaluable antique. And why Pelly didn't think to sell it to Griselda rather than give it to her for safekeeping? I can only suppose he didn't feel comfortable selling the pearl for what it was really worth to his.... his... lady friend." He paused and looked earnestly at Adam. "You believe you've found the statue?"

"The lady that miscreant of a rodent was abusing claims she'll have it by tomorrow," Adam replied. "Just in time for the drop."

Pork's face reflected his mixed emotions of jubilation and fear. "That's cutting it close. You think your antique dealer will come through for us?"

"After rescuing her from Sum Ting Wong, I can reasonably count on it." He paused a moment. "Nothing in life is for certain, Chief."

"No, it's not." Pork fished in his inner breast pocket for the lucky frog's leg, then recalled it was no longer there.

"So what about the pearl that those two guys stole from the pawnshop?" Cal asked. "I'm betting it was Pelly trying to get the statue back after he found out Griselda no longer had it."

Adam thought for a moment before replying. "We can only suppose that it was another fake. Demeris cheated the poor dumb warthog out of a hundred bucks."

The phone rang again, but this time Lieutenant Cluck was able to snatch up the receiver before Pepy did. He spoke for a few minutes then placed the receiver back into the cradle. "That was the city morgue. A murder victim was just brought in. They're requesting an investigation, but I thought you'd like to identify the body, Chief."

Adam and Cal gasped. Pork's mouth went slack and his eyes widened in horror.

"No, no, sorry, Chief," the rooster continued sheepishly. "It's not Griselda." The other three visibly relaxed. He briefly explained the phone conversation.

Pork jumped to his feet and pointed to Pepy. "Hold down the fort, Old Boy," he said, following the other three out the front door.

"I need...a raise," Pepy mumbled under his breath, drawing the chair away from Pork's desk and sitting down. The phone rang once more. "Hello,...Sheriff," he said into the receiver.

SCENE SEVENTEEN: DEAD WRONG

Chief Pork surreptitiously squinted to conceal his weak eyesight and leaned forward over the gurney. The mortician pulled the white sheet back from the body, revealing the murder victim.

"It looks like him, but there's a way to be sure," Pork said, motioning to the attendant to roll the arm over. There it was on the shaved left forearm: a faded blue tattoo of an anchor and gull. Pork swallowed anxiously, then asked the mortician to pull the sheet back over Pelly.

"I don't want to handle this one," Pork said to Adam. Outside the morgue he sat down on a white cement bench near the sidewalk. "Let's bring the County in on it." He paused, fingering breast pocket where his police badge would normally be. About twenty yards away Lt. Cluck and Cal waited in the hog's Chevy, straining their necks to catch a glimpse at what the other two were doing. "Adam, to be honest, I'm worried sick about Griselda, even though she dumped me for that schlep in the morgue. I don't know what that pearl is worth and I don't want to—would make me nervous to know. But there must be some serious money involved. We've got one murder on our hands and also an assault, possibly a murder attempt." He looked up wearily into Adam's angular face. As expected, he found compassion in the large brown bovine eyes. "I'm afraid she might be hurt, might not be returned to us tomorrow night." He lowered his head, grieving silently.

Adam didn't know how to respond so he remained quiet. He was also anxious for the ostrich's safety, but voicing that concern wouldn't bring the chief any consolation, and they had to remain focused on the resolution of the case. Patting the hog gently on his left thigh, Adam rose to his feet. "You're right. There's no point pursuing Pelly's murderer. Either he was killed to rob him of the statue or someone discovered he was passing a fake. In either case, our captors don't have the original yet and neither do we. There's nothing more we can really do until tomorrow. Let's go get some dinner and head on to bed, get an early start in the morning."

They walked toward the car. Lt. Cluck, with a solemn look upon his face, stepped out of the Chevy and pulled the driver's door open for his police chief. There were times when Cluck did the right thing and remained silent; he wasn't a total idiot, Adam thought, though was darned close to it.

Chief Pork grabbed the wheel and, as Adam slid in next to him, announced, "There IS something we've got to do tonight." He put the key into the ignition and peeled out of the parking lot.

Pork was returning from the front desk at the Cowlitz County Regional Justice Center when he heard Sheriff Hoggsbutter's annoyingly piercing voice coming from the hallway to the right of the main lobby. Scanning the room for a quick exit, he ducked behind the counter, pushing the pink flamingo, who was watching the desk, to the side.

"If I get one of my hooves on that hog I'm going to strangle him!" he heard Sheriff Hoggsbutter hollering as he stomped into the lobby. The flamingo peered curiously at Pork who responded by placing a forefinger to his lips, signaling for silence. He heard the sheriff's cowboy boots slamming against the Formica floor and steadily growing dimmer. He heaved a sigh of relief and was nearly to his feet when the boots stopped pounding the floor. There was a pause, and the boots began pounding back toward the desk. In panic, Pork ducked back down and grasped the bird's two legs as if he could somehow hide behind the long slender toothpicks.

"Did they release Chief Pork from the infirmary already?" he heard the unnaturally thin hog ask the desk attendant.

"If I recall correctly, and I usually do, I believe so," the flamingo said. Pork's fingers on his calves tickled him and he giggled.

"What's so funny?" the sheriff asked, his voice rising in volume and coming closer. Pork pictured the hog leaning over the desk, pushing his mangy snout into the bird's beak in his usual attempt to bully those poor souls who were inferior in rank. He shivered, which caused the bird to giggle once more.

"Supervisor isn't keeping you busy enough if you've got time to play games on the job." There was a pause. "You hiding something behind that desk, a pack of cards or one of those handheld computer games?"

Pork ducked to the left, sidling up alongside the short end of the desk, a snug fit as it was close to the wall. He held his breath as the sheriff peered over the top of the counter.

"Nah, just two of the ugliest legs I've ever seen," Hoggsbutter said. Pork pictured him pulling away from the counter and slipped back behind the desk once more. He breathed a sigh of relief, which tickled the flamingo's legs. The bird pulled one leg up into the air and hugged it close to the underside of his body.

"You dissing me in that bird language of yours?" the sheriff asked again.

Holy cow, is this guy sensitive or what? Pork thought to himself.

"No, no, just tired," the bird replied nervously.

"Don't see how, standing behind the desk and playing games all day," Sheriff Hoggsbutter growled, but Pork heard his boots clomping against the floor once more and out of the lobby. He waited a few minutes then popped up from behind the counter.

"Thanks. I owe you one, big time," Pork said to the bird as he fled the building.

Fortunately, the other three had seen the Sheriff exiting through the revolving door; Adam had driven the chief's Chevy off into the maze of the parking lot before the fuming hog had spotted the familiar automobile. When Pork emerged from the building, Adam drove the car cautiously toward the curb and picked him up.

"That polar bear I was telling you about, the one that claimed he never saw Pelly when I was in the infirmary," Pork announced as he slid into the car beside Adam. "He hasn't shown up for work since Wednesday night. It seems highly likely that he was Pelly's accomplice in the pawn shop robbery and assault."

"We should report that," Cluck interrupted.

"To whom?" Pork responded. "We're the critters everyone usually reports to."

"Sheriff..." Cluck stopped speaking when confronted by Pork's glare searing toward him from the front seat.

"They've got an officer on that robbery already," Adam said, turning the steering wheel. Cal held onto the door handle, anticipating another wild ride through the city, but Steer, considerate of the chief's nerves, kept the car at five miles below the speed limit. "Some big hippo of a guy. I'll tip him off tomorrow, keep him busy while we make our final pick-up."

Cal's request that they eat at a MooAsian restaurant didn't go over too well with the others and a few minutes later Adam dropped Lieutenant Cluck off at the Precinct to relieve Pepy of duty for a few hours. Minutes later, relieved of the burden of the fastidious rooster, the two cattle reclined in Pork's living room around his oak coffee table while their host rustled up some dinner in the kitchen. Cal was silently hoping to himself that the hog didn't mean actual grubs when he had made his pronouncement about "fixing some grub." Hogs would eat anything that was organic and didn't move. He was pleasantly surprised to find a plate of steaming broccoli and cauliflower, dribbled with melted feta cheese, placed before him by the chief. Pork handed Adam a similar plate then slumped back into an overstuffed avocado-colored armchair.

"Aren't you going to eat?" Adam asked, sucking a piece of broccoli into his mouth. The room was dark, illuminated only by the harsh glow of the television set. There was a famous rooster and crow comedy team movie playing, but no one appeared to be paying attention, the cattle's focus turned down toward their plates, the hog splayed like a starfish and staring toward the ceiling.

"Not hungry," was the reply. Adam and Cal continued to eat without engaging in further conversation while a cacophony of inane words embellished by a laugh track spewed out from the television. Suddenly inspiration hit Adam. What the chief needed was a little encouragement. Some faith.

"You like pickles?" he asked the chief.

"What?"

"Pickles?"

"Yes, got a whole jar of them in the fridge. Why're you asking?"

"Just a moment." Adam flew off of the couch and into the kitchen. He returned a moment later with a half-gallon sized jar of baby dills.

"See these pickles, Chief? This label here says that they're kosher. Do you know what that means?"

"That you're going goofy?" the hog retorted, which prompted a giggle out of Cal.

"No," Adam protested. He twisted off the lid and pulled out a single plump pickle. "They're blessed."

Pork rolled his fingers toward his temple in the "he's crazy" signal; Cal nodded in agreement.

"You're tired, Adam. Stress of this case. Maybe you ought to pack it in early for the night."

But the master detective wasn't listening. He pulled a small knife out of his coat pocket, pierced a hole into the small end of the pickle, and pulled a loose piece of yarn from the multi-colored afghan on the sofa. He threaded the yarn through the hole and tied the resulting loop to a close with a knot. He proudly held the amulet in the air before the police chief.

"The pickle factory, I kid you not, has a rabbi fly over once a week to bless the pickles. That's what makes them kosher. You wear this and you'll have good luck."

Pork looked at the pickle, dangling in front of his face. Then with a sigh he snatched the makeshift necklace out of Adam's hands and plodded off to his bedroom.

"Reminds me of the frog leg." Cal seized the remote and changed the channel. "Except it tastes a lot better. Give me that jar, will you, Steer? My stomach needs blessing."

Lt. Cluck sat in his chair, cursing the detectives and his chief and even Pepy for leaving him to watch the jailhouse for another evening. Sure, he was making time-and-a-half, but once in awhile he needed a chance to relax and have a little fun himself. He fed the two sulking prisoners in the back, remembered to remove the key from above the toilet before allowing Demeris to use the bathroom, then found himself sitting alone with nothing to do for the evening. As luck would have it, the phone finally rang shortly before midnight. There was a riot at the Boville City Hall, some hapless city clerk was screaming through the receiver. A cop was needed right away. With glee Lt. Cluck grabbed his oversized flashlight from behind his desk and dashed through the lobby, making sure that the front door was locked before he climbed into his Cheep Rangler.

Adam was having difficulty sleeping. It wasn't because Crazy Cal was laughing to himself in his sleep or that Chief Pork's snores rumbled into the room like a thunderstorm robbed of its lightning. He had met Betsy for the first time in months last night, and all he could come up with for conversation was business. He saw the look of disappointment in her eyes when she turned away from him while promising to speak to Lenny. If only he had the nerve to tell her that he missed her, had wanted to telephone or e-mail her, but didn't want to intrude into her privacy—but he didn't and couldn't. Cal thought he was brave and smart, but Adam knew the truth about himself: at heart, he was just a craven coward, afraid of rejection. He could face down violent assailants like Sum Ting Wong or tolerate the rantings of irrational superiors like Sheriff Hoggsbutter, but he couldn't muster up the courage to reveal one honest feeling to the one cow, the only critter, he loved. But perhaps he feared that his heart held only a chimera, the image of the cow he wanted Betsy to be, and confronting her honestly might destroy that dream he treasured.

Or with such an excuse he attempted to comfort himself.

Sighing, he squinted his eyes in the wane moonlight struggling between the Venetian blinds and began to count the knotholes in the ceiling.

Hundreds of signs flickered in the lamplight of the courtyard surrounding the City Hall and angry voices filled the still evening air.

If you bent your ear toward the ground to hear them.

Cluck was pleasantly surprised to discover that his initial assumptions regarding the phone call were correct: The surviving earthworms had finally accomplished their trek to the City Center and were demanding the immediate presence of the mayor. As he stepped out of his Rangler, a flustered white-tailed stag accosted him, pulling at the collar of his night guard uniform as if being strangled.

"My, my, my, I don't know what I would've done if you hadn't shown up. I certainly don't want to disturb the mayor at this hour, but I can't seem to quiet them down."

Lt. Cluck stood, winged hands at his hips, surveying the melee. The courtyard was filled with thousands of worms chanting slogans. Signs proclaiming: "Obey the Law" and "Worms are Critters too" gave a silent voice to their complaint. A few odd signs in red ink also read, "Down With Crows."

"Nothing that a flock of birds can't handle. We could rustle up a few gulls from the pier," Lt. Cluck replied. The guard was overreacting a bit.

"Is violence the only solution you coppers can come up with?" an earthworm said as he smacked the rooster in the shins with his tiny sign.

"See what I mean? Cantankerous little creatures, aren't they? Would never have guessed it." Cluck rubbed at his wounded ankle.

The stag wrung his two hoofed hands together. "Why can't they stay down in the earth where they belong?"

The rooster swept down and plucked the hostile worm from the ground. The orange-ringed worm dropped its sign as it soared through the air toward the open beak.

"Snack time," Cluck announced, the worm dangling between his feathered thumb and forefinger. "I've been waiting all week for this. If it wasn't for your wriggling little butts, the ostrich would never have been snatched."

"I found your squad car," his intended victim announced nonchalantly.

Cluck paused, anxiety creasing his forehead. "Dang. You must be the worm Adam told me about."

"Must be."

The lieutenant had to give the earthworm credit for its pluck and refusal to be eaten when all hope appeared to be lost. Licking the edges of his beak, he pulled the worm away from his salivating mouth and slipped it into his breast pocket. "Guess this is your lucky evening."

In response his guest pushed its head out from beneath the pocket flap.

The stag danced about on its hooves, attempting to avoid stepping on the slithering throng of worms.

In the background the protesters proclaimed, "Fruits and Nuts! Fruits and Nuts! Obey the Law and save our Butts!"

SCENE EIGHTEEN: HOME STRETCH

The following morning Chief Pork emerged from the kitchen with a sizzling hot skillet; the smell of greasy hash browns filled the dining room air. Cal lifted up his plate toward the hog, eager to receive his share of the potato bounty while Adam sat at the head of the small Formica table, transfixed by the newspaper held before him in his two hoofed hands.

"Did you take a look at last night's *Cloverleaf Gazette?*" Adam asked, seeming oblivious to the dollop of spuds Pork slapped onto his plate.

"Another article by Wiley?"

"Uh-huh."

"Better not tell me while I've got a hot skillet in my hands," Pork said, placing the pan upon a crocheted trivet in the center of the table and sitting down next to Adam.

"Give it here. I'm starving this morning." Cal took the wooden spoon from the iron skillet and began heaping more potatoes onto his plate."

"I'll soon be sending you my bill for the bed-and-breakfast," Pork said, delaying Adam's recitation of Wiley's article. Part of him wanted to get the statue, rush to the Westwind Hotel, and scope out the lobby for the best location to apprehend the kidnappers—and another part was afraid of sitting in the hotel for too long, anxiety mounting while waiting for the time of the ransom. Still a third part was wishing he didn't have to deal with it at all, that it was Sunday morning and he was loafing in his jockey shorts, the fateful night behind him. He fingered at the lucky pickle hanging from the yarn around his neck. It felt rubbery and a little sticky to the touch, but he needed all the luck he could get. He was afraid that the kidnappers would double-cross them, take the statue, and not return Griselda. Feared that perhaps she was already dead.

Like Pelly.

He'd slept soundly the night before, but only because of the two sleeping pills he had taken before retiring to bed. He had needed a good rest. It was important to be alert tonight.

For her sake.

Adam interrupted the chief's musings. "I know you don't want to hear this…"

"Go ahead and read it; I'm ready," Pork replied, sticking his spoon into the skillet.

> "It has been confirmed by confidential sources that Ms. Griselda Portentsky, publisher of this fine newspaper, was kidnapped last Monday morning. The ransom note demands her return in exchange for a priceless pearl, nicknamed the MooMoo. It is rumored that the statuette is now in the possession of the Boville Police who intend to make the exchange tomorrow night in Barkerville (exact location concealed to protect the victim). A local antique dealer, Mr. Higsnickle of Real Purdy Furniture, believes that the pearl could be valued in the range of a million dollars, but would have to examine the item himself for a more precise estimate.

> "The MooMoo pearl, carved in the distinctive pose of a dancing cow, has an interesting history…"

"I'd like to make Wiley history!" Pork shouted, jumping up from the table. "Not only will we have Sheriff Hoggsbutter breathing down our necks today, but every greedy little creep in the county will be crawling around Barkerville tonight, hoping to get their hands on that pearl before we can make the drop! Just what the heck does he think he's doing?"

"Causing you an enormous amount of trouble, and, I hate to say it, perhaps ensuring he remains in control of the *Gazette*," Adam replied.

"I'd believe anything of that smarmy creep!"

The beeping of a car horn in front of the townhouse interrupted Pork's ranting. The chief opened the front door and remained on the stoop, motioning for Lt. Cluck to come inside. But the rooster shook his head in refusal. He rolled down the window and yelled, "Get the guys! The squad car's been found!"

"You're kidding me?"

"No. And there's somebody on the seat next to me I'd like you to talk to."

A few minutes later the two cattle walked down the front walk while Pork stood on the stoop, locking the front door. As he turned to follow, the bushes edging the brick exterior rustled. Pork stopped, puzzled. He lifted his right hand toward the sky to test for the presence of wind. But there was none.

"What's the problem? Let's go!" Cluck yelled from the Rangler.

Squinting his eyes, the chief bent downward and examined the scant bottom of the row of rhododendron bushes. Despite the absence of wind, he detected another movement of the shrubbery. With a cry he did a belly flop into the bushes, ripping his green khaki shirt and dirtying his black slacks.

"Too many greasy potatoes," Cal said to Adam, who merely shrugged in response.

Pork sat there in the midst of the rhododendrons feeling silly. He could have sworn there was someone hiding near the porch, but had merely succeeded in destroying years of plant growth and imbedding a few slivers into his derriere.

"You feeling all right?" Adam walked back toward the embarrassed hog.

Pork immediately realized that Adam believed he had been throwing up and played along to protect his wounded ego. "Uh, yes, yes indeed. I feel much better now."

Cal opened the front passenger door and dropped into the seat before a horrified Cluck could protest.

"Oh, great Moogah, I think you just killed the worm that was taking us to our squad car!"

As the vehicle left the curb, a whiskered nose emerged from the lilac bush at the corner of the townhouse.

Cluck was relieved to discover that the worm had been sitting on the stick shift handle when Cal leapt into the passenger seat.

Cal apologized and asked for their guest's name.

"We don't give ourselves names," he announced.

"I believe Lucky will do," Cluck answered.

"I like that," agreed the worm.

"Watch it, Lucky," Adam laughed, "or the chief will be wearing you around his neck!"

Taking a position on the dashboard, the earthworm gave directions to where Big White had been abandoned. Turning right off Hells Highway and down what resembled more a dirt rut than a road, Cluck brought the 4x4 to a halt near an abandoned farmhouse. The squad car sat beneath an aged apple tree, the boughs sagging beneath unpicked and rotting apples, which apparently had been dropping down and pounding the car's roof. Wheat fields, trampled by errant hungry critters, lay to the east.

With an enthusiastic bound the chief was the first to reach his old steel comrade—and froze. Propped in the front seat was Buster the polar bear, his muzzle embedded in his chest, the white fur splattered with blood. After recovering from the initial shock, Pork walked up to the driver's side and, finding the car unlocked, opened the door. A note, hastily scribbled with black ballpoint ink, was literally pinned to the bear's chest with a diaper-sized safety pin.

"You could have warned us." Lt. Cluck said to Lucky, sitting in his breast pocket. He and the cattle joined the chief at the tainted automobile.

"What was I to say? By the way, there's a large dead body in your car?" Lucky answered sarcastically.

Wriggling his nose in disgust, Pork carefully unpinned the note from the furry chest, although the bear was beyond feeling any pain, and scrutinized it. His right hoofed hand trembling, he handed the note to Adam who read it aloud to the others.

> "The statue you deliver to the Hotel had better not be
> another fake, or the ostrich will shortly be saying "hello"
> to your friend here."

"I think the bear found our kidnappers," Cal said, to which comment Adam nodded in assent.

"He deserved it," spat Cluck. "He must've killed the pelican for the fake and then tried to sell it himself and take all of the money."

"Whether he deserved it or not," Adam interrupted, aware of the anxiety the chief must be experiencing, "is not our main concern here. What do we do with the corpse?"

"Call the Sheriff's Office," Cluck replied, opening the passenger door and reaching for the police radio. "This is out of our precinct."

Pork slapped the receiver out of the lieutenant's hand.

"How are we going to explain this? We never reported the car missing. You want to explain this to Hoggsbutter—or to Judge Bookem?"

The rooster's eyes widened in horror. "So what are we going to do? If we move the car or the body, we're destroying evidence."

"We'll have all the evidence we'll need when we catch those creeps at the hotel tonight. Besides, we're just moving him. It's not like we're tossing him out. Adam give me a hand, will you?" Pork grabbed at the shoulder and forearm of the bear and struggled to drag the lifeless body out of the car. "We'll pin the note back to his chest and stick him in the trunk for now, then drop him off in the dumpster behind the precinct house. Afterwards we'll dust Big White for prints and claim we found them on the dumpster. Let's just pray for a heavy rain in case someone from the County decides to check things out further and dust the dumpster for prints."

"I'm horrified beyond words," Cluck said.

"We could be so lucky. Right now, my primary concern is Griselda. We don't have time to waste, and I don't want to give Hoggsbutter a reason to interfere."

"We're darned fortunate that we found the car before someone from the Sheriff's Department did," Adam grunted, grabbing one of the bear's legs.

"We might be committing a felony here," Cluck remonstrated as Pork and the two cattle struggled under the weight of the bear as they carried it to the trunk.

"So who's going to tell—you?" Pork asked, slamming the trunk lid shut. "You're just as culpable as we are. And if you try to rat on us, I'll lie and you'll go to prison alone."

"And I'll back him up," Adam added, still breathless from the exertion of moving the bulky body.

"You've convinced me," Cluck said.

"Boy, he corrupts easily," Cal whispered to Adam.

"Maybe I should ride in the trunk and verify the condition of the body," Lucky volunteered, sliding out of the rooster's pocket.

"No!" the other four shouted.

"Oh, gross. I think I need to find a bush to puke into," Cal added.

"And you were going to eat him. Just think where his mouth has been," Adam said.

While Cluck drove off in his Rangler to return Lucky to the City Hall to continue his protest, Pork and Adam searched the yard of the farmhouse for something to clean the blood from the front seat of the squad car. They discovered a rusted bucket buried in a garden of dandelions and, after filling it with water from the creek running along the backyard, washed down the seat.

"Moogah, I forgot we needed to check for prints first," Pork said after sliding into the damp driver's seat.

"You know, I think this air freshener's shot." Cal was dangling the ubiquitous green evergreen tree from its string and holding his nose. The three of them traveled to Precinct Thirteen-and-a-half with all of the windows rolled down.

Cluck kept Pepy distracted with a recitation of the details of the evening's planned ransom drop at the Westwind Hotel while pretending not to notice the banging of the dumpster lid in the alley behind the precinct house wall. He also kept the officer preoccupied by pulling a codebook from the back wall and dropping it on the hapless sloth's head, while Pork retrieved the fingerprinting equipment from the front desk and scampered out of the room. Replacing Pepy for afternoon duty rewarded the rooster's efforts.

"You want in on the action tonight, then you let Pepy go home and get some shut-eye so he can take the night shift," Pork threatened.

Cluck sighed and took his seat at his desk. Don't cause too much trouble and one day he would be the Chief of Police at Precinct Thirteen-and-a-half, ordering around some other hapless underpaid schmucks, he thought to himself. And taking the shifts HE wanted.

After the other three left the building, Cluck called the Regional Justice Center and requested a transfer of the two prisoners in the back room.

"You know, I just can't shake the feeling that we're being followed," Pork said as the squad car pulled out onto Main Street, which led directly to the shops on the pier.

"Could it be because Wiley is on his moped behind us?" Adam asked, turning around from the front passenger seat and looking out the back window.

"With his brother," Cal added, also looking through the rear window. Wiley steered his powder puff blue moped behind a truck in the other lane, but he was still visible in Adam's side mirror.

"Drop us off," Adam commanded, banging on the dashboard. "Now!"

Pork stopped the vehicle. The two cattle jumped out as the moped raced nearer.

"We've got to scatter to throw him off the trail. Chief, pick us up on this same corner in about an hour. Keep circling till you find us. Cal, you head for the antique shop."

As Pork drove Big White off, Adam slapped Cal on the back and the two ran in opposite directions. Wiley pulled his moped up to the same corner and turned around in his seat, apparently engaged in a quarrel with his brother perched behind him. But just as Adam had surmised, Wiley decided to follow after him and not the other two. After Wiley parked the moped in one of the motorcycle slots on the adjoining street and disembarking, the two weasels rushed toward him. So while the master detective led the two miscreants on a wild goose chase through the various tourist shops leading away from the waterfront, Cal slipped down the back alleys to the Reel Deal to retrieve the pearl.

SCENE NINETEEN: THE OBLIGATORY CHASE SCENE

When Cal entered the antique shop, Kuniko hurried the transaction at the front desk with a dowdy-looking leopard, who was purchasing a beaded silk purse from the flapper era. After the feline left the building, Kuniko locked the door, placed the "Closed" sign in the window, and pulled the green shade. Motioning the bull to follow her, she led him to the backroom and, stopping near her oak desk, asked about Adam.

After Cal explained their need to ditch the nosy reporter and his brother, the elderly rat smiled and opened the top right drawer of the desk to retrieve an ancient double-pronged key. She walked to the opposite wall and slid the key into the slot of what appeared to be a fuse box. It was actually a false cover to a hidden wall safe.

"You've got the payment?" Kuniko asked over her shoulder, her right paw lightly touching the dial to the safe.

"No. Monday, soon after the banks open. Adam will be getting in touch with you," Cal lied. He hadn't the faintest idea how payment was to be arranged or how much. He would leave the details to the Master Detective. If the unthinkable occurred, and they didn't recover the ostrich in exchange for the statue, perhaps they could get the pearl back somehow. He hoped that Griselda was still alive and able to repay the rat for saving her life. If not, he'd feign senility and return to Lilah's Happy Farm.

Kuniko paused.

"Hey, we're the police. Think we're gonna rob you?" Cal asked.

Kuniko appeared to accept the answer and dialed the combination numbers to open the safe. Cal gasped as the door swung open to reveal the pearl. There was no doubt it was the original. Though the light in the back room was sparse, illuminated by aged fluorescent bulbs and upper windows, the black statuette gleamed, as if exuding an inner glow. The image of Tea Blossom came alive on the carved pedestal; Cal could easily imagine two young cattle battling for the love of the young cow. Kuniko picked up a felt bag and slipped it over the statue without touching its surface. She then placed it into a musty gym bag.

His face clearly mirroring awe, Cal received the strap of the bag from the elderly rodent with his two hands.

"How did you manage to get it?" he asked.

"Vee have our vays," she laughed, leading him out of the back room.

Adam was drenched in sweat from leading Wiley and his brother astray. He wasn't sure if the weasel was trying to follow a good story lead or wanted to steal the statue for himself, but regardless of the reason, he dashed under picnic tables, slipped through employee back rooms in fast food huts, and wove between rows of molding clothing in thrift shops. Finally, he leapt over the railing at the pier and dangled over the bay by grasping two wooden slats of the railing in his hands. After feeling assured that the angry voices of the two weasels had disappeared in the distance, he pulled himself up and, landing on the wooden pier, found himself alone, save for a small flock of sparrows.

Soon he met Cal at the corner pick-up site and nearly missed Pork driving by in a two-door green compact, scarcely larger than a coffin on wheels. With some effort the two cattle wedged themselves into the vehicle.

"Swapped cars with Pepy back at the precinct. He moves so slowly he had just made it to the parking lot when I arrived. Didn't want to take Big White to Barkerville," Pork explained, "or else every greedy fathead searching for the statue would have followed us to the Westwind. So you got it?"

"Yes," Cal replied, handing the sports bag from the backseat to Adam in the front.

"Thank Moogah." Pork heaved a loud sigh, releasing a week's worth of anxiety in one breath.

"And it's beautiful. Hard to believe that it's considered bad luck."

"Bad luck!" Pork squealed as the whining rattle of Wiley's moped buzzed up behind them.

"Ditch the creep!" Adam yelled, tapping on the chief's shoulder.

"Why don't we just offer him an exclusive and take him along with us tonight?" Cal asked as their rattletrap car roared into high gear. "Make him our friend instead of our adversary?"

"Because we don't trust him!" Adam yelled back. "Show us what they taught you at the Academy, Chief!" And he hugged the gym bag to his chest.

Cal pulled his head away from the window just before the compact took a hard right in the first intersection. The back end swung to the left then right, nearly knocking into a fire hydrant on the corner. Their pursuers easily followed by cutting across the same corner on the sidewalk. The green bomber then sailed through the red light in the next intersection and into an alley between a grocery and coffee shop. Garbage cans flew in all directions, one can bouncing off of the hood and depositing its slimy and filthy contents across the windshield. Pork continued driving blindly, the car wipers sweeping back and forth in an unsuccessful attempt to remove the crud. The moped dodged between the cans. Finally the wipers cleared the windshield to a tan smudge, leaving enough of a semi-clear spot for Pork to peer through by hunching down behind the wheel.

"I think Wiley's done this a few times," Cal said, looking out the rear window at the weasels. The moped hit a chunk of brown grunge; its riders held on tightly as the bike slid to the right. But the agile driver avoided a total wipeout and righted the bike to continue the pursuit.

"Wiley can't survive this one!" Pork yelled. "Hang on!"

"Neither will we!" Cal screamed as the automobile squealed to the left then soared down a cement staircase toward the waterfront park. The three occupants bounced their heads off the ceiling as the car stumbled down several hundred closely spaced stairs; the sports bag slipped out of Adam's hands. It swung forward and nearly hit the dashboard, but fortunately it was roped around his wrist and fell back into his lap. The rusty compact hit the last step with a bang, the bumper tearing loose in front and flying off to the left. The impact didn't seem to faze the hog at all, for he swung the steering wheel in a near circle; the car tore off to the right down the park lawn fronting Foggy Ghost Bay.

Cal watched with chagrin as Wiley took his bike down the smooth rim alongside the staircase and avoided the bumpy ride down. Figmund shrieked as they soared off the ledge, several steps up from the bottom, and came to a crashing halt near the base of a maple tree. Which didn't bother Wiley in the least. He backed the bike up with his legs and the cycle roared to life down the lawn after the automobile.

Pepy's car raced faster down the lawn than its collective week of mph, scattering picnic baskets and young lovers to and fro.

"Look out! Watch the kids!" Adam yelled as a mother duck and her ducklings emerged from the bay into the path of their car. Once again Chief Pork spun the wheel and the automobile did a 180, two cattle screaming in unison, and raced back toward Wiley and Figmund. The moped soared up and over the roof of the car. Cal turned around to watch the two weasels bounce off the trunk with the motorbike skidding after them.

As Pepy's car spun into action in the opposite direction, the statue slipped from the bag and landed into the chief's lap.

"Critters! Bad luck, bad luck!" Pork shouted, slapping the statue out of his lap without considering what he was doing, engrossed in controlling the speeding car.

Adam ducked down to the floorboard and fished for the bouncing statuette while praying to Moogah that it would not get damaged. Finally his hoofed fingers grasped the head and he slipped the bag over it. At that very moment the car hit a large bump as Pork brought the vehicle back onto Hells Highway, which caused the bag to swing out toward the open passenger side window.

With a cry of alarm Adam leapt out the window and clutched the bag's strap just before it hit the concrete speeding by beneath. He held it outward in his two hands for protection as his body bounced back and forth against the passenger door; his fedora flew off his head and rolled down the highway. Adam slipped further out the window.

"Stop the car, stop the car!" Cal shouted, leaning forward over the front seat and grabbing Adam's tail. The detective held onto the window ledge with his bent knees, grinding his two horns against the concrete. Sparks flew. Pork slammed his foot down on the brake. Momentum sent Adam and the pearl down the highway in a live leather ball that quickly went flat.

As Pork and Cal exited the vehicle, a County squad car, sirens blaring, skidded to a stop alongside. The hippopotamus, which the two sleuths had run into investigating the incident at the Pawn 'n Spawn, lumbered out of the car with one hand upon his holster, the other upon his ticket book.

"Know how many driving laws you broke?" the County cop, chewing a large wad of gum, asked.

"All of them?" Pork replied, pulling a wallet out of his back pocket and flipping it open to expose the police badge to his interrogator.

"Well, heck," the cop said, tossing his ticket book back into his squad car. "I thought I was gonna win an award for this traffic stop."

"What vehicle did you train in at the Police Academy: a tank?" Cal asked Chief Pork.

Their attention was distracted by Adam's groans as he lay on the highway several yards away. Cal ran down and bent over him. "You O.K.?" Without waiting for an answer, Cal snatched up the sports bag from the detective's clasp and examined the statue inside.

"Holy hogs in heaven, is it all right? Is it damaged?" Pork, running up to Cal, asked with alarm.

"No, no, looks like it's O.K."

"Adam, can't you be more careful? Grissie's life depends upon that statue!" Pork said.

"Thanks. I'll remember that after the hospital binds up all my broken bones. Please go back and retrieve my hat so I'll look presentable for my entrance into the Emergency Room."

In their preoccupation with the two weasel brothers, Pork and his comrades didn't notice the sleek black compact sedan that had been trailing from far behind. The car pulled discreetly into a weigh station on the side of the highway; its occupant waited for the trio of investigators to continue their journey to Barkerville.

SCENE TWENTY: THE BIG DROP

Lt. Cluck, dressed not in his uniform but in black sweats, joined the other three at a nondescript diner a few miles short of Barkerville. It was nearly 6 PM, a mere nine hours before the ransom drop. Over a dinner of greasy alfalfa burgers and onion rings, the police officers and two cattle avoided the topic of the ransom and discussed Department politics with nervous abandonment. But finally reality could no longer be avoided; they emerged from the metal cocoon and piled into the dark blue sedan the rooster had rented at Pork's request to take them all to the evening's big event. Fearing that the weasel would subsequently discover Pepy's automobile in the vicinity of the hotel (not realizing that Figmund had overheard Betsy and already revealed the information to his brother), Pork demanded they leave it at the diner. And just in case the weasels, or perhaps even Lenny, would recognize Cluck's red Cheep Rangler, it, too, had to remain parked at home.

"You think Pepy will notice the missing bumper right away?" Pork asked, examining the front grille of the sloth's car.

"We can super glue it back on later," Cal suggested. "Did anyone remember to pick it up off the lawn near the bay?"

Pork and Steer shrugged their shoulders.

"You would've been with us if we had," Adam said.

"Then I think he might notice," Cal continued. "But we can outrun him!"

A mile down the highway they found that both lanes going into Barkerville were backed up with traffic.

"Dang, you don't think this has anything to do with Wiley's article in the *Gazette* last night do you?" Pork asked. "It's a Saturday night, for crying out loud."

"I don't know, but I haven't seen this many old junkers on the road since the last tornado whipped through the wrecking yard," Cal commented, peering out the back passenger window and down the highway.

"We don't have tornados around here!" Cluck replied in an exasperated tone. His winged hands hurt from gripping the bulling wheel in anxious excitement. He wished that the bothersome fruitcake of a bull hadn't been permitted to interfere in tonight's official police business. It was almost criminal to allow that novice to be involved in the investigation: Tonight they were going to interact with the kidnappers and rescue an important lady from harm. But Pork was the boss and he didn't appear to mind that protocol was being ignored. One day the old fool would retire and he'd get Precinct 13-and-a-half into proper shape.

"I'm not from around here," Cal replied without a hint of animosity. "Duck!" he yelled suddenly.

"What the..." Cluck exclaimed as Chief Pork grabbed the rooster's top comb and shoved his beak into the seat between them. The two cattle also hid down below view from the outside. A moment later Wiley in his rumpled trench coat and Figmund, looking a little banged up about the face, slowly cruised by on the moped on the shoulder of the road, bypassing the traffic jam. Cal popped his head up just as Figmund looked back. He hoped Figmund's eyesight was too poor to have spotted him.

As the four of them returned to an upright position, Adam commented, "Well, I bet those two weasels didn't notice anything strange at all about a car sitting on the highway with no driver as they rode by."

It took more than ninety frustrating minutes to negotiate the sedan into Barkerville through traffic that would test the most patient driver in the best circumstances, which this was not. The city resembled a disaster zone: Stray cats and dogs and all types of critters were rummaging through dumpsters, garbage cans, telephone and electrical boxes—almost anything that could hold a small statuette. In the car they passed a trio of possums struggling with a crowbar, attempting to lift the lid off of a sewer in the middle of the street. Suitcases fell from the balcony of a hotel and crashed open onto the sidewalk below. An abandoned couch in an alley was torn to pieces with a sharp instrument, white piles of foam scattered everywhere.

Having checked out the location of the Westwind earlier during the week, the lieutenant soon pulled their vehicle into the main parking lot of the hotel.

"You two go through the front, check for potential hiding places. Cluck and I will come through the back," Pork commanded, looking over his shoulder at the two cows in the backseat.

"Always leave yourself multiple avenues of escape," Steer explained to Cal as they exited the vehicle.

A few minutes later the four of them stood in the center of the Westwind Lobby. Adam proffered the sports bag with its priceless content to Pork. "She was your gal."

Pork took a wary look at the bag. One hand wanted to reach for the pearl, but superstition pulled it back. "Best that someone who's not emotionally involved make the drop."

"I'll take..." Cluck began but the hard look the detective gave him stopped his tongue.

"So what do we look for?" Cal asked.

"It's nearly nine o'clock," Adam replied, looking at his wristwatch. "We need to determine how many entrances there are into the lobby. Give ourselves a fighting chance to figure out a way to block their escape and retrieve the statue. If not, we can just trail them back to their lair. We know that whoever kidnapped Madam Portentsky may have also killed Buster, the polar bear. Whoever it is needs to pay for both crimes."

No one mentioned the greatest fear preying on their minds: a possible third crime, Griselda's death. Only the impending events of that evening would reveal her condition.

They discovered five main entrances into the main lobby: the front door, the hallway leading from the back door past the banquet halls, the door leading from the employee's entrance to behind the front desk, the hallway leading to the elevator lobby and the guest quarters, and the double glass doors to the swimming pool. The pool, the central focus of the hotel, was circumvented by a walkway to various banquet rooms, the bar, and the restaurant. Facing the lobby were also two bathrooms, one for each gender. Steer volunteered to enter the ladies' room: It was empty, as was the males'.

"So tell me," Cal inquired about the ladies' room, "did you find the powder in there?"

Surprisingly, there were two identical blue flowerpots in the lobby instead of just one as inferred by the ransom note: one near the telephones by the entrance to the pool and one near the entrance way leading to the elevators.

"Which one?" Cluck asked.

"Maybe there was only one when they wrote the ransom note," Cal offered. "Let's ask the attendant at the front desk if the custodian has dropped one off lately."

"We don't need to," Adam said. "Think for a moment. Pretend you're the kidnappers and you're going to pick up a valuable statue in a public hotel. Do you choose the flowerpot near the telephones where someone, speaking on the phone, might absentmindedly look into the pot and see the sports bag? Or do you choose the pot near the double doors leading to the central poolroom, a room itself with several entrances—and escape routes?"

"That's exactly what I was thinking," Cluck said, covering his butt.

Adam stepped out of the lobby through the double doors and returned with four steaming mugs of espresso from the bar. The front desk clerk, a pelican with an odd black knot of feathers on his head, gazed at them with apparent apprehension. Cluck, noticing the stern glare of the bird, stepped toward the desk, but Pork grabbed his arm and pulled him backward, causing the rooster to spill coffee down the front of his sweat top.

"We can't tell the hotel staff what we're up to," Pork hissed to the rooster. "They might fear events will escalate out of control and interfere with the drop. Act nonchalant."

The four of them sat down on two white patent leather sofas crowded around a circular coffee table. The typical travel magazines and national newspapers were strewn across its glass surface. Cluck picked up the *Cloverleaf Gazette*, peered over the top edge, and waited. Ever so often Adam would poke him in the side to remind him to turn the page as the suspicious pelican kept a distrustful eye trained on them.

"Boring convention," Pork explained to the pelican. "We just need to log in our hours for the…" He squinted his eyes to read the blackboard near the front desk, "Canary Kay seminar and then head on home."

"Whatever," the pelican replied, but didn't look convinced.

"You realize that Canary Kay is a cosmetics firm, don't you," Adam, grinning, whispered to Pork. "Their sales staff are known for driving yellow Catillacs." Pork's face grew red with embarrassment, while Cluck looked mortified.

"And I hear the cosmetics are priced 'cheep'," Cal added.

With such nervous, inane chatter the four of them kept vigilant watch over the critters walking in and out of the lobby and waited for 3 AM. They couldn't see the black compact sedan pulling into the parking lot in the back of the building nor its whiskered driver hopping out onto the sidewalk.

At 2:50 Adam was shaken to alertness by an obviously anxious hog. "It's time to place the pearl into the flower pot. We don't want to cut it too close." He held up a pocket-sized walkie-talkie. "I sent Lt.

Cluck up to the roof a little over two hours ago." And added, pointing toward his right ear, "I've got a wireless receiver. We won't be caught by surprise."

"Rather big roof. Maybe we should send Cal up there also."

"No. I don't want conflicting reports. Best to have only one trained eye up there."

Adam winced. The rooster was more like a trained dog than trained eye: good at obeying precise commands but not at improvising.

Pork noticed the unspoken commentary on Steer's face. "I know. I thought about involving Lt. Sparrow tonight but the less association with other police departments, the more confident I feel we can keep this drop confidential and under control. You're sure that the statue is undamaged?"

Steer pulled the zipper apart and peered inside the bag. "I believe so. But even if it wasn't, what could we do about it now?"

"I think it's best we stay away from the pot: Don't make the kidnappers feel crowded. And away from the entrances: Don't make them think we're going to prevent them from escaping. I don't give a fig about the pearl. Let the sons-of-biscuit-eaters have it. It's only a means to an end."

"The couch works for me."

Pork held his breath as Adam walked across the lobby and slipped the bag into the flowerpot by the doors to the central pool.

"Hey, we don't allow dumping trash into the flowerpots!" the hotel clerk yelled, hopping over the top of the front desk and running toward the pot. He seemed happy to finally have an opportunity to castigate the errant loungers.

Pork intercepted him, whipping out his badge and shoving it into the nosey bird's beak. "Shut the hell up," he hissed. Wide-eyed, the pelican shut up and slunk back behind the desk.

"I hope no one observed you flashing the badge," Adam said, sliding back into the couch.

"What's the difference? The kidnappers already know who's making the drop." The chief was becoming noticeably irritable.

"You think that's them?" Cal whispered to Adam. A Doberman, a patch over one eye, walked into the lobby from the elevators and commenced sniffing each object in the room. A weather-beaten calico pranced after him.

"No. Act nonchalant, as if we don't care. They haven't the foggiest idea whether the pearl is in this hotel or not. Wiley was smart enough not to print THAT detail in the paper."

Cal immediately began whistling—to Pork's annoyance.

"Oh, that works, Cal. Really nonchalant."

The dog lifted his head, gave them a curious glance, then followed the cat toward the back hallway.

"What the blazes! I'll kill him! I'll absolutely kill him!" Pork roared, jumping to his feet.

Wiley, closely tailed by his brother Figmund, slunk into the room. His embattled fedora was pulled down low over his eyes, a camera hung down upon his chest, and his hands were thrust deep into the front pockets of his trench coat.

"Calm down," Adam said, grasping the back of Pork's shirt as he leapt to his feet. "He couldn't know where the statue is. Perhaps we can use him for a shield, if need be." He winked, but the chief wasn't in the mood for humor.

"It's nearly 3 AM. It couldn't possibly get any worse." He put the walkie-talkie to his mouth. "Cluck? Cluck! Why didn't you warn us that the weasels were entering the hotel?" His rebuke was responded to with a symphony of snores. "I can't believe it! How could anybody fall asleep after drinking three espressos? Darned pickle." He pulled it out from beneath his shirt and, before Adam could intervene, yanked it off the string of yarn and dashed it to the lobby floor. "Didn't bring me any luck at all!"

His smile sliding into a sneer, Wiley turned his attention to the three couchant critters and sauntered toward them. He lifted his SLR camera to his face. "Cheese!" The flash caught a picture of Chief Pork's fist raised in the air in the first throws of a punch. But his attention diverted, the hog didn't complete the throw: A furtive rat, glancing to and fro, slipped into the lobby from the direction of the elevators.

"If you want your big exclusive, hide behind the sofas, NOW!" Adam hissed to the weasels. Wiley leapt behind Adam's chair while Figmund, without invitation, seated himself next to Cal.

Bingo! Adam caught a definite look toward the flowerpot by the grey rat. The rodent, apparently contemplating its next move, scratched at its chin and stood for a moment in the middle of the lobby. Adam held his breath in anxious anticipation. This was it. He hoped Wiley would merely observe, get his big exclusive, and not interfere with police business. Fining the weasel for hindering an investigation would not save Griselda's life, no matter how much personal satisfaction the penalty would bring.

Unexpectedly, the rat skittered up to Chief Pork and shoved a folded piece of white paper into his hands. "Take a hike," the rodent squeaked.

As Pork began to pull his hand away, Wiley leapt up from behind the couch and snapped a photo of the transaction. The flash momentarily stunned everyone into a frozen pose.

Then the rat scampered across the lobby toward the flowerpot. At that same moment two rhinoceroses with silver-plated horns came barreling from the back employee rooms and smashed through the front desk, tossing aside a very bewildered pelican. Broken bits of wood flew throughout the room. The rat leapt to the rim of the flowerpot while bathed in the surreal intermittent light of Wiley's camera flashes. The larger rhino lowered its head and rammed the flowerpot, sending the squealing rat and the ceramic flying. Before the pot hit the floor, a walrus on a moped sped into the lobby through the glass doors of the central atrium and caught it midair with his flippers.

"Holy guacamole, I hope Wiley doesn't run out of film. I'd like to see this again," Cal quipped.

"Hey, Walrus! Like hell I'm gonna let you have the pearl!"

As if standing in a crypt when the iron door suddenly slams shut, every critter in the room froze in fear as the largest mole anyone had ever seen smashed through the main front window and rushed into the room in an obvious rage. The floor buckled and shook as the colossal rodent, apparently heedless of the broken glass strewn about, ran toward the moped and yanked the flowerpot out of the walrus' hands. A pint-sized white rat ran up over his right shoulder from his backside, hopped to the rim of the pot, and pulled out the bag.

"I thought you could handle a simple job!" the giant bellowed, intentionally stepping upon the tail of the first grey rat. "I shouldn't have had to come in here!"

"Aren't you going to pull out your gun or something?" Cal asked Pork. Adam and Figmund merely sat speechless in disbelief.

"I don't have my gun, remember? Besides, this is all I care about," Pork replied, holding aloft the note that the rat had given to him.

"What is that?"

"Tells me where Griselda is. I'm off. Enjoy the show." And Pork dashed out of the lobby toward the back entrance past the banquet halls. A moment later he walked backwards into the room with both hands held high, the two guns of Sheriff Hoggsbutter pointed into his snout. Several similarly armed County Police officers followed them into the lobby.

"Ain't nobody going anywhere!" the sheriff shouted in his high-pitched nasal twang. "This is in MY jurisdiction! I want to know just what the hell is going on here! Pork, you've got some explaining to do!"

At that moment Wiley snapped several photos, the flash momentarily blinding the sheriff and his cronies. Pork made a run for the front doors. The white rodent ran down the back of the colossus and high-tailed it toward the elevators. Figmund came to life and intercepted the rat, snatching the bag out of his hands. But before he could turn to exit the lobby, Lenny came flying out of the men's room, banging the door against the wall.

"It's mine! It's mine!" he squeaked, grabbing the sports bag from the surprised weasel. The mountainous mole pounced and the walrus on his moped roared to life, while Lenny ran for the front doors. With a squeal the hapless rodent evaded the walrus on the speeding bike and the outstretched arms of the giant villain, only to stumble upon the pickle Chief Pork had angrily tossed to the floor minutes before. He slipped and fell backward; the bag went limp in his two paws as the statuette went soaring through the air.

Everyone stood mesmerized by the beautiful black pearl, the wane light of the early morning bathing it in an ethereal glow. No one made a move to rescue the statue until it nearly hit the marble floor.

As if a circuit breaker had suddenly been thrown, every critter in the room ran forward in a vain attempt to prevent the statue's destruction. But it was too late: The priceless MooMoo Pearl smashed against the marble and broke into thousands of scattered pieces.

Tears flooding his eyes, Lenny lay flat on his stomach on the floor. He groaned as in physical pain. The giant mole, in an obvious rage, slapped the little white rodent across the face. "Stupido!" His violence was rewarded with a savage bite planted into the back of his paw.

With all eyes in the room following him, Adam walked forward, bent down, and picked up a broken piece of the pearl. He placed it between his teeth and bit down. The shard turned to powder between his front teeth. "Ceramic," announced the master detective.

"It's a fake!" shouted Wiley.

Cal laughed while Lenny's mouth dropped open in surprise and the flow of tears stopped.

"Hey!" The pelican with the odd black top notch emerged from under a pile of broken wood, which had once been the front desk, and walked to the center of the lobby. "Who's gonna pay to clean up this mess?"

Episode Four: Wrapping It All Up

THE FINAL SCENE

Out in front of the Westwind Hotel, Chief Pork screamed into the walkie-talkie until the drowsy rooster responded. Shortly thereafter the two of them hopped into the blue rental and sped out onto Hells Highway and out of Barkerville. The sun struggled to come to life over the tops of the distant hills. Apprehension held Pork's heart in a tight-fisted grip.

"This is it," announced Lt. Cluck, bringing the sedan to a stop. "The address on the note the rat gave you."

To their right lay a field of thousands of pecking, scratching, wing-flapping ostriches: several acres of fowl that all looked alike, multitudinous mottled brown backs being warmed by the glow of the rising sun.

"What the heck is this place?" exclaimed Chief Pork.

Lt. Cluck brought the sedan forward so the two of them could read the semi-circular wooden marquis hanging between the two posts over the main gate. The engraving read: Mavis' Egg Hatching Sanitarium.

Pork could picture Adam laughing his head off, but he, himself, could not stretch his mouth into even a wry grin. Apparently the kidnappers wanted to ensure that Griselda could not be located too quickly in case the ransom drop had gone badly. And it had. He didn't know if she was left to fend for herself, alone, in the gaggle of maternal hens or was closely guarded. Most likely it was the latter. She had to be found before her guardian heard about the catastrophe at the Westwind Hotel.

Pork opened the passenger side door and stepped out onto the soft ground of the shoulder. He lifted a pair of binoculars to his eyes, scanning the yard and its environs. To the left of the ostriches there was a large hatchery, a plume of smoke rising from its chimney, signaling the near arrival of breakfast. A barbed wire fence ran the circumference of the farm to a height of five feet, apparently to ward off any carnivores that chose to violate the Fruits and Nuts Law.

"We've got to find her—now!" Pork signaled the rooster to follow him. He tried the handle on the gate, but it was stuck fast. Looking upward, he noted a small green sign on the side post which read, "Visiting hours: 10 AM to 5 PM. If dropping off a hen, please ring bell for service."

Lt. Cluck leaned forward and extended a feathered finger to ring the bell, but Pork slapped his wing away. "We don't know if the owners of the farm are in cahoots with the kidnappers or not," he warned. Pulling up his black slacks at the waist and, placing a foot into the bottom slat of the metal gate, the portly hog climbed up and over. Soon Cluck was at his side. They darted amongst the flock of birds, examining each face for Griselda's features. Twenty minutes and several hundreds of beaks later, neither officer had found Madam Portentsky.

"You don't think this is some sort of sick prank, do you?" asked Lt. Cluck.

"After their poor performance at the hotel, I don't know if they're sophisticated enough for a gag like this. But ignorant enough to kill? Possibly."

Pork shuddered visibly as he spoke his last words. With a look of grim determination on his face, he held his hoofed hand out, palm up, to the rooster.

"Give me your gun."

"What? I can't give you my gun. You've been banned from carrying a sidearm for two weeks. I'd get into big trouble with Judge Bookem."

"I don't plan to shoot it off. I just want to look threatening."

Cluck frowned. "You think I'm dumb enough to believe that line?"

Pork lunged forward and grabbed at the rooster's holster. Cluck cupped his wings protectively over his sidearm, but the chief managed to grab the weapon's handle. With Cluck's fingers tightly wrapped about his own, Pork and the rooster waved the gun back and forth in the air between them, fighting for control. The gun accidentally discharged.

The shot rang throughout the valley like the first drumroll of thunder in a lightning storm. Thousands of avian heads thrust themselves into the ground in search of safety.

All except one.

The solitary ostrich stood about a hundred yards away amidst a sea of raised and exposed feathered butts. She swayed back and forth upon her two wobbly legs. With mixed feelings of glee and anxiety, Pork ran toward the lone figure. Holding his gun, Cluck appeared uncertain whether to follow or allow the chief a moment of privacy.

"I knew it!" the ex-lover shouted, swinging an arm around Griselda's neck. "I knew you were too stubborn to shove your head into the ground like the other birds. You wouldn't run away from anything, you willful old dame."

"Who are you?" Griselda asked, spittle dribbling from her chin. She was obviously drugged.

Another shot rang out. The bullet nearly missed Pork's left foot, knocking up a cloud of dust.

"Cluck! Watch where you're pointing that pistol!"

"It wasn't me, Chief!"

Several yards to the east stood a cloaked figure. Pork hadn't noticed the critter in his delight at spotting Griselda. Shouldering a rifle, the miscreant prepared to fire again. As the shot rang out, Pork knocked Griselda to the ground and buried his face into the stiff feathers of her back. He prepared himself for the impact of a bullet, but none came. With trepidation he looked up: The cloaked critter was lying on the ground, the weapon flung several feet from its outstretched right paw. Another common grey rat.

Lt. Cluck walked over to Pork and replaced his gun into his holster.

"I really hated to do that, but I had no choice," the rooster said.

"You know,...it's the weirdest...thing, sir," Pepy said as the Chief of Police walked into Precinct Thirteen-and-a-half. It was late Sunday morning. Pork had dropped Griselda off at the Boville Hospital for observation and returned to the station to await the pending wrath of Sheriff Hoggsbutter. "This gang of...crows wandered in...early this morning and asked...if they could have the contents...of the dumpster in...the alley behind us. I figured,...what the heck,...these guys want to haul off...our trash for free,...why not let them?"

Lt. Cluck came into the room to catch the tail end of Pepy's announcement.

"What do you think, Cluck?" the chief asked his second-in-command. "Should we chase the crows down?"

The lieutenant looked squeamish. Pepy could swear that the rooster's face, despite the feathers, turned green.

Cluck sat down on the wooden bench in the lobby. He pulled nervously at the neckline of his sweat top then gripped his rib cage with his winged arms as if in pain. "What the heck. Let someone else clean up our mess for once!"

"So how's Griselda doing?" Pork asked, strolling into the visitor's waiting room of the Boville hospital. He sat down on the couch between Adam and Cal.

"Besides a sore throat from having her stomach pumped, she seems to be doing all right," Adam replied. "The nurses are doing some tests right now; we have to wait until they're done before they'll let us back into the room."

The three of them sat in silence for a few minutes.

"So, Chief, did Griselda seem happy to see you?" Cal asked.

"I don't know. Didn't appear to recognize me. She was really out of it. Didn't say a single word in the car on the way to the hospital." Pork turned toward Adam. "And you know she doesn't normally keep quiet for long."

"And how about you?" Cal asked the master detective. "Think you'll go back to the Backdoor Club to say 'hello' to a special someone?"

"I'm not sure. She didn't appear much more aware of my presence that night than Griselda was of Pork's this morning. She's got the drug of anger in her system, and you can't pump that one out."

"Flowers would be a good start."

"Humph."

The three of them lapsed into silence again.

"Where's Cluck?" asked Adam.

"Filing a report with the County for discharging his weapon. Guess I'll have to consider giving him a raise after saving our butts this morning."

"Saving two lives: that does sound good on a resume," Cal retorted, bending forward. He gave a soulful look at Adam. "So this is it, isn't it? Time to go back to Lilah's?"

"You know, Cal," the hog interrupted with a wink. "If you want to be a private detective in this state, you've got to do a year-long internship with a licensed sleuth. Think you might be talked into it, Steer?"

Adam raised a hoofed hand to his chin as if pondering the question. Then, with a broad smile, he placed an arm around Cal's shoulders. "Since I'm going back into business, I could use a sidekick to do the boring stuff."

"Hey, I'm your patsy!"

Pork rose from the couch with a slight limp. He'd bruised his leg when pushing Griselda to the ground. "I'm going to check on the old bird before I put in my own report to the Sheriff. Gotta explain why he's got all of those jerks warming up the beds in the Justice Center."

"Have you forgotten? You're defrocked for two weeks. Hoggsbutter will have your butt in a sling if he finds out you've been interfering with official police business."

"That's right. You want to fill the paperwork out, then, Steer?"

"Let's volunteer Cluck."

"I'd love to, but the Sheriff already caught me at the hotel. I've got a lot of explaining to do," Pork replied. "May as well get right to it."

"Did they throw Lenny into prison, too?" Cal called after the hog. "Isn't he the innocent one in all of this?"

Pork chuckled under his breath. "Hoggsbutter doesn't know that yet. And Adam, don't think you're getting out of this one without filing your own police report." He walked through the double doors leading to the west patient wing and disappeared from their view.

"We've got one problem remaining," Adam said. "Kuniko. We owe her for the statue."

"That's right. But she didn't really seem concerned about it. Said it was O.K. to pay her Monday."

"How much?"

"She didn't specify."

Adam tilted his head backward and laughed out loud, a very welcome, cheery laugh after the anxiety of the last 48 hours. "You mean she didn't press you for payment? Just let you have the statue without a promissory note or anything?"

"Yes." Cal thought for a moment. "That is rather odd, but I was in such a hurry I didn't consider it. You don't think she knew that the statue was another fake, do you? She risked Madam Griselda's life if she did."

"She fooled me."

"Fooled all of them. Think there ever was an original? Maybe Lenny never did find it in MooAsia."

"Who knows for sure? Although I can't believe that the old rat came all the way from Singapork to harass Kuniko over a fake," Adam said, leaning back into the couch. "I'm betting that if we don't show up tomorrow to pay her, she's not going to press us about it."

The two of them stood to leave. Pork had offered his living room for their humble abode pending the two cattle scraping enough money together to rent their own place. But until dinner hit the table at the hog's townhouse, the afternoon was theirs to enjoy.

"After all that's been said and done," Cal said as he followed Adam out of the waiting room, "I still think the butler did it." He sighed and pulled his paper detective's hat out of his coat pocket and placed it upon his head. "It feels good to have a friend."

"Let's go get us some jelly donuts," Steer said with a smile. "You like lemon?"

Kuniko closed the shop early that afternoon and walked to the back room. Although alone, she pulled the double doors gently to a close with the barest audible click as the lock snapped into place. She looked out the windows to note any pedestrians passing by, then pulled down the shades. With a sense of awe she slid the shoebox out from under the oak desk and set it onto the center of the desktop. After placing her dainty paws into soft white gloves, she took the top off the box and spread aside the tissue paper. With trembling fingers she lifted the MooMoo Pearl out of its paper safe, the most unlikely hiding place for a priceless heirloom. Turning it slowly to catch the rays of sunlight coming through the upper windows, Kuniko admired the way the glittering light made the cow seem to come alive and dance on its pedestal. Soon the Dalmatian would arrive with the promised payment. She only hoped that Dudley would find a home worthy for the cursed antique.

NOT THE END

PLEASE BE ON THE ALERT FOR CATTLE CAPERS #2: THE CHEEP BRIGADE

The carnivores are getting restless.

A little background for those who are interested

    Cattle Capers began in 1990 as a series of notes and drawings. Adam Steer and Betsy Moo have retained their original names, Lenny's and Chief of Police Ignatious Pork's original names are too embarrassing to admit to. There was a mouse detective that didn't make the cut in this first novel and Lt. Cluck wore eyeglasses. The original concept was to create a humorous adventure comic strip. The first strip is below.

    Subsequent research revealed that there was no market for new adventure strips in the newspaper field. Adventure strips don't sell to editors. When it comes to the newspaper market, you are selling to the editor, not to the public.

    The next step was to create a comic book. I listened to, and consulted with, experts in the field. There was positive response to my concept. But I wasn't excited about drawing hundreds or thousands of pictures and promoting a comic book. And to keep an audience interested, you have to put out a new comic book bi-monthly. I knew that I could not keep that pace and hold down a full-time job.

    Finally, in early 2000, I wrote the first chapter of this novel and submitted it to my unsuspecting "Writing For Children" teacher, Ms. Peggy King Anderson—who enjoyed it.

    And so, after a long gestation period, the cartoon novel you have just read was born. I hope that these characters were as real to you as they became to me over the years.

    And may life smile upon you as you strive toward your dreams.

Dawn

LaVergne, TN USA
20 November 2010

205737LV00003B/34/A